LINDA HOWARD

HEART OF FIRE

POCKET STAR BOOKS

New York London Toronto Sydney Tokyo Singapore

An *Original* Publication of POCKET BOOKS

A Pocket Star Book published by
POCKET BOOKS, a division of Simon & Schuster Inc.
1230 Avenue of the Americas, New York, NY 10020

ISBN: 0-671-72859-8

First Pocket Books printing July 1993

10 9 8 7 6 5 4 3 2 1

POCKET STAR BOOKS and colophon are registered trademarks of Simon & Schuster Inc.

Cover art by Yuan Lee

Printed in the U.S.A.

Prologue

"Who's that, Daddy?" Jillian's small finger poked insistently at a picture in the book her father held. She was ensconced on his lap, as she often was, for even though she was only five years old she was fascinated by his tales of long-ago people and faraway places, and had been since she was a toddler.

"That's an Amazon."

"What's her name?" Jillian knew the figure was female because of the way it was shaped. When she was real little she had sometimes been confused by the length of the hair, until she realized that almost everyone in Daddy's picture books had long hair, boys as well as girls. In search of a better means of gender identification, she had soon discovered a much more dependable clue: chests. Men and women had different chests.

"I don't know her name. No one knows if she ever truly lived."

"So she may be a pretend person?"

"Maybe." Cyrus Sherwood gently stroked his daughter's small round head, lifting her thick, shiny hair and letting the dark strands drift down to fall once more into place. He delighted in this child. He knew he was biased, but her understanding and her grasp of the abstract were far beyond what was normal for her age. She was fascinated by his

1

books on archaeology; one of his favorite memories was of her, at the age of three, tugging on a book that weighed almost as much as she did, wrestling it to the floor, and then spending an entire afternoon lying on her stomach, slowly turning the pages as she pored over the pictures, utterly oblivious to everything else around her. She combined childhood innocence with a startling logic; no one would ever accuse his Jilly of being muddleheaded. And if her primary personality trait was pragmatism, her second was stubbornness. He fondly suspected that his beloved daughter would turn out to be more than a handful for some unsuspecting man in her future.

Jillian leaned closer to study the picture in greater detail. Finally she asked, "If she's a pretend person, why is she in here?"

"The Amazons are classified as mythical figures."

"Oh. Those people that writers make up stories about."

"Yes, because sometimes myths can be based on fact." He usually tried to simplify his vocabulary when he was talking to Jillian, but he never talked down to her. If she didn't understand something, his fierce little darling would demand explanations from him until she *did* understand.

Her little nose wrinkled. "Tell me about these Amazings." She settled back in his lap, making herself comfortable.

He chuckled at her accidental but on-target pun, then launched into an account of the warrior women and their queen, Penthesilea. A door slammed somewhere in the house, but neither of them paid attention, caught up in the old world that was their favorite playground.

Rick Sherwood bounded into the house with unusual enthusiasm, his customary sullenness lost in excitement. The cleats on his baseball shoes made a strange metallic sound against the wooden floors as he ignored the housekeeper's oft-repeated demand to take the shoes off before coming inside. God, what a game! It was the best game he'd ever played. He wished his dad had been there to see him, but he'd had some student appointments and couldn't make it.

Up to bat five times, and he'd had four hits, one of them a home run. That made his batting average for the day a stupendous .800! Math wasn't his strong point, but he could figure *that* batting average easily enough.

He stopped in the kitchen to down a glass of water, gulping it so thirstily that rivulets ran down his chin, then ran another glass. As he brought it to his mouth he heard voices and paused. It sounded like his dad.

Still impelled by excitement, he clumped rapidly toward the library, where he knew his dad would be. He burst the door open and rushed through. "Hey, Dad! I got four hits today, one of them a home run! I had seven RBIs and made a double play. You shoulda been there!" The last was said on a burst of excitement, not as a complaint.

Professor Sherwood glanced up from the book and smiled at his son. "I wish I had been. Good boy!"

Rick ignored his little sister, perched on their father's lap. "Your student appointments didn't take as long as you thought, huh?"

"They were postponed until tomorrow," the professor said.

Rick stood there, his excitement fading. "Then why didn't you come to the game?"

Jillian had been listening with interest, and now she said, "I like baseball games, Daddy."

He smiled down at her. "Do you, Jillian? Perhaps we'll go to the next one."

She was satisfied with that, and her story had been interrupted long enough. She poked at the book to redirect his attention. "Amazings," she prompted.

Obediently the professor responded to the demand in that piping voice, something easy to do when the story was so close to his own heart. Thank heaven Jillian preferred myth to fairy tale, or he couldn't have been nearly so patient.

Rick's happiness died, to be replaced by fury as he found himself once again shut out by that brat. Okay, so she was smart; so what? She couldn't handle a double play. Frustration welled up inside him, and he stalked out before he gave in to the urge to grab her out of their father's lap. The professor wouldn't understand; he thought the little darling was wonderful.

Little darling, my ass, Rick thought viciously. He'd disliked and resented Jillian from the moment she was born, just as he had disliked her mother. Her mother had died a couple of years ago, thank God, but the brat was still here.

Everybody made a fuss over her because she was smart. They treated him like some dummy just because he'd been left back a grade in school. Okay, so he was seventeen, and would turn eighteen just after starting his junior year in high school; he wasn't *stupid,* he just hadn't tried real hard. Why bother? No matter how good he did, people still gave the brat all of their attention.

He went upstairs to his room, where he pulled off his baseball shoes and hurled them against the wall. Now she'd even ruined the best game he'd ever had. If Dad's student appointments had been postponed, he could have come to the ball game after all, but instead he'd come home to tell stories to that little brat. The injustice of it made Rick want to hit something. He wanted to hit the brat. He wanted to make her hurt, the way she made him hurt. She'd stolen his father from him, she and her stupid mother, and he would never, ever forgive her.

Impulse jerked him to his feet. His socks muffled all sound as he padded out of his room and down the hall to Jillian's room. He stood in the middle of it, looking around. Like all children, she gathered her treasures around her; the room was littered with her favorite books and dolls and other mementos with meanings obvious only to her. Rick didn't care about any of that; he just looked for her special doll, the one she loved more than any of the others, a bedraggled plastic playmate she had named Violet. She usually slept with it snuggled against her cheek.

There it was. Rick grabbed the doll and slipped back to his own room, trying to decide what to do next. He wanted to whack the thing to pieces and leave it on Jillian's bed, but animal cunning told him he would be blamed for it, because there was no one else who could have done it. Still, just hiding the doll from her wasn't enough. His jealousy demanded more; he needed to destroy something she loved, even if he was the only one who knew about it.

Smiling, he got his pocket knife from the top of the dresser and opened it. Sitting down on the bed, he calmly and thoroughly dismembered the doll. Jillian wouldn't know what he'd done; she would cry because her favorite doll was lost, but no one would accuse him of anything. He would hug the knowledge to himself, and every time he looked at her he would gloat, because he would know and she wouldn't.

1

Jillian Sherwood was tight-lipped with anger as she let herself into her condo. It was less than two years old, and she usually felt a surge of pleasure and achievement on stepping over the threshold, for the condo wasn't only great looking, it was *hers,* but today wasn't a usual day and she didn't even notice the cool, soothing interior. She slung her canvas bag onto the foyer table and stalked straight through the living room to the balcony. Her anger was so overwhelming that she felt as if she had to be outside so it could expand.

She stood rigidly still in the late spring heat of Los Angeles, her hands braced on the rim of the waist-high concrete wall. She had a good view of the city, and normally she loved it, both the pastels of daytime and the glowing neons of night, but she was too angry right then to even see it.

Damn those narrow-minded bastards!

She had paid her dues, earned the right to work on the Ouosalla dig in east Africa; it was the biggest new archaeological find in decades, and her mouth literally watered at the thought of being involved. She had never wanted anything as much as she wanted to help excavate the buried ancient village that had only recently been discovered on the African coast of the Red Sea. The dig was being funded by the Frost Archaeological Foundation, the very foundation she worked for, and she had been almost giddy with excitement when she submitted her name for consideration for the team being chosen to work on the Ouosalla site.

Why shouldn't she have expected to be chosen? Her work was excellent, and so were her reports; her papers had been printed in several reputable publications. She had a doctorate in archaeology and had already been on several minor digs in Africa; her experience would be of considerable value to a dig as important as the one at Ouosalla. Only the best would be chosen, but she knew that she *was* one of the best. She was experienced, dedicated and hardworking, and possessed the kind of nimble, commonsense mind that allowed archaeologists to piece together ancient lives from the fragments left behind. There was no reason why she wouldn't be chosen.

But she hadn't been, because to the pinheads who ran the foundation, there was one very good reason not to include her: her name was Sherwood.

The head of archaeology at the university had put it to her point-blank: The daughter of Cyrus "Crackpot" Sherwood wouldn't be a prestigious addition to any archaeological team. Her own work and reliability were overshadowed by her father's reputation for propounding wild theories.

She was beating her head against a wall and it infuriated her. Her father had always said that she had enough determination for three people, but in this instance she was frustrated by a lack of options. She didn't want to leave the field of archaeology; she loved it too much. But the upper levels of her chosen career were closed to her, because of who she was. Archaeological digs cost a lot of money, and there weren't many sponsors around; the competition for the available funds was murderous. Therefore no reputable team could afford to send her on a major dig, as her very presence would call into question the validity of the findings, and the team would then lose the funding.

Even changing her name wouldn't do any good; the world of archaeology was a small one and too many people knew her. If only it weren't all so political! The funding went to the big names that got the publicity, and no one would take the chance of getting bad press by including her. She had been on plenty of minor digs, but all of the important finds had been closed to her.

Not that she would have changed her name, even if it would have done any good. Her father had been a wonderful man and a brilliant archaeologist. She had dearly loved him, and still missed him even though he had been dead for half of her twenty-eight years. It infuriated her that his many contributions to archaeology had been virtually ignored because of his wilder schemes and theories, none of which he had been able to prove. He had died in an accident in the Amazon jungle while on a trek that he'd hoped would provide incontrovertible proof of one of his more outrageous theories. He had been called a charlatan and a fool, but after his death the more sympathetic had decided that he had merely been "misguided."

Cyrus Sherwood's reputation had followed Jillian throughout her college days and her career, so she had often felt as if she had to work harder than anyone else, to be more accurate, more conscientious, to never show any of the flights of fancy that her father had reveled in. She had devoted herself to archaeology, never even taking a vacation, using every possible moment to pursue her goals.

All for nothing.

"Crackpot" Sherwood's daughter wasn't welcome on any major digs.

She banged her hands down on the wall. He hadn't been a crackpot, she thought fiercely. He had been a little vague, a little off-key, but a marvelous father, when he was home, and a damn good archaeologist.

Thinking of him made Jillian remember the boxes of his papers that she had never gone through. After his death, Professor Sherwood's papers had been packed up and the house sold, and her half brother, Rick, had taken the boxes to his dingy apartment and simply stacked them in a corner. He had no interest in them, and as far as she knew, they had never been touched. When Jillian finished college and moved into her own place she had offered to take them, to get them out of his way, but Rick had refused—more, she thought, because he liked the idea of having something that she wanted than because he himself wanted their father's things.

In that, as in most things, Rick's reasoning had been faulty. Though she would never have destroyed her father's papers, she hadn't been panting to get at them. Quite the contrary. By then, Jillian had been forced to full, painful acknowledgment of her father's reputation as a crackpot, a joke in the profession, and she hadn't wanted to read anything that might make her believe it, too. Better to keep her memories of him as they were.

But now she felt a surge of curiosity and a need to bring his memory closer. He had *not* been a crackpot! Some of his theories were unconventional, but five hundred years ago the theory that the earth was round was also considered a crackpot idea. Her father had spent countless hours poring over maps, charts, and journals, tracking down clues, to help formulate theories. And in the field he had been superb, able to tell so much about the past by the few shards of evidence that had survived to the present day.

She wished she had those boxes right now. Her father had never given her anything but support, and she needed that. He was gone, but those old records were more a part of him than the few mementos, mostly photographs, that she had.

She wavered for a minute. This was the blackest moment of her career, the angriest and saddest she had been since she had learned of the professor's death. She was independent by nature, but even the most independent person sometimes needed comfort, and this was one of those times for her. She wanted to feel closer to her father, needed to refresh her memories of him.

Making up her mind, she moved briskly back inside and looked up Rick's number in her address book, thinking wryly that it was an accurate comment on their relationship that she didn't know it. In essence, there was no relationship between them in any emotional sense. He had borrowed money from her a couple of times, but on average she saw him maybe once a year, which was plenty for both of them.

She let the phone ring for an entire minute before hanging up. Always realistic, she knew that it might take her a couple of days to get in touch with him, so she controlled her impatience and changed into her gym clothes. A workout was always good for stress, and she liked staying in shape anyway. Visits to the gym three days a week, plus jogging, kept her fit.

Still, as soon as she returned home a couple of hours later, she picked up the telephone and hit the redial button. To her surprise, after the first ring there was a click as the receiver was lifted and a brusque, only slightly slurred "Yeah?" barked into her ear.

"Rick, it's Jillian. Are you going to be home tonight?"

"Why?" The second word was guarded, suspicious.

"I want to look through those boxes of Dad's old papers."

"What for?"

"Just to look through them. We never have, you know. We don't know what's in there."

"So what does it matter now?"

"I don't guess it does. I'm just curious." Instinctively she didn't let Rick know how much she hurt inside or how she needed that contact with their father.

"I don't have time to sit here and watch you trip down memory lane," he said, totally bypassing the possibility of letting her pick up the boxes and carry them home with her. Rick would never give up what he perceived as an advantage over her.

"Okay," she said. "Forget it. It was just an idea. Bye."

"Wait," he said hurriedly. She could almost feel him thinking, picture the idea forming in his mind. "Uh . . . I guess you can come over. And, uh, do you think you can spare some cash? I'm a little short."

"Well, I don't know," she said, not wanting him to think it had been too easy and maybe change his mind. "How much cash?"

"Not much. Maybe a hundred."

"A hundred!"

"Okay, okay, make it fifty."

"I don't know," she said again. "I'll see what I have."

"Are you coming over now?" he asked.

"Sure, if you're going to be there."

"I'll be here." He dropped the phone, crashing it in her ear. Jillian shrugged as she hung up. Every contact with Rick was like that. Sometimes she wondered if he would ever see the futility of trying to spite her.

She checked her wallet to make sure she had fifty dollars in cash; she did, but it would wipe her out until she could get to an automatic teller, something she didn't like to do at night. She had plenty of gas in her car, though, so she wouldn't need cash for anything that night. It was worth fifty bucks to her to be able to go through her father's papers right away, when she needed bolstering. She seldom did, being solidly planted on her own two feet, but sometimes even the most resilient plant wilted. Tonight her leaves were definitely drooping.

She didn't bother changing out of her sweats because she was certain it would be a dusty, dirty job, sorting through those boxes after all these years. It took her forty-five minutes to reach Rick's apartment complex. It was a trio of two-story buildings, the stucco painted a pale salmon that had probably looked fresh lo, those many years ago when the complex was new but now was stained and faded to an unappetizing pinkish tan. Rick lived in the building on the left, on the bottom floor. The parking lot was crowded with vehicles in various stages of disassembly. Those that did presumably run were mostly in need of bodywork or were evidently in the process of getting it, since the main color was paint primer. The apartment occupants were in much the same shape, except for the paint.

She knocked on Rick's door. She could hear the television, but nothing else. She knocked again.

"All right, all right," came a faint, disgruntled answer, and a minute later Rick opened the door.

She was always surprised by how pleasant and boyish Rick's features were, how well his face had resisted the effects of cigarettes, booze, and his general life-style. His looks were fading a bit now, finally being worn down, but he was still an attractive man.

11

"Hi," he said. "You bring the money?"

"I don't have much more than fifty, but I can get by if you need it," she said, while thinking, *Hello, I'm fine, how are you?* She could smell the alcohol on his breath. Rick wasn't much for manners when he was sober, but he had none at all when he was drinking. Unfortunately, that was most of the time.

"Sure, I need it," he snapped. "I wouldn't have asked for a hundred to begin with if I didn't need it."

She shrugged and took out her wallet, opening it so he could see that she was giving him every bill she had. Fifty-seven bucks. She would never see it again, but she didn't expect to. She gave him the money and said, "Where are the boxes?"

"Back there. In the other bedroom."

The second bedroom was a junk room, without any hint of ever having seen a bed. Rick used it for storage and, evidently, as a convenient place for tossing anything that got in his way, including dirty clothes. The boxes were stacked in a corner; she fought her way over to them and began clearing out a space so she would have room to unpack them.

"What're you looking for?" Rick asked. She heard the suspicion in his voice and knew he hadn't quite believed her before.

"Nothing. I just want to read them. Why don't you bring in a couple of chairs and go through them with me?"

"No, thanks," he said, giving her a "get real" look. "I'd rather sip a cold one and watch the tube."

"Okay," she said, reaching for the first of the boxes; there were five of them, water-stained and fittingly coated with dust since most of the things the professor had loved had been dusty. She sat down on the floor and began tearing off the brown masking tape that had been used to seal them shut.

A lot of the material was research books, which she arranged around her according to subject. Some of the books, she noted with interest, were rare editions, which she handled with appreciative care.

There were notes about various digs, articles he had thought interesting and saved, maps and charts of varying ages, and several spiral notebooks in which he'd recorded his own ideas. These she opened with a smile tugging at her lips, for in the cramped handwriting she found again the essence of her father. He had had such enthusiasm for his work, such a boundless joy in reconstructing lost civilizations. He had never tried to rein in his imagination but had let it flow, trusting that it would take him toward the truth, which to him had always been much more fantastic than the most clever of lies.

His zest for his work had led him to try to track down several legends, and he had accorded each one a chapter in his notebooks. Jillian remembered the many evenings she had spent as a child, sitting enthralled at his feet or in his lap while he spun his wondrous tales for her entertainment. She hadn't grown up on fairy tales, though in a way perhaps she had, but her fairy tales had been of ancient civilizations and treasures, mysteriously vanished. . . . Had they ever really existed, or were they exactly that, tales grounded only in man's imagination? For her father, even the faintest glimmer of possibility that they could be true had been irresistible; he had had to track down the smallest of threads, if only to satisfy his own curiosity.

She skimmed the notebooks, her eyes dreamy as she remembered the tales he had told her associated with each legend, but she noted that he had discounted most of the legends as myth, with no factual basis. Some few legends he had decided were at least possible, though further research was needed and the truth would probably never be known. She became furious all over again; how could anyone dismiss him as a crackpot, when the evidence was right here that he had weighed the facts very carefully and wasn't influenced by the glamour or mythic proportions of his targets. But all anyone had ever talked about was his Anzar theory, his spectacular failure, and how his pursuit of it had cost him his life.

The Anzar. She hadn't thought about the legend for a long time, because it had caused his death. He had been so excited about it. The last time she had seen him, that morning before he left to travel to the Amazon in pursuit of the Anzar legend, he had been so exuberant, so enthusiastic. She had been a thin, awkward thirteen-year-old girl, almost fourteen, sulky at being left behind, pouting because he would be gone during her birthday, but he had hugged and kissed her anyway.

"Don't pout, sweetheart," he had said, stroking her hair. "I'll be back in a few months, half a year at the most."

"You don't have to go," she had replied, unrelenting.

"But I have this chance to find the Empress, to prove that the Anzar existed. You know what that would mean, don't you?"

At thirteen she had already had an alarmingly realistic outlook on life. "Tenure," she had said, and he had laughed.

"Well, that too. But think of what it would be like to prove the legend true, to hold the Heart of the Empress in my hand, to give its beauty to the world."

She had scowled. "You'd better be careful," she had scolded, shaking her finger at him. "The Amazon isn't a cakewalk, you know."

"I know. I'll watch every step, I promise."

But he hadn't. That morning was the last time she had seen him. They got the news about three months later, and it took another two months before his body was retrieved and returned for burial. Great-Aunt Ruby had come to stay with Jillian while the professor was gone, so Jillian's schooling wouldn't be interrupted, but after his death the house was abruptly sold and she found herself permanently installed in Great-Aunt Ruby's tiny bungalow. Rick, though he was her closest relative, hadn't wanted to burden himself with an adolescent girl. Besides, Rick had never forgiven his father for remarrying after the death of Rick's own mother, and he had moved out as soon as he finished high school. Rick and Jillian had never been close; he had barely tolerated her. The situation had never improved.

Her father's pursuit of the Anzar legend had ended his life and totally changed hers, not just in losing her father but in uprooting her from everything she had known, and even in the present his last quest overshadowed her own career. She flipped through the notebook, wanting to see his most personal thoughts about the legend that had cost her so much, but there wasn't a chapter devoted to the Anzar. She laid the notebook aside and picked up another, but it didn't contain anything about that ancient tribe either.

She went through two more notebooks before she found it, lying under the third notebook, which she had just picked up. It was plainly labeled on the front of the notebook in a heavy black script: *The South American Anzar Civilization.* It alone, of all the legends he had investigated, rated a notebook by itself. A thrill of excitement went through her as she lifted it out of the box and carefully opened it, wondering if she would be able to see what had so captured his interest that he had risked his reputation and his life to pursue it, and lost both.

He had collected several fables and legends from various sources, she saw, all of which contained some reference to the Empress or the Queen's Heart. The origins of these fables were impossible to pin down, though Cyrus Sherwood had meticulously researched them. They were neither Incan nor Mayan, yet seemed to originate from some advanced civilization. The fables had also referred to "the city of stone under the sea of green, the land of the Anzar." In several versions of the fable, with minor variations, a great warrior queen fell in love with a fierce warrior from another tribe, but he was killed while defending the city of stone, and his warrior queen, from a tribe of bloodless winged demons. The warrior queen, or empress, was devastated by his death and swore on his body that her heart would never belong to another, in this life or the next, through all eternity. She lived to a great old age, and when she died, her heart turned into a red jewel, which was taken from her body and placed on the tomb of her beloved warrior so it would belong to him through all eternity, just as she had pledged. Supposedly the red jewel had magical powers; it cast a spell of protection over the Anzar that kept them forever hidden in their city of stone under the green sea. It was the sort of tale that had sprung up in endless variations all over the world, with nothing to set it apart that would explain Professor Sherwood's intense interest in it.

Or her own. Jillian sat back on her heels, staring at the notebook. Her heart was pounding, and she didn't know why, unless it was because her father had thought this legend important enough to devote a separate notebook to it. She felt tense, caught up in the almost painful anticipation that still colored his words fifteen years later. She began reading again.

Almost an hour later she found the code. She stared at it, the childhood memory clicking into place. She grabbed her purse, scrabbled around for a pencil, and began transcribing the code. Only a few words into it, she folded the paper and crammed it into her purse, not wanting to go any further until she could do it in private.

No wonder he had been so excited.

She was sweating, her pulse racing. Her heart was slamming against her rib cage, and it was all she could do to keep from lifting her head in a primal scream to release the tension that had built within her.

He had done it. She knew it as she had never known anything else in her life, with a bone-deep conviction. Her father had found the Anzar.

And so, by God, would she.

2

Ben Lewis was kicked back at his favorite bar in Manaus, Brazil, a bottle of his favorite whiskey on the table and his favorite waitress on his knee. Life had a way of going in cycles from pure shit to really great, and this was one of the great times. As far as he was concerned, there wasn't anything like good whiskey and a willing woman to make a man feel mellow. Okay, so there was one part of him that wasn't feeling mellow, but hell, his dick hadn't felt mellow since puberty kicked in. And that was where sweet Thèresa came in. Since she was blond and spoke bad Portuguese with an American accent he figured she was really just plain Teresa, but that didn't matter. All that mattered was that she would get off work soon and lead him to her room, where she would spend the next hour or so under his pumping butt. Yep, he was definitely feeling mellow.

Christus, the bartender, yelled for Thèresa to get her ass back to work. She pouted, then laughed and gave Ben a hard, deep kiss. "Forty-five minutes, lover. Can you hold off that long?"

His dark eyebrows lifted. "I reckon. I'm usually worth the wait."

She laughed, the sound full of warm female anticipation. "Don't I know it. All right!" she said irritably to Christus as he scowled at her and opened his mouth to yell again.

As she left his lap, Ben patted her butt and then settled back contentedly to do justice to the smoky whiskey. Like any cautious man, he sat with his back to the wall. The dim, dingy, smoke-filled bar was a favorite with expatriates. Somehow people always managed to find other people like themselves, in any country, in any city, like floatsam washing ashore at one particular place. Brazil was a long way from Alabama, where he'd grown up, but he felt right at home here. The bar was lined with men who had seen it all and done it all, but for various reasons no longer felt the need to watch their backs. He liked the mix in Christus's bar: guides, rivermen, mercenaries both retired and active. It could reasonably be expected to be a rowdy joint, had been at times, and would be again in the future, but for the most part it was just a dim, comfortable place to take refuge from the heat and be with your own kind.

He supposed he'd be safe enough if he sat on one of the barstools; there wasn't anyone in here likely to kill him, and Christus would watch his back. But Ben didn't sit with his back to the wall because he was expecting a knife or a bullet, though they had been possibilities a few times in his life. He sat where he did so he could see everything that went on and everyone who came in. A man could never know too much. He was naturally observant and a lot of times it had saved his life. He wasn't about to break a lifelong habit now.

So when the two men entered the bar and stood for a minute letting their eyes adjust to the darkness before they chose a seat, he noticed them immediately and didn't like what he saw. One was a stranger, but he knew the other man's face and name, had heard a lot about him, none of it good. Steven Kates was a crook, unburdened by any principles or morals, uncaring of anything and everyone except himself. Their trails had never crossed, but Ben's habit of gathering information and keeping tabs on everything going on around him had brought him a lot of talk about Steven Kates. The thing was, Kates operated in the States; what was he doing in Brazil?

The two men moved to the bar. Kates leaned across it and

addressed a low comment to Christus. The burly bartender shrugged, not saying anything. Good old Christus could be as closemouthed as a clam if he didn't like the looks of someone, another reason why his bar was so popular.

Kates said something else, and this time Christus growled an answer. The two men held a brief discussion between themselves, nodded to Christus, then went to a table and sat down.

Thèresa drifted back over to Ben's table several minutes later. "Those two guys are trying to find you," she murmured as she bent over and wiped the table, which didn't need it.

Ben admired the view, looking forward to the moment when she would take her blouse off completely and he'd have unlimited access to those lush breasts.

"Something about a guide job upriver," she continued with a smile on her face, knowing exactly what he was looking at and thinking. She shrugged her shoulders, letting the blouse slide a little farther down and reveal even more of her cleavage.

"I don't need a job," he said.

"What *do* you need, lover?" she purred.

There was a lazy, slow-burning fire in his eyes. "A couple of hours of screwing would take the edge off," he allowed.

She shivered, and her little cat's tongue licked out. That was what he liked about Thèresa; she wasn't any great shakes in the brain department, but she was good-natured and completely sensual, always ready for a good time in bed. She was already getting turned on. He knew the signs as well as he knew them in his own body, though it was kind of difficult for an iron-hard dick to go unnoticed or be mistaken for anything else. Thèresa had to have a steady supply of sex, just as he did. When he wasn't around, someone else would do. Hell, just about anyone else would do. Sweet Thèresa wasn't particular, she liked all men, as long as their equipment was in working order.

She was beaming as she went back to work, her face lit with anticipation.

Ben studied Kates and the man with him. It was the truth; he didn't need a job now. He had plenty of money in the bank, and his life-style wasn't extravagant. Fancy sleaze could cost a lot of bucks, but plain sleaze was dirt cheap. As long as he had food, a bed, good whiskey, and plenty of sex, that was all he asked out of life. Ben Lewis was a contented man.

Like hell.

The nose for adventure, which had led him into one hellhole after another for most of his life, was working at full strength now. If a slime ball like Steven Kates would put himself out by tramping through the Amazon basin, there had to be a mighty important reason behind it. The Amazon wasn't an ordinary river and any expedition wasn't exactly a walk in the park. From what Ben knew of him, Kates was the type who hung back and let others do the work; then he stepped in and relieved them of their hard-earned loot.

It had to be something big to entice Kates to active participation.

Ben got to his feet and ambled over to their table, snagging the bottle of whiskey from his own table as an afterthought. He tipped the bottle up and let a small amount run into his mouth where he held it on his tongue, savoring the taste for a delicious moment before swallowing it. Damn good whiskey.

Kates was staring at him with cold disdain. Ben cocked one eyebrow at the two men. "I'm Lewis. Y'all looking for me?"

He almost laughed aloud at the look on Kates's face, and he knew what the other man was seeing: someone who hadn't shaved, whose clothing was stained and wrinkled, and who was cradling a bottle as if he never let it out of his arms. Well, he *hadn't* shaved, his clothes *were* dirty and wrinkled, and he didn't intend to let that bottle go just yet. He'd come straight here from a bitch of a trip upriver, and the shaving and bathing would wait until he got to Thèresa's place, because she liked to take a bath with him. And this was, in fact, fine whiskey; he hadn't had even a taste of booze in a couple of months, and if he'd left it on the table some son of a bitch would have swiped it. He'd paid for the bottle, so where he went, it went.

The other man, though, was looking at him eagerly. "Ben Lewis?"

"Yep." This guy looked to be in his mid-thirties, maybe older but with boyish features that disguised his age despite a certain look of dissipation. Ben sized him up immediately: a do-nothing, the type who whined about being dealt a bad hand in life rather than getting up off his lazy ass and doing something about it. Even if he did do something, it would be along the lines of robbing a convenience store to improve his finances; actually working hard at a job wouldn't occur to him. Ben wasn't much on the nine-to-five routine himself, but at least he was solvent through his own efforts, not someone else's.

"We heard you're the best guide available for an expedition we're planning," the other man said. "We'd like to hire you."

"Well, now." Ben hooked an extra chair around and sat down in it backwards, his arms propped on the back of it. "I'm the best, but I don't know if I'm available. I just got back from a trip, and I'd planned on a little R and R before I went back up."

Steven Kates seemed to have recovered from his distaste, maybe figuring that anyone who had just returned from a guide trip was entitled to look dirty and unshaven. "It'll be worth your while, Mr. Lewis."

Mr. Lewis? It had been so long since Ben had been called "mister" that he almost looked around to see if someone was standing behind him. "Just 'Lewis,'" he said. "My while is worth a lot right now. I'm tired and looking forward to sleeping in a real bed for a couple of weeks." A real bed with a woman in it.

"Ten thousand dollars," Kates said.

"For how long?" Ben asked.

Kates shrugged. "We don't know. It's an archaeological expedition."

That was doubtful. Ben couldn't imagine Kates being involved in anything as high-minded as an archaeological expedition. He might use it as a cover, but that was it. This was getting more interesting by the minute. "What's the general area? I'll be able to judge the length of the trip then."

The other man pulled out a map of Brazil and laid it on the table. It wasn't a large or detailed map; in fact, it looked as if it had been torn from an encyclopedia. He tapped his finger on an area far inland and north of the Amazon. "In here somewhere. We don't know exactly where."

Ben stared at the map with half-closed eyes and took another sip of whiskey. Damn, that was good stuff. It burned all the way down. Appreciation of it kept him from laughing out loud at the preposterousness of the situation. These goofballs had come down here with a grade-school map and no idea what they were getting into. "It's uncharted up there," he finally said. "I've never gone into that territory, and I don't know anyone who has."

"You can't do it?" the second man asked, looking disappointed.

Ben snorted. "Hell, yes, I can do it. Just who are you, anyway?"

"I'm Rick Sherwood. This is Steven Kates."

So Kates wasn't going by an assumed name. He apparently thought no one would know of him down here. That meant he felt safe.

"Well, Rick Sherwood and Steven Kates, I can take you up there. I've never been, but I know how to get along in the jungle, and I don't suppose it makes any difference that I don't know exactly where I am if you don't know exactly where you're going. The problem is, ten thousand is peanuts. You won't be able to hire anyone who knows his stuff for that amount. You're talking about two, maybe three months in hell. My price is two thousand a week, and you pay for all the supplies and extra help. I'll cost you roughly twenty, twenty-five thousand, and the rest of it will come to about another ten. So, are you still so all-fired set on this 'archaeological expedition'?"

The two exchanged looks. They hadn't caught his faint

emphasis on the last two words. "No problem," Kates said smoothly.

Ben was now past curious, he was flat-out intrigued. Kates hadn't even blinked an eye, which meant that whatever was up there was worth so much money that thirty-five thousand dollars was a drop in the bucket in comparison, and Kates sure as hell wasn't involved out of a burning desire to be written up in any archaeological papers. Scavenge the site was more like it, assuming there really was an archaeological site up there, which Ben thought was doubtful. The jungle destroyed evidence of man almost as fast as man could leave it. Still, until he had a better idea of what was going on, he was going to assume there was a site up there, because there sure as hell wasn't anything else in that area. But what could be so valuable that it would lure someone like Kates into going for it? The jungle abounded with tales of lost treasure and fantastic myths, but as far as Ben knew, none of them were true. People were always looking for lost treasure; except for the odd shipwreck, none of those treasures were ever found. It was a fact that people believed whatever they wanted, regardless of the evidence. Ben certainly wasn't going to risk his profits on finding a pot of gold at the end of the rainbow.

"Payable in advance," Ben said.

"What the hell? Forget it," Sherwood blustered.

Significantly, Kates didn't say anything, though he was frowning. Ben tilted the bottle up for another sip. "I don't skip out on my clients," he said. "If I did, I wouldn't get any more. The same isn't true the other way around. I learned that the hard way. I get my money up front or it's no deal."

"There are other guides, Lewis."

"Sure there are. But none as good as I am. It's your choice if you want to get back alive or die in there. Like I said, I just returned from a trip. It won't hurt my feelings to have a little vacation before I take another job."

Ben was aware that he wasn't telling the exact truth, but bluffing was part of the game. If these fools didn't know how to play it, that was their problem. There were Indians in the region who knew more about living in the jungle than he ever would, but those Indians just might be the biggest danger to anyone trespassing in their territory. There were still bands of natives deep in the interior who had never seen a white man, still huge areas that were uncharted. No one knew what was in there. At least, no one who had come back out to describe it. Hell, for all he knew, the region was infested with headhunters.

"Ask around," he said carelessly, getting to his feet. "Like I said, I don't need a job, but you need a guide pretty damn bad."

It was real funny the way most people valued something more if they thought it was hard to obtain. Just as he'd thought, his indifference to the job convinced them that he was the best available.

"Don't be so hasty," Kates said. "You're hired."

"Fine," Ben said just as carelessly as before. "When do you want to leave?"

"As soon as possible."

He sighed. Damn. He'd hoped for a few days to relax, but twenty-five thousand was twenty-five thousand. "Okay." He glanced at his watch. Three-thirty. "Meet me back here at seven and we'll go over the logistics." That would give him at least two hours with Thèresa, and time for cleaning up as well.

"We can do that now," Sherwood said.

"You can. I can't. Seven o'clock." Ben walked away and approached Thèresa. "Give me your key," he said, and nuzzled her neck. "I'll clean up and be waiting in bed for you."

She laughed as she fished the key out of her pocket. "Well, all right, but I was planning to climb into the tub with you."

"Got things to do, sugar. If I'm already cleaned up, we'll have more time in the sack."

"In that case, get a move on." She winked and kissed him, and Ben sauntered out of the bar, aware of three sets of eyes watching him, but he was interested in only one. Women. Damn their sweet little hides, if they ever figured out just how wild men were for them, the power structure of the entire world would turn upside down. Maybe that was why men had been made bigger and stronger, just to give them a fighting chance.

Rick had given Jillian instructions to have their belongings stored while they were away; then he and Kates had left the hotel to find the guide they had heard about. She was glad of the time alone, because she had some things to take care of that she didn't want either of them to know about. First she arranged for storage, searching out the hotel manager, who didn't seem overly pleased with the idea of holding their stuff. But as they wouldn't be leaving a great deal behind and since she paid him for two months' storage in advance, he was willing. After a few moments of conversation in a mixture of Portuguese and English, she understood that he disapproved of her going on the expedition at all.

"Many men do not come back, senhora," he said seriously. He was very Latin in looks, short and stocky, with straight black hair and large dark eyes. "The jungle eats them up, and they are never seen again."

Jillian didn't correct his assumption that she was a married woman, for it would only have embarrassed him and didn't matter to her. It wasn't an unusual assumption, that she was Rick's wife rather than his sister. They didn't resemble each other at all, except that they both had brown hair. The manager seemed like a nice man, and she wanted to pat his hand to comfort him. "I understand your concerns," she said. "I share them. Believe me, I don't take the jungle lightly. But I'm an archaeologist, and I'm used to rough conditions. I've probably slept more nights in a tent than in a bed, and I'm very cautious."

"I hope so, senhora," he replied, his fine eyes worried. "Myself, I would not go."

"But I must, and I promise you I'll take every care."

She hadn't lied. Though she had done most of her work in dry, dusty climates, she knew the obstacles that faced them. Both flora and fauna could prove deadly. Her vaccinations were up to date, she had a good supply of antibiotics and insect repellent, a more than adequate first-aid kit, and was competent at stitching up minor wounds. She had also taken the precaution of getting a prescription for birth control pills and had brought along a three-month supply, smuggled into the country in her first-aid kit, disguised as antihistamines.

Still, she didn't try to fool herself that she could cope with everything the rain forest would throw at them. She would be careful, but accidents could always happen, as could illness. Despite every caution, snakebite could happen. She also had antivenin in the first-aid kit, but there were some poisons for which there was no antidote. Hostile Indians were also a possibility, since there were great stretches of the Amazon basin that had never been explored or mapped. They literally had no idea what they would find.

She quickly finished her business with the manager and left the hotel with one purpose in mind: to purchase a reliable weapon. She thought it would be a relatively easy task in Manaus; after all, the city, with its wide avenues and European ambience, was a duty-free port. Practically any mass-produced product in the world could be found in Manaus.

Living in Los Angeles probably helped her endure the heat better than if she had lived in, say, Seattle, but still she found the humidity enervating. They were here in the best season, the winter months of June, July, and August, which meant this was the driest time of the year and the heat was marginally less intense. She suspected that "dry" meant that instead of raining every day, perhaps it would rain only every other day. If they weren't so lucky, it would rain only twice a day rather than three times. She hoped for the first, but was prepared for the latter.

She walked around for a while, not straying far from the hotel but keeping her eyes open. She overheard at least seven different languages before she had gone two hundred yards. Manaus was a fascinating city, a deep-water port situated twelve hundred miles inland, with all the worldliness of any seaport visited by cruise ships. Indeed, the cruise ships probably accounted for the variety of languages she had encountered. So what if they were smack in the middle of a continent? The mighty Amazon was a law unto itself, so deep in some places that four hundred feet of water still lay beneath the hulls of the ships.

Rick was still sullen over her insistence on keeping the map to herself, scarcely speaking to her at all except to give orders, but she didn't let that sway her determination. This expedition was as much for their father as it was for her—more, in fact. She was strong and could fight her own battles, but the professor couldn't protect either his reputation or his memory. He would be forever remembered as a crackpot unless she could prove that his theory about the Anzar had been valid, and that meant not trusting Rick with the information.

She wished he weren't involved at all, but circumstances had been against her. Rick had reentered the room only moments after she'd realized what she had, probably to make certain she wasn't up to something, and she hadn't been able to hide her excitement. He had looked at the papers scattered around her, seen a general map of the area, and for once leaped to the correct conclusion, though he had called it a "treasure map."

He had badgered her for days to give him the coordinates, but she knew her brother; he was what in the old days had been called a ne'er-do-well. He would probably have sold the information to some ambitious fortune hunter without thinking or caring about the professor's reputation. He certainly wouldn't have been inclined to preserve the findings for careful excavation by trained archaeologists or to catalog the finds or to turn any valuables over to the Brazilian government as required by law. If she could have lined up any outside sponsorship she would have done so, and she'd have gotten the documents even if she'd had to resort to burglary, but all of her feelers had been either ignored or laughed at. She could just hear them all now: Crackpot Sherwood's daughter had gone off the deep end too.

In the end, it was Rick who had brought Steven Kates into the picture. For reasons of his own, Kates was willing to finance the project. Jillian had insisted on coming along to protect the find as best she could, but she couldn't help feeling bitter that she had been forced into such a position by the blindness of some members of her chosen profession. If they had given any credence to her father, or to her, the expedition would have been staffed by trained archaeologists and reliable guides rather than the unscrupulous riffraff she was very much afraid Rick and Kates had hired. If she had had any other option she would have used it, but she had to make do with the resources available to her. She was a pragmatist, yes, but she was a *prepared* pragmatist. She had committed the location of the Stone City to memory, so they *had* to take her along, and she would also make certain she was armed.

It was a logical precaution. She was competent with a firearm, a competence that came in handy in her profession. Snakes and other dangers were part of the job. She was concerned that this time the snakes would be two-legged, but that was a risk she would have to take. She only hoped she could contain the damage; after all, they were hardly likely to kill her or leave her behind in the jungle to die. Despite Rick's failings as both a man and a brother, he wasn't a murderer. At least, she *hoped* he would balk at any attempt to harm her. She reserved judgment on Steven Kates, but on the surface he seemed to be civilized. If he proved to be otherwise, she would be prepared.

Finding a weapon in any large city wasn't a difficult task, and Jillian wasn't timid about it. She would have brought one from the States if she had been confident of getting it through customs, but smuggling a weapon was rather different from smuggling birth control pills, especially if she'd been caught.

She walked slowly past the line of taxis in front of another hotel, studying the drivers without making it obvious. She was looking for one who didn't look quite as prosperous as the others, though none of them looked well off. Maybe "seedy" was the word. Finally she selected one; he was unshaven, a little more slovenly than the others, his eyes bloodshot. She walked up to the vehicle with a smile, and in her imperfect Portuguese asked to be taken to the docks.

The driver wasn't inclined to talk. Jillian waited a few moments as he negotiated the traffic in the crowded streets before calmly saying, "I want to purchase a weapon. Do you know where I can find one?"

He glanced quickly in the rearview mirror. "A weapon, senhora?"

"A pistol. I prefer an automatic, but it doesn't matter if it's a . . . a—" She couldn't think of the word for "revolver" in Portuguese. She made a circle with her finger and said "revolver" in English.

His dark eyes were both wary and cynical. "I will take you to a place," he said. "I will not stay. I do not want to see you again, senhora."

"I understand." She gave him a reassuring smile. "Will I be able to find another taxi back to the hotel?"

He shrugged. "There are many tourists. Taxis are everywhere."

By that she assumed she might or might not be able to catch another taxi. If necessary, she would walk to a public telephone and call for one, though she didn't relish the idea of walking in this heat. She had dressed sensibly in a thin cotton skirt, and her legs were bare, but a steam bath was a steam bath no matter what you were wearing.

He drove her to a rather seedy section of town, run-down but not yet a slum. She gave him a generous tip and didn't look back as she walked into the shop he had indicated.

Within half an hour she was the owner of a .38 automatic, easy to clean and maintain, and an impressive supply of ammunition weighted down her shoulder bag. The man who had sold it to her hadn't even looked curious. Perhaps American women bought weapons from him every day; it didn't take much of a stretch of imagination to visualize it. He even called a taxi for her and allowed her to wait just inside his door until the vehicle appeared.

When she got to the hotel she found that Rick and Kates still hadn't returned, but she hadn't expected them. Rick was still so put out that he might well leave her on her own all night, a prospect she knew he hoped would alarm her, but it didn't. She wasn't there to sightsee, and the room service menu was more than adequate; it wouldn't bother her at all to remain at the hotel for the rest of the day. She would even welcome the chance to rest.

But Rick and Kates returned to the hotel late that afternoon and came to her room, both of them smiling and in a good mood. Jillian smelled liquor on their breath, but they weren't drunk.

"We found a guide," Rick announced jovially, having finally come out of his sulks. "We're supposed to meet him at seven to do the planning."

"Here at the hotel?" It seemed convenient to her.

"Naw, at this bar where he hangs out. You'll have to come. You know more about this planning stuff than we do."

Jillian sighed inwardly. She could think of better places to discuss this than in a crowded bar where any number of people might overhear them. "Who is the guide? I don't believe I heard you mention his name."

"Lewis," Kates said. "Ben Lewis. Everyone we asked said that he's the best. I guess he'll do. If he leaves the bottle alone, he should be all right."

That sounded truly encouraging. She sighed again. "Is he an American?"

Rick shrugged. "I guess. He did have kind of a southern accent."

To Jillian's way of thinking, that pretty well nailed down the man's country of origin. She managed to keep the comment to herself.

"He was born in the States," Kates said, "but who knows if he still considers himself an American? I believe the term is 'expatriate.' No one seemed to know how long he's been down here."

Long enough to have gone completely tropical, Jillian would have bet. Slower, less concerned with detail. But most places in the world lacked the obsession with speed and efficiency that characterized the States, and she herself had learned to slow down when in other countries. She had been on digs in Africa among people who had no word for "time" in their language; the concept of putting themselves on a schedule would have been utterly alien to them. It had been a matter of adapt or go insane; it would be interesting to see which option Mr. Lewis had chosen.

"He's the type who wants to run the show," Rick said. "If half of what we heard about him is true, I guess he does what he damn well pleases."

She could tell that Rick had been impressed by this Lewis person. Her brother's taste had been frozen in mid-adolescence, however, so she decided to reserve judgment. Rick was impressed by any swaggering bully, believing machismo to be the essence of manhood. She began to lower her expectations of the guide they had hired.

At Rick's request, she was ready at six-thirty. She knew him well enough to realize he wished she were some sort of blond bombshell who was willing to use her body to dazzle and influence this man, who had somehow impressed him, but even if she were willing to bleach her hair she just didn't have the basic material to be a bombshell. One of the requirements was voluptuousness, and Jillian fell far short of that. She'd always been glad, too, because it looked like a lot of effort to haul around the large breasts that seemed to turn men into slavering idiots.

She was what she was: neat, trim, pleasant to look at but not a raving beauty. If anyone had asked her what her best feature was, she'd have said it was her brain.

As a concession to the heat, however, she wore a halter-top dress; it was, in fact, the only dress she had packed. Except for the skirt and blouse she had worn on the flight down, she'd brought only sturdy trousers, shirts, and boots.

During the taxi ride through Manaus with Rick and Kates she took the time to look around and admire what she saw. It was a beautiful city and she wished she had time to explore it, but then, she always felt that way. She never had enough time in the cities of today's world; her work was with those of past worlds—dead cities, burial grounds—trying to piece together the past so as to learn how those long-ago people had lived as well as how the human race had come to be in its present position. Archaeology tried to find the roadway humans had traveled to the present, and to learn how they had changed over the millennia. It was a puzzle she never tired of trying to solve.

The bar she and Rick and Kates stepped into wasn't the ritziest joint she had ever been in, but neither was it the worst. She took it in stride, even the way the men at the bar all turned to survey her with hooded eyes. Had she been alone she wouldn't have entered the place except in an emergency. Still, it was dim and blessedly cool and filled with the low hum of voices. The scents of alcohol, tobacco, and sweat swirled around with the lazy movements of the two ceiling fans.

She was flanked by Rick and Kates as they moved toward a table set against the wall, where a lone man lazed as if half asleep, an open bottle of whiskey in front of him. His appearance was deceptive, however. Even from beneath those half-lowered lids she could see intensity gleaming in his eyes. As they approached, he shoved out a chair with his foot and gave Jillian a look that had about as much in common with the looks from the men at the bar as a shark had in common with a trout. The men at the bar might have speculated, but they kept their thoughts to themselves. This man, in his mind, already had her stripped, spread-eagled, and penetrated, and didn't care if she knew it.

"Well," he drawled. "Hello there, sweetcakes. If you aren't taken, why don't you sit down over here by me?" He nodded at the chair he had just kicked out.

Now that they were closer, Jillian could see that his eyes were either blue or green; it was difficult to tell which in the dim light. He was darkly tanned, but his jaw had the freshly scraped look of a man who had just shaved. His hair was dark and too long, hanging over his collar at the back of his neck and almost touching his shoulders. His clothes, though clean, were badly wrinkled and well worn; he had the unselfconscious air of a man who didn't give a damn how his clothes looked.

Without even a flicker of an eyelash to indicate that his blatant once-over had discomfited her, she pulled out her own chair and sat down, ignoring the one he had kicked out.

"I'm Jillian Sherwood," she said in a cool tone, instinctively refusing to let him know that he had ruffled her. She wasn't even certain why he had bothered, since God and everyone else with eyes could see that she wasn't anything special. Some men, however, felt compelled to make a play for every woman who entered their vicinity.

"Ah, hell. You're married."

"She's my sister," Rick said. "This is Lewis, our guide."

Ben lifted his eyebrows as he looked at her. "Sister? So why are you along?"

Jillian's eyebrows mirrored his. Surely Rick and Kates had told him something about the expedition. Absently she noticed that Rick had been right about the southern accent. Aloud she said, "I'm the archaeologist."

He gave her a pleasant smile that still managed to be dismissive. "You can't go," he said.

Jillian remained cool. "Why not?"

Mild surprise reflected in his eyes, as if he hadn't expected a protest. He slowly sipped at his whiskey as he studied her. "Too damn dangerous," he finally said.

Rick and Kates had both taken seats by then. Rick cleared his throat, and Ben looked at him. "It's not that simple," Rick said.

"I don't see what's complicated about it. I don't take women inland. End of discussion."

"Then it's evidently the end of your employment, too," Jillian murmured, her composure intact. She had met chauvinistic jerks like him before, and she wasn't about to get ruffled by this one.

"Oh?" He didn't seem perturbed. "How's that?"

"She has to go," Rick interjected, and scowled at his sister. This was a sore point with him. "She's the only one who knows where we're going."

3

Ben looked unimpressed. "So she can tell us and then we'll all know, and she can toddle on back to the hotel like a good little girl and leave the rough stuff to us."

"I'm perfectly capable of carrying my own weight," Jillian said calmly. "And the decision isn't yours whether I go or not. I'm going. All you have to decide is if you want the job or if someone else gets the money."

Kates had said the same thing, but Ben realized Jillian Sherwood meant it. She didn't care if he backed out.

He leaned forward and propped an elbow on the table, cupping his chin in his palm as he looked at her. "Sweetcakes, if you think this is going to be a romantic adventure, you're dead wrong. There's no way I'm taking a woman on a two- or three-month trek into that part of the jungle."

She looked amused. "Protecting the little woman?"

"You got it, honey. In my opinion, there isn't enough prime pussy in the world as it is, and a man needs to protect the supply."

He was being deliberately crude, hoping she'd get huffy and tell him she wouldn't walk across the street with a jerk like him, but again she didn't even blink. Her face was as calm and blank as a statue's; even the expression in her eyes was shielded. "If I don't go," she said, "the expedition's off.

34

At least as far as you're concerned. As I said, if you want to throw away the fee, that's fine with me. There are other guides."

There were, but none he'd trust with a lone woman for that long a time. He doubted her brother could be counted on to keep her safe. He decided to try another tack, one that was bluntly truthful. "Honey, you don't want to spend two months inland—"

"On the contrary, that's exactly what I want to do. I'm not a stranger to archaeological expeditions, Mr. Lewis. I'm used to bugs and snakes and being dirty, to bad food and bruises. I can walk all day and carry a hundred pounds doing it. I can shoot my own food if necessary, stitch up a cut, and use a machete."

He placed his free hand over his heart. "My God, the perfect woman."

She gave him a cool look but didn't snap at his bait. He leaned back in his chair and studied her with narrowed eyes. He'd really only given her a cursory inspection before, enough to know that she wasn't his type despite his automatic raunchy remarks, but she was becoming more interesting by the moment. Her cool composure made him want to do something that would *really* rattle her, like pull her onto his lap and kiss her until some of the stiffness left that backbone.

At second look she still wasn't anything outstanding, except for the intelligence in her eyes. God save him from intelligent women; they *thought* too much, instead of just following their instincts. She was pretty enough but not flashy, just a rather lean, smallish woman with sleek dark brown hair and regular features. She was wearing a neat but unremarkable dress that managed not to be sexy even though it was a halter-top. Even worse, she revealed absolutely no awareness of him as a man. He was accustomed to all women being aware of him, even if they weren't receptive, but Ms. Sherwood appeared not to have an active hormone in her body. Dead from the neck down, as the saying went. Pity.

On the other hand, if she could walk all day while carrying

a heavy pack, then that trim body was probably all taut, finely tuned muscle. He had a sudden image of strong, slim thighs wrapped around his hips and, to his surprise, felt an answering tension in his groin. He'd left Thèresa asleep in her tumbled bed, exhausted from an afternoon of rather vigorous sex, and he'd returned to the bar feeling completely satisfied. His penis, however, seemed to have a different opinion. Well, the damn thing had never had any sense anyway. No matter how firm and tight she was, he didn't want Ms. Archaeologist Sherwood along on his trek.

"Let me get this straight," he drawled. "You want to be the only woman alone with a group of men for a couple of months?"

"Sex doesn't enter into it, Mr. Lewis."

"The hell it doesn't. Men get into fights over women every day, all over the world."

"How silly of them."

"Yeah, I've always thought so, but face the facts: if you're the only woman, then you pretty well have the monopoly, and men get a little crazy when it's around and they don't have any."

She gave him an ironic look. "I won't be prancing around in negligees, Mr. Lewis, and I'm prepared to defend myself. I would also expect you to hire people who aren't rapists."

Rick and Kates had been sitting silently while she and Lewis battled, Rick looking uneasy and Kates merely looking bored. But Kates sat forward now. "This is pointless," he said. "She has to go. Do you want the job, Lewis, or not?"

Ben thought about it. He didn't need the money or the hassle. He could tell them to find someone else; then he could spend the next few weeks resting and banging Thèresa, just as he'd planned. On the other hand, his instincts were telling him that something was going on, that though *she* was on the level, these other two were working their own deal, and he wanted to know what it was. He smelled money, a lot of it. He had a few scruples, but they seldom got in the way of making money, certainly not when it came to perhaps conning a couple of con men.

"All right," he said abruptly. "I'll do it. Let's get this figured out." He slugged back a hefty swallow of whiskey and gave his full attention to the business at hand. Laying in supplies for a long trek into the interior was serious stuff and had to be carefully calculated. How many people were involved? How far were they going? How long did they expect to stay once they got there? He always took extra supplies in case something went wrong, which always happened—he had to plan for all possibilities.

He pulled out a map and spread it on the table, a larger and much more detailed map than the one the men had produced earlier. "Okay, show me where we're going."

Jillian leaned over and drew a large circle with her forefinger. "This general area."

He looked at her as if she were crazy. The area she had indicated covered thousands of square miles. "Shit, if you don't have a better idea than that where we're going, we're likely to wander around for months without finding what you're looking for, and that's not an area where we can stroll at our leisure. It's uncharted territory, sweetcakes. Nobody knows what the hell is in there. If any white men have gone in, they haven't come out."

She remained unruffled. "We'll have to work out the exact course en route, Mr. Lewis."

"Well, I can't lay in supplies *en route*," he drawled with almost visible sarcasm. "I have to know beforehand where I'm going."

She leaned forward and tapped a spot on the map beyond the area she had indicated before. "Then get sufficient supplies to last us to this point, and that will be more than enough."

He showed his teeth, but not in a smile. "We have to *carry* the goddamn supplies. The more we have to carry, the longer the trip will take. The longer it takes, the more stuff we'll need. Is any of this making sense, sweetcakes?"

"I'm sure you'll find a satisfactory median."

"A median isn't what would give me satisfaction right now." Throttling her struck him as a damn satisfactory idea. Or climbing on top of her. He was definitely getting hard. Arguing with a woman had never caused that response before; it must be true that a man couldn't resist a challenge from a woman, and Ms. Jillian Sherwood was a challenge from head to foot.

"Then you'll have to do as you think best," she said blandly. "I've given you all the information I can."

Or would. He suspected she knew a hell of a lot more than she was telling, but none of it was given away by those cool green eyes. He wondered why their destination was so all-fired secret that she hadn't even told her brother. On second thought, he decided that he wouldn't share any valuable information with Rick Sherwood either, especially when he had friends like Steven Kates. Maybe Ms. Sherwood was even smarter than he'd thought. But just what the hell did she think she was going to do when they got to wherever she wanted to go? Stand guard twenty-four hours a day?

He dropped the subject, knowing she wasn't going to say anything else in front of the other two. She didn't trust *him* either, come to that. Definitely a smart woman. If he had to be honest with himself, which he usually was, he had to admit that she was right in that, too. If she let her guard down just a fraction, he'd have her drawers off before she knew the game was going on, much less that she'd lost it. Since she insisted on going with them, he'd have a couple of months to work on her, and he had no doubt about the success of his seduction plans.

Who knows, if he sweet-talked her just right, she might even tell him what she was looking for. If whatever was in the jungle was so valuable to her, well, hell, it would be valuable to him, too. A man never had too much money. Ben had a few limits as to what he'd do to get it, but that didn't mean he wasn't willing to seize every opportunity that presented itself.

He made arrangements to meet them the following day for his advance payment as well as the money he would need to start laying in supplies and hiring porters. Now that the decision was made, he was ready to get on with it.

* * *

"Did you have to come on like such a bitch?" Rick asked resentfully when they were back at the hotel.

Jillian sighed. She was tired, and dealing with Ben Lewis had just about used up her store of patience. "I was more polite than he was."

"You were throwing your weight around, making a point of showing him that the big-shot archaeologist is the one calling the shots."

Big-shot? She almost laughed aloud. Her professional prestige was almost nil; if the foundation had had any respect for her or confidence in her opinion, she wouldn't have been forced to deal with roughnecks like their guide. But Rick had always been jealous of the fact that she had followed in their father's footsteps, and he was quick to flare up at any perceived slight.

"I wasn't throwing my weight around. I was just letting him know that he can't intimidate me. And anyway, I don't think he's such a good choice. He was drinking this afternoon when you saw him, he was drinking tonight, and he's probably been drinking every minute in between. A sot isn't our best bet."

"So now you want to run this part of it, too?" Rick sneered.

It was difficult, but she held on to her temper. Maybe she did so out of guilt, because she knew the professor had preferred her over her brother. She couldn't help feeling sorry for Rick, though at the same time she had to fight her impatience with him. Whatever was wrong with his life was always someone else's fault, and usually she was the someone else.

"What I want," she snapped, "is to find the Anzar city and clear Dad's name. And I think we'd have a better chance of doing that if our guide is at least sober."

He scowled at her. "I suppose you think I don't care about Dad's name? He was my father too, you know."

She did know it. No matter how angry Rick made her, she never forgot that he really had loved the professor. That more than anything was what kept her from writing him out of her life.

"Let's forget about it, okay?" Kates cut in. "We're all tired. I know Lewis looks and talks rough, but his reputation is the best. I'll see him tomorrow and tell him to lay off the sauce. Why don't we call it a night?"

His tone was soothing, the peacemaker at work, but his cold eyes signaled a warning to Rick. Jillian saw it, though she pretended not to. Kates worked hard at presenting an innocuous front, but she couldn't quite buy it, maybe because the eyes never fit the image. Because it suited her to cut the conversation short before it degenerated into a real fight, she murmured good night and went into her room.

Kates jerked his head at Rick, and the two men went down the hall to their own rooms. "Don't get her back up," Kates warned. "If she decides to cut a separate deal, we're left out in the cold with nothing for our trouble."

Rick turned sulky, as he always did in the face of criticism. "She's not going to cut any deals with Lewis," he muttered. "She can't stand him."

"Lewis isn't the only guide. If she convinces someone else that those jewels are really there, they might get the financing and go after the treasure on their own. Try to keep your temper under control, at least until we're on our way and there's nothing she can do about it."

"All right, all right. That attitude of hers just pisses me off."

Kates managed a tight smile. "Just think of the money." Kates himself couldn't think about anything else; it was the only reason he was there. He was out of familiar territory and didn't like it at all, but was willing to do whatever it took to get those jewels. When Rick had first come to him with a wild story about his old man finding a lost city with a fortune in gems just waiting for whoever got there first, he'd wondered what kind of ha-ha powder Sherwood was taking. But Rick had had details, enough that Kates had begun to realize he was dead serious.

He was desperate enough to jump at the chance to involve himself; he needed money, lots of it. He was literally at the end of his rope, jumping at every unexpected noise. His last big shipment of coke had been seized by the police. They hadn't been able to nail him, but the cops were the least of his worries. He owed millions to the people who had fronted him the money for that coke shipment, money that would have been earned back several times over if he'd been able to get the coke on the street, and his creditors were tired of waiting for him to make good on the debt. Those people made the cops look like Mister Rogers.

Rick's mad scheme was a godsend, in more ways than one. Kates had just enough money to finance this crazy project. If it panned out, then he could save his ass. At the very least, being in Brazil would give him a breather from looking over his shoulder every few minutes, waiting for his head to be blown off.

If Rick was right . . . damn, a deal like this came along once in a lifetime. The gems—especially that big red diamond—would bring in a pile of loot that would make his coke debt look paltry. He dreamed about that damn rock, dreamed about holding it in his hands. It was his ticket to easy street, if he could just get Sherwood to keep his stupid mouth shut. The sister wasn't a fool; from what Kates could tell, she'd gotten all the brains in the family. But she was keeping all the information to herself, and the instructions were written in some kind of code that only she could read. He wasn't worried about her, though. All he wanted was for her to get him there. Then he wouldn't have any use for her or any of the others. He had plans that didn't include them, big plans. He was tired of always being pissed on by the big boys; this was one time when *he* was going to get the lucky break.

The next day Steven Kates showed up at the bar alone. Ben hid his instinctive distrust of the man behind a facade of good-old-boy affability. A lot of people were fooled by his slow southern drawl and seedy, hard-drinking act; it was a useful disguise. Oh, the drawl was real, but people who knew him long enough gradually realized that behind it lay a sharp brain and ruthless determination. He doubted Kates was smart enough to figure it out.

"You nearly screwed things up bad last night, talking to

Jillian like that," Kates snapped as soon as he sat down at Ben's table. "She's not one of your cheap whores. Keep in mind that we need her to find the site."

Thèresa was working her regular day shift again, and Ben didn't like the way Kates had glanced contemptuously at her when he'd said "cheap whores." She was a warm, fun-loving, sensual woman who adored sex; she was not a whore. He kept his mouth shut, though, because now wasn't the time to get in Kates's face. After they were in the interior, there would be plenty of time to let the jerk know who was boss, and it sure as hell wouldn't be Kates.

"Buttoned-up lady archaeologists turn me on," Ben drawled.

"Well, keep your mouth shut and your pants zipped, at least until it's too late to turn back. Then you can do whatever you want."

"Sure thing, boss," Ben said, and grinned inside, knowing Kates wouldn't hear the mockery in the title. "Where's her brother?"

"I didn't need him this morning. I'll handle this part of it."

Which probably meant Kates was up to something. Ben pulled a pen and sheet of paper out of his shirt pocket. He'd already worked out what they would need and how much of it; he turned the sheet around so Kates could read it. "That's what I've figured for the supplies, and how many people we'll need. We'll go upriver by boat as far as we can. We'll need two boats; I'll line them up today."

"Fine." Kates handed him a brown envelope. "Twenty thousand for ten weeks. If the trip goes over that time limit, I'll pay you the rest when we get back."

"Fair enough." Ben took the envelope and pocketed it. He would count it later.

"I'll be hiring one man myself, someone who has been recommended to me. Now, how do we handle payment for the supplies?"

"I'll arrange for the supplies and bring you the receipts. Then you pay for everything and it'll be released for loading." Ben was highly curious about this one man Kates wanted to hire himself, but he didn't ask. Let Kates think he wasn't interested.

When Kates left the bar, Ben let the door close before he got to his feet. His pickup truck, a ten-year-old Ford, was parked in its usual spot outside the back door. He was out the door and in the vehicle before ten seconds had passed. He circled the building and pulled out into traffic just in time to see Kates getting into a taxi.

He hung back, something that was easy to do in the Manaus traffic. South American traffic, while it tended to be chaotic, lacked the grim purposefulness of its North American counterpart. He rolled his windows down and let the hot breeze blow through the truck while he wove in and out, dodging bicycles and pedestrians and always keeping an eye on the taxi several vehicles ahead of him.

Christus's bar wasn't in the best section of town, but the taxi was heading into the truly rough area. Ben reached under the seat and drew out a pistol, placing it beside him. It was a Glock-17, mostly plastic, with a seventeen-shot magazine, and it was one smooth-working piece. Just one look at it tended to effect an attitude adjustment in unfriendly individuals.

He shielded his eyes with a pair of very dark sunglasses, taking the precaution even though he suspected Kates was so sure of himself that he hadn't even considered the possibility of being followed. Stupid bastard.

The taxi pulled over to the curb and stopped. Ben drove past without looking directly at the vehicle, then turned the corner. As soon as he was out of sight, he parked and jumped out of the truck, smoothly tucking the pistol into the waistband of his jeans at the small of his back, with his loose shirt hiding it.

He didn't know in which direction Kates would go. He stood by the truck for a couple of seconds, waiting to see if Kates would come by, but he didn't dare wait any longer. When the man didn't appear, Ben strode quickly to the corner, walking close to the side of the dilapidated building. Kates had crossed the street; he was going into a bar, Getulio's, which was so seedy that Christus's place looked like a four-star establishment in comparison. Ben had been in the bar a couple of times several years ago, and hadn't liked the atmosphere. A man could get dead in a hurry in Getulio's.

Well, hell. He couldn't follow Kates into the bar without being recognized, for he'd have to remove the sunglasses in the dim interior. Frustrated, Ben looked around.

Less than a minute later he was the owner of a stained khaki safari hat, bought from a swaggering teenager for twice what the damn thing had cost brand-new, assuming that the kid had bought it rather than stolen it, which Ben didn't. It still wasn't much of a disguise, but it would have to do.

He ambled across the street and stepped aside when the bar's rough plank door opened and two burly dockworkers staggered out. Despite the relatively early hour, neither of them was feeling any pain. Before the door could slam shut, Ben slid inside, immediately reaching up to remove the sunglasses, both so he could see and so his hand would hide his face. Without looking at anyone, he moved to his left and took a seat at the table closest to the corner. There weren't any windows in Getulio's; there were a couple of naked low-wattage bulbs hanging from the ceiling and another couple of lights over at the bar, which was manned by a bartender who looked even meaner than the one Ben remembered. This one was a big bruiser who stood six and a half feet tall—easy—and probably weighed close to three hundred pounds. His left ear was missing.

Ben's butt had scarcely settled on the chair when a sullen-faced boy appeared beside him. "Drink?"

"Beer." He didn't want to give the kid anything to remember about him, so Ben limited his response to that one word and didn't even glance up. He also resisted the urge to look around. He just sat slouched in the chair, doing his best to look sleepy or drugged.

The kid brought the beer. Ben laid the money on the table, the kid's nimble fingers made it disappear, and then he was left alone to nurse the drink.

The glass probably hadn't been washed in a week. Mentally Ben shrugged and took a sip, figuring the alcohol would kill any germs. He shifted his position until he was hunched over, elbows resting on the table, his head dropped forward. The hat shielded his face. Ever so slowly he moved his eyes, trying to penetrate the shadows of the room.

There were fifteen, maybe twenty men there, half of them standing at the bar. No one was paying any attention to him. The conversation was the usual bullshit; the country and language changed, but the bullshit never did. A radio on the shelf behind the bartender blared out some Brazilian rock song. The singer wasn't any good. No one cared.

Kates was sitting at the very last table, his back to the door. Stupid move. But then Ben recognized the other man at the table and realized that Kates wouldn't have had any choice about where he sat. Ramón Dutra would automatically put his back to the wall, with good reason.

Dutra was a murderous thug. He was known to kill for hire, and took pleasure in being as brutal about it as he could. If Dutra was the one man Kates personally wanted to hire, then this was rapidly getting much rougher than Ben had originally thought. What was Kates planning? To leave everyone else dead in the jungle and keep all of the—what? —gold, maybe, for himself. But gold was heavy. One man couldn't carry out enough to make the trip worthwhile, and not only that, Kates wouldn't be *able* to make it out by himself. The man knew nothing about the jungle.

Dutra did, however. He regularly vanished upriver, probably to evade either some other thug or the law. Maybe Kates was fool enough to think he could hire Dutra to do his dirty work, then guide him out of the jungle with the loot before he himself killed Dutra. Probably Dutra was planning on roughly the same scenario, but with a different dead person at the end of it.

This made the situation a lot more serious than Ben had anticipated, and the prim, serious Ms. Sherwood was in over her head. Damn it, how had she gotten involved with a slime ball like Kates, anyway? Her brother, of course. Didn't the man care that he was putting his sister in so much danger? Obviously not, because he didn't seem to have an inkling that Kates was double-dealing all the way. Sherwood thought of himself as a full partner, when he was nothing but a patsy.

Once again Ben thought about bailing out, knowing all along that he wouldn't. Then he thought about dumping Kates and Sherwood while he and the sister did the trek on their own, but he discarded that idea because, for one, he didn't want to throw that much money into a project that might not pay off as big as he hoped, and for another, she probably wouldn't go along with it. She hadn't seemed overcome by his charm.

Not that he'd made any effort to be charming. He'd been deliberately crude and insulting. Well, she was just going to have to get over her distaste for him, because they were going to have to work together to get back from this trip alive and in one piece.

Having seen what he'd come in there to see, he slugged back the beer, wiped his mouth, and slid the sunglasses back into place as he stood. No one paid any attention to him as he walked out as unobtrusively as he'd entered.

Dutra's presence didn't simply mean that he would have to be more alert and take more notice of Jillian's safety; the men he had been planning on hiring would refuse to go if Dutra was one of the party. Now he would have to hire less reliable helpers, and that would increase the danger. There was a fifty-fifty chance that the helpers themselves would be in danger; if Kates was indeed after gold, he would need the extra manpower to haul it out of the interior. A small percentage of the money would keep them happy. Once Dutra got out with the gold, the helpers would be expendable. This sort of theft happened all the time; archaeological sites were continually being looted.

Ben crossed the narrow street and went around the corner to his truck. As usual, it was being swarmed over by a crowd of youngsters. He shooed them off and got inside. Even with the windows down, the heat had built up under the metal roof, but he had been in the tropics so long that he no longer even noticed how hot it was. Sweat trickled down his back as he sat there for a few minutes trying to put the pieces together.

He and the two Sherwoods were the three most in danger, Rick Sherwood less so than his sister. When they got to the site, assuming it existed, Kates would act. If they didn't find anything, then there wouldn't be any danger.

It was a crapshoot no matter how he looked at it.

But what the hell; he liked crapshoots. He hadn't chosen this life because of the safe nine-to-five routine. He didn't have anything else to do except keep Thèresa's sheets warmed. Instead, he'd work on warming Jillian Sherwood. Now *that* looked like a challenge.

4

Jillian went back to her hotel room early that night, leaving both Rick and Kates still drinking in the hotel lounge. Tension was wearing on her nerves; she didn't trust Kates or that man they had hired to guide them, but Kates was financing the trip, so she had to go along with him. The temptation to call it off was getting stronger by the minute, but deep down she really wanted to continue, since she had come this far. If they could just get started, then it would be too late to call the trip off and she could forget about that and focus on the job at hand—finding the Stone City.

Just being by herself was a relief; as she unlocked the door to her room she could feel her face relax now that she didn't have to keep every reaction to herself, guarding every word and expression. Maybe she was in over her head, but she had to remember that she had no other course of action.

She switched on the light and turned to bolt and chain the door.

"Don't bother with that," a deep voice said. "Unless you want me to stay the night."

She jumped and whirled, automatically drawing back to belt the intruder with her purse even as recognition flared. Ben Lewis! Odd that she knew his voice after meeting him only that once, but she did, instantaneously. He was rising from the chair across the room and coming toward her, his darkly tanned face creasing in a smile.

"Whoa, sweetcakes. You could do some serious damage with that thing."

That deep voice was warm and teasing. Jillian looked up into his lazy blue eyes, and fury roared through her, clean and hot; without thought or hesitation she swung the purse like a major leaguer at the plate, hitting him square on the side of the head with it. He staggered sideways into the wall, his face registering complete surprise.

"That's for scaring me," she snapped and drew back for another go at him. "What are you doing in here anyway?" *Whap!* "You broke into my room!" *Whap!*

He threw one arm up to protect his head, and the second blow hit him in the ribs. He yelped as he caught his balance and turned toward her, but not in time to prevent taking the third blow full in the chest, making him grunt. Quick as a snake he darted his hand out, seized the strap, and jerked the purse out of her grip, pulling her forward at the same time. He caught her full against his body, the purse in his right hand, his left arm wrapped around her waist like a steel band. "Good God," he said incredulously. "You've got a black belt in purse attack, that's for damn sure. And here I've been worried about taking care of you, when it looks like I'm the one who needs protecting."

Jillian didn't find his remarks amusing. She put both hands against his chest and shoved, hard. He didn't budge. The wall of muscles beneath her hands was rock hard. "Let go of me," she growled.

Instead of doing as she said, he actually chuckled, his warm breath stirring the hair at her temple. "Now, now," he chided.

"Don't 'now, now' me!"

"What do you want me to do to you?"

Jillian took a deep breath and grimly regained control of her temper. She seldom lost it, but that didn't mean she didn't have one. She said very clearly, "If you don't turn me loose right now, I'm going to bite you, *hard.*"

The arm around her waist loosened and he grinned down at her, totally unabashed. "Mind you, if we were both naked I probably wouldn't mind if you bit me, but under these circumstances I'll pass."

She stepped back and straightened her clothing, then ran a hand over her hair, searching for unruly strands. To her surprise, everything felt as neat as when she had walked in the door.

"You look just fine," he said, still grinning. "All prim and buttoned up. You sure had me fooled!" He began laughing.

She turned and wrenched the door open. "Get out."

He reached past her and flattened his hand on the door, closing it with a thud. "Not yet, sweetcakes. We need to talk."

"I can't imagine why."

His eyes sparkled at her acid tone, and he leaned closer to her. His breath was warm and smelled, not unpleasantly, of fresh whiskey. "Come away from the door," he murmured. "Kates or your brother might come up, and I don't want either of them to hear what we're saying. Are their rooms next door to yours?"

Jillian silently studied him, noting for the first time the shrewdness in those blue eyes. Despite the whiskey on his breath, he was sober and in perfect control of himself. Not only that, his comment had made it plain that he didn't trust the other two men, which was very perceptive of him. Instantly she saw that she had underestimated him, but that didn't mean she trusted him now.

Still, she answered his question. "No. Rick is two doors down; Steven is across the hall."

"Good. But just to be on the safe side, let's turn on the television and get away from the door."

He suited actions to words, moving to the television and turning it on. Rapid Portuguese filled the room. Then he settled comfortably into the room's one chair, lifting his booted feet to the bed and crossing them.

She shoved them off. "Keep your feet off my bed."

She had the impression that he wanted to laugh again, but instead he said, "Yes, ma'am," in a suspiciously meek tone.

She sat down on the bed. "All right, what did you want to talk about?"

He didn't answer for a moment, and she read the lazy interest in his eyes as he looked at her and at the bed. He made no effort to hide it, as if he didn't care that she knew what he was thinking. Jillian took her own satisfaction by refusing to give him any sort of reaction.

His mouth twitched a bit in amusement as he hooked his hands behind his head. She couldn't help noticing what a well-shaped mouth it was, wide and clearly outlined, with blatant sensuality in the curve of his upper lip. He was a raffish-looking scoundrel, with his hair tousled and his jaw already showing the need for a razor. His clothes looked as if they had never seen an iron, and maybe they hadn't. His lightweight khaki pants were stuffed into scarred brown boots, while his sweat-stained white shirt hung loose outside his pants. An even worse-stained khaki hat lay on the small table.

But she remembered that cool assessment in his eyes, and knew how alert he was behind the image he projected. This man knew *exactly* what he was doing.

That didn't mean she was going to trust him, or start this talk. He wasn't going to sucker her into telling him everything she knew without revealing anything himself.

The silence stretched between them for a few minutes, but it didn't seem to make him uncomfortable. If anything, the amusement deepened in his eyes.

"Not a blabbermouth, are you, sweetcakes?" he finally drawled.

"Should I be?"

"Well, it might simplify things, that's for certain. Let's start showing our cards."

"You first," she said politely.

Again the flash of that quick grin, but it quickly faded as a rather grim expression crowded the amusement out of his eyes. "Steven Kates is a crook," he said bluntly. "I saw him a couple of times back in the States a long time ago. He doesn't know me, but I make it a point to keep tabs on people. He's pure slime, and he sure isn't interested in going

51

on any archaeological expedition to photograph burial grounds. As soon as he and your brother offered me the job, I figured they planned on doing some looting, assuming that this site is really there and we can find it."

"It's there."

"So you say. What you have to understand, sweetcakes, is that knowing it's there and finding it are two entirely different things. Hell, even knowing exactly where *you* are once you're in the interior is a pretty fancy trick. There aren't any maps or experienced guides, and global positioning devices won't work because of the triple canopy."

"I can get us there."

"Maybe. We'll find out. I figured I wouldn't mind seeing what's so all-fired interesting at this archaeological site, and I figured I wouldn't have any trouble keeping an eye on Kates and your brother. What about your brother, by the way? Do you think he's planning to loot whatever you find?"

Jillian had long since faced the truth about Rick. "Probably."

"Would he be willing to kill you to do it?"

Her breath caught in her throat at actually hearing the words said out loud, but the thought had been needling her for a couple of days now. "I don't know. I hope not, but . . . but I don't know."

He grunted. "He may figure that you aren't going to do anything to incriminate him, so he isn't worried about you. Kates is a different matter. I followed him today; guess I'm just a naturally nosy son of a bitch. He met up with a hired killer, a thug named Ramón Dutra, and hired him as one of our party. The way I see it, Kates doesn't plan on you, me, or your brother making it out alive."

She could call it off. The thought ricocheted in her mind. It wasn't too late to call it off. There was no expedition without her, though she had no idea what Kates would do if she backed out after he'd spent so much money.

But she might never get another chance to find the Anzar and their Stone City, or the Heart of the Empress. She might never get another chance to verify her father's theories and clear his reputation, and her own. She knew she could find the site. She had the map and the precise instructions, written in code, and she had committed the key to memory. Even if Kates found the map he wouldn't be able to read it.

Ben Lewis was closely watching her. She clenched her hands in her lap and forced herself to say calmly, "What else?"

He rolled his eyes a little. "The men I usually hire are honest and dependable, but they won't go on any expedition that involves Dutra. I've had to hire a different bunch, not as dependable, or skillful, and sure as hell not as honest. With my own men I wasn't much worried about anything Kates could cook up, but it's a different situation now. Since we can't depend on your brother, it'll be you and me against the rest of them. We'll have to call a truce, sweetcakes, and you'll have to cooperate with me."

"Why should I trust you?"

The corners of his mouth lifted in a mocking smile. "Because I'm all you have. Now I've spilled my guts, so it's your turn. Just what in the *hell* are we looking for out there?"

"A lost city."

He stared at her in disbelief before tilting his head back and letting deep, rich laughter pour out of that strong brown throat. "Don't tell me you've fallen for one of those fables that float around out there like pollen. According to the tales you'll hear, there are a thousand lost cities in the interior. You'd think no one would be able to step on the riverbank without kicking a bone, but it just isn't so."

"This tale is true."

"What makes you so sure?"

"My father found the city."

"Did he bring back evidence of it?"

"He died trying."

"So you don't have any proof."

"That's what *I'm* going to get." Pure stubbornness steeled her voice. "I'll find proof that he was right."

"Or die trying."

"You don't have to go, Mr. Lewis. But I am."

"I'm going, I'm going. This is better than a circus any day.

So why don't you tell me about this famous lost city. Just which one is it? I've probably heard about them all."

"It's possible," she said grudgingly. "Have you ever heard of the Anzar or the Stone City?"

He thought about it, pursing his lips and tapping them with his fingertips. Her gaze followed his fingers, lingered on his mouth, before she realized what she was doing and looked away. Had he done that deliberately, to draw her attention to his mouth? She wouldn't put it past him, but she didn't look at him to see if that wicked amusement was back in his eyes.

"Can't say that I have," he said. "Want to tell me about it?"

She quickly told him the legend of the Anzar and the warrior queen, and of her heart, which now guarded her lover's tomb. He began to look bored.

"That isn't all," she said. "My father was an archaeologist too, and he had a passion for investigating old legends like that, to satisfy his own curiosity. All of the others he dismissed as just that, legends. But not the Anzar."

"So what was it about that particular fairy tale that made such a believer of him?"

Anger glinted in her eyes for a second, but she tamped it down. If her father's own colleagues hadn't believed him, why should someone who had never known him?

"Do you know how the Amazon got its name?" she asked. He shrugged. "From the jungle, I guess."

"No, the jungle was named for the river."

"What about it?"

"In 1542, a group of Spaniards set out to explore the river. It didn't have a name then. There was a Dominican friar with them, Gaspar de Carvajal. The friar kept a journal of what they saw. A lot of it is typical of the tales the Spaniards carried back to Europe: gold and treasure for the taking."

"It pretty much was," Ben said. "When they found it. Look what they did to the Incas."

"The friar told about gleaming white cities and royal highways paved with stone, which would describe the Incan empire pretty well even though it was a lot farther west. It's possible the friar was just repeating tales that *he* had heard. But then the friar mentioned something that was out of place, different from the rest of the stories being told. Carvajal said that they met a tribe of 'fair female warriors who fought as ten Indian men.'"

"Don't tell me," Ben said, closing his eyes. "Let me guess. They found the Amazons, and that's how the river got its name."

"Exactly."

"Bullshit."

"Most of it. Carvajal's journal is entertaining, but discounted by historians. It was the other tales, from different sources, that tied in and made my father curious."

"Such as?"

"He found five different sources for the Anzar fable. He couldn't find any connection between them, but the fragments of information fit together like the pieces of a puzzle. One tale was about the 'bloodless winged demons,' but that one also called them 'the devils from the great water.' It doesn't take much imagination to see the pale Spaniards coming ashore from their ships, with the white sails puffing in the wind like wings."

"All right, I'll give you that." He looked bored. "That isn't much of a stretch."

"The city of stone under the sea of green is obviously a city in the jungle, hidden by the canopy—so well hidden that the Spaniards couldn't find it."

"All of this is an interesting mind game, sweetcakes, but don't you have any hard evidence? I suppose you're trying to build a case that the friar's Amazons were really this Anzar tribe."

"Dad ran across a reference to the 'Stone City map.' He tracked that reference down and found another thread. It took him three years to actually find the map. He had it authenticated, and it dates back to the seventeenth century. It doesn't give the name of the country or even the continent, but it's quite detailed, with landmarks and distance notations."

He snorted in disbelief. "There aren't any landmarks in

the jungle, none that last. The vegetation swallows every-thing up. 'Dust to dust' takes on real meaning here; you can almost watch it happening."

She ignored him. "The map refers to the Queen's Heart and pinpoints its location."

"So you think this Queen's Heart is some huge gem that's been sitting in the jungle all this time, and the map will take you right to it."

"It will," she said confidently. "Dad plotted out the course and encoded it."

"Say you actually find this place; I don't much think it exists, but let's say it does. What do you do then?"

"Photograph everything, document it, bring the proof back. My father was called a crackpot; his reputation was ruined by this theory, and so was mine. I'm going to prove that he was right. I don't care if there actually is a huge gem of some sort guarding a tomb; I want to find this city and prove that the Anzar existed. I love what I do, Mr. Lewis, but unless I can clear my father's reputation I'll never be anything but Crackpot Sherwood's equally loony daughter."

"Call me Ben," he said automatically, rubbing his chin while he considered the situation. "Even if there is some sort of lost city out there, what if it didn't belong to this Anzar tribe? What if the Anzar weren't really Amazons—and I gotta tell you, sweetcakes, the Amazons are way down on my list of possibilities—but just your ordinary, isolated Indian tribe that died out several centuries ago?"

"It doesn't matter. A lost city is a lost city." She had to make an effort to keep her voice brisk. His lazy speech cadences were contagious. "All I have to do is bring back proof of it."

"You know you're likely chasing a rainbow."

She shook her head. "My father did meticulous research. He wasn't a treasure hunter; he was a truth hunter. He didn't care if the myths he investigated were real or not; he just wanted to prove it one way or the other."

"But Kates is betting on finding a fortune in gold or gems. How did he get involved, anyway?"

She hesitated, then sighed. "Rick. He had all of Dad's old papers. I was at his place going through them when I came across the Anzar information. I admit, I was so excited I couldn't hide it—"

"Wish I'd been there."

She didn't let the lazy comment distract her. "Rick asked me what I'd found, and like a fool I just blurted it out. He grabbed the papers from me, but he couldn't read the instructions because they're in code. He got a little sarcastic then, asking me what made me think this told how to find lost treasure when I couldn't even read it. I told him I *could* read it, that Dad had taught me the code. I refused to tell him what it said, though."

"Bet that livened things up."

She smiled at the understatement. "I tried to interest several of my colleagues in the project. Everyone just laughed. I could tell what they were thinking; they were comparing me to Dad. An expedition like this takes a lot of money, and I couldn't do it on my own, but I couldn't find a backer. Not even the foundation I work for, and the Frost Archaeological Foundation is the biggest. Basically, they patted me on the head and told me to go away. I was so disappointed and depressed after being turned down by everyone I knew that I called Rick and told him there wouldn't be any expedition. I don't know why, except that I think he really loved Dad too, so he deserved to know. The next thing I knew, Kates was in on it and we were making plans to come down here."

"They didn't try to talk you into giving them the map and instructions?"

"Of course they did." She gave him a cool glance that told him how successful *that* effort had been. Then she bit her lip. "I don't know for certain, but I think someone searched my place."

"Kates, probably. Or someone he hired. He doesn't like to do the work himself. Did he get the map?"

"No. No one will find it where I put it."

"You don't have it with you?"

"Of course not! I'm not about to bring a four-hundred-year-old map along. I copied down the instructions, but as I said, they're in code."

He muttered something under his breath.

"What?" she demanded.

"I said, 'You must think you're Jane Bond.' They can't read the code and you won't tell them what it says, so they're forced to bring you along."

"Exactly. They would just loot the site rather than trying to preserve it, and Dad's reputation would never be cleared."

Abruptly his lazy facade fell away and he sat up, glaring at her with narrowed eyes. "And just how in the hell do you plan on stopping them?"

She braced her shoulders. "I don't know. But I bought a pistol."

He swore viciously. "And you thought that would solve your problem? Jesus. You bought a pistol. What kind, a pearl-handled derringer?"

"A .38 automatic."

"Do you even know how to use it?"

"I do. I'm an archaeologist; my work isn't in civilized places. I wasn't lying about having to kill my own food a time or two, and I've had to scare off some unfriendly creatures, both the two-legged and four-legged varieties."

He looked suspiciously at her purse.

"No, it isn't in there," she said, and smiled at him. "And I'm not buying your act. You found it when you searched my room, so you know I have a pistol, you know what kind it is, and you know *where* it is."

He smiled back at her, not denying the charge. Of course he had searched her room while he'd had the chance. "You have nice underwear."

"I'm glad you enjoyed it. Did you try it on?"

"Nah. Just rubbed it against my face."

Damn him. He probably had, too. The picture flashed into her mind and her stomach tightened. She still didn't want to show any reaction to him, but it was getting more and more difficult. He was wicked and blatant, and so damn masculine her nerve endings were tingling despite herself.

He was watching her, still smiling a little as he picked up the way her eyes dilated. Some reactions couldn't be hidden. Ben felt more than a little satisfaction at finally having gotten past her guard.

But there were more important things to talk about than sex. "Considering the situation," he said slowly, "why don't you decipher this code for me and I'll find this lost city, if it's really there, while you stay here out of danger?"

She laughed in his face. She didn't try to be polite about it, either. She crossed her arms over her stomach and absolutely hooted at the ridiculousness of the proposition.

"I take it that's a no."

"I don't know how you even said it with a straight face," she replied, still snickering. "Do you think I trust *you?*"

"You'll learn," he said cheerfully. "After all, since you insist on going along, we'll be sharing a tent. Yep, you'll learn real quick that you can trust me in a lot of ways. For one thing, I won't ever leave you hanging, sweetcakes."

5

She shot off the bed, control forgotten in the renewed surge of fury. *"Share a tent!"* she half yelled. "With *you?*"

"Shhh." He motioned toward the door. "Anyone out in the hallway can hear you." He hid his satisfaction at her reaction, because if she saw it she would clamp down again. She sure had fooled him the night before with that iceberg image. The pure volcanic rage he'd seen on her face right before she'd begun walloping him with her purse had made his entire body tighten with excitement, just as it was doing now that he had breached her control again.

"I don't care if they can hear me down in the lounge."

"That's a possibility. Settle down, sweetcakes."

She lowered her voice to a furious whisper. "We're going to get something settled, and I'm not it. I'm not sharing a tent with anyone, and certainly not with you!"

"I figure that's the only way Dutra will leave you alone."

"I appreciate your gallantry, Mr. Lewis, but I'm not falling for this little gambit. Did you really think it would be that easy to line up your 'supply,' as you so charmingly phrased it last night?"

Damn, she wasn't going for it. But these were the early stages, and he was enjoying the game. He grinned at her, totally unabashed. "It was worth a try."

"I'll be sleeping with the pistol in my hand," she informed him.

"That's good to know, because I really wasn't kidding about Dutra. You may be safe enough on the trip in, because Kates won't want Dutra to harm you, but as soon as we find this place, *if* we find it, you'd better stay right with me. Okay?"

"Okay."

He looked surprised at her ready agreement. "What? No arguments? You'd better watch it, or I might start thinking you like me."

Jillian gave him a mockingly sweet smile. "I think I can prevent that from happening. I wouldn't want you going so far off track."

He gave a deep chuckle of appreciation and got to his feet. Instantly she felt a little overwhelmed by his nearness and tried to take a step back, but the bed was right behind her. He noticed the movement and sauntered even closer, so close that she could feel the intense heat of his muscled body.

Her breasts brushed against the hard wall of his upper abdomen and a hot tingle shot through her nipples. She stopped breathing, because even that small movement was too potent.

He wasn't doing anything, just standing there so close that his body was touching hers. She could feel his gaze on her face but refused to look up, both because she didn't want to see the sensuality of his expression and because she didn't want him to see her own involuntary response. His heat was wrapping around her, beguiling her, sapping her strength. She hadn't realized he was quite so big, but he had to be a couple of inches over six feet, and she already knew that he was all muscle. He would overwhelm a woman in bed—

No. She halted the wayward thought, appalled that it had slipped into her mind. She didn't want to think about him in bed.

"Jillian." He said her name in a softly cajoling tone. "Look up at me."

She swallowed. "No."

Another of those deep chuckles rumbled from his chest. "Stubborn." He moved then, sliding his left hand into her hair at the back of her head and pulling gently, forcing her face up. Just for a second she saw his eyes, glittering and intent, all amusement gone; then he bent his head and firmly angled his mouth to fit over hers.

She quivered, then stood very still, her eyes closed. The sudden flood of pleasure took her unawares. She had expected to endure it, nothing more, but found instead that she was tempted to open her mouth to his probing tongue. In a flash she saw that she had vastly underestimated his seductive skills. His mouth tasted clean, and smoky with whiskey; his lips were firm-textured but gentle in the way they moved over hers. She could have withstood brute force without even a scintilla of response, but force wasn't what he used; he lured with light, tender kisses that lingered; he tempted her with a hint of passion that she only glimpsed before he controlled it, beguiled her with his animal warmth and hard strength, invited her to rest against him.

Oh, God, he was dangerous.

She clenched her hands into fists, sinking her nails deep into her palms with her inner effort to resist. She didn't open her mouth to him, she refused to open her mouth, but she wanted to so fiercely that she shook under the strain.

He ended the torment himself, lifting his head after one last, lingering kiss that almost broke her resolve. "Sweet," he murmured, and brushed his thumb over her lower lip. Then those blue, blue eyes met hers, and he seemed satisfied by what he saw there.

"I'll have you yet," he said lazily. "Be sure to lock the door behind me."

But she just stood there, trying to get herself under control, as he walked to the door. He stopped and lifted his eyebrows at her, then took a step back toward her. Jillian was recovered enough that she narrowed her eyes warningly at him. He laughed and lifted his hand in a little salute, then left without saying anything, a forbearance she appreciated.

After a minute she crossed to the door and obediently set

the bolt and chain. Then she sat down in the chair he had just vacated and tried to bring order to her scattered thoughts. It was difficult to think, however, when all she wanted to do was *feel,* to revel in the wickedly delicious sensations he had aroused.

Why couldn't he have been simply what he had appeared at first, a raffish, disreputable guide who was too fond of his whiskey? She could have easily resisted that man, but the one he had revealed to her tonight, the real one, was something else. Despite that sexual brashness he was charming, or maybe that was part of his charm. She had never met anyone before who was so totally at case with his sexuality as Ben Lewis was. But even worse, he was intelligent and tough; he had seen immediately that Kates was up to no good. Unfortunately, he had also seen how easily he could slip past her guard, and he'd taken fiendish delight in doing so.

She had to be a fool to willingly spend two months or longer in his company. She had supplied herself with birth control pills not because she was looking to have an affair but because it was common sense and basic self-protection. Anything could happen to a woman in a foreign country, in uncivilized circumstances. She would be alert, try to protect herself, but her relentless realism told her that the worst could happen. Protecting herself against Ben Lewis, however, would be more difficult, because she would have to resist herself, too. If he made love as well as he kissed, a woman could die of pleasure.

She could also die of other means, if she insisted on continuing. Dutra's presence made the expedition even more dangerous than before. But she was committed; she refused to stop now. If this meant her life, she was willing to take the risk, because this was her one chance to vindicate the professor and resurrect her own career. It was for herself, and for her father, the one gift he would appreciate above all others.

She was going to find the city of the Anzar. The others, Kates and Rick, were in it because of the lure of the Empress jewel, but she hoped it didn't really exist. It had been useful as the lodestone that had drawn so many people to search for the Anzar, searches she hadn't told Ben about, but if the Empress really existed it put them in grave danger from Kates and his henchman. If she was lucky, she would find only the city.

She was very much afraid, though, that the Empress was real. The professor had thought so. He had written that he suspected it was a huge red diamond, as colored diamonds were mined in Brazil. It would still be there, indestructible and undisturbed, possibly the world's largest specimen of the rarest diamond of all, the red diamond.

Red diamonds were of poor quality, because of the imperfections that made them red, but their rare color made them extremely valuable. The professor had been interested not in the Empress itself but rather in what it would prove. There would be no riches in it for him, only vindication, since archaeological sites belonged to the country they were found in rather than to the person who found them. The government of Brazil would be extremely pleased if the Empress was found.

She hadn't told Ben of all the references to the Empress, for if he realized how likely it was that the thing existed he might refuse to put them in such danger. As it was, he thought they would explore the jungle for a couple of months and find nothing. No Empress, no danger.

But the professor had found another map, far more detailed than the seventeenth-century one. That was where the actual instructions had come from, the instructions that he had copied. He had never lost his professional spirit of competition, and the slight paranoia that went along with it, so he had written the instructions in the code he had devised. Jillian's eyes filled with tears; she could just picture him, quivering with suppressed excitement and glee, as he encoded the information, making it all the more mysterious. He had loved things like that, which was why he had developed the code in the first place and then shown Jillian how to decipher it. She remembered the key, and the key was all that was important to breaking any code. Her father had called it a running code, since it changed with every word, but with the key memorized she could take a pad and pencil and decode it. The key itself was simple, if a bit obscure. She had no doubt that an intelligence agency could break it in little time, but it had served her father's purpose well, just as it was now serving hers.

The last map he had found, the one with the precise details of latitude and longitude, miles and yards, had been made in 1916 by an explorer who had ventured deep into the rain forest and found incredible ruins, a city that had rivaled those of the Incas, with what seemed to be a palace carved deep into a cliff of stone. The explorer had made it out of the jungle alive, but had succumbed to malaria. Tossing in high fever right before he died, he had muttered about seeing "the heart on the tomb," which everyone had taken to be a forecast of his own death. A pity, but not a difficult prediction.

Her father had been certain the explorer had stumbled on the hidden city of the Anzar, and had actually seen the huge red diamond but for some reason had been unable to retrieve the gem. After reading his papers, Jillian was also certain of it.

She had thought she would be able to protect the site, but now she didn't know. As Ben had said, the situation had changed. The odds were loaded on Kates's side now. The thought of the site being looted made her tremble with rage. She had pointedly told Rick before they left the States that the laws against stealing antiquities and national treasures were severe, but that countries often offered rewards for new finds as a means of preventing theft. He had shrugged off her concerns, carelessly swearing that he didn't intend to steal the diamond. Why go to all the trouble to steal something when you could make money from it legally?

In her occupation, she was well aware of all the angles. Why settle for a reward if you had a contact who would pay much more? She didn't think Rick had those kinds of contacts, but she was certain Kates did. Her opinion of him hadn't improved on acquaintance, rather had steadily gone downhill. He was too smooth, too . . . cold. She had no trouble believing the things Ben had told her about him.

She had to go through with this. For her father, and for herself. But just in case the worst happened and she didn't make it back, she would *not* let Kates get away with both murder and looting. The idea of looting infuriated her almost more than the thought of getting killed.

Briskly she got out a pen and pad and began writing. Twenty minutes later she sealed two envelopes, feeling grimly triumphant. She scrawled the hotel manager's name on one and the address of a colleague in the States on the other. She would privately give both envelopes to the hotel manager, with instructions to open the one addressed to him and promptly mail the other if she didn't personally return to retrieve their belongings. Inside, in both letters, she had outlined the circumstances. The Brazilian government might not pull out all the stops on her account, but she hoped they would at least investigate something as valuable as the Empress. And in a further effort to make certain the truth was known about the Anzar, and about her father, she hoped her letter, coupled with her own death, would cause enough interest that her archaeological colleagues would investigate the Anzar. It was a hope, nothing more, but she felt better having made the effort.

She thought about using the letters as a guarantee, telling Rick and Kates about them once they reached the site, but then realized that Kates would simply not return for his belongings. The hotel manager would assume that they had *all* died in the interior. If he ever did open her letter, it would be too late; Kates would already have left the country.

She would have to keep her precautions to herself, and her pistol close at hand. It was the best she could do. She was scared, but only a fool wouldn't have been. At least Ben would also be keeping his eyes open. She couldn't trust him sexually, but she thought she could trust him to try to keep her safe. After all, his neck was at risk, too.

"How long will we be on the boats?" Jillian asked, standing on the docks and watching the black waters roll past. Manaus was actually located on the Rio Negro, seven miles upriver from where the river would add its clear black waters to the yellow of the Amazon. The two currents were so strong that the rivers flowed side by side without mixing, black and yellow moving sinuously along like a huge serpent, for about fifty miles before finally merging their forces.

"Two weeks, give or take a day," Ben replied without looking at her. His attention was on the loading of the last of their supplies.

Inwardly she groaned at the thought of two weeks cooped up on board, but didn't complain out loud. There was no help for it. Riverboats were the only way to get their supplies upriver to where they could begin the trek on foot.

"Coming back, that time will be cut in half," he said. "We'll be riding with the current rather than against it, for one thing. For another, we won't be bringing all of these supplies out, and the load will be a lot lighter."

They had eight helpers, counting Dutra. Ben had hired an additional seven, five Brazilians and two Indians from the Tukano tribe. The two Indians, one on each boat, were silently distributing the weight of the supplies so the loads were evenly balanced. Ben divided his time between the two boats, his eyes shaded by dark sunglasses but missing nothing. He knew exactly where every item was, how much they had of it, how long their supplies should last. If they hadn't found this lost city by the time half of the supplies were gone, tough. They were coming back out anyway. He figured he'd have more trouble with Jillian than with any of the others if that happened, but he'd bring her back if he had to string her up on two poles like a peccary and carry her out.

When she had arrived on the docks this morning, ready to leave, it was the first time he had seen her since he'd left her hotel room two nights before. She had clubbed her shoulder-length dark hair, and in the bright sun it gleamed as lustrously as mink. "Put your hat on," he said automatically. He himself was bareheaded, for he hadn't wanted to take the chance that Dutra would recognize him if he wore a hat and sunglasses. He'd gotten rather fond of the khaki hat and had brought it along, but for now, if the sun got too hot for him, he would put on his usual baseball cap.

She obeyed. He liked the way she looked in her sturdy canvas pants and white short-sleeved shirt. With the straw fedora set firmly on her head, she was brisk and no-nonsense, her experience showing in every move she made. The canvas pants also revealed every delicious curve of her rounded buttocks, and he whistled silently to himself. She'd be sleeping beside him on the crowded deck for two weeks, and every night of those two weeks was going to be pure temptation. Nothing else, though, damn it. Not with four other people right beside them.

"What do you think of our friend Dutra?" he asked in a low voice.

She didn't have to look at the man in question to see him in her mind, and she suppressed a shudder. "We'll be lucky if he doesn't kill us all," she murmured.

A few inches shorter than Ben, Dutra probably out-weighed him by thirty pounds or more. He wore a shirt with the sleeves ripped out, and huge sweat stains ran from his armpits to his waist. His head looked too small for his massive shoulders, even though his skull was covered by a thick mass of dull, unruly black hair, more like an animal's in texture than a human's. His brow ridge was as prominent as a Neanderthal's, but his eyebrows were sparse, almost nonexistent. His deep-set eyes were small and mean and cunning, his jaw unshaven, his teeth stained brown. His incisors were as pointed as an ape's. Between those teeth and his hair, he didn't appear quite human. She couldn't look at him without feeling her stomach roil with distaste and fear.

Dutra wasn't working, though he was supposed to be one of the helpers. He leaned against a post, his massive arms crossed as he stared unceasingly at Jillian. Ben let it slide; for one thing, the boats had to be precisely balanced, and Dutra would deliberately screw it up. For another, let him make Jillian uneasy; she might reconsider her decision about sharing a tent.

Rick Sherwood was on the second boat, sitting lazily on the prow with his feet propped up. Steven Kates, however, was pacing back and forth on the docks as if he were personally directing the placement of every box that went aboard. Ben spared both of them a disgusted look, knowing that the sunglasses hid his eyes. Those two would be in for a shock when they got upriver.

The humid heat had bathed them in steam by the time everything was loaded. Jillian took pleasure in seeing that the knife-edge creases in Kates's pants had wilted. She could have told him that having his clothes pressed was a useless effort in the tropics. She suspected both Rick and Kates were in for a rough time when they reached land upriver, for neither of them was used to hard physical labor and they would have to carry a load through the jungle just like everyone else. She kept herself in good physical condition, but she wasn't looking forward to the first few days.

"That's it." Ben said something to the two Tukano tribesmen in their language, and they murmured soft replies. One would be in the lead boat, the other in the second, piloting it. Both of them knew the rivers. He put his hand on Jillian's arm as he turned to Kates. "Kates, you and Sherwood go in the second boat. Jillian and I will be in the front one."

"I'd planned to be in the front one," Kates said.

"Won't work. You don't know how to navigate the river. I do."

"I meant, put Jillian in the second boat with Rick."

"Nope. Since she's the only one who knows where we're going, she has to ride with the navigator."

It was an argument Kates couldn't refute, but he didn't like it. Being on the second boat offended his sense of self-worth. Ben didn't give a damn; he didn't want Jillian on the same boat with Dutra. She walked calmly aboard the first boat, surefooted in her deck shoes, cutting off further discussion.

"We're casting off," Ben said impatiently, and Kates stalked aboard the second boat.

Ben took the wheel and started the engine. The boats didn't look like much, but the engines were first-class. They had to be, to buck the current. They surged to life with deep, guttural roars. The two Tukanos slipped the mooring lines, tossing them on board and following with agile leaps as the boats eased away from the docks.

"Talk to me," Ben said to Jillian as he deftly steered through the maze of ships and boats in the harbor. The idea had come to him that morning. "I've been thinking about something. Can you find this place as easily if we go in on the Rio Negro rather than the Amazon?"

She cleared her throat.

He took the chance of looking at her rather than at what he was doing, and her expression made him swear softly under his breath. "Goddammit," he muttered. "Just when were you going to say, 'Oh, by the way, Mr. Lewis, we need to go up this river rather than the other one'?"

She made a show of looking around. "Actually . . . right about now."

"And what if I didn't know anything about the Rio Negro?"

"You aren't the only one who can snoop around," she replied easily. "I asked around about you. You've guided as much up the Rio Negro as you have up the big river."

"So why didn't you bother to say something before now?"

"To throw off anyone who might have been nosing around, anyone Kates or Rick might have told. I had my reasons."

"Yeah, lack of trust being at the top of the list."

"You got it."

He frowned, but only for a minute. What the hell, so she'd been one step ahead of him all along. It happened. Not often, but it happened.

"Well, I agree with you," he said. "Not only will it give us an advantage, but it'll be more comfortable. No mosquitoes."

"Really? Why not?"

He shrugged. "Something in the water. Black-water rivers tend to have fewer insects."

She'd already had experience with the swarming black clouds of mosquitoes that inhabited tropical areas. If the

Rio Negro had fewer of the insects, she was all for traveling on it. It would certainly make sleeping on deck much more comfortable,

Ben whistled as he handled the wheel. Manaus sat on the Rio Negro, but he hadn't actually thought of going up the black river until that morning. He had assumed they would head downstream for seven miles and pick up the Amazon. But upstream the rivers penetrated similar regions. And if they took the Rio Negro, Ben would have a significant advantage. From what all his contacts had said, Dutra always went up the Amazon when he disappeared upriver. As far as he'd been able to find out, the thug didn't know anything about the Rio Negro. But Ben knew both rivers. Little things added up; if putting Dutra on unfamiliar ground would give Ben even the slightest advantage, he'd take it.

All in all, he was pleased with himself. He pulled his baseball cap out of his back pocket and put it on. They were on their way; they likely wouldn't find anything in the jungle worth stealing, so they wouldn't have anything to worry about from Kates and Dutra; and he had Jillian Sherwood in his constant company for about two months. He figured that by the time they left the boats, he'd have her so hot for him that they could leave one of the tents behind, as they wouldn't be needing it.

He was so pleased, in fact, that he reached out and gave her bottom a caressing pat, briefly clenching his hand on the enticing fullness. Less than half a second later, the heel of her shoe connected violently with his shin. She gave him a smile that showed a lot of teeth, and moved away to the prow of the boat.

Jillian remained in the prow for most of that first day, so she could see everything. The excitement of actually being under way drowned out—at least for the moment—the concerns that had been keeping her up nights. She watched the roiling waters of the massive river in awe. The Rio Negro was the largest of the Amazon's tributaries, so she felt a deep connection to that great river, which really only became the

Amazon when it met with the Rio Negro seven miles downstream from Manaus. One fifth of all the fresh water on earth was contained in the Amazon and its tributaries, ten of which carried more water than the Mississippi. The great Nile might be considered the longest, by a small margin and depending on which course of the Amazon was measured, but the African river paled in comparison to the South American giant. The river was a law unto itself, so strong that when it emptied into the Atlantic it pushed back the ocean's salt water for about one hundred miles. Jillian was thrilled to actually see this part of it, to feel the power of the water humming through the wooden boards beneath her feet.

The riverbanks were lined with shanties, some of them little more than a few pieces of tin and wood nailed together. As they got farther from Manaus the number of shanties diminished until there were only a few of the dismal dwellings spaced here and there.

The heat became suffocating. She finally moved to sit under the roof of the boat, but the shade couldn't diminish the humidity.

The three Brazilians were talking quietly among themselves, while the Tukano sat on the deck a few feet away from Ben, completely silent but not missing anything. Her excitement had ebbed; the heat and the motion of the boat made her drowsy, but she didn't want to nap.

She pulled off her hat and fanned herself. After a while the slow, hypnotic motion of her own hand became so soporific that she had to stop.

Her sleepy gaze wandered to Ben. She couldn't find a single thing wrong with the view. He stood solidly at the wheel, his back to her, his feet planted apart to brace himself against the sway of the boat. Thick dark hair curled over his collar; unless he got his hair cut sometime during this expedition, it would be touching his shoulders by the time they got back. Broad shoulders strained the fabric of his sweat-dampened shirt. His khaki pants revealed powerfully muscled legs and clearly outlined his tight buttocks. She smiled a little to herself. She did so admire the sight of a nice, tight, muscled male derriere, and Ben's was perfect. Aesthetically speaking, of course. Beauty was where one found it.

As if he were clairvoyant, he turned and gave her a slow, knowing, lascivious wink.

6

Kates was furious that they were going up the "wrong" river, yelling his protests over the radio.

After a while Ben got tired of listening to him and took the microphone long enough to say, "Sorry, this is the way Ms. Sherwood says we have to go," neatly placing all the blame on Jillian's shoulders. After a while, accepting the uselessness of his protests, Kates shut up.

It was well before dusk when Ben steered the boat into the shelter of a cove. "Storm," he said briefly to Jillian. "This is a good place to tie up, so we might as well spend the night here. There won't be much light left by the time the storm is over."

It had rained almost every day they had been in Brazil, so the weather didn't come as a surprise. Jillian had been watching the purple clouds gather on the horizon and march steadily closer. Now that the boat engines were silent, she could hear thunder rumbling.

The Brazilians on both boats began unrolling the heavy tarps that were secured to the flat roofs. Neither boat had a closed cabin, just a simple roof over the cargo area, with all four sides left open except for a tiny, crude toilet area. She had noticed the tarps and thought they were meant to provide shade during the late afternoon when the angled sunlight could penetrate beneath the roof, but as the wind began to pick up she saw the real reason for them. When they were unrolled, they were tied down to rings on the deck to keep out the blowing rain. One side, away from the wind, was left open.

But the storm hadn't yet arrived, and Jillian didn't want to remain in the dim, close shelter. She moved out on the deck with the men. One of the Brazilians smiled shyly at her and she returned the smile. Ben had said that these men weren't top notch, not his regular helpers, but she couldn't help liking this one man. From listening to their conversation, she had learned that his name was Jorge. The other two were Floriano and Vicente; Ben had called the Indian Pepe, though she was certain that wasn't his real name. It didn't seem to matter to him, though. He replied to the name and kept to himself. The other Indian, Eulogio, was piloting the second boat, which carried Joaquim and Martim, the other two men Ben had hired.

Because of the heat, no one would take shelter behind the tarps until the storm was actually upon them. She looked at the other boat and saw that the preparations on it mirrored their own. Likewise, everyone was on deck. Rick's face was flushed and he was talking too loud. He had probably been drinking ever since they left Manaus.

Thunder began booming continuously, much closer now. A sudden breeze lifted, delightful in its coolness. She took off her hat and let the fresh wind lift her hair. The sky was darkening dramatically.

Then the darkness was split by great sheets of lightning, brightening the dim jungle with dazzling white. The wind died and a great calm settled on them. The hot, still air was heavy with the decaying odors of the thick vegetation that loomed on the bank.

"Here it comes," Ben said. He turned and took her arm, holding her steady as the boat began to surge beneath their feet. "Get under the roof."

A huge blast of wind pressed against the boat, and the temperature plummeted. Even sheltered behind the tarps, Jillian began to shiver. The cove was much calmer than the open river, but even so, the water was churning and lifting under the boat, whipped by the wind. A few heavy raindrops pounded against the roof like hammers; then the deluge hit. There was no talking; the effort would have been useless in that din, as overwhelming as if they had been inside a huge drum.

Everyone seemed to take the storm as a matter of course, having been through similiar ones more times than they could count. Pepe, the Indian, squatted in a corner and calmly waited. The Brazilians found comfortable niches and settled back to smoke. Ben sat down beside her and put his arm around her shoulders, pulling her against the solid heat of his big body.

She started to pull away, but his arm tightened and she looked up to protest. He was looking down at her, his blue eyes steady, warning her to sit still. In a split second, she realized that the others had noted his action. Ben had marked her as his woman. She might not agree, but she was realistic enough to see that, considering the prevalent macho attitudes, he had just given her a measure of protection.

So she sat there, letting her weight rest against him, letting his heat protect her from the chill, and against her will she was swamped by primitive female satisfaction. Women had felt the same way thousands of years before, sitting in firelit caves and leaning against their rock-hard, muscled mates, men who used their strength to keep their families fed, to guard them, to stand between them and danger. Her field might be archaeology rather than anthropology, but she was well aware of the seductiveness of his strength. A few hundred years of civilization couldn't override instincts developed over years that numbered in the millennia.

In a flash she saw how easy it was for the dominant male in a group to have his pick of the females. His very dominance made him *their* prime choice. Ben was definitely the dominant male in this little group, and she was the only female. He had been right to warn her about being the lone woman on an expedition, an uneasy situation he had instinctively recognized, while she had let her advanced education and life-style blind her to the basic nature of life.

It would take some very fancy footwork on her part to keep him out of her tent, because everything about the situation would work to force them together. He seemed certain she wouldn't be able to long resist giving in to him, and she had to admit he probably had the upper hand in this old battle. She had to fight him as well as herself and her own sexual instincts that had been stirred to life. Physically she was strongly attracted to him; mentally she didn't want to have an affair, didn't want to become involved in messy emotional tangles. She was strong and whole as she was. An affair would be too much trouble.

Not only that, his self-assurance ticked her off. He was so certain that he was eventually going to wear down her resistance and tempt her into having sex with him that he didn't even try to hide it. His confidence showed itself in every cocky, heart-stopping grin, in the wicked gleam in those deep blue eyes. He was challenged by her resistance, but she was equally challenged by his assurance, and her female pride had immediately battened down the hatches to weather a strong blow. Everything about him was saying, "I'm gonna get you," and her instinctive mental response was a truculent "Oh, yeah?"

She had a strong competitive streak in her nature. She liked to win, whether it was at cards or beating someone to a good parking spot. She liked most team sports and absolutely loved football. Seducing her was just a game to Ben, so that was the way she would play it too: to win.

She had woefully underestimated him at their first meeting, but now she had his measure and wouldn't make *that* mistake again.

They were in a dicey situation; they needed to keep their wits about them and their eyes wide open rather than waste time on the Adam and Eve stuff. Of course, as he had pointed out, they were safe enough on the trip in. It would be on the trip out that they would be in danger. Still, she didn't intend to let Ben distract her.

Night crashed down with stunning abruptness. One moment it was twilight, the next it wasn't. The impenetrable jungle seemed to press harder against the boats where they were pulled up to the riverbank. The level of noise began to build, complete with shrieks and howls, coughs and rumbles, until she wondered how any of them would get any sleep.

Battery-operated lanterns were turned on. Each boat carried an alcohol stove, and a quick, simple meal was supplied. Vicente did the cooking on their boat, throwing together rice, fish, and seasonings to make a dish that wouldn't win any awards, but was edible. It would fill their bellies and give them energy; nothing else was required of their food, certainly not good taste or an elegant presentation.

Afterward, the tin plates were quickly cleaned and stored, and hammocks efficiently hung, taking up most of the deck space. "This one is yours," Ben said to Jillian, indicating the hammock closest to his. They were virtually side by side, close enough to hold hands if either of them was so inclined. Jillian wasn't.

She expertly maneuvered herself into the swaying hammock and arranged a swath of mosquito netting over her. Even though she had to admit the night was wonderfully free of the pests, she didn't want to take the chance that there might be a stray bug out there just waiting to jump on her. The mosquito netting was her own form of a security blanket.

Ben settled into his own hammock. "Bet you think you're safe, don't you?" he whispered a moment later. "Ever done it in a hammock?"

"Of course," she said, and was vastly pleased with the precise blend of unconcern and boredom that she had managed. Let him wonder about *that!* He hadn't specified which "it" he was talking about, so she felt free to apply her own interpretation. She had definitely slept in a hammock before.

The immediate blasé response brought a scowl to Ben's face as he relaxed with the slight swaying of the hammock. What did she mean, "of course"? Did more go on during her archaeological expeditions than he'd imagined? It made sense; people were together for long periods of time, so it would be human nature for their gonads to act up. He was sympathetic to the condition; his own libido wasn't the best-behaved in the world.

But the thought of Jillian swaying in a hammock with some bare-assed, bony-kneed archaeologist humping her wasn't pleasant. In fact, he didn't like it worth a damn. His scowl deepened, and a strange kind of anger flared deep in his belly. The incredulous thought surfaced that he was feeling *jealous,* but he dismissed the idea almost as soon as it had formed. That was ridiculous. He'd never been jealous of a woman before in his life, and he sure wasn't jealous of Jillian Sherwood. She wasn't even his type. Her main attraction was that she was the only woman available—that and the almost irresistible urge he had to show her that he could have her anytime he wanted. All he had to do was turn up the heat.

He reached out and nudged her hammock. "Where?"

"Where what?" she murmured, rousing up from a light doze.

"Where did you do it in a hammock?"

"Oh. On the balcony of my condo." Knowing that he couldn't see her in the dark, Jillian allowed herself a triumphant smirk. It was true; she did have a hammock on her balcony, and she had, on occasion, napped out there.

He lay in his own hammock and simmered as his image of a bony-kneed archaeologist was transformed into a vision of a trendy West Coast type with sun-bleached hair, whose clothes bore all the right labels. On the balcony. *In public!* Jesus Christ, even he had never done it in public. He couldn't believe his initial impression of her had been so far off base; he knew women, read them easily, but Jillian kept disconcerting him. That night in her hotel room, when he had kissed her, he had sensed her arousal but she had refused to open her mouth to him and return the kiss. Such self-control baffled him. Why would anyone want to resist pleasure?

The night wasn't clear, but there was a faint hint of light, just enough to keep the darkness from being complete, as it was under the canopy. He couldn't make out her features even though her hammock was only a few inches from his, but she was lying in the limp stillness that meant sleep. Damn it, how could she tell him about screwing in a hammock on her balcony and then just drop off to sleep? How in hell was *he* supposed to get to sleep now?

He couldn't stop thinking about that hammock, but somewhere along the way his imagination did away with the trendy West Coast type and substituted himself. He had touched her at various times, held her against him, so he knew how firm and sleekly muscled she was; he could easily visualize that neat, tight body naked, perky breasts high and nipples tightly drawn with excitement as he moved in and out of her.

His erection pushed painfully against his pants. In the darkness he scowled at her sleeping form and reached down to adjust himself to a more comfortable position.

He lay awake for a long time, scowling and shifting uncomfortably. Another storm built up in the distance and he listened to the rumble of thunder for a while, waiting to see if they would need to move to shelter, but the storm drifted by at a distance. Once he heard a faint scratching against the side of the boat; both he and Pepe got up, and he shone a flashlight over the railing. A startled turtle promptly disappeared underwater again. The nightly serenade hummed on undisturbed.

Ben settled into his hammock again. The interruption had served to take his mind off Jillian. He yawned and finally went to sleep.

The howler monkeys made certain that no one slept past dawn. At the first screech, Jillian bolted up from her hammock, swiping away the cocoon of mosquito netting as she whirled to face the attack she was sure was coming. Next to her, Ben grunted and cursed but showed no alarm as he swung his feet to the deck.

After her initial response she quickly realized what the uproar was; she had read about the howlers, but hadn't realized their dawn ritual to establish territory was so loud. The howls quickly spread until the monkeys sounded like thousands of people screaming at once. She was embarrassed by her fright, though a quick glance at the other boat, moored next to them, showed that both Rick and Kates had also started to their feet. From their expressions, she could tell that they still didn't know what was going on.

"Scared you, huh?" Ben asked, yawning as he rubbed his hand over his face.

There wasn't any point in trying to lie about it. "I nearly jumped out of my skin," she admitted. "I wouldn't believe anyone could get used to it, but all of you acted as if it were nothing more than an alarm clock going off."

"That's basically what it is. How did you sleep?"

"Better than I'd thought I would. I must have been tired." Or maybe she'd felt safe sleeping beside him. Now, there was a ridiculous thought.

He stretched like a sleepy tiger, then draped a heavy arm across her shoulders and turned her to face the east. "Look," he said, his early morning voice deeper and slower than usual.

She caught her breath. The sun was a huge, gleaming ball hanging in a pearly sky with the trees silhouetted in stark black against it. The river was as smooth as dark glass, a ribbon of serenity curling through the teeming jungle. A few misty clouds seemed caught on the treetops, as if they were the last remnants of steam formed in the creation of the world. That was what it felt like, the beginning of time, caught here on this river where nature still ruled supreme.

Ben left her standing there, lost in the dawn, while he set about getting things organized.

Breakfast was coffee, scrambled eggs, bacon, and toast, absurdly normal fare considering where they were, even though the eggs were powdered and the bacon was canned. Under Ben's efficient supervision, preparing the meal, eating, and cleaning up took less than forty-five minutes. Before she would have thought it possible, they were idling out of the cove, back into the river's current.

She had learned the day before that there wasn't a great deal to be done on board the boat to keep herself occupied, but the newness of the experience had kept her from being bored. She expected to be bored, though, on the second day. She expected to be, but she wasn't, even though the unbroken, towering tangle of vegetation lining the riverbanks like a living green wall never seemed to change. She caught glimpses of color in the dark green as bright-feathered parrots flew from perch to perch, and occasionally an extravagant orchid or some other flower would take her attention, but for the most part there was nothing to see but the unending jungle. And yet she was enthralled by the lushness and incredible scope of nature.

It could have been any number of things. Maybe it was the hypnotic throb of the engine, maybe it was the somnolent spell cast by the warmer climes that made it so treacherously easy to go tropical, but she was oddly content with the circumstances. The river itself was fascinating. It wasn't black at all, but the color of tea, changing in shade from a clear brown to gleaming amber. While the morning was still relatively cool, she made herself comfortable in the bow and let herself be lulled by the swirling patterns of the water as it rushed past.

A dolphin leaped beside the boat, startling her, and she scrambled to her knees with an exclamation of delight.

Ben turned the wheel over to Pepe and came to sit beside her. "Pink dolphins," he said, smiling at her expression.

She gave him a suspicious, half-warning look, but the lure of the dolphin was too strong and she turned back to watch. Now she could see that there were several of the playful mammals racing effortlessly alongside the boat, darting and jumping as if playing tag with the vessel. She propped her elbows on the side of the boat and leaned farther out so she could see them better. Immediately a big hand grabbed the waistband of her pants and tugged her back.

"Sit down," he ordered. "You'll see a lot of dolphins over the next couple of weeks. It isn't worth going overboard. The river's filled with piranha."

She sat, because it was only common sense to do so. He stretched out one leg to brace his booted foot against the other side of the V of the bow.

"Don't try to scare me with piranha," she said mildly. "You know and I know that I could go swimming and be perfectly safe."

He grinned, not at all abashed. Most people new to the Amazon basin were terrified of piranha, thinking that if they dipped a toe in the water it would be snapped off before they could draw back. But Jillian knew that it was blood that attracted piranha; if you weren't bleeding, you could splash around as much as you wanted.

"It'd be a lot of trouble to have to stop and fish you out," he said.

"That sounds more like it."

He sucked in a deep breath and let his head fall back as he exhaled. There was an expression of pure contentment on his face. "Damn, I love this river," he said, spreading his arms wide and letting them drape over the sides of the boat. She noticed cynically that the movement "accidentally" brought her within his embrace, albeit an open one, with his left hand just brushing her shoulder. "The Amazon's always a challenge, the way you have to read the currents and deal with the tides. A storm on the Amazon can be as wild as one on the open sea. But this river right here is damn near perfect. Great water. It's almost as pure as distilled."

His enthusiasm wasn't feigned, and she let herself relax back into enjoyment, watching the dolphins as they continued to play around the boat.

"The river's still in high water," Ben said, "or you'd see a lot more of them. Most of them have spread out in the palm swamps. During low water, obviously, they're a lot more concentrated."

"When is low water?"

"The rainy season's over, so the water has already started dropping, but the lowest levels start around October and extend through the end of the year. The natives like that season best because fishing is so much better. The river will drop about twenty feet from now until the rains start again. This area here will be nothing but white sand."

Long-tailed macaws, in brilliant shades of blue and yellow, sailed among the tall palms. A snowy egret stood poised, waiting for breakfast to swim by. The light was so clear, the morning so fresh, that it almost hurt.

"This is probably paradise," she said.

"For the flora and fauna. It can be damn hard on humans. But as many times as I've been up this river, it's never been the same yet. Neither has the Amazon. Guess that's why I'm still hanging around after all these years."

She looked at him curiously. "How long have you been in Brazil?"

"Fifteen years. Since I was twenty. I hopped a freighter, and got off in Manaus. The only job I could get was helping a river guide. The life suited me, so that's what I've been doing ever since."

She wondered at the wealth of information he had left out, such as what a twenty-year-old had been doing hopping freighters in the first place. "What were you doing on a freighter, seeing the world on the economy plan?"

"Something like that." His voice was placid, and he seemed as laid back as it was possible for a good old boy to get, but she wasn't fooled. She frowned at him as he began to brush his fingers against her shoulder, and sat forward away from the contact. He gave a cheerful "well, I tried" type of shrug and continued as if the little byplay hadn't happened. "I lit out as soon as I finished high school. Home was okay, just not enough going on."

"Where was home? Somewhere in the South?"

"Alabama. It's still home, always will be."

"Obviously." A strand of hair blew across her face and she pushed it back as she smiled at him. "Fifteen years in Brazil, and you still have a southern accent."

"As Popeye says, I yam what I yam. What about you? Where's the place you call home?"

"Los Angeles. I'm one of those rare creatures, a native-born Californian."

"How did you settle on being an archaeologist? That's kind of like being a river guide; it's not a mainstream occupation."

"Dad was a professor of archaeology, so I grew up with it. Maybe it's in the genes, but I never wanted to do anything else. It's a lot of fun."

He looked doubtful. "Yeah, I can see where digging up bones would be a barrel of laughs."

The boats moved steadily through the water. They passed by an assortment of other vessels, mostly canoes of all sizes but also some other motorized craft. During high water, all travel was by boat. He told her how, when the river was low, the natives netted cardinal tetra for the huge aquarium trade, supplying the colorful tropical fish for the world's enjoyment. Not that the natives made much from it; most of the money was on the other end. River traders would stop by the villages and trade supplies for the fish, but at such a low rate of exchange that the villagers were often deeply in debt.

She wasn't foolish enough to relax her guard around Ben, but she enjoyed the conversation so much that she sat there long after the heat had grown uncomfortable. Finally she couldn't stand it any longer and moved to the shade under the roof, where she made a comfortable seat from the boxes of supplies and settled back. Ben took over the wheel from Pepe. Idly, Jillian decided that this wasn't a bad life at all.

If there were just this one boat making its way upriver, she would have been blissfully happy. Her private little contest with Ben was exhilarating, though of course she wouldn't let him know that. She would be on her way to find proof of the Anzar, an accomplishment that would not only clear her father's reputation but would raise her own stature dizzyingly high. It would be the find of a lifetime, something any archaeologist would give an arm for and the vast percentage could only dream about. There just weren't that many old civilizations left undiscovered.

All of her problems were in the second boat. She didn't turn around and look, but she shivered a little knowing it was back there. The time spent on these boats would be the most peaceful, for once they took to the land she wouldn't have any time away from Rick, Kates, and Dutra. Were they using the opportunity to plan, or were they already getting on one another's nerves? Were any of the other men likely to throw in with Kates, or would they find a way to tell Ben anything they overheard?

They had scarcely gotten under way again after lunch when the wind picked up and a fast-moving storm came into view. The rain was normal; only the time the storms hit differed from day to day. Ben immediately began searching for a safe place to tie up, for the waves during a violent storm could turn the boats over. If they had had larger boats they could have proceeded, though the ride would definitely have been a bit rough, but he wasn't going to chance capsizing when he didn't have to.

He started to edge toward a protected bank when he saw another boat already moored there. There was plenty of room, but he swung back into the current.

"Why did you do that?" Jillian asked, appearing at his elbow. "Shouldn't we be mooring too?"

"Not there," he said.

"Why not?"

He glanced briefly at her before returning his attention to the rapidly worsening weather, but she saw the way his eyes gleamed. "Smugglers."

"How do you know?" She swiveled to get another look at the boat in question before it disappeared from view. Nothing about it distinguished it from fifty other boats they'd seen since leaving port.

"I've been running the rivers for fifteen years. Experience."

"Would they actually shoot at us?"

"It's possible," he drawled. "I wouldn't push it."

"Are there a lot of smugglers on the river?"

"Enough, sweetcakes. The safest bet is to keep to ourselves."

An abundance of smugglers meant that Kates, if he should get his hands on the Empress or any other artifacts, would find it fairly easy to get the contraband out of the country. She was sure he would have noted this, too.

A sheet of rain swept toward them as lightning crackled. Ben put his hand on her shoulder and turned her toward the shelter of the tarps. "Get behind the tarps and hold on. It could get a little rough before I find a place to tie up."

Since she saw no point in getting wet when she didn't have to, she did as he said, seeking shelter and bracing herself against one of the poles that held up the top. The boat began pitching as the waves increased, and the wall of rain hit them without any warning pattering of drops. Jorge, holding tight to another pole, shouted something at her, but she couldn't hear what he was saying over the pounding rain and reverberating bass of the thunder. The boat pitched forward into a trough, then rose alarmingly. It was like white-water rafting, only she didn't have either a helmet or a life jacket, and she couldn't see a blessed thing inside the sheltered area.

She wasn't frightened; the storm didn't seem rough enough, or the waves high enough, for them to be in real peril. Discomfort, yes, but nothing more. Of course, everything was relative; if she'd been in an airplane and it had been pitching the way the boat was currently doing, she'd have been saying her prayers.

After a few minutes she felt the boat begin to turn and ease its way into more sheltered waters. The pitching settled down, though the battering of the rain still made normal conversation impossible. The chill brought goose bumps to her arms and she hugged herself, drawing her knees up to preserve as much body heat as she could.

Pepe and Ben tied the boat securely and ducked under the shelter to wait out the rest of the storm. Both of them were as soaked as if they'd jumped into the river. Ben pushed his dripping dark hair out of his eyes and made his way over to where Jillian was sitting. When he got close, she could see the brightness of reckless excitement in his eyes.

"Good ride," he said, raising his voice so she could hear him. He hooked his sodden shirt off over his head and tossed it aside. Jorge threw a towel to him and he deftly caught it, rubbing it first over his hair and face, then down to his chest and shoulders. All the while he stood right in front of her, never taking his eyes off of her.

The sight of his naked torso was causing her to entertain

87

definitely impure thoughts, and he knew it, too, damn him. That was why he was watching her with that expression of taunting delight, waiting to catch every slip she made. Deliberately she looked right at his tight little nipples, half hidden in dark curly hair, and licked her lips. She saw his own involuntary response in the tightening of his abdominal muscles, and glanced up at him with her own taunting smile. It wouldn't hurt him to realize that two could play that game.

"Want to dry my back?"

He pitched his voice lower this time, so low that she didn't actually hear him, but read his lips quite well. She smiled. "I'm sure you can manage."

Inwardly she stifled a sigh. The urge to touch him was almost irresistible. He had the kind of body that literally made her mouth water, strong and hard without being indecently muscle-bound. A man's body, not a boy's: heavy in the shoulders, dark hair on his chest and down the center of his abdomen. His skin was sleek and tanned, glowing with health.

He picked up her hand and put the towel in it anyway, then turned his back. She stared at the deep furrow down the center, at the hard muscles that flexed with his slightest movement. She didn't want to touch his bare skin, didn't want to feel his living power, the seductive warmth. . . . Yes, she did. Too much. She also wanted to lean forward and press her open mouth against that intriguing furrow, run her tongue over the sections of his spine. It would serve him right if she did, but it might cost her more than it did him.

So she contented herself with briskly running the towel over his back, not letting her hand touch his skin at any time. "There."

"Thanks." He turned around and took a seat beside her, draping the towel around his neck.

"You're getting the supplies wet."

He looked at the box he was sitting on. "No problem. It's the tents, and they won't mildew."

Because the rain continued to beat down so loudly, he sat beside her without saying anything else until it slackened.

When it did, he spoke to Pepe in dialect, and the small, lean Indian silently got to his feet and slipped out of the shelter. A moment later the engine started and they began moving. The tarps were quickly rolled up out of the way, letting sunshine and fresh air sweep over them.

As they chugged upriver, Ben lounged lazily on the boxes, casually resting his forearm beside her thigh. Jillian looked down and just as casually shifted away.

He gave a low laugh. Conversation was possible now, even one quiet enough to be private. "Stop being so jumpy," he said. "We're in this together, remember?"

"I remember that you're a better bet than either Kates or Dutra," she corrected.

He looked hurt. "You don't trust me?"

"As much as I would a cat in a cage full of canaries."

"Give me the chance, and I'll sure eat you up," he purred, his tone making the promise so lascivious that her heartbeat speeded up. He should have had a net thrown over him a long time ago, for the safety of the planet's female population.

"Now that we're under way and you can't be left behind, why don't you tell me what that tricky little map of yours says? There may be something in it that you haven't deciphered right, something that I would spot because I'm familiar with the jungle."

"Good try," she said, loading her tone with admiration.

"I'm serious." He moved his hand a little and lightly stroked the side of her thigh. "Why not tell me? It'll be safer if two of us know."

She pushed his hand away. "I won't tell you because you'd probably maneuver me into the other boat and leave us behind while you race ahead to see if you can find any gold or jewels."

"You really *don't* trust me!" Now he sounded frankly incredulous.

"You bet your ass I don't. Nothing's changed. If I don't go, no one goes. I'm sorry you wasted your little seduction routine."

7

Little seduction routine. Ben ground his teeth every time he thought of that dismissive, condescending phrase. All right, so he'd been trying to work on her, but those not-so-accidental touches had been making his heart race, and he'd actually been getting a hard-on. From barely touching her! He hadn't felt like that since high school, as if he had to sneak up on some delicious but forbidden fruit to get even the slightest taste of it. There he'd been, going down for the count in that damn, stupid, inexplicable fascination he felt for her, and she'd been as cool and unaffected as if she were shooing away a fly. She kept throwing him with that; damn it, was her coolness real or not? He'd seen exciting passion in her when she erupted in anger, felt her respond to his kisses—he thought—even though she'd stubbornly refused to admit it. And she'd kept him up half the night with that enraging tidbit about making love in a hammock on her balcony, just the sort of thing a man liked to hear, how a woman he was interested in had made love with someone else.

His body, his instincts, insisted that she was a passionate woman, but his mind couldn't come up with any corroborating evidence. She was making him doubt himself, the way she shrugged off his advances as if they were nothing more than ploys—all right, so maybe they were, a little. But only a little, and only on the surface. On a deeper, more fundamental level, he was dead serious. His relationships with women had always been light and fun, a good time, but he didn't feel at all lighthearted about Jillian. His determination to have her was getting stronger by the day.

Damn it, what was it about her? In looks she was fairly ordinary, average height, not voluptuous at all. Her thick, straight brown hair was glossy and attractive, but not head-turning. Her green eyes were nice, with long dark lashes. But overall, the thing about her that struck him most was the lively intelligence in her face, and he sure as hell wasn't used to being attracted to a woman's *mind*. That was a good line for the glossy magazines, but it had little to do with reality. The thing was, he could see that she was attractive, nothing more, but his hormones insisted that she was the most fascinating, seductive woman on earth.

He didn't like it. He'd always loved women, loved sex; he would rather be with a woman than buddying around with a bunch of men, but at the same time he'd always been able to cheerfully walk away and find another woman who meant just as much to him. It was a good way of life and he didn't want to change it. He didn't want to have one woman occupying his thoughts to the exclusion of all else, especially a woman who didn't seem to feel any spark of desire for him in return.

He didn't like it and he spent the next several days telling himself that it was just an aberration, brought on by the fact that she was the only woman along. If, say, Thèresa had also been on the trip, he'd never have looked twice at Jillian. But she wasn't, and he couldn't get Jillian out of his mind. He'd never had that trouble before; if one woman he'd had his sights on hadn't worked out, something that seldom happened, he had simply moved on. He couldn't move on here, and that was the problem. That, coupled with her resistance, was what was making her stand out. Once he'd had Jillian a few times she would become just like any other woman to him, and the obsession would go away.

* * *

On their sixth day out, when they tied up for the night Ben rapped out a few orders and the Brazilians on both boats leaped ashore with machetes in hand. Jillian watched them hack a small clearing out of the tangled vegetation that crowded every inch of earth and hung out over the water. Ben had spoken too rapidly for her to follow, so she went over to him. "Why are they doing that?"

"We're going to eat dinner ashore tonight," he tersely replied. "I'm goddamn tired of this boat and I figure everyone else is, too."

He had a point. Ben had been in a bad mood for the past few days, Floriano and Vicente had been growling at each other for a day or so, and God only knew how bad the tempers were aboard the second boat, given who was on it. Every night she had heard curses and arguments from the companion vessel, though voiced low enough that she hadn't understood what they were saying. She looked back at the bank and noticed that Dutra wasn't doing any work, but wore a sneer as he watched the others labor.

Ben noticed it at the same time. "Dutra, get a machete and help." His tone was even but inflexible; Jillian had never heard him sound like that before and she gave him a swift glance. His eyes were hard, without even a hint of the roguishness that usually lightened them.

Dutra spat dismissively and leaned against a tree. "Do it yourself."

The six other men on the bank stopped and looked at Ben. They were very still, waiting.

Ben smiled, but there was nothing pleasant about his expression. "Fine. Then get the hell away from this camp. If you don't work, you don't eat, and you sure as hell don't take up room on these boats. We'll leave in the morning without you."

"Hold it right there, Lewis!" Steven Kates leaped ashore, his good-looking face hard with anger. "Dutra is my employee, and so are you. I'll decide who stays and who doesn't."

"No, you won't." Ben turned that humorless smile on him. "You haven't been in command since we cast off in

Manaus. I'm in charge of this trip, just as a surgeon is in charge of an operating room and a pilot's in charge of an airplane. You pay me to get things done, but we do them my way. Either Dutra works or he stays here. We can't carry food and equipment for someone who doesn't work."

Jillian saw Dutra's eyes, small and mean and gleaming like those of an animal sensing a kill. She edged slowly away from Ben and squatted down beside her pack of personal belongings. Only her head was visible from the riverbank, if anyone was paying her any attention. They weren't; probably they thought she had prudently removed herself from danger. Instead she unzipped the pack as quietly as possible and ran her hand down inside it, rummaging around for her pistol. She touched metal, the butt fitting comfortably, reassuringly, in her palm.

Dutra spat again and drew a machete from the scabbard behind his back. "Perhaps you will be the one who stays here," he said, his wolfish canines showing as he started toward the boat.

"Perhaps not." Ben's move was as smooth as silk, his expression still calm as he reached behind his back, under his loose shirt, and came out with an authoritative automatic of his own. Jillian gave it a half-startled, half-admiring look. That was a serious piece of action, not so big that it couldn't be concealed but with the hefty look of a 9mm. She hadn't even suspected its presence, and she could tell from the way Dutra froze in his tracks that he hadn't either.

"Both of you back down," Kates snapped, stepping forward.

"I wouldn't get in the line of fire if I were you," Ben advised.

Kates halted. Rick, still on the boat, leaped to the bank and stumbled, falling to his knees. He struggled to his feet. "Hey!" he said belligerently. "Hey! What th' hell's going on here?"

He was drunk. Jillian's lips tightened, but she remained where she was. She hoped he wouldn't stumble into the line of fire, but she wasn't going to worsen the situation by throwing herself out there in an attempt to head him off.

"What's it going to be, Dutra?" Ben asked pleasantly. "Do you work, or do I blow your kneecap off? There won't be any chance of a murder charge against me that way, not that the police in Manaus give a damn what happens to you. They'll probably shake my hand. I'll just leave you here on the bank. Maybe you'll be able to get a ride back to Manaus before your leg rots off, but maybe not. You don't have many friends on the river. Then, too, a jaguar might get you the first night, what with the smell of fresh blood and all."

"You're going too goddamn far, Lewis," Kates said. He was enraged, his face dark red at what he saw as the usurpation of his rightful authority.

"Just laying the ground rules, Kates. This is *my* expedition. My job is to get everyone in and out alive, and for me to do that, everyone has to do what I say, when I say it. No arguing, no negotiating. A split second can make the difference between living and dying out here, and if you think your buddy Dutra has the experience to take over, let me tell you right quick that he doesn't. He doesn't know anything about this river or the territory we're going into. His expertise, such as it is, is limited to the Amazon and its banks, and any back-alley murdering you want done. Maybe he told you he knew his way around in the interior, but he lied."

Jillian glanced at Ben. He knew better. He knew that Kates had hired Dutra specifically for his killing skills. She saw at once why he had said it, however. Let Kates believe that Ben thought Dutra had duped Kates by lying about his expertise. It made Dutra the bad guy while allowing Kates to still pretend that he was on the up-and-up. As long as Kates didn't realize how suspicious she and Ben were, they weren't in as much danger. If he ever decided they were on to him, he might well tell Dutra to kill them the first chance he had.

It would be simpler, she thought, if Ben could just kill Dutra where he stood. But he was right in that he'd be risking a murder charge, assuming that they all made it back to Manaus. Kates, enraged at having lost his treasure, would definitely have charges brought. The police might privately thank Ben for ridding them of a big problem, but publicly he would have to be charged.

If Dutra made another step toward the boat, Ben could legitimately shoot him in self-defense. Why hadn't he done that when Dutra took out the machete and started toward the boat? Then she realized that Dutra hadn't said anything that could be taken as a direct threat, and Kates could have sworn that he had only taken out the machete to do the work that Ben had ordered him to do in the first place.

Rick lurched forward and stumbled again.

"Stop him," Ben said quietly, and automatically Kates turned to catch Rick's arm.

Rick threw him off. "What's goin' on?" he demanded.

"Rick, shut up and stand still." Jillian's voice snapped like a whiplash.

He turned toward her, his face twisted in an ugly scowl. "Don't tell me to shut up. No one wanted you to come along anyway."

"But she is along." Ben didn't take his eyes off Dutra, nor did the pistol waver. "And none of us can get where we're going without her. That battle's already been fought, and she won. Except for me, she's the one person this expedition can't succeed without. Everyone else is expendable."

"Nice of you to include yourself," Jillian murmured.

"I try to think of everything," Ben replied in a tone just as low, before raising his voice to say, "What's it going to be, Dutra? I'm not going to stand here all night waiting for you to decide. Either start work *now*, or I'll blow your kneecap off and leave you here."

Dutra stood there for another two seconds, glaring, his small head thrust forward as if preparing to charge. From where she was crouched, Jillian could see Ben's finger start to tighten on the trigger. Maybe Dutra could too, or maybe he just decided this wasn't a fight he could win, because he abruptly turned and started hacking at the undergrowth. With an almost visible sigh of relief, the others did the same.

"He'll just wait for a better chance," she said.

"I know. But maybe Kates is smart enough to figure that he needs me, at least on the way in." Again, their voices were low so those on the bank couldn't hear. Ben gave her a quick smile. "Good thinking, to move away like that."

Deliberately she pulled her hand out of her pack just enough for him to see the handle of her own weapon, before she replaced it and zipped the bag up again. He gave her a long, level look, as if trying to decide whether or not she was truly willing to use it. She returned the look, in spades. If he thought she was exaggerating about knowing how to use a weapon, or about having used it in the past, then he had better think again. The woman who looked back at him wasn't someone who would shrink from protecting her own life, or the lives of others, and she saw the knowledge flare in his eyes.

A slow grin spread across his face, one that lit his entire expression. All of a sudden the ill temper that had shadowed his eyes for days was gone. For some reason, Jillian didn't trust that glowing smile. If Ben Lewis looked that happy, then he had just thought of something that she knew she wouldn't like.

Ben started whistling as he leaped ashore, taking care not to get too close to the machete Dutra was swinging with lethal power. Jillian had just told him a lot more than she thought she had, and it was all he could do to keep from chortling.

But he had some serious problems on his hands that he had to handle right now, and his face turned expressionless as he approached Kates.

"Walk over here with me," he said, and moved toward the other boat, away from Dutra. Reluctantly Kates followed, and Rick lurched to accompany them.

"Can you handle Dutra?" Ben asked brusquely. "If you can't, I'm going to leave him at the next settlement. I can't watch my back and pay attention to everything else, too, and I'll get damn tired of having to hold a pistol on him to make him work."

"Perhaps you've forgotten who's paying the way here. Don't give me that captain-of-the-ship shit again." Kates lit a cigarette and eyed Ben through the smoke.

"That's exactly the shit you're going to get. If you don't

like the way I do things, *I'll* bail out at the next settlement, and you can go to hell for all I care."

"Fine," Kates snapped. "You do that. Dutra says he's familiar with the interior and I believe him. We don't need you."

Ben snorted. "Then you deserve what you get with him. I hope you enjoy your little outing, because you sure as hell won't find what you're looking for."

"That's your opinion, and we all know what your opinion's worth," Rick put in belligerently.

Neither Ben nor Kates even glanced at him. "Oh, we'll find it," Kates said with assurance.

"Not without Jillian."

That gave Kates pause, and his good-looking face went cold. "What about Jillian?"

"She'll stay with me. Let's just say that Dutra hasn't made a favorable impression on her."

"And you have?" Rick hooted. "She thinks you're slime."

Ben allowed himself a complacent grin. "But good in bed."

Again Kates gave him a considering look. "You're bluffing," he finally said.

"What makes you think so?"

"Jillian wants to find this place more than any of us, so she can clear her old man's name," Kates said. "She won't give up the chance just because you're screwing her."

Rick frowned. "My sister? Gotta be kidding. Jillian's probably queer. She hangs around with a bunch of weirdos. Know what I mean?"

Sherwood was beginning to get on Ben's nerves, but he continued to ignore him. "Not just because of that, no," Ben agreed. "But take a good look at Dutra; if you were a woman, would you want to go anywhere with him in charge? Why the hell do you think I insisted that Jillian be on my boat? She flatly refused to get on the same boat with Dutra."

He *was* bluffing, of course. He'd already learned enough about Jillian to know that "stubborn" was her middle name. She had her mind set on finding this lost city, and God help anyone who got in her way. But he figured that both Kates and her brother underestimated her. Now, having been on the receiving end of her temper, and having seen the look of calm determination in her eyes when she showed him the pistol, he had an entirely different picture of the woman. It suited him, though, for the others to underestimate her.

He shrugged negligently. "Ask her, if you don't believe me."

Rick turned to obey. "Hey, Jillian!" he yelled. "Is Lewis really—"

Ben divined what the idiot was about to say a split second before the words came out, and that was exactly how long it took his fist to connect with Sherwood's gut. Rick's breath left him in a big whoosh, and he doubled up, clutching his belly. He coughed and began vomiting. Ben immediately stepped back, as did Kates.

When the spasm had ended, Ben knotted his hand in Rick's shirt and hauled him up on his toes. "Get sober," he advised in a voice that was devoid of his usual I-don't-give-a-damn tone. "And stay sober. Because if you say anything to Jillian that I don't like, I'm going to stomp your ass into the mud, whether you're in any condition to fight back or not. Is that clear?"

Rick tried to shove Ben's hand away, but Ben just twisted the fabric tighter. "I said, is that clear?" he barked.

"Yeah," Rick finally panted. "Uh—yeah."

"You'd better remember it." Ben released him with a little shove and turned slitted eyes to Kates. "Well, what's your decision?"

Kates didn't like it—in fact, he hadn't liked anything about this damn expedition since the minute the boats left the dock in Manaus—but what he saw in Lewis's narrowed eyes made him back down. He would cut the big-shot guide down to size, he swore to himself, as soon as they found the jewel and didn't need him *or* Jillian Sherwood any longer. He'd see how good Lewis grinned at him with an extra mouth sliced into his throat. But first maybe he'd let him watch while Dutra had fun with the broad.

"All right," he muttered. "I'll talk to Dutra."

"You'd better do more than just talk. If he even looks at me cross-eyed, he's out." Ben walked back to the first boat, aware of Jillian's sharply curious gaze on him. He was grateful that she had remained where she was, rather than coming ashore to see what the altercation was about. Probably she had done so in order to keep watch on Dutra. The idea of her guarding his back gave Ben a warm feeling.

Rick and Kates watched him go, both wearing expressions of anger and hatred in varying degrees.

"Son of a bitch," Rick said, wiping his mouth. "I'll kill him."

Kates gave him a furious look. Rick Sherwood was ineffectual, strictly small-time, though he swaggered and tried to pass himself off as a real hard-ass. His whining was getting on Kates's nerves; getting rid of him would be a pleasure, but for right now he had to endure the aggravation. "You're too drunk to kill a goddamn bug. He's right. Why the hell don't you sober up? You're no good to me like this."

"This stupid river is boring," Rick said, voice and expression turning sullen. "Nothing to do all day but just sit and watch the trees go by."

"Even Dutra is staying sober. Maybe we should leave *you* behind."

Still seething at how he had been outmaneuvered, Kates went over to where Dutra was swinging the machete with murderous power.

"I want to talk to you," he said, jerking his head to indicate they should step out of hearing, for all of the Brazilians spoke some English and he didn't want any eavesdroppers.

Dutra halted the swing of the machete and walked a few paces away. There was a chilling gleam in his eyes, an expression at once empty and savage. It even gave Kates an uneasy feeling. "I will kill him tonight," Dutra said, hefting the machete. His upper lip curled, showing his incisors. "With one swing, his head will bounce across the bottom of the boat."

"Not yet, damn it," Kates said. "The woman won't

cooperate without the bastard, and we have to have her. Just play along until we find the jewel. Then you can do whatever you want with both of them."

"I can make her cooperate," Dutra replied, his small eyes swinging to the trim figure aboard the first boat.

Kates was getting tired of having to deal with stupid people. "Just do what I tell you," he snapped, and walked away. Dutra's chilling gaze settled on his back, and the thick lips twisted into a feral smile.

"What was that about?" Jillian asked Ben quietly.

"We got a few things settled."

"Such as?"

"Such as, who's running things."

"Is that why you punched Rick? What was he about to say?"

Ben looked at her and was caught by her shrewd, level eyes. He could lie to her, but she'd know it. "He was going to ask you if it's true we've been . . . uh, having sex."

From the way her mouth quirked, he knew that she'd noticed the way he'd modified his phrasing at the last second. "What gave him that idea?"

"I told them we were," he said casually.

Instead of blowing up as he'd expected, she turned to watch the men working. "Any reason for that, or was it just the usual male bragging?"

"They were thinking about leaving me behind. I told them you wouldn't go on without me."

"Smart. But it won't get you inside my tent."

"It'll have to, at least occasionally. What we do in there is our business."

Again she gave him that look that pinned him to the wall. "You think you've outmaneuvered me, don't you? I can always stage an argument as an excuse to kick you out."

He put his hand over his heart. "You'd endanger me like that?"

"You're a big boy; from what I've seen, you can hold your own."

"Just remember," he said with a grin, "you're choosing between me and Dutra."

"Don't let it go to your head," she advised. "I'd choose a slug over Dutra."

The men had finished hacking out a clearing large enough so that they could sit comfortably and enjoy a measure of security. Within a month after they'd gone their way, the undergrowth would have taken over again and erased any sign of their having been there, but for now the vegetation was held at bay. Pepe swung aboard to begin unloading the alcohol stove, the lanterns, and the supplies for supper.

Jillian moved to help him, startling the lean little Indian, who ducked his head and shyly muttered his thanks in Portuguese, the first words in that language she'd heard him speak.

Ben was well satisfied with the day. He had backed Dutra down and gotten some control over the situation, at least until they found the lost city—*if* they found it. Kates was a smart man; he would keep his hired killer on a leash as long as he thought he still needed Ben and Jillian.

But more than that, he'd gotten his answer about Jillian. She was cool, all right, with that air of being indifferent, but a woman who was unaffected by a man wouldn't have been willing to pull a weapon and shoot somebody in his defense. A cold, passionless woman wouldn't have had the guts or the fire. She was a sham, hiding all that heat behind that cool act, but he had her number now. He'd known it from the time she swung at him with her purse, or at least his body had, but he'd let his mind fall for the charade. Hell, his body had known from the first time he'd met her.

Good old chemistry was a mighty funny thing. Whoever would have thought he'd have the hots for a too-slim, stubborn woman? A woman who seemed to see straight through even his best lines?

But she'd been willing to shoot Dutra to protect him. Something like that warmed a man's heart.

The meal ashore went smoothly, partly because everyone was glad of any excuse to get off the boats and partly because whatever Kates said to Dutra evidently had worked. After the meal was finished they lingered, reluctant to go aboard again. Jillian produced several decks of playing cards, which the men received with appreciation. She declined to join any of the games and sat a little apart from them, content to watch the fire. Ben decided not to play either and moved over beside her.

"Good idea. I didn't know you had the cards. Why haven't you brought them out before?"

"If I had, everyone would already be tired of playing. Now it will keep them occupied for several days."

"So you're a psychologist, too."

"Just common sense. I've been on digs before, so I know how boredom works."

"Aren't you bored, too?"

The firelight flickered on her face, revealing the little smile that barely moved her lips. "A little, but not as much as they are. I like this kind of life. Eventually I'd have to have some books, but I don't need television or telephones, things like that."

"Why didn't you bring a few books?"

She looked incredulous. "Give me a break. I'll be carrying enough weight in my pack as it is. I have two cameras, a supply of film, a tape recorder and microcassettes, extra batteries, a blank notebook, and waterproof pens."

"Don't forget your other little item," he said blandly, meaning the pistol.

"I won't, don't worry."

"Why two cameras?"

"In case something happens to one. In my experience, something usually does."

"So what else do you have in your personal stuff?"

This time her smile was bigger. "A whisk broom and a trowel."

"A *what?*"

"You heard me."

"What in hell do you need a broom for?"

"Those are standard tools for an archaeologist. What did you think we used, shovels?"

"Well, when I think of 'dig,' I sure don't automatically think of a whisk broom. Guess it takes a while to uncover anything at that rate."

"It can," she agreed. "But that way we do the least possible damage to the find. When everything lost is irreplaceable, you learn to be cautious. We won't be doing any actual excavating, anyway. I just want to find the place."

Her eyes were shining with enthusiasm for her work, though he didn't see how she could get so excited over old bones and buildings. Gold and jewels, now that was different.

"There's been a major new find in east Africa," she said. "At Ouosalla. It looks like an entire village, thousands of years old. I'd have given anything to be included on that team, but I was turned down. Wasn't even considered, really. So much is going to be learned about how people lived back then, and there's nothing like helping to put the pieces together."

"Why weren't you considered?" he asked. "Because of your father?"

"Yes." Her eyes lost their sparkle and she watched the fire a little longer. He almost regretted bringing up the subject, because he had reminded her of why they were there. A few minutes later she excused herself and went back aboard the boat.

8

For the first time since they had started out, it rained at night. Ben had been expecting it, as night storms weren't unusual. What was unusual was that the rainstorms, because of their timing and position, had thus far missed them at night, allowing them to sleep on deck.

Ben swung out of his hammock as the first cool wind hit him, and to his left Pepe was already on his feet. Ben shook Jillian awake. "It's going to rain," he said. "Get under the top."

The men unrolled the tarps and fastened them down, then turned a lantern on low to relieve the darkness. Sleepily they made themselves as comfortable as possible on the boxes of supplies; Jorge and Vicente almost immediately dozed off, snoring their unconcern over the weather. Floriano yawned and nodded off, woke with a jerk at a clap of thunder, then dozed again.

The rain began its loud drumming on the metal top. Jillian hugged herself into a knot to conserve body heat, and tried to curl up on the boxes. A sharp edge dug into her side, keeping her awake. Fretfully she sat up and shoved cartons around to arrange a better nest.

"Here." Ben moved over next to her and pulled her against his side, fitting her head into the hollow of his shoulder. "Better?"

"Mmm." His body heat was wonderful, liking pulling a blanket around her. She closed her eyes and began to sink into sleep.

"How 'bout this?" he whispered, but she could hear the smugness in his voice. It brought her eyes open. "I knew you'd be sleeping with me sooner or later."

Without a word she moved away and pulled a couple of extra shirts out of her pack. One she rolled into a ball and used for a pillow, the other she used to cover her bare arms. Before she went to sleep she had the regretful thought that she wished he had kept his mouth shut, because he was much warmer than her thin shirt.

Ben watched her curl up with her back to him, and he wished he'd had the sense to keep his mouth shut. She'd have been sleeping peacefully in his arms if he had. *He* might not have slept, but he'd've enjoyed the hell out of being awake. Now he was still awake, but there was nothing about it to enjoy.

Pepe turned the lantern off. The rain continued, the darkness lit only by the flashes of lightning as the storm moved on, the rumble of thunder gradually becoming fainter. A few minutes later Ben noticed that the rumble was growing louder again, as if another storm was blowing up. But the night air was calm.

"Pepe," he said quietly.

"I hear," the Indian replied.

"Wake the others."

Pepe moved silently about in the darkness, shaking the Brazilians awake. Ben did the same to Jillian. He put his mouth close to her ear. "We have unexpected company. Try not to make any noise. Just get down on the floor and stay there."

"Smugglers?" she whispered.

"Maybe."

He made certain she was in a sheltered position and then, going only by his sense of touch, fetched his shotgun. Around him in the darkness he could hear the faint clicks as the others found their weapons and readied them. He didn't dare use the radio to alert the second boat; the noise could have cost them the advantage of surprise. He only hoped that Eulogio, the Tukano who was piloting the other boat, had heard the engines and roused the men.

The approaching boat might not be smugglers. It might be pirates. It might even be some totally innocent people, caught out late on the river and looking for a safe place to tie up for the rest of the night. He didn't think the last scenario was likely, but just to be on the safe side he whispered for the others to hold their fire until they knew for certain, but to be *ready*.

The engine cut off, and silence fell. Ben felt his muscles tighten as he pictured the unknown boat drifting closer and closer. He whispered another command, and caught the edge of the covering tarp with his left hand, holding the shotgun steady in his right. He didn't want to let the new-comers get too close, but he wanted them within range of the shotgun's lethal power. Steady, steady . . .

"Now!" he barked, and the five of them simultaneously threw the tarps up and trained their weapons on the black bulk of the silently approaching boat. His eyes well adjusted to the dark, Ben could plainly see the dark figures poised on deck, as if ready to jump aboard the instant the hulls touched. A startled shout came from the unknown vessel as the dark figures scrambled into action.

An instant later, a flashlight clicked on from behind and to Ben's left, pinning the scurrying strangers in a beam of light and plainly revealing the weapons in their hands.

Jillian! The realization flashed in his brain at the same time one of the pirates halted, brought a rifle to his shoulder, and jerkily fired in the direction of the flashlight beam.

"Get down, damn it!" Ben roared at her as the night erupted in gunfire. The pirate craft was only twenty feet away. He pulled the trigger on the shotgun, hitting the shooter and slamming him backwards. Ben pumped anoth-er shell into the chamber and fired again, this time splinter-ing the top edge of the hull and sending long slivers of wood flying.

The flashlight beam still hadn't wavered.

Combat was an almost purely physical experience, without room for much thought or reason as instinct and learned technique kicked in. He felt the shotgun bucking in his hands, the heat of it like something alive. He felt the power of the gunpowder exploding, smelled the acrid tang of it hanging in the night air, heard the thunder of it. He also heard the screams and curses, the yells, the groans of pain. All of his senses were painfully acute, time slowing and stretching out so that seconds were like minutes, everything happening in slow motion. He saw and felt and heard everything, was aware of everything. He knew that the men on their second boat were also firing, their attack splitting the pirates' efforts at defense. He felt the hot rush of a bullet close to his head and instinctively fired again even as he dodged to the side, so they couldn't zero in on his muzzle flash.

Then, even through all of the noise, he heard the deep cough as the pirates started their engine and threw it into reverse, slowly backing the vessel away from the riverbank. Ben fired the shotgun a few more times to speed them on their way. When the pirates had enough maneuvering room, they swung the boat around and headed out at full speed. The wake washed against the two moored craft, setting them to bobbing.

Ben shouted at Pepe to check for any wounded. Then he whirled back to Jillian and grabbed that damn flashlight, but to his horror there was no hand holding it. "Jillian!" he said hoarsely.

"Here."

Her voice was amazingly calm, and came all the way from the stern of the boat. He turned the flashlight around so that the beam shone full on her face, making her blink as she crawled out from behind her shelter.

Confused, he looked down at the flashlight in his hand. If she hadn't been holding it, who had? "Are you all right?" he finally asked.

"Not a scratch. How about you?"

"I'm fine." Damn if they didn't sound as if they were about to sit down to tea.

Then she held out her hand. "May I have my flashlight back?"

He didn't release it, but instead kept it shining in her face. He was beginning to do a slow burn. "This is your flashlight?"

"Yes, and you're running the batteries down."

He clicked it off. "I told you to stay down," he said in a very level voice. "Instead you got up and flashed a light right in their faces. Goddammit, you made a perfect target of yourself."

"I did not," she shot back. "I braced the flashlight on some boxes, then reached up and turned it on. I was behind cover the entire time."

He thought about covering her behind with his hand and then maybe she would get some idea of just how serious he was. She didn't seem the least bit excited, as if she got shot at by pirates every day of the week.

"Don't you *ever*— " he began, his voice low and tight, but she coolly interrupted.

"The flashlight trick works every time as well as letting you see what you're shooting at. I've used it on grave robbers before."

He stopped. "Grave robbers?"

"Sure. Any new site is a target for grave robbers. Humans tend to bury a dead person's valuables with the body."

He had a mental picture of her crouching in an open grave, flashlight in one hand and pistol in the other. He rubbed his face and gave up. "Shit."

Pepe approached with a report. Floriano had been hit in the arm, but the wound wasn't serious. Everyone else was okay. The pirates had been firing wildly, their attack plan thrown into total confusion when they had, in effect, been attacked first. Both boats had taken some rounds, but the damage was slight. All in all, they had escaped very lightly.

Excitement made the men jumpy and they were slow to settle down, chattering excitedly between the two boats and rehashing the events over and over. Eulogio, as Ben had hoped, had also heard the pirates approaching and had the men on the second boat ready, so they had all been in on it from the beginning. After a while, though, when it became apparent that the pirates weren't coming back, they began to settle down. As a safety precaution, Ben set a guard, scheduling a change every hour so everyone would have a chance to sleep. The short watch time also ensured that the guard would be alert, just in case the pirates were stupid enough to double back for a second go at them.

Once the lanterns were out and everyone quieted down, the snoring began surprisingly soon. Ben wondered if they would have been as lucky if that thunderstorm hadn't roused them. Probably, since both he and Pepe slept like cats, awakening at the slightest unusual noise. But if the pirates had been smarter, if they had cut their engines a lot sooner and paddled in, things could have been a lot nastier. This time, chance had been on their side.

Jillian had settled down in her previous position on the boxes, and had dropped off as easily as the others. When he thought she was sleeping soundly, Ben moved closer to her and stretched out beside her, straightening his long legs. He wasn't actually touching her—not quite—but he was close enough to hear her breathing, and that let his taut nerves finally relax.

The damn boxes were fairly comfortable, he thought drowsily. Or maybe he was sleepier than he'd thought. He dozed, and woke up half an hour later to listen carefully. Everything was calm, the night denizens carrying on undisturbed. Jillian was soft and warm beside him. Instinctively he turned on his side and draped his arm across her waist, cuddling her closer to him. She made an incoherent noise of protest at being disturbed, but didn't awaken. Instead she adjusted her position against his warmth and then the deep breathing rhythm of sleep resumed.

Jillian woke up just before dawn, only minutes before the howler monkeys would begin their daily uproar. They were such effective alarm clocks that, after the first morning, she had invariably woken before the noise started, evidently in self-defense against being startled out of her skin.

Her first rational thought was that she was stiff and cramped from sleeping on the boxes; the second was that, regardless, she didn't want to move. There was something so comforting about waking up in a man's arms—

Whoa.

That conniving rat.

She didn't doubt for a minute that he'd waited until she was asleep, then slipped over next to her so as to give credence to his lie about their sleeping together. It was also a sneaky way to cop a few feels, if he was so inclined, and nothing she had seen about him yet made her believe that he *wasn't* inclined. The man was a walking hormone.

His arm was lying heavily across her rib cage, his wrist snuggled between her breasts, his hand tucked into the little pocket between her neck and shoulders, but he was utterly still and she thought he must still be asleep. The strong, even movements of his chest as he breathed were so soothing that, even considering everything, she was a little reluctant to move. But she had to; it was time to get up.

Then she felt a definite movement that wasn't soothing at all, and she realized that she wasn't the only thing getting up. Ben was definitely awake. He thrust his hips firmly against her bottom, tightening his arm to hold her still.

She didn't waste time trying to tug his arm away, because he was far too strong for that. Instead she reached up and back, closed her fingers in his thick, tousled hair, and pulled with all her might.

"Ouch! Hey!" he yelped. "Hey!" He was up on his knees, trying to relieve the pressure on his scalp.

Jillian released him and rolled away, getting to her feet with a lithe bound. She gave him a pleasant smile. "Good morning. Did you sleep well?"

He rubbed his head and scowled at her. "The sleeping was fine. Waking up was hell, though."

"Then you'll learn to behave."

"It's not something I can control, damn it. Every man I know wakes up with a hard-on."

"Maybe so, but they do not—repeat, *do not*—rub it on me."

"'Every man I know' wasn't rubbing it on you! It was just me!"

"And it was just your hair that I pulled, wasn't it?" she asked sweetly.

He growled something under his breath and turned away. Pleased with the exchange, Jillian turned around and saw four pairs of dark eyes regarding her with expressions varying from complete puzzlement to shock to amusement. Pepe was the puzzled one, while Jorge looked as if he might laugh aloud. Not knowing what else to do, she shrugged in a questioning manner as if it were all Ben's fault and she didn't understand any more than they did, and picked her way to the rear of the boat where the tiny closet of a toilet was.

The howlers began their serenade, and as if on cue everyone swung into action. While breakfast was being cooked, Kates came over to the lead boat, with Rick right on his heels.

"That was some firefight last night," Rick said excitedly, still caught up in the rehashing of the event.

Ben sighed. He tended to take it personally when someone shot at him, but Rick had obviously built the skirmish up in his head until it was on the same level as the Battle of the Bulge. Ben wasn't in the mood to listen to it again. His head was still hurting where Jillian had pulled his hair, and frankly he was pissed.

"It was minor," he growled. "Except to the bastard I shot. With a wound like that in this climate, he might not make it back to Manaus to see a doctor, even if there is one willing to treat scum like him."

"Will you have trouble about that when we get back?" Kates asked with a concern that Ben didn't believe for a minute.

He gave him an incredulous look. "For shooting a river pirate? This isn't the first time it's happened and won't be the last." Irritated, he turned away. "Breakfast is almost ready. Let's get moving."

Kates smirked as he and Rick went back to the second boat. "The bastard's worried," he half whispered, "and trying not to let us see it. That's why he's so touchy this morning. He probably killed that man, river pirate or not."

111

Rick paused and looked at Lewis standing in the bow of the lead boat, studying the river. "I don't think that's it. Joaquim said last night that Lewis is famous on the river for handling these problems, and that the authorities steer clients to him because he'll take care of 'em. That don't sound like he gets in trouble for it."

Kates's cold eyes flicked at him. "You're spending a lot of time with the greasers," he said. "They're filling you full of hot air." He boarded the boat, blond hair gleaming in the soft morning light. He couldn't tolerate it when an idiot like Sherwood contradicted him.

They were soon continuing upriver. Ben was satisfyingly surly, and Jillian knew he was still smarting. It served him right. If she hadn't pulled his hair, he probably would have done something extremely embarrassing.

He was in such a fit of pique that she hadn't properly appreciated his gesture of admiration that he scarcely spoke for the next several days. Ben, she decided, was a sulker. He would instantly turn sunny again if she approached him and cuddled up to show how sexy she found him, but for now he was behaving as if he had offered her his favorite toy—come to think of it, he had—and she had spurned it. She bit her lip so often to keep from snickering that it became sore.

But even though he was pouting, he was still protective of her. She thought some of it was show for Kates's benefit. He wasn't always around, but the men talked to one another whenever they halted, so presumably those on the second boat knew that Ben kept a sharp eye on her. He always warned her away from the railing well before they hit any even slightly rough spots in the water, he slept between her and the other men at night, and he made certain none of them bothered her when she was bathing or attending to other functions in the closet-sized toilet cubicle.

She knew the interpretation the others would put on his behavior, but her own view was more cynical. She was the only one who knew how to get to the Stone City; Ben would take very good care of her for that reason alone.

By the tenth day on the river, Jillian began paying very

close attention to the passing jungle and studying the course of the river. Sometimes she retired to a corner by herself, pulled out some papers, and worked at her indecipherable notes. They had to be getting close to the place where they should put ashore. It might take them another two to four days to reach it, but she wanted to make certain they didn't pass it by due to carelessness on her part.

"Tell me if you want to slow down so you can study a particular place," Ben said, abandoning his sulk in favor of taking care of business. He had immediately noticed the change in her behavior now that they were so far upriver. They had to be getting close to the point where they would leave the boats and continue by land. It had been two days since they had passed the last settlement, and they had seen only one raft in the same length of time. The jungle was pressing in closer as the river narrowed, and the air, if anything, was even hotter and more humid. At noon it was almost impossible to breathe. By his reckoning, they were dead on the equator.

They were also heading toward the mountains. The great Amazon basin was mostly flat, but the Rio Negro rose out of mountains that extended into Colombia and Venezuela. Green, mysterious mountains, largely unexplored. The Yanomami tribe had been discovered in those mountains not so many years ago, after living isolated for centuries in Stone Age conditions.

Jillian didn't look away from the jungle. "The river forks again not too far from here, doesn't it?"

He laughed. "According to the aerial maps. I've never been this far up, sweetcakes. Nothing up here except isolated Indian tribes, who may or may not have ever seen a white man before and who may or may not be headhunters."

She ignored that last comment. "Take the left fork."

"Yes, ma'am. And then what?"

"I'll tell you when I see it."

When he thought about it, he realized that she hadn't been exactly straight with him when she indicated on the map the area that they would be going into, the distrustful little wench. But she was smart; he had to give her that. With the information she *had* given him, he had laid in sufficient supplies to get them to where they really were going.

An hour later they reached the fork, and Ben took the left one. Navigation was trickier now that the river was getting shallower and narrower with every passing mile, and he cut the engines back until they were barely making headway. Jillian stood in the bow, leaning over the rail in mingled anxiety and eagerness, searching for the landmark. Ben said sharply, "Don't lean over like that. If we hit a snag you'll go overboard."

Obediently she moved back, but it was difficult to restrain herself. She was afraid she would miss the sign, afraid she hadn't decoded the professor's notes correctly, even though she had repeated the process several different times to check herself.

Ben appeared beside her, and she looked back to see that Pepe had taken the wheel. Immediately she jerked her head back around. What if she had missed it, in that split second when she looked at Pepe?

"Tell me something," Ben drawled. "If Carvajal went up the Amazon and found the Anzar, why are we going up the Rio Negro? I realize you haven't told me the truth about anything so far, but there's no reason now not to tell me, is there?"

"I just didn't go into all the detail when I was telling you about Carvajal's journal. Orellana and the men on his expedition had a brief skirmish with the Tapua tribe, and the Indian women fought alongside their men. Carvajal called them Amazons."

He sighed. "So you made up all of that about the Anzar?"

"No. There are more sources for it than just Carvajal. There's the incident with the Tapua, which most people think is how the name came about. But there were other sources, other tales, about a separate tribe of warrior women deep in the interior. The Anzar. The names, Anzar and Amazon, are similar. It's easy to see how the tales about the Anzar would be discounted as Amazonian myth."

"It's still pretty damn easy to discount them," he muttered.

114

She smiled, her eyes on the horizon. "Don't you see? It doesn't matter. What matters is that if the Stone City exists, then I've proven Dad right. It doesn't matter if the tribe was made up of warrior women or a normal mix of male and female. What's important is that I'll have found proof of a lost city, a lost civilization."

"So an army of one-eyed bandits could have lived there for all you care?"

"Exactly, though that would bring to mind the old myths about Cyclopes."

"I think I have all the myths I can handle here. Forget about the one-eyed bandits."

She straightened abruptly. "Here!" she said.

"Here?"

"Yes, *here!*" She whirled toward him. "Here, damn it!"

He gave a quick, disbelieving look at the impenetrable tangle on the banks and said, "My opinion exactly," before he yelled a command to Pepe, who instantly turned the boat toward shore.

There wasn't a good place to leave the boats, but Ben hid them as best he could, pulling them into a cove and securing them with chains to sturdy trees. Even so, he was well aware that the boats were just as likely as not to be missing when they returned. It was a problem he'd foreseen, though, so they dragged two large, inflatable rafts about fifty yards inland and hid them, too.

The tangle of vegetation was always thickest on the riverbanks, where more sunlight was available; they had to hack their way off the boats, but once they were in the dimness under the triple canopy, they found it much easier to move around. Plant life didn't linger on the jungle floor; it had to reach upward, toward the sunlight, to survive. It was a different world under the canopy, a world of climbing orchids and still, humid air. Giant buttressed roots anchored trees whose limbs stretched far overhead, lost in a sea of green. The brightest noon became a twilight in this dim world where vegetation reigned; thick liana vines trailed from overhead, sometimes swaying with the invisible

115

movements of monkeys far above. Occasionally a ray of sunlight would dapple the leaves. Sound seemed to flatten and die; though they could hear the chirping and chattering of the jungle denizens, it had a muted, faraway quality to it. The jungle had the same hushed expectancy as a cathedral.

Jillian worked with the men to unload the boats. Each of them would carry a pack that included their own lightweight tent, a foam sleeping pad, their personal belongings, and some of the general supplies. The remaining supplies would be loaded onto four two-man litters, to be carried by the eight helpers. Ben had also left enough supplies with the rafts to get them back to Manaus.

It took most of the remaining hours of daylight to unload the boat and divide the supplies, so rather than push on, Ben decided they'd spend the night there. They set up the tents in their first inland camp and built a fire. They would leave the alcohol stoves behind, as they added too much weight. Henceforth, they would cook on a campfire.

Late in the afternoon Kates left the camp to attend to a call of nature. Less than two minutes later they heard his hoarse scream. Ben grabbed his shotgun and plunged in the direction of the screams, with everyone else streaming behind him.

The vegetation was so dense that Kates hadn't gone far. Jillian plainly heard Ben say, "It isn't poisonous."

"Goddammit, don't tell me it isn't poisonous!" Kates was screaming when they all got there. "It's a coral snake!"

"False coral," Ben said patiently. "It's a river snake. Unless you're small enough for it to swallow, you aren't in any danger. Just calm down, and from now on carry a stick with you."

The Brazilians were already heading back to camp, trying to hide their smiles. Jillian turned to do the same, and bumped into Dutra.

Instantly she jumped back, her stomach roiling with distaste at having touched him. She hadn't realized he was standing so close behind her, though as his rank smell rose to her nostrils she wondered how she could have missed him. He didn't say anything, just grinned at her, showing his stained teeth. The long incisors made a chill prickle her spine. His eyes were flat and malevolent as he stared at her breasts; Jillian had the sickening intuition that he was thinking of biting them.

She started to hurry back to the camp, but then halted. Though the tents were only about twenty yards away, the thick vegetation would hide her from view for most of the way. With Dutra so close, there was no way she would take the chance of being caught alone even for those few steps. Instead, she deliberately stepped close to Ben's side. He gave her a surprised look; then his gaze slid to Dutra, and she saw instant understanding replace the surprise.

He slipped his arm around her waist. Jillian thought wryly that she should have expected that. Ben Lewis wasn't one to let any opportunity pass.

Leaving Kates there to accomplish what had been interrupted by his sighting of the snake, they turned back to the camp. Dutra was nowhere in sight, and she was surprised at how silently he could move.

Ben squeezed her waist. "All right?" he asked in a low voice.

"Sure," she replied, giving him a grateful smile. "I was just being cautious."

"Smart girl."

He halted when they could just see the tents through the foliage, holding her in place beside him. "I'm going to kiss you," he murmured, already bending his head. "Play along."

Play along, indeed. Caught in his strong arms before she could react, she didn't have much choice. She tried to protest, but then his lips were on hers, and he slipped his tongue into her mouth before she could prevent it.

A wild shudder of pleasure racked her, and she had the disjointed thought that it should be against the law for anyone to kiss the way Ben Lewis did. She knew she should push him away, but couldn't resist the temptation to let herself enjoy the moment. She wound her arms around his brawny neck and sank against him, reveling in the hardness of his muscled body.

He made a rough sound of surprise and satisfaction in his throat and gathered her even closer, adjusting her hips to fit his. One hand slipped down to squeeze her buttocks.

Quick as a flash Jillian slipped away from him, giving him a wink over her shoulder as she stepped into the camp clearing. Behind her, she heard his groan of frustration. It was just what he deserved. She hadn't evaded Dutra just to put herself in Ben's hands, skillful though they were; he needed to learn not to take advantage of a damsel in distress.

After eating, she retired early to her tent, deciding that Ben still looked a bit put out and it would be best to avoid him. Inside, she unrolled the foam pad, which was only about an inch thick but surprisingly comfortable. The nylon tents were small; high enough to sit up in, four and a half feet wide. The sleep pads were thirty inches wide, so that left two feet on the side for personal gear. The open end of the tent could be closed by a heavy-duty, two-sided plastic zipper. To secure it, she took a roll of electrician's tape from her pack, cut off a three-inch strip, and placed it across the zipper right below the head. That way no one on the outside could unzip it; it made a cheap and effective security device. With sturdy nylon between her and the jungle, and electrician's tape between her and Ben Lewis, she felt fairly safe.

She carefully plotted the coordinates that she would give Ben the next morning, then packed everything away and undressed. From experience she knew enough to get comfortable, and that meant stripping down to her underwear, which consisted of cotton underpants and a cotton tank shirt. She didn't carry bras on expeditions.

She switched off the flashlight; faint light from the fire filtered through the nylon, so it wasn't completely dark. She reached into her pack and got the pistol, putting it close by her head. She could hear Ben retiring to his tent, which he had positioned right next to hers, and the low murmur of voices from those who remained around the fire. If they were smart, they would try to get as much sleep as they could, because tomorrow would be grueling. Taking her own advice, she stretched out and promptly went to sleep.

* * *

Rick stared resentfully at the two tents set up right next to each other. "She's told him about the treasure," he muttered to Kates. "He's going to try to cut in on us."

Kates had had the same thought, but Lewis hadn't said anything to indicate that he thought there was anything in the jungle other than ruins. He wouldn't have worried about it if Lewis hadn't turned out to be completely different from the man Kates had thought he was hiring. The Lewis who had taken charge of the expedition was a far cry from the careless booze hound he had seemed at first.

"We'll have to watch him," Kates finally said. That was about all they could do right now. After they found the treasure, though . . . that would be a different situation.

"I never thought Jillian would take up with *him,*" Rick mused with a bitter undertone. "Trust her to do whatever will screw me up the most. She was a pain in the ass from the day she was born."

Kates gave the other man a long, considering look. Rick Sherwood wasn't distinguished by his intelligence. Kates rather looked forward to the time when Dutra would shut that whining mouth forever.

"I doubt she spared you a thought when she became involved with Lewis," he replied. No, more than likely this was just another of her maneuvers. Jillian was nothing like her half brother; she was both shrewd and closemouthed, and she might sense that Kates had his own agenda. Getting in tight with Lewis might be a form of self-protection, a way of lining up a bodyguard, so to speak. Like Rick, he never would have suspected it, given the animosity between the two of them when they first met, but she wouldn't be the first woman to take an opportunity when she saw it. Evidently she was smarter than they were, in seeing Lewis's true character before they did, and taking advantage of it.

Lewis would be a problem. He was tough and wily and already watched Dutra like a hawk. As far as Kates could tell, he was never unarmed. They'd need an ambush to take him out.

There had been nothing but problems from the minute they left Manaus. Rather than the expert on the interior he had claimed to be, Dutra had turned out to be a murderous thug who had sometimes gone upriver to hide out from the law. The river he had gone up, however, wasn't the one they were on. His skills in the jungle were mediocre at best. Kates only hoped Dutra was skilled enough to get them back out when they found the treasure, because Lewis wouldn't be making the return trip.

9

Even though she had known what the day would be like, Jillian couldn't believe how rough it was. The pack on her back was so heavy that by the time they stopped at noon she felt as if she could barely lift her feet. The straps pulled at her shoulders, and her thighs were burning. Trekking through a jungle wasn't easy even without a pack, and with one it approached torture. It even took extra effort to inhale the heavy, wet air. She had to look out for roots that might trip her, avoid trailing vines that might sting, and carry a heavy stick to ward off any creatures that their passage disturbed.

Ben and the two Tukanos, Pepe and Eulogio, seemed tireless, although Ben was drenched with sweat while the Indians remained dry. Jillian felt proud that she fared at least as well as the porters, and better than Dutra. Rick and Kates, as she had expected, had the hardest time of all, for they had been utterly unprepared for the sheer physical effort of it. Ben wasn't setting a very fast pace on the first day, but even so, they were gasping for breath in that deep, hoarse manner of complete exhaustion. When Ben called a halt, they sat down right where they stood, without even removing their packs.

Jillian shrugged out of her pack and set it down. "Drink

some water," she said, taking in Rick's pallor. "And take a salt tablet."

Neither of them moved. "Drink some water," she said insistently.

Rick opened one eye to glare at her. "Who put you in charge?" he demanded nastily. "Bossy bitch."

"You should listen to her." Ben's tone was hard. "She knows a hell of a lot more about what she's doing than you do. If you want to feel better, you'll do as she says, because I'll leave you here if you aren't ready to go when the rest of us are."

Kates didn't join the argument, and after a minute he reached for his water. Jillian also saw him take a salt tablet. But the expression on his face when he looked at Ben wasn't pleasant, and she realized he probably hadn't liked the idea of being left behind, since he had financed the expedition. When she considered it, she had to admit that Ben had more gall than any two normal people put together.

Sullenly Rick followed Kates's lead and soon began to feel better; well enough, at any rate, to eat a fair amount when Pepe had the food ready.

When they began preparing to start out again, Rick walked over to Jillian's pack. "I think I'll carry yours and let you carry mine," he said, still in that nasty tone. "I don't think you'll be so perky then. I doubt you'll last an hour. You couldn't have kept up if you'd been carrying your fair share of weight."

She couldn't think of anything she had done to trigger such outright hostility, and she turned away to hide the hurt she couldn't keep from her eyes. It was silly, because she knew Rick and knew better than to expect any kind of regard from him, but he was her brother, and she couldn't write him out of her life. That day might come, but it hadn't arrived yet, and she was surprised to find herself vulnerable to his attacks.

She didn't like the idea of Rick having her pack, since her pistol was in it, but she wouldn't fight him over it. It wasn't that important.

"Don't touch her pack," Ben said, stepping in once again. He didn't care about anything Rick Sherwood might say or think. "You stupid jerk, she's carrying just as much weight as you are, and maybe more. On second thought, you can pick both packs up, so you can compare the weight, but then you'll very gently put hers down and keep your fucking mouth shut from now on."

Rick stood over her pack, glaring at him.

"Pick it up!" Ben snapped.

Slowly Rick leaned over and hefted the pack. A surprised expression crossed his face and he darted a quick look at Jillian. Then his mouth twisted into a sneer again and he started to dump the pack on the ground.

"Hold it!" Ben rapped out the words. "I said *gently.*" He stood with his feet squarely planted, his head lowered just a little. His hands hung loose at his sides, but he looked like a man who was coiled to act.

His fury was plain in his eyes, but Rick gently lowered the pack as he had been ordered. Without another word he moved to his own pack.

"I agree with Lewis," Kates said in a hard, low voice as he grabbed Rick and pulled him off to the side. "Keep your fucking mouth shut. I don't care if you hate your sister's guts. If you keep it up, she's going to start thinking that she doesn't have to put up with us, that there's no reason why she and Lewis can't go on alone. Do whatever you have to do to get on her good side, and I mean it."

Rick's expression was both sullen and furious, but for once he took the advice given him: he kept his mouth shut.

Jillian picked up her pack and silently slipped her arms through the straps, then buckled the one across her chest to anchor it. Ben came over to her. "All right?" he asked.

She wasn't certain how he meant the question. Was he asking if she was upset about Rick or if she was handling the pace okay? It didn't matter, she decided, because the answer was the same either way. "All right."

He moved around, making certain everyone was loaded up and nothing was left behind. He had changed since they left the boats; he was as wary and alert as a wild animal, his narrowed eyes sweeping from one side of the trail to the other, missing nothing. His tone was brisk and commanding, and now she had no trouble believing that he was the best guide in the Amazon. Even his appearance had changed: his pant legs were tucked into his boots, which came up to midcalf, and his shirt was neatly tucked into his pants. He wore the pistol openly now, in a holster strapped to his lean hip, for all the world like an Old West gunfighter. A machete with a two-foot blade hung in a scabbard from his belt, and he carried the pump shotgun slung over his left shoulder. All of that armament could have had something to do with the way Rick had backed down.

"Everyone ready," Ben called. "All right, let's go."

He led, using his machete to clear the way when necessary. Pepe and Eulogio followed with a litter, and Jillian fell in behind them. Directly behind her were Jorge and Floriano with another litter. Vicente and Martim were teamed, then Joaquim and Dutra. Rick and Kates brought up the rear, struggling to keep the pace.

The rest had allowed Jillian to recoup her strength, but by the time two hours had passed she was feeling the strain more with each step. The straps of the pack dug into her shoulder muscles, and the discomfort quickly became real pain. She tried shifting the straps around, but that also shifted the weight of the pack and made it difficult to carry. She began hooking her thumbs under the straps to move the pressure points, because otherwise she didn't know how she was going to be able to bear it for several more hours. For tomorrow, she promised herself, she would make some kind of padding to protect her shoulders.

Her legs, though aching, were holding up. She was accustomed to running five miles a day at home, and she regularly lifted weights, but nothing got you accustomed to packing a load except packing a load. The days spent on the boat without exercise hadn't helped, either. She knew that things would be better by the third day; it was just a matter of enduring until then.

Behind her, Jorge said softly, "The straps are causing pain, senhora?"

She looked over her shoulder with a smile. "Yes, they are. I'll pad them tomorrow."

"Perhaps you would like to put your pack on our litter. We would not even notice the weight."

"Thank you for the offer," she replied, touched by his consideration. "But if I can't carry my portion, I don't deserve to be along."

"But you are a woman, senhora. You should not have to carry a man's burden."

"On this trip, yes, I should. I am really very strong; soon I won't even notice the weight."

"Very well. But if it becomes too much, we will carry it for you."

Hearing their voices, Ben looked over his shoulder at them. He swiftly skimmed Jillian with an expert eye, gauging her endurance. She had no doubt that he had heard enough to understand the gist of the conversation. Without saying anything, evidently satisfied, he returned his attention to the trail.

Perhaps it was consideration, though there was an equal possibility that it was sheer caution, but Ben called a halt for the day while there were at least two hours of light still remaining. Jillian unbuckled the chest strap and gingerly eased the pack off her shoulders, wincing at the protest of her muscles. She would gladly have dropped straight to the ground, but there was still work to do. An area had to be cleared for the tents, and she pulled on a pair of gloves before taking up a machete and hacking at the undergrowth.

"Keep an eye out for snakes," Ben called.

"Thanks for the warning," she muttered. "I will."

"The fer-de-lance likes to lie on the ground among fallen leaves and wait for its food to come tripping along."

Damn him. She stopped and gave the ground an extra-sharp perusal, then went back to hacking. She knew about snakes and had automatically looked before she began, but he had made her uneasy enough to look again. Not that that was a bad thing, she was forced to admit. She would rather suffer a little uneasiness than a snakebite. Though they carried antivenin, a bite from a fer-de-lance could mean a painful death, and the bushmaster was even deadlier.

When they had made a sufficient clearing, they quickly set up the camp with the tents in a circle around the campfire. Rick and Kates unfolded their lightweight chairs and sat down, their faces and posture telling of their utter exhaustion. Ben didn't prod them to help, as they were clearly beyond it.

Pepe began the meal, and everyone gathered around. Conversation was sketchy, as they were all tired from the exertion of the first day. As soon as they had eaten, Jillian once more retired to her tent. She had shown Ben on a map the location of the next landmark, and he had said it would take at least three days to reach it. Until then, she had no other calculations to make or recheck. All she had to do was rest, and that was exactly what she intended to do.

After securing the zipper with tape, she undressed and used moist disposable towels to clean up as best she could, paying special attention to her feet. A blister or fungal infection could make life miserable. She dusted her feet and boots with antifungal powder each morning, but every little irritation had to be treated immediately, before it became a major problem. Clean socks were as necessary as food. Thank God her boots were old and well broken in.

Feeling better, she pulled on clean underwear and, with a deep sigh, stretched out on the sleep pad.

"Jillian."

It was Ben. She sighed again, but this time not in relief. "What?"

"You need a rubdown." She heard him tugging at the zipper. "The damn zipper is stuck."

"No, it isn't. I have it jammed from in here."

"Well, unjam it."

"I'm okay. Forget about the rubdown."

"Open the zipper." His voice was quiet, but again there was that unmistakable tone of command.

She scowled in his direction, even though she knew he couldn't see her. "I'd rather be sore tomorrow than deal with your so-called rubdown," she said bluntly. "I'd have to be an idiot to let you in here."

Ben sighed. "No funny business, I promise. No wandering hands."

"Why should I believe you?"

"Because I gave you my word."

That wasn't much reason, but she found herself hesitating. A rubdown would be heaven; she was so sore now that every movement hurt. Tomorrow would be torture if she didn't do something about the muscle strain. Why should she endure pain when she didn't have to? Common sense was sometimes uncomfortable. If she denied herself the rubdown she could feel virtuous and long-suffering, but "suffering" was the key word. Being entirely practical, however, she couldn't find any sense in refusing.

"Well, all right," she muttered. "But if you make even one wrong move, I'll brain you with something." Wincing as she moved, she sat up and peeled the tape back, then slid the zipper down.

"You mean you brought your purse?" Ben crawled into the tent, making it suddenly seem child-size. He brought one of the lanterns and a bottle of liniment with him. One eyebrow climbed as he studied the strip of tape, and he grinned.

"It works," she pointed out.

"So it does. Okay, down on your stomach."

She obeyed, though stiffly. "I'm all right, really. I expected to be sore."

"No point in having pain when I can relieve at least part of it. By the way, I like the outfit."

She hadn't blushed in years, but suddenly she felt her face heating up. More was covered than would have been if she'd been wearing a bathing suit, but the fact that her panties and shirt were underwear made the moment far more intimate. Trust Ben to mention that. Trust him to be incapable of refraining from making suggestive remarks. She pressed her hot face into the pad, thinking that if she could have moved fast enough she would have belted him one just on general principle.

The pungent scent of liniment burned her nose when he opened the bottle. He poured a liberal amount into his palm and began massaging it into her legs. He started at her ankles and worked upward, rolling and prodding the tight muscles. She moaned with delight when he kneaded her calf muscles, then caught her breath on a sharp inhalation of pain when he moved up to her thighs.

"Easy," he murmured soothingly. "Relax and let me work the soreness out."

His touch was slow and lingering, for all the power in his fingers. She had been wary, expecting his hands to wander where they shouldn't have, but they didn't, and after a while the pleasure of the massage was so great that she couldn't resist its drugging spell any longer. Slowly the tension drained out of her with each long stroke of his hands. She heard herself making little sounds in her throat, and tried to stop, because it sounded lewd.

"Roll over," he said, and she did.

He massaged the fronts of her thighs, rubbing in the liniment, easing the soreness. "I knew you'd be in good shape," he commented. "Nice, strong legs. I was beginning to think your brother and his cohort weren't going to make it, though. They crawled into their tents right after you did. They wouldn't even have taken off their boots if I hadn't made them."

"They don't know anything about what they're doing," she said drowsily.

"That's an understatement. Okay, on your stomach again so I can do your back. Pull your shirt off."

She was sleepy, but not that sleepy. She opened her eyes and glared at him.

"I can't rub in the liniment if you don't," he pointed out. "Look, I'm not going to jump your bones tonight. I like my women a bit more lively than you are right now. Your shoulders and back are sore, and if I don't rub them down tonight they'll feel even worse tomorrow. You know it, so don't argue."

She didn't trust him an inch, but he had behaved so far, and the massage felt like heaven. After giving him a warning look she turned onto her stomach again, then wriggled her tank top off.

She heard him chuckle, but he kept any comments to himself. He poured a small amount of liniment on her back, then settled himself into position astride her buttocks. She closed her eyes, berating herself. She should have known.

But all he did was lean forward and begin a strong massage that almost brought her off the pad, especially when his fingers dug into her sore shoulders. She groaned aloud at the exquisite pain.

He worked on each muscle, forcing them into relaxation. She felt herself going limp and was helpless to stop it. Along with the soreness he rubbed out every bit of strength. He prodded until he found every sore spot, then lingered until the last vestige of tension was gone. He was good at this. Oh, was he good. He didn't hesitate to use the strength necessary to do a thorough job.

She would almost have believed sympathy and a desire to help were his only motives, if it hadn't been for the swelling hardness she could feel against her buttocks. Every time he leaned forward, his erection pressed against her. But he didn't do anything else that she could object to, and he had done such a good job of relaxing her that she was incapable of responding, either in welcome or in rejection. All she could do was lie there, drifting in and out of a doze, and wishing those powerful hands could stay on the job for another hour or so. It was pure heaven. . . .

Ben looked down at her, and his lips moved into a strained, rueful smile. She was asleep. He was astride her firm, deliciously rounded, barely covered ass; he had been rubbing his penis against that ass for half an hour, he was so hard that he was shaking with the need to have sex, and she was asleep. Blissfully, peacefully asleep.

He would be lucky if he slept at all that night. He'd caught a glimpse of her breasts when she pulled off her shirt, and the image was torturing him. Lush, heavy breasts had always been his favorite, and hers were on the small side, firmly erect without the voluptuous sway that had always turned him on, so he was perplexed by this almost painful fascination with hers. He wanted to see her nipples, roll them between his fingertips, maybe even suck at them a little. He had always loved the feel of a woman's nipple in his mouth. She was lying there almost naked and sound asleep. All he had to do was gently roll her over and look his fill. He wouldn't even touch her.

He began muttering curses from between his clenched teeth as he moved from astride her and capped the liniment bottle with barely restrained violence. He'd given her his word. Something had to be wrong with him. He couldn't believe he'd actually promised her he wouldn't touch her; that in itself was proof of something serious going haywire in his brain. What was even more ridiculous was that he had her at his mercy and wasn't even going to roll her over for a sneak preview of her breasts.

He looked down at her, at the thick swath of shiny brown hair spread across her bare shoulders, at the way her dark lashes rested on her cheeks, at the relaxed softness of her mouth. The sounds she had made while he was massaging her sore muscles had sounded so much like intense sex that he couldn't stop thinking of a time when he would be deep inside her, finally, and those low, husky moans would be sounding right in his ear. This firm, sleekly muscled, deceptively strong body would be vibrant with arousal beneath him, her hips rolling and lifting into his thrusts. She would be clamped so tightly around him that it would be all he could do to move in and out of her, and when she came . . . God Almighty, when she came . . .

He shuddered and forced the fantasy from his mind. He was only torturing himself, and damned if he knew why. He'd never been this obsessed with a woman before. Obsessed. He didn't like the word, or the meaning behind it. It was stupid to be obsessed about any one woman when there were hundreds of millions of them in the world and he deeply appreciated a great many of them. To be obsessed with one would mean that others had lost their appeal for him, and he couldn't see that ever happening. Hell, what man in his right mind would *want* it to happen?

Maybe that was the problem. He wasn't in his right mind. If he had been, he never would have made that stupid promise.

But he was oddly content just to sit in that cramped space and watch her while she slept, to enjoy the maddening nearness of her almost naked body.

Damn her. What did she think he was, a damn gelding? How could she have gone to sleep like that, as if she weren't wearing only her panties and he hadn't been astride her firm little ass with a throbbing hard-on? She should have been awake, on guard against the possibility that he would toss her onto her back and make a serious effort at convincing her to slip out of those panties, too. Did she discount his masculinity to the point that she wasn't even *worried* about being seduced?

He should show her how wrong she was in that kind of thinking. He could have her almost ready to climax before she was even awake; she would be twisting in his arms, begging him to enter her and finish the delightful torture. He could spend the night here rather than in his own tent.

Except for that damn promise.

Sighing, he picked up that flimsy little undershirt she'd been wearing and draped it across her back, so he couldn't see the swell of her breast beneath her arm. No point in making this any harder on himself than it had to be, both literally and figuratively. Then he put his hand on her shoulder, pausing a moment to feel the smooth, silky curve, before he shook her slightly.

"Wake up, sweetcakes." His voice sounded strange even to himself, with an oddly husky tone. He cleared his throat.

"Hmmm?" she murmured.

"I'm leaving now. Wake up so you can put the tape back across the zipper."

Heavy lids drifted open and sleepy green eyes looked up at him. For a moment the expression in them was soft and welcoming; then they sharpened and narrowed. Immediately she reached for her shirt, and momentary confusion crossed her face when she found it already draped across her. Not that it was much of a shield, being both too small and too flimsy, but it was comforting for all that.

"Don't worry," he drawled. "Nothing happened. When I get around to fucking you, sweetcakes, you can bet you won't be able to sleep through it."

She fumbled at the shirt and finally got it positioned, holding it across her breasts as she sat up. Her cheeks turned pink at his crude remark, but she contented herself with merely glaring at him.

"Thanks for the rubdown," she said stiffly. "It helped a lot."

He lifted his eyebrows. "It was my pleasure."

"Probably, but thank you anyway."

"My services are available for tomorrow night, if you'd like to make an appointment in advance."

She started to tell him that she'd be just fine, thank you, but prudence made her pause. She hoped most of the soreness would be worked out by then, but if it wasn't, a rubdown would be more than welcome.

"I'll wait until tomorrow night to see," she said smoothly. "If you're already booked up I'll just have to wait."

He winked. "Just remember that my services are much in demand."

"I'm sure they are."

He leaned forward and kissed her. "Look, Ma, no hands," he murmured against her lips, and despite herself she chuckled. Ruthlessly he took advantage of it, deepening the pressure and pushing his tongue past the relaxed barriers of lips and teeth.

It was as wonderful as before, damn it. She shivered and helplessly returned the kiss, luxuriating in the feel and taste of him. Her breasts tightened in instinctive preparation, ready to receive their share of attention from him. What would it feel like if he moved his mouth down to her nipples? If he did that as skillfully as he kissed, she wouldn't be able to bear it. If he made love with the same slow sensuality, she would go mad from the pleasure.

She should never have let him kiss her, because her worst enemy was temptation, and oh, was she tempted. She was a woman, not a statue, and Ben Lewis was all man. She wanted him.

So she kissed him too, her mouth sweet and warm with wanting, her tongue joining his. She felt him shudder and was intensely satisfied that she could make him writhe under the same lash of desire.

Then he pulled away, his eyes glittering, his face hard. His mouth was wet and sensual, as if it still molded hers to his passion.

"Goddammit," he said violently, and snatched up the lantern and the bottle of liniment. He jerked the zipper down and started to crawl out, then turned and glared at her. "I'll *never* make such a goddamn stupid promise again," he barked. "And put the tape back over this son of a bitch."

"I will," she said faintly as he exited the tent. She fumbled in the darkness for the strip of tape still attached to one side of the flap, and smoothed it in place over the zipper. Then she stretched out on the pad and tried to sleep, but her heart was pounding way too hard. Her breasts ached; her nipples were tight and throbbing. She found the twisted undershirt and finally managed to pull it on, hoping that the light covering would ease the ache.

No matter how sore she was, she couldn't allow him to give her another rubdown. She knew exactly what would happen. She was too physically aware of him to resist that kind of closeness, and *he* wouldn't try to resist at all. Instead he would use every opportunity to undermine her defenses —not that they were all that strong. Right now they were definitely tottering.

10

On the third day the terrain began getting rougher as the flat basin started to give way to mountains. Jillian moved up so she was right behind Ben, her eyes anxiously searching ahead.

"What are you looking for now?" he grumbled. He knew what he was looking for: danger. It could be lying in wait overhead or on the ground right in front of him. It could come charging at them from the underbrush. It could arrive in the shape of an arrow, for the more isolated tribes could get distinctly irritated when anyone trespassed on their territories, or the danger could be as simple as swarming bees. It was his job to note every detail, to be prepared for everything. Earlier he had caught the strong acrid scent of huangana, and swung on a wide detour to avoid the ill-tempered and dangerous animals. Pigs from hell, that's what they were. The detour had made Jillian nervous, even though he assured her they had returned to their original course.

"I'm looking for a flat-topped mountain," she replied.

"How close are we supposed to be to it?"

"I don't know. It doesn't matter, anyway, since we won't actually go to it. It's just a means of lining up our position. It's supposed to be visible within one day's walk of the time when the terrain begins rising."

"Gosh," he said sarcastically, "I didn't realize the instructions were that precise."

She narrowed her eyes at his broad back, thinking how she would like to hit him with a rock, right in the middle of that sweat-stained expanse, though the rock would probably bounce off, considering how hard the man was. He had become aggravated with his shirt-sleeves the day before, because they restricted his motion as he swung the machete at obstructing vines, so he had simply torn the sleeves out. His bare arms were roped with muscles—muscles that rippled and bulged with each movement, muscles that made her abdomen tighten in reaction.

"I suppose," he continued, "if you don't see this flat-topped mountain within one day's walk, we'll turn around and march back and forth until you do find it."

Maybe she'd aim at his head, she thought with pleasure. Granted, his head was probably the hardest part of him, but if the rock was big enough it might make a dent and get his attention. Aloud she said sweetly, "What a good idea! Now I won't worry so much about finding it the first time."

He had learned that the saccharine tone in her voice meant she was thinking up something particularly nasty to say or do to him, and he threw a wary glance over his shoulder. Her expression definitely was not sweet. She looked as if she was contemplating dismemberment—his—and reveling in anticipation. Damn it, he'd never met a woman like her before. She was strong and confident and levelheaded, certainly not qualities he'd ever been particularly attracted to; he'd always looked more for a good sense of humor, a lack of inhibitions, and big hooters. Jillian definitely didn't qualify for the last two, though she did have a subtle, slightly warped sense of humor that kept him on his toes. He couldn't intimidate her, couldn't embarrass her, couldn't seduce her. He was beginning to wonder if there was anything he *could* do to her.

For over two weeks he had seldom allowed her to get more than ten feet away from him, and she had been out of his sight only during calls of nature and when she had zipped herself into her tent the past three nights. Even during the calls of nature, he had made a point of being close by, and keeping a lookout for Dutra at the same time. Such enforced close contact with any other woman would have driven him crazy with boredom by now; Jillian was driving him crazy, all right, but not with boredom.

The truth was, he felt alarmed and annoyed that she wasn't right beside him during the nights so he could keep an eye on her. What if Dutra tried to get into her tent? Sure, Kates had evidently gotten it through the bastard's head that he had to be on his best behavior on the trip inland, but that didn't mean Ben trusted him for a minute. Jillian had her little trick with the tape to jam the zipper on the tent flap, and she had her pistol, but what if Dutra simply sliced his way into the tent? Would Jillian hear him and wake up in time? She had shown herself to be more than capable; in fact, she had been one step ahead of him most of the time, and that was aggravating as hell. But he still worried and fretted, because if he didn't have her soon he was going to either explode or turn into a babbling idiot.

When he had her safely back in Manaus, he was going to lock himself in a hotel room with her and not come out until he had another guide job, which might be a month or more. A whole month of making love . . . He indulged in some very graphic fantasies for a moment; then his eyes narrowed as he realized that another job would mean leaving her behind, and she probably wouldn't be there when he got back. No, independent Ms. Sherwood would hop a flight back to the States, or she'd be haring off to dig up some old bones somewhere.

He halted in his tracks and turned around to glare at her. Behind her, the entire column lurched to a halt, but he didn't spare them a look. "You'll damn well stay where I put you," he snapped, and turned back around to slash viciously at a vine.

"You've lost it, Lewis," she muttered as she started after him again. "The heat has gotten to you."

"It's not the heat," came his return mutter. "It's a critical buildup of sperm."

She had to bite her lip to keep from laughing. "Oh, I see. Your brain has become clogged."

"Something's clogged, all right, but it isn't my brain."

He sounded so irritable that she wanted to pat him on the head and say, "There, there," but she didn't think he would appreciate the gesture. Instead she asked, "If celibacy is so difficult, how did you manage on your other expeditions?"

He glanced at her over his shoulder again, the intense blue of his eyes flashing in the green-tinted dimness. "Usually it isn't."

"Isn't what?"

"Difficult."

"So what's different about this trip?"

"You."

"Keeping you reminded, huh?"

"Something like that." He was muttering again.

She fell silent, but she was smiling. So he was feeling frustrated, was he? Good. It was no less than he deserved.

He stopped again, suddenly motionless, and she skidded to a halt to keep from knocking into him. Behind her, everyone else also stopped, and something about his alert stillness made them abruptly wary. Slowly Ben unslung the shotgun.

He whispered something to Pepe in the Tukano language, and the wiry little Indian whispered a reply.

"Back up," Ben murmured to her. "Very carefully. Don't make a sound."

Easier said than done, but under the silent urging of Pepe and Eulogio they were all retracing their steps, carefully placing their feet to avoid twigs, using their hands to keep limbs from swishing, inching backward with far more caution than they had used while advancing.

Ben stopped again. Jillian tried to see past him, but his broad back blocked most of the view. He made a slight motion with his hand that told her to freeze.

Then she saw it, her eyes suddenly picking out the details from the forest surrounding it. Fierce eyes, golden and predatory, locked on Ben who was at the head of the column. A magnificent golden coat, dotted with black rosettes and blending almost perfectly with the dappled foliage. A thick tail with the tip twitching as if with a life of its own.

The jaguar crouched in wait, powerful muscles bunched. Jillian's muscles were so tight that she could barely breathe. She wanted to look away from the big cat, feeling as if it were mesmerizing her, but she didn't dare break eye contact in case it charged.

The humidity seemed to increase now that they weren't moving, and the intense smells of the jungle crowded in on them, with another scent added: the acrid smell of a big cat. Sweat trickled down her temples and stung her eyes. They stood motionless for so long that the birds in the area, which had initially taken alarm, began to sing again. Tiny brilliant hummingbirds darted close by, and a giant butterfly with six-inch iridescent blue wings fluttered over the barrel of the shotgun, even briefly alighting before continuing its leisurely flight through the jungle. Monkeys high overhead were barking at one another as they normally did. Lizards went about their business of snaring ants and termites, tongues flicking out with hypnotic regularity.

And they stood there, pinned by the big cat's unblinking yellow gaze.

If the jaguar charged, Ben would have to kill it. If anyone behind her made a reckless movement, that might trigger an attack. She began praying that, for once, Rick would control his impatience.

Then suddenly the monkeys began screaming in alarm, making her glance upward, and there was a great scramble aloft; unseen tree limbs high above began swaying with the commotion, making the dangling lianas dance and tremble. Ben still didn't move. She heard a deep, rough cough, and the fine hairs on the back of her neck lifted in primal warning. When she looked back, the jaguar was gone.

They stood there for what seemed like an hour, and probably was. Behind her, either Rick or Kates made an impatient sound that was quickly silenced by a warning gesture from Eulogio. Finally Ben motioned for Pepe to move up beside him; the litter was carefully set down, and Pepe edged around Jillian. He and Ben slipped forward and returned ten minutes later walking normally, though their eyes were still warily searching every bush and tree.

"Jaguar," Ben said succinctly.

"Oh, hell." It was Rick, his disgust plain in his voice. "You mean we stood here for an hour because you saw a damn cat? Why didn't you just shoot it?"

"I would have if it had attacked. It didn't. No point in killing it." Not to mention there were strict laws against killing the big predators. He didn't figure that would matter to Sherwood, so he continued, "I don't want to fire any shots if we don't have to; not only are there tribes in here who sort of worship the jaguar and wouldn't take kindly to us killing one of them, but I don't want to pinpoint our location for anyone."

Those two reasons apparently made sense to Rick, and he dropped the subject. Without any more fuss they started forward again, but for the next several miles everyone was jumpy, staring hard at the foliage in an effort to see if it hid a big spotted cat.

Jillian didn't see a flat-topped mountain. She told herself not to panic, that they hadn't had a full day's walk from the time the terrain had started rising. Probably she wouldn't find the mountain until tomorrow. But there weren't any breaks in the triple canopy, and she couldn't see more than a few feet in any direction. She began to fret that if they were even a little off course the mountain would be blocked from view. Also, the ground was becoming increasingly uneven so she had to devote more time to watching her feet. If they'd had to do this kind of walking on the first day, she wouldn't have made it half so far. They were all more accustomed to the exertion now, though it was only the third day, but she could feel her breathing becoming more and more ragged, and her legs were aching.

Perhaps he could hear her breathing, for Ben slowed the pace. She knew now how he had developed that rock-hard body. If there had been an ounce of fat anywhere on him, he would have burned it off during the first hour. The machete was never still, effortlessly hacking out a clear path for those who followed him. His stride never faltered, his alertness never diminished.

Ben and the two Tukanos hadn't lost any weight since they started walking, having already been down to pure muscle, but the rest of them had. Jillian suspected she had lost at least five pounds; her pants were looser around the waist and hips. She might not lose much more weight, for her muscle mass would increase from the exercise and make up the difference, but she would lose even more inches, and she began to wonder how she would hold up her pants. Her web belt was in the last notch now; she would have to resort to braiding vines to tie around her waist.

Thunder began to rumble overhead, and they could hear the first raindrops pattering in the canopy overhead. The umbrella of trees was so thick that little rain actually fell directly to the ground; instead, it eventually dripped from the leaves or ran in rivulets down tree trunks and lianas. There was no way to avoid getting wet without losing a couple of hours waiting for the forest to stop dripping, but they halted during the worst of it and took shelter under the tarps they had brought along. She dreaded the first hour after the rain, for that was when the humidity was at its absolute worst, the jungle literally steaming under the intense equatorial sun.

The storm was brief that day, and they were on their way again within half an hour, struggling to breathe the heavy air. The humidity was so irritating that conversation was always at a minimum during this part of the day, and the added effort of having to scramble over rougher ground made it worse.

She didn't realize how high they had climbed until suddenly the vegetation thinned and the sun broke through, almost dazzling her with its brightness. They were on the side of a ravine, with a sparkling, shallow stream at the bottom of it. Mountains loomed overhead, silent and primitive, undisturbed since their creation millions of years before. And right in front of her, smaller than the others, was a mountain with a broad, flat top, an understatement in a land of superlatives. A rather insignificant mountain, drowsy and peaceful, no challenge at all in its existence. "Ben," she said. "There it is."

He stopped and looked, his eyes automatically going to the highest elevations, which were rolling and uneven. Then he let his gaze slide downward and focus on the table mountain before him. "All right," he said. "We'll go a little farther and camp for the night while you figure out the coordinates for the next leg. Unless my ears are going bad, there should be a small waterfall ahead. If Pepe says it's okay, we'll be able to clean up tonight."

There was a waterfall, not very big, not very forceful, just a ten-foot spill of water onto a rock ledge that had been hollowed out over the centuries by the constant battering, before the stream flowed on its way to join with the Rio Negro and then the Amazon itself. Pepe and Eulogio pronounced the water safe. Only Dutra was unenthusiastic about the idea of a bath, but he sullenly went along. Jillian remained at the camp, content to wait her turn, but Ben stayed behind also. She gave him a cool look.

"If you're thinking about taking a bath with me, you can forget it."

"Do you want to strip naked and take a bath without a guard?" he returned calmly. "I'll stand watch while you bathe, and you can do the same for me. I would have gone on with them, but I didn't like the idea of leaving you here alone. Of course, if you don't mind Dutra watching . . ."

"You've made your point." She didn't like his plan, but accepted the necessity of it. She wasn't modest so much as private; it wouldn't be comfortable to be naked in front of Ben, nor would it be very safe, come to that, but the alternative was to remain dirty and she could barely stand herself as it was. She would keep her back turned to him and get it over with as fast as possible. He was serious about guarding her, and wouldn't abandon that responsibility to make an attempt at seduction. For the seduction attempt he would probably wait until she finished her bath.

While they were waiting for the others to return, she bundled her soap, shampoo, and clean clothes into a towel, and Ben whistled as he did the same. "Are you going to leave your pack here? You know Kates will go through it."

She gave him a thoughtful look, then took the pistol out of the pack and slid it into her bundle.

"What about the map?"

"He can't read it." She grinned. "Want to see it?"

"I'd be a fool to say no."

She took out her notebook and unfolded a thick sheet of paper. There were a few rudimentary drawings on it, but nothing that would pinpoint location. The instructions were the damnedest bunch of gibberish he'd ever seen.

"You can read this?" he asked doubtfully.

"No. I can deciper it, though."

He chuckled. "Where are we now?"

She pointed to a sentence about halfway down the page. "Right here."

"Great. That tells me so much. You don't have the code written down anywhere?"

She sniffed. "Do I look like a fool?"

"You haven't written it down when you've been decoding this mess?"

"Remember, I decoded and memorized the entire thing before I ever came to Brazil; this is just so I can recheck. Anyway, the code changes with each word. Unless you know the key, which I also have memorized, none of it is going to make sense."

"This is really going to piss Kates off," Ben said with satisfaction. "He's probably twitching with anticipation, knowing that we'll both be away from the camp for at least half an hour."

"Longer than that," Jillian corrected. "I'm going to wash my clothes while I have the chance."

"Good idea. You can wash mine while you're at it."

"You can wash your own."

Wearing a pained expression, he placed his hand over his heart. "You're an unnatural woman. Don't you know you're supposed to *want* to do things for your man?"

"I don't remember ever claiming you as mine, so the issue doesn't arise. But I can't think of a reason why any woman would want a man who was too lazy to do his own laundry."

His expression became mournful. "No wonder you aren't married."

"And no wonder you aren't."

"I've never wanted to be."

"Neither have I."

He watched her for a moment, his eyes gleaming with satisfaction at the exchange. Then he lightly flicked the tip of her nose. "Ever been engaged? Had a serious relationship?"

She thought about it, then shrugged. "Nope. A guy once asked me to marry him, when I was in college, but I wasn't interested."

"No one since then?"

"I've dated," she said. "But not steadily with any one man."

"So what do you do for fun?"

"Work."

She had to laugh at his disbelieving look. "Working is more fun than dating," she said. "I'm not interested in getting married, so I don't see the point in dating much. If I like someone's company, that's fine, but it would be silly to tie up a lot of time in a relationship that won't go anywhere."

He got to his feet and glared down at her. "So you were screwing on the balcony with some guy you barely know?" he demanded wrathfully.

She felt completely at sea for a moment, without any idea what he was talking about. Then she remembered the hammock and began to laugh. "I've never had sex on a balcony with a *stranger.*" Or with anyone else, for that matter.

She had that sweet tone in her voice again, Ben noticed. He felt like shaking her. "Great. At least you'd been introduced."

"What are you getting so sarcastic about? Haven't you ever had a one-night stand?"

"Plenty, back when I was young and stupid, but I'm a lot more careful now."

She shrugged, as if she couldn't understand his problem. "So am I."

He stalked away, muttering to himself. A minute later he stalked back, and stopped so close that his boots were nudging hers. "So why won't you have sex with *me?*" he demanded, his jaw set.

He was in an absolute fury, she saw. The urge to laugh again was almost uncontrollable, and she bit the inside of her cheek to hold it back. "I don't want to have children right now," she said with perfectly feigned bewilderment, "so what would be the point in having sex?"

His jaw dropped, and he stared at her in disbelief. "Holy shit," he finally said, as if to himself. A strange look entered his eyes. "You've never had a climax, have you?"

Too late, Jillian saw what she had done. Appalled, she jumped to her feet. "You stay away from me," she warned, backing away. To Ben, the thought that no other man had been able to give her pleasure would be an irresistible challenge. He was so sure of his own masculine sexuality that now he would be doubly determined to have her, to show her the pleasure of it. She had just meant to tease him, but instead she had all but issued a direct challenge to his ego.

Sure enough, he moved closer, unconsciously stalking her. "So that's what it is," he murmured. "Sweetcakes, don't you know I'll take care of you? I'm not one of those men who jump on and jump off again five minutes later. I like to take my time, stretch it out for an hour or so."

An hour. Dear God. She began to tremble at the thought of it. Not only was he sexy, he was slow.

"I don't want you to take care of me," she cried, holding

up her hand to ward him off. "I just want to be left alone. Ben Lewis, don't come another step closer!"

He did, stalking her as surely as any jaguar.

"All right," she said desperately. "I lied."

He stopped. "Lied about what?"

"I was just teasing you."

"Teasing me." It wasn't a question. "You sure as hell have been doing that."

"No, not like *that.*"

"That's what you think."

"Ummm." She tried to gather her thoughts. "It's just . . . your attitude gets on my nerves."

"My attitude?"

"Don't sound so bewildered. Your attitude. You know, the attitude that you're God's gift to women and can have who you want, whenever you want."

He crossed his arms. "I pretty much can."

She crossed her arms. "Except for me."

"So that's it," he said slowly. "You're doing it just for spite."

"Is that any worse than what you're doing? You're *trying* to seduce me just to up your score."

"I am not."

"Oh?"

"Yes, oh."

"Do tell." She waited patiently.

He leaned so close that she could see the bright striations in those devilish blue eyes. "I've been *trying,*" he said, emphasizing the word just the way she had, "because you turn me on so much I've had a hard-on since the day we met."

She didn't want to hear that. It was almost impossible to keep from looking down. What if he did? She took refuge in sarcasm. "You would be *trying* just as hard with any other woman under these circumstances, so am I supposed to be flattered?"

"Now, there you're wrong. I don't mess around with married women."

"Well, I don't want to be messed around with, period."

"Sure you do," he said, a cheerful grin breaking across his face. "You just want to be talked into it so you'll feel more appreciated."

The sound of voices as the men returned from their baths was probably all that kept her from knocking him in the head. She turned away and snatched up her bundle, and he did the same. They didn't speak as the men filed into the camp. Ben slung the shotgun over his shoulder. "Anyone who tries to sneak a peek will get his head blown off," he said casually.

It was easy for Jillian to follow the path the men had made. It angled down the ravine for perhaps a hundred yards, which in the thickness of the jungle was well out of sight. The path ended just beside the narrow waterfall.

Ben studied the situation. "We'll cross over to the other side," he said. "That way I can see the path better. There's room behind the waterfall to get past."

There was, and they picked their way over the rocks to the other side. Ben took the shotgun off his shoulder and gave it to her. "I'll go first."

She didn't protest, because she was rather relieved. She was especially nervous about undressing in front of him after the conversation they'd just had. Somehow, if he bathed first, it wouldn't be so hard when she did it, and she was grateful that he'd suggested it. Sometimes, such as when he'd massaged her sore back, he could actually be considerate.

11

Considerate, my foot, Jillian thought five minutes later. Diabolical was more like it. She couldn't take her eyes off him and he knew it.

He had stripped down to the skin with an utter lack of modesty that told her he was accustomed to being naked with a woman. Why would any woman in her right mind want him to wear clothes anyway? He was tall and lean and superbly muscled, and his buttocks were so round and taut that her hands instinctively curled into fists in an effort to resist patting them. He had the shoulders of a stevedore and the legs of an athlete, long and powerful. She had never enjoyed looking at a man more.

He stepped under the waterfall and let the water splash over him while he tilted his head back and shook his hair. Sunlight dappled on the flexing muscles of that marvelously strong body, and the water droplets spraying through the air glittered like diamonds. His genitals hung heavily between his thighs, and he was so perfectly, utterly male that her chest constricted, making it difficult for her to breathe.

Then he looked straight at her, the blue of his eyes so intense that she could see it even across the forty feet that separated them. He stepped forward a little, so that the main force of the water was hitting his back; he was right on the edge of the rock shelf above the pool of water. He was totally exposed to her, without the stream of water to blur the powerful lines of his body. As he stared at her, his shaft began to stir, to grow thick and long, to rise fiercely toward his belly.

Damn him, she thought feverishly. A more graphic demonstration of desire wasn't possible. Nothing was so seductive as knowing that you were wanted, and he knew that. The potent reaction of his body to simply looking at her did ten times more damage to her resistance than any of his slick, playfully profane cajoling, or even those bone-melting kisses.

Her gaze went irresistibly to his erection and she felt herself literally grow weak. Her mouth began to water, and she swallowed convulsively. That thing was impressive, the shaft thicker than the bulbous head. She almost moaned aloud.

She dragged her gaze back up and met his, bright and expectant. Oh, yes, he knew exactly what he was doing to her. The man was so diabolical that she had another almost irresistible urge to throw rocks at him.

Humming, he finished his bath and even scrubbed his clothes, taking his time about it. Jillian's hands tightened on the shotgun that lay across her lap, and she forced herself to scan the path that led back up to the camp, to see if any interlopers had dared test the strength of Ben's casual threat. Birds sang and flitted from tree to tree without concern, the iridescent hues of their feathers glittering whenever they winged their way through a shaft of sunlight. It was peaceful and wildly beautiful, and the naked man standing under the waterfall was as much at home here as any of the jungle creatures.

What would it be like to live out here with him, she wondered, just the two of them, no one else around for hundreds of square miles?

No sooner had the thought formed than she scoffed at herself because of the ridiculousness of it. This *wasn't* Paradise, and he wasn't Adam. This was Ben Lewis, ruffian and adventurer. A woman would have to be crazy to even dream of any sort of permanence with him. All he wanted was a woman for the moment, someone to satisfy his immediate desires. Any woman would do. And afterward he would disappear on another of his treks. She supposed he would reappear occasionally, expecting to be fed and bedded, and he would seldom have any trouble finding a woman willing to do that for him. But that woman wouldn't be Jillian.

Finding the Anzar city would be the making of her career. She would be able to pick her position, though she hadn't decided yet what her inclinations were. She had no ties with the foundation, not after the way they had treated her concerning both Ouosalla and the Anzar. She had taken an extended leave of absence to make this trip, but she wasn't certain she ever wanted to return. She definitely wouldn't return to her same position.

She had decisions to make, decisions that didn't concern Ben Lewis, no matter how magnificent he looked standing naked under a waterfall.

He had finished bathing and left the water to stand on the bank while he dried himself. He made no effort to turn his back, so she made no effort to look away. Instead she accepted his unspoken invitation and appraised him brazenly.

"You aren't a very good guard," he charged, a smile lurking around his mouth. "You spent more time looking at me than at the surroundings."

"Well, you were doing everything but waving a flag at me to attract my attention," she replied. "I didn't want to disappoint you."

"A flag wasn't what I was waving," he pointed out. "Now, if you said flag*pole* I'd have to agree, but—"

She snatched up a rock and threw it at him before he could finish the sentence. She had played on softball teams in high school and college, so she had a good arm and good aim. The missile struck him on the thigh, disconcertingly close to the flagpole.

"Ouch!" He gave her a horrified look. "Good God Almighty!" he bellowed. "Watch what the hell you're doing."

"I was watching. I'm very good at hitting what I aim at." She picked up another rock. "Want me to show you?"

Hastily he turned his back, not wanting to take any chances with a wild pitch, or even one that was carefully placed. She'd had that dangerously sweet tone in her voice again, and he didn't trust her for a New York minute. He pulled on his clothes before she could think of anything else, but soon found himself smiling again. All in all, he was pleased. He'd seen her reaction to his nakedness, and his arousal. She wanted him, all right. She didn't have a prayer of holding him off much longer. He couldn't believe her reasoning in holding him off this long, just to show him that he *couldn't* have her. What in hell did that accomplish, except causing them both a lot of frustration?

But he had to admit it had been interesting. Jillian might drive him mad, but he'd certainly never die of boredom around her. He had to keep his wits about him whenever he was dealing with her in any capacity; he was used to being able to seduce women to his will, to effortlessly charm them, but Jillian refused to be either seduced or charmed.

He finished dressing and approached her, lifting the shotgun from her grasp. He gave the area a thorough survey before leaning down to kiss her. "Okay, it's your turn."

Her mouth throbbed from even that light touch. "Do you swear you'll stay here and keep guard?"

His blue eyes turned cool. "This is something I take seriously, sweetcakes."

"You're right. I'm sorry," she said contritely. He had protected her from the moment the trip started, with dedication and determination. He wouldn't relax his guard or move from his post while she was bathing. Afterward, he might jump her himself, but he'd make damn certain no one else did. She had to be losing her senses, because the realization made her feel oddly secure.

Ben settled back and got comfortable, ready to enjoy the show, though he gave the area another intense survey before returning his attention to Jillian. His heart began pounding heavily at the prospect of seeing her naked.

Jillian stepped down to the edge of the water and took a deep breath. There was no getting around it: she had to take her clothes off in order to bathe, and she was *not* going to deny herself a bath. But if Ben Lewis thought she was going to put on a show for him, he was going to be disappointed.

She sat down and removed her boots and socks, then turned her back to him as she took off the rest of her clothes. She accepted that there was only a certain amount of modesty she could preserve, but she did what she could. Before removing her shirt, she took the towel and wrapped it around her hips. Then she slipped out of the shirt and undershirt, and adjusted the position of the towel so it covered her breasts. She didn't dare glance up at him; she knew the scowl on his face would be as dark as a thunderstorm.

Then she slipped behind the waterfall and undid the towel, snagging it on a high rock to keep it dry. Naked, she stepped under the force of the water and had to hold back a startled cry at the power of it. It was cooler than she had expected, and it battered down on her head and shoulders. It was almost painful at first, but then her tight muscles responded to it and began to relax with pleasure. Taking care to stay near the back of the waterfall, and keeping her back turned, she grasped the bar of soap and happily began to scrub.

Ben watched the blur of her body in an agony of anticipation. *Turn,* he kept thinking, as if he could bend her to his will with his thoughts. *Turn.* He wanted to see her; he needed to see her. Not that he didn't enjoy looking at her ass, what he could see of it through the water, but he wanted more. He wanted to see her breasts, to have an image of reality to replace his fevered imagination. He wanted to know exactly how the plane of her belly curved down to her mound, if her hair was straight or curly, thick and lush or a neat little covering.

His hands were sweating, and he wiped them off on his pants. His chest was heaving with the harshness of his breathing. Damn the perverse little witch, she wasn't showing him *anything.* Didn't she know how much he needed to see her?

A tiny movement in his peripheral vision caught his attention and he jumped to his feet, the shotgun ready as he searched the far bank with narrowed eyes. The movement came again, and he relaxed as he made out the spots and stripes of a paca, a rodent somewhat bigger than a rabbit. The Indians hunted them for food. Ben had eaten them more than once, liking their porklike taste. Pacas liked to make their homes on riverbanks, so it wasn't unusual for it to be there. He wouldn't have seen it at all if it hadn't moved. The meat would make a welcome change in their diet, but he didn't shoot. They still had food; he would hunt only when it ran out.

Just to be certain, he took the time to look over the area again, but the birds were flitting about undisturbed, so he returned his attention to Jillian.

She had her head tilted back, rinsing her hair. He watched every move she made, intently focusing on the lines of her body, the graceful economy of her movements. After a few minutes his eyes actually began to ache from the effort of trying to pierce the blurring veil of water, but he didn't look away. He'd never felt so damn hungry in his life, desperate for any small glimpse of her, the way a starving man pined for the tiniest scrap of food. He couldn't help resenting it, because no woman had ever had that much power over him before. If one turned him down, there were always others who were willing. But now there were no others, and he had the sinking feeling that it wouldn't do him any good if there were. He wanted Jillian, and no one else would do. He hadn't even gone back to Thèresa's bed the night he'd first met Jillian; he hadn't thought much about it then, because he'd just spent the afternoon screwing, but looking back, he decided it was a bad sign. Normally he would have returned to Thèresa's apartment and crawled on top of her again. Instead, he had gone to his own place and brooded over the possibilities of what he'd just gotten himself into.

Up until now he'd been enjoying the game, absolutely sure that he'd have her eventually. The chase was part of the fun, and Jillian was so elusive she challenged every male instinct in him. He wasn't feeling so lighthearted now. His determination had a grim edge to it, and that was what he didn't like. If for some reason—God, even the idea was unthinkable—he didn't eventually have her naked beneath him, he would feel seriously deprived. That deprivation would change him somehow, make his life less complete. For the first time, he felt no other woman could make up for the loss of this one.

No, he didn't like that possibility worth a damn. Thinking about it made him feel helpless, something he wasn't familiar with and tried to thrust away.

She had finished bathing and emerged from behind the waterfall with that damn towel wrapped around her again, her heavy dark hair sleeked back like an otter's coat, her bare shoulders gleaming wetly in the reddish glow of the setting sun. She didn't even look at him as she picked up her dirty clothes and disappeared back behind the waterfall.

She wanted him as much as he wanted her. He knew it, he'd seen it in her eyes when she watched him bathing. So how could she just shrug her desire away like that? She hadn't even glanced at him to get his reaction to her maddening maneuvers. She was one cool customer, so cool that he just might have met his match. The thought gave him a panicky feeling, because that meant his chances of having her were only fifty-fifty, and he wasn't comfortable with that. Ninety-ten would be better; no, hell, why give her any chance at all? He wanted to be one hundred percent certain that she'd be his. Anything less was unacceptable.

Laundry done, Jillian emerged again from behind the waterfall and walked to her pile of clean clothes. He wondered if she could manage to dress with the same now-you-see-it, now-you-don't technique she had used undressing. Watching her, he discovered that she could. How did women learn to do that? It was aggravating, that was for sure.

Feeling smugly satisfied with herself, Jillian sat down to put on her boots, and only then did she look over her shoulder at him. "I'm finished. Are you ready to go?"

He wasn't, but the light was fading fast and they had to get back to the camp. He moved lithely down the bank and across the rocks until he reached her side. "You're a little smart ass, you know that?"

"Oh?" Her green eyes were wide and innocent. "Why is that?"

"Don't give me that wide-eyed look." His own eyes were curiously grim as he put his hand on the small of her back. "C'mon, we have to get back; it's almost dark. I hope Pepe's saved us something to eat."

They gathered up their bundles of wet clothes, and Jillian made certain that her pistol was tucked out of sight. She was a little puzzled. Something about Ben had changed, but she couldn't put her finger on it. He just seemed . . . different.

They climbed out of the ravine and made their way back to the camp. When they walked into the circle of light, Jillian was struck by the rather exaggerated nonchalance of Kates and Rick, while Dutra was even more sullen than usual. Probably Dutra had wanted to spy on her but Kates wouldn't let him, not wanting to bring Ben down on them while they were trying to decipher the coded instructions. None of the others seemed to have noticed anything, but Kates was slick enough to have grabbed the map without drawing attention to himself.

From the sly glances that everyone gave her and Ben, she knew what they thought, but there wasn't anything she could do about it. Ben had gone out of his way to make certain everyone believed they were having an affair; it would have been a waste of time to deny it, even had she been so inclined. She wasn't so silly that she would throw away the bit of protection he had given her.

She retired to her tent immediately after eating, as she had made it her custom to do. When she opened her pack, she found the map in the same pocket, but not in the same position. So they had looked at it, for all the good it had done them. She double-checked the next portion of the code to make certain she had deciphered it right the first time. Then, satisfied that everything was okay, she undressed and stretched out to sleep. She felt more exhausted than normal; dealing with Ben Lewis took a lot of a woman's energy.

The next set of directions took them deeper into the mountains, and the way became increasingly torturous. They had to scramble up and down ravines, and the footing was so slippery that Ben resorted to linking them together with rope like mountain climbers. The amount of ground they could cover in one day was cut at least in half. Most worrisome of all, they had to take so many detours that Jillian was constantly fearful that she would miss the next landmark. Still, she couldn't see any other way they *could* have gone. It would have taken expert mountaineers with rappelling equipment to scale some of those cliffs. They were taking the path that was open to them; there was no other choice.

On the fifth day of such climbing, they were caught on a narrow, winding trail on the side of a mountain when a storm blew up, hard and fast. There was no way they could get to shelter, and there wasn't any room on the trail to even get under one of the tarps. The trail was little more than a natural ledge carved into the mountainside, with vertical walls above and below. They were totally exposed to the wind and pelting rain, with the lightning stabbing around them and thunder booming right over their heads.

"Get as close against the wall as you can, and crouch down!" Ben bellowed, working his way down the line so all could hear him. Then he returned to where Jillian sat with her back against the cold stone, her head and shoulders hunched against the rain. He crouched beside her, wrapping his arms around her and shielding her as best he could from the stinging force of the rain. A tropical rainstorm wasn't a gentle thing; it roared and battered, the immense force of it tearing leaves from trees and sending creatures scurrying for cover.

She huddled in his embrace and stoically prepared to wait out the storm. It would have been suicidal to try to negotiate the ledge in such violent weather, not to mention useless, for the storm would certainly be over long before they could reach any sort of shelter.

Minutes dragged by while the deluge beat down on them. Rivulets from above began to grow in width and strength, sluicing down on them, swirling muddy water about their feet. The storm seemed interminable as they crouched there for what seemed like hours, cowering from the lightning and on edge at every sound. But suddenly it was gone, moving on through the mountains with metallic echoes of thunder. The rain stopped, and the sun came out, almost blinding in its brightness.

Cautiously they stood, stretching cramped legs and backs. Just as they did, Martim shook a cigarette out of his waterproof pack and reached for his lighter. The wet metal slipped from his fingers and fell across the path. In a reflex, without thinking, he stepped forward to get it.

It all happened in an instant.

"Not so close," Ben called sharply.

There was a whooshing, sodden sound, and Martim had time only for a strangled cry of terror as the ground collapsed beneath his feet and he disappeared from view. It seemed as if they could hear his scream for a long time before it abruptly ended.

"Shit!" Ben exploded into action, unlooping a section of the rope he carried slung over his shoulder. "Get back!" he roared. "Everybody stay away from the edge. The rain softened it." Obediently they moved to huddle once again against the mountain, their faces blank with shock.

There was nothing on which to anchor the rope, so he tied it under his arms and tossed one end to Pepe. "Don't let me go over," he said, and stretched out full length to slither to the edge.

Jillian started forward, her heart lodged in her throat, but forced herself to stop. Her added weight would only increase his danger. Instead she poised herself, ready to jump and add her strength to Pepe's if the ground beneath Ben gave out too.

Cautiously Ben peered over the edge. "Martim!"

There was no answer, though he called twice more. He twisted his head around. "Binoculars."

Swiftly Jorge found them and slid them across the sodden ground to Ben's outstretched hand, taking care not to go too close.

Ben put the binoculars to his eyes and focused them. He was silent for a long minute, then tossed them back to Jorge and began slithering away from the edge.

"Sherwood, take Martim's place with the litter," he said tersely, and Rick was shocked enough that he moved to obey without complaint.

Jillian's face was white and strained. By chance she had been looking right at Martim when he went over, and she had seen the expression of utter horror and helplessness in his eyes as the earth gave way beneath him. The knowledge of his own death had been there, and there hadn't been anything he could do. Her father had also died from a fall in these mountains. Had it been on this very ledge? Had that same sick, helpless look of realization been in his eyes, too?

"What are we going to do?" she asked in an almost toneless voice.

Ben gave her a sharp look. "We move on. We have to get off this ledge."

"But . . . we have to go down. He might not be dead." She felt they had to at least make the effort, even though, logically, she knew it would have taken a miracle for Martim to have survived. "And if . . . if he is dead, we have to bury him."

"We can't get to him," Ben replied, edging closer to her. He didn't like the way she looked, as if she were going into shock.

"But we have to. He might just be hurt—"

"No. He's dead."

"You wouldn't be able to tell if he's still breathing, not even with the binocu—"

"Jillian." He put his arms around her and pulled her close against his muddy body, stroking his hand over her wet hair. "He's dead. I give you my word." Martim's skull had broken open like a ripe melon on the rocks below. There was nothing they could do for him, and he didn't want Jillian to see the body.

"Then we have to get his body."

"We can't. The ledge wouldn't hold up even if we had the equipment we'd need. It would take a team of experts to get him up."

She was silent for a minute, but he felt the fine trembling of her body and held her closer. "We'll come back for his body?" she finally asked.

In this case, he had to tell her the truth. "There won't be anything left to come back for." The jungle would have destroyed all traces of Martim's body by the time they could get back.

"I see." She squared her shoulders and pushed away from him. She did see. If she hadn't been so shocked and upset, she would never have asked such a foolish question. There was nothing they could do for Martim. All they could do for themselves was to continue on the expedition.

12

It was a subdued group that moved on. Ben kept even closer watch on Jillian than usual, worried by the tension on her face. It wasn't just Martim's death that had upset her, though that had been bad enough; there was something more, something that went deeper.

He was also beginning to worry that they wouldn't be able to work their way off this damn ledge before dark, forcing them to sleep there. There wouldn't be any room for tents, so they would be exposed to the swarms of mosquitoes that had begun plaguing them as soon as they left the river, as well as any other menace.

Ben called a break and sent Pepe on ahead to scout, wary of their situation. He crouched down and stared at the surrounding mountains looming over them. He felt as if he were in a hole, with only a circle of sky directly overhead. The situation wasn't that bad, but it was the way he felt. They couldn't get off the ledge soon enough to suit him.

Jillian was also staring silently at the mountains. Ben went over to her, taking care not to come too close to the unstable edge.

"What is it?" he asked quietly, hunkering down beside her.

She had plucked a leaf and was unconsciously shredding it. She didn't look at him, but kept her gaze on the

159

mountains. "My father died in a fall," she finally replied. "In the mountains, we were told. It had to be *these* mountains, somewhere along the trail we've been following. Perhaps even here on this ledge. God knows it's dangerous enough."

He wanted to comfort her, to just hold her close until the pain eased, but there was nothing he could do. The urge was a new one for him; he'd never wanted to take care of anyone before. It was a little startling. "There's no way of knowing for sure," he said. "Don't let yourself think about it."

"It isn't something I can shut off like a faucet. I loved him, you know."

"I know." Her love for her father must still be strong, for her to expend this much time and energy in an effort to restore his good name, to risk this kind of danger. Most people wouldn't even have contemplated an expedition this dangerous, this rigorous, but she was doing it for a dead man. A sharp pang hit him as he realized that when Jillian loved, she loved forever.

"Hey, Lewis." It was Rick, approaching them. "Why do we have to carry all of Martim's personal supplies? It makes the litter too damn heavy for this kind of walking."

"We may need them," Ben explained patiently. "We don't know what's ahead of us. Anything can happen."

"We could at least leave his tent behind. What do we need an extra tent for?"

"In case something happens to one of ours."

"But we didn't have any extras before; everyone carried his own."

"The tents don't weigh that much," Ben said sharply, rapidly losing his patience. "What are you complaining about?"

"With Martim gone, we don't need to carry as much food, do we?"

Both Ben and Jillian stared at him in disbelief, and finally Ben shook his head at the man's stupidity. "We don't leave food behind. Ever."

Rick's face was sulky. "I was just asking."

"And I just answered."

Rick turned sharply to leave. Jillian, watching him, saw the way he suddenly lurched to the side, heard that sodden whooshing sound again. She didn't think, didn't pause, simply launched herself forward in simultaneous motion as the ground gave way beneath her brother. Her scrabbling hands caught at his shirt as he plunged downward; the fabric tore and he slipped through her grip, only to catch again as his hands locked on her forearms.

She heard screams, cries, curses, but couldn't tell where they came from. Rick was screaming, surely; she could see his open mouth as she was inexorably dragged through the mud toward the edge by his weight. Maybe she was even screaming herself; she simply didn't know. There was a strange dreamlike quality to it as he pulled her farther and farther over the edge, time moving in slow motion, sounds far off and distorted.

Then vises clamped around her ankles and stopped her slippery progress over the edge of the precipice. Her shoulders were burning with agony from the strain. Rick's hands began to slip on her arms and desperately she tightened her own grip.

The cursing was still going on above and behind her, lurid, inventive curses that included every swearword she'd ever heard and some, in Portuguese, that she hadn't. She closed her eyes as the pain in her shoulders and arms became worse, gasping from the fierceness of it.

More ground gave way beneath them, plunging them farther down. Rick's weight jerked on her shoulders and she screamed in pain.

"Don't let me go, please, Jill, don't let me go," he was babbling, his face white and twisted in panic.

"I won't," she whispered. He slipped some more, until their hands were locked around each other's wrists. His grip was so tight that she could feel the delicate bones in her wrists grinding together.

"Pull her back!" Ben was roaring. "I'll kill every one of you bastards if you let her go!" He had dug his heels into the mud, straining backward with every ounce of strength in his body, holding her ankles in a death grip. His threat was empty, because if she went over, he'd be with her; he sure as hell wouldn't let go.

Jorge was on his knees, stretching forward to hook his fingers in the waistband of Jillian's pants, and he added his considerable strength to the effort.

"Try to get a loop around Rick's feet," Ben ordered, his teeth clenched. Veins bulged in his forehead, and sweat ran in his eyes. "We'll pull him back upside down if we have to."

For an instant no one moved; then Floriano grabbed the rope. Kates had stood back at first, fear for his own neck outweighing the knowledge that, without Jillian, there was no point in going on; now he evidently decided that the risk was worth the possible gain and threw himself down beside them, also grabbing her legs.

Floriano wasn't skilled enough with the rope to get it around Rick's feet, given how the panic-stricken man was kicking. He was also hampered by not being able to get close to the edge himself. He moved as close as he dared, but still couldn't see Rick's feet. He dangled the loop blindly, to no avail.

"Take her ankles," Ben ordered, his voice tight with strain, and Joaquim hurried to do so. Ben staggered to his knees and rapped out a demand for the rope; Floriano gladly wriggled backwards, out of danger, and thrust the rope into Ben's hands.

Ben stretched out on his stomach. "Hold my legs." Vicente and Floriano instantly obeyed, clamping their hard hands around his boots.

He leaned out as far as he dared, and the weak ground began crumbling beneath him. He could see Jillian's face, utterly colorless except for the mud that caked it, etched with pain. She wasn't making a sound. Rick was still screaming and kicking wildly, pleading with them not to let him fall.

"Goddammit, hold still!"

Rick either didn't hear or didn't understand, senseless to everything except his panic and the emptiness beneath him.

Ben swung the heavy loops of rope as hard as he could,

hitting Rick on the head. "Shut up! Shut up and listen to me!" The raw fury in his voice must have gotten through, for Rick abruptly stopped screaming. The sudden silence was as nerve-racking, in its way, as the screaming had been.

"Hold still," Ben ordered, his voice tight. "I'm going to try to get a loop around your feet. Then we'll be able to pull you up. Okay?"

Rick's gaze was blank with terror, but somehow he focused on Ben. "Okay," he said, the word barely audible.

Jillian turned her head to look at him, her eyes pleading and almost blind with pain. Ben had to grind his teeth to hold back more curses as he realized what Rick's weight must be doing to her more fragile joints. *She* should have been the one screaming, but of course she would bite it back, self-controlled even now.

Ben coiled the rope, moving fast, intensely aware that every second must feel like an eternity to both Jillian and Rick. He wasn't too happy to be hanging over the edge like this himself, feeling the mud crumble away under him. He shook out a loop and twirled it sideways, toward Rick's swaying feet. Catching both feet would be a miracle, so Ben didn't expect it. All he wanted was to get the rope around one foot; that would be enough. He'd roped plenty of calves and steers in his day, growing up on a ranch in Alabama, and this wasn't much different, except he was hanging upside down.

The loop swung under Rick's swaying right boot and Ben expertly flipped it upward; the rope caught his foot and Ben jerked to tighten the slipknot. It was a good catch, just below the ankle. "Pull me up," he yelled, and the hands on his legs began tugging him backward.

Once he was on stable ground again he lurched to his feet and thrust the rope into Floriano's hands. "You and Vicente hold him. Hold tight, goddammit, because it's going to be a strain when all of his weight pulls on you."

Floriano's black eyes were steady. "We understand."

Eulogio had been standing back out of the way, but now he moved to also take hold of the rope. The wiry little

Indian was pretty strong, so Ben estimated Rick was safe enough. The problem now would be pulling Jillian back to safety.

Cautiously he crawled as close to the edge as he dared. "Rick, listen to me. I got the rope around your foot. We have three men holding it up here, so you aren't going to fall. We have you. Do you understand?"

"Yes," Rick gasped.

"You have to let go of Jillian. You'll drop, but only for a few feet."

The thought of releasing his grip on Jillian was impossible; Rick's panicked eyes rolled in his head. Jillian was solid, a link to safety that he could feel; what if they didn't really have a rope around his foot? He couldn't tell if they did, couldn't marshal his panicked thoughts into any sort of calm decision, couldn't even look down to see for himself if the rope was there. Jillian's face filled his vision, white and strained, his own desperation mirrored in her eyes.

"No, I can't," he wailed.

"You have to. We can't pull you up until you do."

"I can't!"

Fury burned through Ben like lava. Jillian was hurt, in pain, and he couldn't do anything to help her until Rick released his grip on her. "Turn loose, you son of a bitch," he said in a guttural voice. "I'll knock you in the head with a rock if I have to."

"Rick." It was Jillian's voice, a barely audible whisper. "It's okay to turn loose. I can see the rope around your foot. They have you. It's okay."

Rick stared upward at her for a long agonizing second, then let go.

The sudden release of his weight sent the men holding Jillian tumbling backward, but thank God Jorge retained his grip on her waistband and his backward momentum jerked her back, too. The three men holding the rope dug in their heels, braced against the brutal jerk as all of Rick's weight swung against them. Rick was screaming again, his voice hoarse with terror.

"Pull him up!" Ben yelled, but his own attention was on

hauling Jillian the rest of the way onto the ledge and then pulling her to safety against the wall of the mountain.

As gently as possible he turned her over onto her back. Her face was ashen, even her lips. She wasn't screaming, but each inhalation of breath ended in a harsh, almost soundless groan.

"Can you tell me where it hurts worst, sweetheart?" Ben began feeling each joint, starting in her right hand and working upward. There was a deeply tender note in his voice.

"Left . . . shoulder," she panted. She had broken out in a cold sweat. "I think it's . . . dislocated."

It was, and no wonder, with all of Rick's heavy weight jerking on her sockets the way it had. He was careful in his examination, but even so she cried out every time he touched her. His attention was so focused on her that he was barely aware when the groaning, heaving men finally pulled Rick back onto the ledge, though they were only a few feet away.

"I have to get the joint back in place," he murmured. "This is going to hurt like a son of a bitch, but it has to be done."

Her pupils had contracted to tiny points from the pain. "What do you think . . . it feels like . . . now? Go ahead . . . do it."

Shit, he hated this, knowing how much it was going to hurt her, but she was right; nothing could be gained by waiting. It wasn't as if they could have her at a hospital within the hour; they might make it in a month, if luck was on their side. Her shoulder had to be put back into position, now. He knew how to do it, had done it before, and had himself once been on the receiving end of the maneuver. It wasn't any fun. Before he let himself think about it too much, he lifted Jillian's arm, keeping it straight, and put his free hand on her shoulder.

She screamed as he snapped the joint into place, her slim body arching rigidly. The hoarse scream echoed around them. He hoped she would faint, but she didn't. Instead she rolled convulsively to the side and began gagging from the nauseating agony. She'd been pale before, but now she was chalky.

"What's wrong with her?" Rick was crawling toward them, his own face pale and still wild-looking.

"Your weight jerked her shoulder out of its socket when she caught you," Ben replied, his tone clipped. He was surprised by the violent urge he had to kick Sherwood off the ledge after all, for being so damn stupid and injuring Jillian, not to mention nearly getting her killed in the process.

Abruptly Rick stopped as his strength deserted him. He flopped on his stomach and lay there shaking like an aspen leaf. "God," he whispered. After a minute he managed to lift his head. "Will she be all right?"

Ben wished he had some ice to put on her shoulder to relieve the pain and swelling, but he might as well have wished for the moon. "She won't feel so hot for a couple of days. That joint's going to be damn sore." He reached for a canteen of water and wet his handkerchief, which he used to wash her face and neck. "She's a little shocky. Prop her feet up on your legs," he directed, and Rick scooted to obey.

Gradually Jillian began to feel better; though her shoulder still throbbed, it wasn't with the agony of before. The nausea faded, and she lay quietly, resting.

"Feeling better now?" Ben asked after several minutes.

"Top of the trees," she murmured.

"Thatta girl. If you feel like sitting up, I'll wrap your shoulder. Once it's immobilized, the throbbing will ease."

He spoke as if he had been through the experience himself. Curiosity stirred in Jillian, but quickly faded; she just didn't have the energy to pursue the subject. Carefully Ben eased her to a sitting position against his knee. Everyone seemed to be standing around, watching her with varying degrees of concern, and for various reasons. Except for Dutra, she noticed. From what she could tell, he was still in the position he'd been in when Rick had fallen. His brutish face was set in a sneer.

The first-aid supplies included stretch bandages in various widths, in case of sprained ankles or wrenched knees. Ben chose the widest one and tightly bound her shoulder with it, then used another to secure her left arm to her side. If she had felt better she would have glared at him, because the binding did not make her shoulder feel better; it just intensified the throbbing. As if he'd read her thoughts he said, "I know it hurts. Give it a minute. It'll start feeling better, I promise."

Thankfully, the pounding ache did begin to ease. Ben gave her a couple of aspirin, which she gratefully swallowed. Pepe returned while she was still leaning against Ben's knee, recovering her strength, and she heard Eulogio telling him in their own language what had happened. Above her head, Ben spoke quietly to Pepe, and she half listened to the reply. It seemed they could soon get off this damnable ledge, perhaps after another hour's travel. So much time had been lost, however, that they might not make it before dark.

"Then we'll make it after dark," Ben replied. "We're not spending the night on the ledge." His head dipped down to hers. "Sweetheart, can you walk?"

She hesitated. "I think so, if you can get me to my feet."

Carefully he helped her to stand, and Rick quickly moved to her other side to steady her. She swayed a moment, but took two deep breaths and then stood firm. She even managed a small smile; very small, but still a smile. "All systems go."

Ben slid his arms into his pack, then shouldered Jillian's too.

"We could divide her load," Rick said.

"I don't want to take the time; we need to be off this ledge before dark. I can manage the weight for an hour."

"I'll help Jillian, then."

"No." Jillian took another deep breath. "It'll be safer if we go single file. I can walk for an hour. It's no problem, since Ben is carrying my pack."

The look Ben gave her told her that he knew exactly how much of a problem it was, but there was no alternative, so he didn't say anything. Jillian was glad of his silence. In an odd way, it was a measure of his respect for her strength and capabilities.

Pepe led the way, and Ben insisted that Jillian go second, while he fell into position right behind her. She knew he wanted to stay close by so he could be there immediately if she started to waver, but she resolutely set one foot in front of the other. The pain wasn't so bad, not as bad as she had feared. Her shoulder throbbed with each step, but it wasn't unbearable. The worst of it was the weakness in her legs; she felt as if she were just recovering from a severe case of the flu. Probably a reaction to the shock of pain, as well as crashing down from an adrenaline high. Everything seemed slightly unreal, even Martim's death. Had it only been a few hours?

Absurdly, she began to feel hungry. Not exactly a delicate reaction, but then she wasn't a delicate person. The hunger was reassuring, a mundane touch of reality.

It was deep twilight when they finally worked their way off the ledge, and completely dark when they plunged once again under the triple canopy. Camp was set up hastily, the men hacking a smaller clearing than usual out of the underbrush, one just large enough to accommodate the tents and the cook fire. Ben set up Jillian's tent for her, then found a comfortable place for her to sit while Pepe prepared the meal.

Jillian had no trouble feeding herself, even with her left arm immobilized from the elbow up, and wolfed down the simple meal of rice and canned fish. She usually didn't drink coffee at night, but Ben handed her a mug of the beverage, heavily sugared, and she drank it without protest. By the time the meal was over, she was feeling much better.

Rick came over and sat down beside her. He seemed embarrassed, looking not at her but at the ground between his feet. "Uh—I wanted to say thanks for what you did," he mumbled.

It was the only friendly gesture she could remember Rick making toward her in her entire life, and she refused to let herself read too much into it. She contented herself with a simple "You're welcome."

He shifted his weight uncomfortably. "Are you feeling okay now?" he asked after a minute.

"My shoulder's sore, but it feels better than it did."

"Good." He couldn't seem to think of anything else to say, and after another uneasy minute he stood up. He still hadn't looked her in the face. "Thanks again," he said as he returned to his previous position.

As soon as he had left, Ben appeared at her side with the lantern and a familiar bottle. "C'mon," he said. "Time for the liniment."

She was more than willing. The pungent stuff, coupled with his strong massage, had worked wonders on her sore muscles the first time. Clumsily she crawled into her tent and Ben followed, taking up most of the space with his big body.

She looked down at her dirty clothes. "I need to clean up first."

"I don't know of a handy waterfall close by." Kneeling beside her, he began unlacing her boots.

"I have some wet-wipes in my pack."

He looked up and grinned, a quick flash of white teeth. "So that's how you've been doing it. I've wondered how you've been staying as clean as you have. The rest of us look and smell like bums in comparison."

"If the shoe fits . . ." she murmured.

"Now I know you're feeling better," he said approvingly as he slipped off her boots and socks. "Let's get your pants off before I unwrap your shoulder. It'll be less jarring that way."

She thought about insisting on doing it herself, but sighed and faced reality. Tonight, at least, she needed help. He unfastened her pants and skimmed them off with speed and efficiency, moving her around very little. Then he began unwrapping her shoulder, since he had placed the bandage over her shirt.

Carefully she held herself very still, fearing that any movement would bring a return of that searing agony. Ben unbuttoned her shirt and eased it off, working the sleeve down her arm without disturbing her shoulder. Then he looked at her undershirt for a second before raising his eyes to hers. A disturbing sort of glee was shining in those blue eyes, but he merely said, "I'll have to cut your undershirt off. You can't raise your arms to pull it off over your head."

It wasn't the thought of cutting her shirt off that was tickling him so much, she thought crossly, but the knowledge that the shirt was coming off, period. They stared each other down like gunfighters before Jillian finally said, "It's real stretchy. Help me to get my right arm and head out of it, and we can work it down my left arm."

His hands were incredibly gentle as he helped her to maneuver her right arm free of the material, then pulled the garment over her head and once again worked it down her left arm without causing any undue pain. His gaze lingered on her exposed breasts, and despite herself she felt them begin to tighten in response. Her pulse began throbbing at the base of her throat.

He knew there couldn't be any lovemaking, considering the shape she was in, but he could no more keep his hands from going to her than he could stop breathing. He slid his left arm around her, gently cuddling her against him, while his right hand cupped each breast in turn, his rough thumb rasping over and around her tight little nipples. He was entranced by the way each firm, plump mound fit into his palm, just enough to fill it. Her nipples were a pale, delicate rose-brown. How tender her skin was, compared to his big, rough, sun-browned hand.

She was holding herself very still, except for the fast, shallow rhythm of her breathing. Ben bent his head and kissed her, unable to prevent himself from doing so. Since he had hauled her back from the edge of the cliff he had been shaking inside from the close call, and the need to hold her was overpowering. Still, he had to keep himself under control. So what if she was—finally—almost naked in his arms? So what if he had a hard-on that was threatening to tear his zipper wide open? She was hurt and he had to take care of her; the sex would have to wait. But not much longer, he thought desperately. He couldn't stand it much longer.

It took every ounce of willpower he had to force himself to release her, to move away from her. She silently watched him, the green of her eyes almost swallowed up by her dilated pupils.

Sweat sheened his face, but he wrenched his mind back to the necessary things. "Where are those wet-wipes?" he asked. His voice was strained and rough, and he cleared his throat.

She swallowed too. "In the front zipper compartment."

He found them, but Jillian held out her right hand for the towelette, silently insisting on the right to wash herself. She cleaned up as best she could, ignoring her seminudity with as much dignity as possible. This was far more intimate than bathing in front of him; that had been almost a contest, to see how much she could thwart him. This was different; Ben was subtly different. The tenderness of his care was unnerving, though it had been right in character for him to seize the first opportunity to fondle her breasts.

When she had finished, he lifted her right hand and somberly examined the dark bruises that completely encircled her wrist. They were repeated on her left wrist, and various other bruises laced their way up her arms. "You won't be doing anything much for several days," he said quietly, and helped her to lie down on her stomach. "Your back and arm muscles will be almost as sore as your shoulder."

"The liniment will help," she said, closing her eyes.

He was silent as he rubbed in the sharp-smelling lotion, taking his time, knowing that every minute he spent massaging her abused muscles would lessen the tight soreness she would have to deal with the next day. He sat her up again and rubbed both arms; they too had been enormously strained. Her left shoulder was swollen and bruised; he bound it again, and she sighed with relief at the support.

"No undershirt tonight," he said. "You'll have to sleep as you are. Do you want me to stay in here with you?"

She was surprised that he asked, rather than bluntly stating that he was going to stay, forcing her to fight with him. It worried her that she actually considered the idea for a moment. "Thanks, but I'd rather stay by myself," she replied. "I don't expect I'll get much sleep tonight."

"I think you'll be surprised. You're exhausted. You'll be able to put the tape across the zipper, but how are you going to lie down by yourself? You need support to get up or down."

She managed a smile. "Lying down is easy; I'll just fall over. But I think I'll leave the tape off tonight, because I don't like the idea of trying to sit up by myself in the morning to let you inside."

He stroked her hair back from her face, his hand lingering. "Why did you do it?" he asked curiously. "You and Rick don't exactly have the warmest relationship I've ever seen."

"He's my brother," she said simply.

"Would he have done the same for you?"

"I don't know. Probably not. But it doesn't matter; I'm not him." If she had let Rick die without even making an effort to save him, she couldn't have lived with herself. Their strained, barely civil relations had nothing to do with it.

Ben searched her face, then gave a short nod, as if he understood. "Okay, let's get you settled for the night. I'll sleep light," he promised. "Dutra won't get anywhere near you."

She snorted. Her injury hadn't made her soft in the head. "It isn't Dutra sneaking into my tent I'm worried about."

The corners of his eyes crinkled as he grinned. "Don't try to fool me. I'm making progress and I know it. You've already invited me back in the morning."

"To help me dress."

"If you insist." He leaned down and kissed her again, his mouth lingering. "Don't bother to get dressed on my account." He traced a finger around her nipple, delighting in the way it puckered up. "I don't know why you've been hiding these sweet things from me. I should have done this days ago."

"You wouldn't be doing it now," she pointed out, "if I had full use of my arms."

"Providence works in mysterious ways," he intoned, eyes dancing. Then he was serious again. "Call me if you need me, sweetheart."

"I will."

He kissed her one more time, then helped her to lie down and covered her with a sheet. The covering had become necessary once they moved into the mountains, for the nights were cooler than they had been before. He took the lantern with him and Jillian lay there in the darkness, tired in both mind and body, wary of this new intimacy between them but accepting the necessity of it. Keeping him at bay would be even more difficult after this. She remembered the intent look on his face when he had cupped her breasts, and her entire body clenched with lingering desire. His hard, warm hands had been like fire touching her, setting new fires, arousing her flesh. He knew just how to touch her, damn him, with the precise combination of firmness and tenderness that was irresistible.

As she drifted into sleep, the events of the day played through her mind like scenes flashing across a movie screen. A jumbled image of the downpour battering them, then the shock on Martim's face just before he disappeared from view, brought her jerking back into wakefulness.

She dozed again, but her mind picked up where it had left off, reliving again those horrible, molasses-slow moments when she had seen Rick begin to fall and had thrown herself wildly at him, clawing at him to find a grip. For a split second of sheer terror she had thought they were both going to die, then those steel vises had clamped around her ankles and halted their downward progress. Ben. He had been right beside her, the only one who could have gotten there that fast.

Ben . . . something was different. She didn't know what it was. And why had she stopped being "sweetcakes" and become "sweetheart"?

13

The sound of the zipper on the tent flap woke her, and she tried to sit up, only to immediately freeze as her shoulder protested. "Bad idea," she muttered.

Ben's head poked in; then the rest of him followed. A steaming cup of coffee was in his hand; he carefully set it down, rezipped the flap for privacy, then turned back to her. Blue eyes sharply examined her face, looking for the telltale signs of pain and fatigue. As deeply as she had slept, she figured she looked dazed, but certainly not fatigued. He must have thought the same, for his face relaxed. "How do you feel, sweetheart?"

She yawned. "If I don't move, I feel fine."

He hesitated. "I think we should rest here for a day."

"That's your decision; we'll do whatever you tell us to do. But you know I'm perfectly capable of walking, even if I can't carry a pack right now." She looked at the coffee. "Is that yours, or did you bring it to me?"

"Both." He slid a brawny arm behind her back and lifted her to a sitting position as easily as if she were a child. She grabbed the sheet and tucked it under her arms, covering her breasts, and a grin teased his mouth. "You didn't worry about that last night," he said as he placed the tin cup in her right hand.

Cautiously she sipped the steaming hot brew. "Of course I did. There just wasn't anything I could do about it."

He rubbed her bare back, his strong fingers digging in and testing for both stiffness and soreness. She closed her eyes in ecstasy, and a low purring sound came from her throat. "Umm, right there," she murmured.

"You're better than I thought you'd be," he commented. "Probably because you're in such good shape in general." He took the cup from her hand and drank, then returned it to her. "Now let's see how that shoulder looks."

It looked much the same as it had the night before, swollen and bruised, but she could move her arm a bit more before the pain kicked in. "I think I'll be okay with it bound," she said. "Give me some more aspirin for the inflammation, though. I never thought a dislocated shoulder would be so much trouble; I thought you just popped it back in, and that was that."

"Not quite," he said dryly.

"So I've discovered. Help me get dressed, and we'll get this show on the road."

"I have a distinct memory of you saying that it was my decision whether or not we moved on today."

"You must be hallucinating."

"I must be. You've never been that agreeable."

As he was talking he firmly tugged the sheet away from her body. A triumphant grin was on his face as he looked down at her, but it slowly faded and an absorbed expression took its place. Very gently he began stroking her breasts, finding them delightfully cool in the morning air, but they rapidly warmed under his touch.

"Don't you ever think of anything else?" she asked grouchily, to hide the response she couldn't suppress. She wanted to sink back and let those hot hands touch her all over.

"Sure." His tone was absent, his gaze locked on her breasts. Slowly he began to lower his head. "I think of how you'll taste."

"Ben!" Her protesting cry was thin, and trailed into

silence. She shivered, all of the strength leaching out of her as his hot mouth closed firmly over a painfully sensitive nipple. She sagged against his supporting arm, her eyes closing as electric prickles spread from her nipple throughout her breast, then darted down to her loins. His heat surrounded her; the musky male scent of his body enticed her to bury her face against his neck and let him wrap his strength around her. His tongue roughly pressed her nipple against the roof of his mouth in a strong suckling motion, and the coffee cup dropped from her hand. She dug her fingers into his back, whimpering with pleasure.

"Shit." He lifted his head, his eyes slightly glazed, his mouth wet and sensual. "I didn't mean to do this." But then he bent to her other breast, cupping and lifting it to his hungry mouth, unable to resist giving it the same treatment.

When he raised his head again, there was an expression of acute discomfort in his eyes. Very carefully he stretched out his right leg and adjusted himself.

Shaking, Jillian drew back. "Serves you right," she said weakly.

"I know." He wasn't quite in control of himself yet, and he sucked in a deep breath. "Like I said, I didn't mean for that to happen. It wasn't fair to either of us."

She knew him well enough to realize he thought all resistance was in the past, that she was his for the taking as soon as her shoulder healed enough to allow lovemaking. Being Ben, in his estimation that would be tomorrow night. Dazedly she stared at the coffee she had spilled, a brown puddle on the nylon floor of the tent, and wondered why she didn't just go ahead and give in to him. She wanted to; she wanted *him,* damn it. But she didn't want casual sex, and she doubted that Ben could offer anything else. He wasn't the type of man with whom a woman could plan a future; he offered hot sex, a good time, but after he got up and put his pants on, he'd be gone. So, despite his self-confident air, the battle was still enjoined. She couldn't afford to lay down arms.

"Help me into an undershirt," she said shakily.

"You can do without one today. No one will know, and it'll be easier to undress tonight."

"I sleep in my underwear, so it won't be a problem. Just wrap my shoulder once I have the undershirt on, then put my regular shirt on over the bandage. If you think my arm still needs immobilizing, you can strap it to my side the way you did yesterday, over my shirt. That way my shoulder won't have to be unwrapped tonight in order for me to undress, and I should be able to dress myself tomorrow."

He didn't move, but the expression on his face was suddenly dangerous as he got the meaning behind her words. She had the impression of a male animal on the verge of violence, rigidly holding himself in check; only the instinctive knowledge that Ben wouldn't hurt her kept her from cringing in fear.

"You can't hold me off much longer." His voice was low and steely. "What's between us won't just go away."

She faced him, seeing the force of his arousal in the hard, taut planes of his face. "I don't have to hold you off forever," she said, a little sadly. "Just until we get back to Manaus. Then I'll be out of your life and it won't matter anymore."

He gave a short bark of laughter, a sound totally without humor. "Getting back to Manaus won't keep you safe from me, sweetheart. You're mine, and you're going to admit it no matter how long I have to keep after you."

"That's ego talking. Once we get back, some other woman will catch your eye, someone who won't mind being easy-come, easy-go."

"There's sure as hell nothing easy about you," he muttered. He looked as if he wanted to say more, but abruptly changed his mind and dug a clean undershirt out of her pack. His hands were as gentle as before when he helped her into it, then tightly wrapped her shoulder and finished dressing her as efficiently as if she were a child. Afterward, to her surprise, he knelt behind her and brushed out her hair, then caught it up in her usual ponytail. He ended by kissing the nape of her neck. "There. Are you ready for breakfast?"

She was, though he'd knocked her a bit off-balance with the sweetness of his care. She didn't want him to be sweet; she wanted him to be the Ben Lewis she was accustomed to: shameless, raunchy, and reckless. Brave, too, she mentally added, to give the devil his due. Intimidatingly capable. Dangerous. Ruthless.

For the first time, she wondered if she had a prayer of resisting him, if it wasn't a question of "when" rather than "if." She was doing something so stupid she could barely believe it of herself. She was falling in love with the man.

He called for frequent breaks that day to allow her to rest, and she did much better than she had expected. Though her wrists and shoulder were sore, she wasn't in any pain from them unless she bumped her bruises. The tight binding prevented movement in the shoulder joint, letting the strained ligaments heal. Since she wasn't carrying a pack, the trek was actually easier on her than it had been before her injury.

That night, when Ben unwrapped the bandage that had kept her left arm bound to her side, she found that she could move it without much discomfort, since the bandage on her shoulder still supported the joint. She managed to undress herself, though with slow care, and, after taking two aspirin, slept well.

The next day she felt well enough to do without restraining her arm and strode briskly along in Ben's wake. They were so high in the mountains that the altitude had eased the suffocating heat somewhat, and though they were still scrambling up and down steep grades she managed without undue difficulty.

They had been walking only a few hours that morning when abruptly they found themselves in what appeared to be a tropical version of a box canyon. The mountains rose vertically around them, and though the coded instructions clearly indicated they should go due north at this point, due north would have been possible only if they'd had wings. They all stopped, watching her expectantly. She looked up at the mountains soaring overhead, bare rock showing through in some places, but for the most part trees and bushes sprouted from every crack, turning the face of the cliffs into walls of green. Lianas thicker than her arm trailed to the ground, and wild orchids bloomed more profusely than anyplace she'd seen them before.

Ben walked over to her, carrying her pack. "Maybe you'd better recheck the instructions," he suggested.

She did, taking out her notebook and reworking the code, but the instructions still read the same. "We're in the right place," she said, puzzled.

"We can't be, unless we're supposed to shinny up the vines like monkeys."

"It says due north." She gestured helplessly. "That's due north."

"Shit." He took off his hat and wiped the sweat from his forehead. "We must have strayed off course somewhere."

"Impossible. The landmark yesterday afternoon was right where it was supposed to be. We're in the right place, I know it."

He tilted his head back and looked upward. "Then you'd better come up with something else, because from my point of view, we're at a dead end. Not that this isn't what I expected, but if you don't change my mind quick, we'll be turning around and going back."

"What do you mean, going back?" Kates had approached close enough to overhear, and his demand was furious.

Ben gave him a sardonic look. "Don't you know that most expeditions like this turn up nothing? It's like drilling for oil. You pay your money and take your chances."

"But—but this was supposed to be a sure thing." Kates's expression had abruptly turned sickly.

Ben snorted. The rude noise adequately expressed his opinion of "sure things."

"We can't go back," Kates insisted. "We have to find it."

Jillian walked away to look more closely at the vertical wall of stone, advancing until the way was blocked by huge tumbled boulders and thick undergrowth. She tried to push away the welling disappointment and *think*. The professor had taught her to always think a situation through, to realistically assess the pros and cons. It was a discipline that had always stood her in good stead. She considered the facts. The way was blocked. They couldn't go up, and according to the instructions, that was exactly how they needed to go. She stared upward, studying each crevice in the rock, each tree, looking for anything unusual that might give her a clue.

Due north. No matter what, they had to go due north. And that was . . . She stared hard at the enormous boulder in front of her. Due north was straight ahead, not straight up.

Jorge was lingering close by. She turned to him and asked courteously, "Would you cut a strong stick for me, please?"

"Of course." He used his machete to hack off a sturdy limb for her. Another few whacks removed the smaller branches, and he handed it to her with the same grave courtesy.

She used the stick to probe the underbrush, making certain there weren't any snakes or other dangerous creatures hiding in there.

Ben came striding forward. "Jillian, wait. What're you doing?"

"Just looking," she said, slipping from view behind an enormous fern.

"Damn it, wait. We'll clear this out if you want."

After being in the bright sunlight, it took her a minute to adjust to the dimness again. The foliage was thick, forming a natural ceiling over her head. A butterfly lit on a leaf next to her hand and folded its quivering wings.

These boulders were huge and covered with vines. She reached out and placed her hand on the cool side of one that had to be at least two stories high. There was no telling how old these monoliths were; if they had tumbled from the top of the mountain, then probably even more of their bulk was buried beneath the soil.

"Jillian, I told you to wait." Ben appeared at her side, swatting away a vine. They were completely hidden from the others, who couldn't have been more than ten feet away. The vegetation was so thick that even the sound of their voices was muted.

She poked with the stick, swiping the ground, and took another step forward when nothing either leaped or struck at her.

"What is it?" he asked, closely watching her.

"Let's work our way behind this boulder."

"Why?"

"Because the instructions didn't say anything about going *up*," she replied.

His brows lifted. "I see what you mean. Okay. But I'll go first."

He squeezed past her. It was a tight fit, because of the closeness of the enormous rocks. He used the machete to clear away the undergrowth and small trees that clogged every square inch of space, making the area almost impassable. It seemed to get darker with every foot they progressed, as the stones loomed closer and closer over them.

Ben stopped, every muscle taut.

"What is it?"

"Feel."

She was silent, concentrating. Feel what? A slight cool breeze . . . A breeze? Here behind these huge stones?

"Where's it coming from?" she whispered.

"Right in front of me." His voice was tight. "It's blowing full on my face."

He swung the machete again, hacking at the green wall obscuring his vision. As the thick tangle of vines and limbs fell away, a narrow black opening was revealed. The cool air blew gently from its mouth.

He stepped back, bumping into her. "Well, I'll be damned."

"Can you see how far back it goes?"

"Sweetheart, I can't see two feet inside that thing. Now that's what I call *dark*."

He had dropped his backpack before joining her, so he didn't have a flashlight with him. Jillian hurriedly retreated to where the others were waiting. They were all a bit anxious about what she and Ben were doing but not curious enough to see for themselves what was behind the big rock. As she fished a flashlight out of her pack Kates said, "Did you find anything?"

"There may be a passageway behind the rock," she said. "Maybe not. We can't tell."

"I'll go with you," he said.

They worked their way back around to where Ben waited. Kates kept casting uneasy glances overhead, but didn't turn back. When they reached Ben, Jillian saw that he had used the time to finish clearing out the space around the opening.

Kates's eyes widened as he stared at the thin black slit in the mountain. The thought of stepping inside that opening was clearly frightening to him.

Ben took the flashlight and shone it around the opening. It widened immediately beyond, and he realized what a good defense this narrow door in the rock was; enemies would have to enter in single file, allowing the occupants to pick them off without effort. The passageway beyond was like a tunnel carved into the mountain, probably seven feet high and five feet wide. He couldn't tell if the dimensions changed as the tunnel went on, for about ten feet in, it made a sharp curve to the right.

"Shit," Kates blurted. "There're probably bats in there."

Ben played the flashlight along the ceiling. He saw cobwebs, but nothing else. "It looks man-made," he said. "No bats, unless it opens up into a natural cave farther on." He raised his voice and shouted, "Pepe!"

Within thirty seconds the little Indian was there. He took one look at the opening and his slanted black eyes widened with alarm. He said something rapidly to Ben in his own language.

"He doesn't like it," Ben translated.

"I'm not crazy about it myself," Jillian commented. Every time she thought about entering the total blackness of that passageway, apprehension tightened her spine.

Kates was sweating as he stared at the black hole.

Ben winked at Jillian. "I'm not worried about bats, but there's no telling what else is in there."

"Only one way to find out," she said.

"You go first."

"You're the one with the flashlight in your hand."

Ben drew his pistol and thumbed off the safety. "I'd rather have this."

"You have both, so do it," she said impatiently. "I'll be right behind you. Or in front, if you really do want me to go first."

"You stay here," he ordered.

"I will not. I found it; it's my hole."

"I beg your pardon. *I* had the machete, *I* cleared out the underbrush, and *I'm* the one who first felt the cool air."

"Only because you bullied your way in and got in front of me. I was doing just fine without you."

As they were bickering, Ben stepped the first few feet inside, with Jillian right on his heels. Her heart was pounding with excitement. Kates followed, rather reluctantly, but he was there. "I told you to stay outside," Ben muttered to her.

"So?"

They reached the sharp curve and edged around it; until then, light from the entrance had shone on their backs, but suddenly they were swallowed by complete darkness broken only by the meager beam of the flashlight. The tunnel didn't change; it was still roughly the same height and width; she trailed her hand over the stone wall and felt the patterns that bespoke human labor.

"I know," Ben said, noting her action. "It *is* man-made."

Or woman-made, she thought. She was so excited that she wanted to scream with joy, just to release some tension.

They went about fifty yards farther, without stumbling across any hidden pits or booby traps, but Ben called a halt. "That's it," he said. "Let's get out of here. I'm not going one step farther without ropes and safety precautions. This thing could snake around in here for miles." His voice echoed back and forth in the tunnel, returning to them from both sides. The effect was eerie.

Kates set a fast pace on the return trip and would have gone faster if that hadn't meant leaving the comforting beam of the flashlight behind. They emerged into daylight again to find everyone else standing outside the entrance, varying expressions of anxiety and excitement on their faces. "What did you find?" Rick asked. He was one of the excited ones, all but jumping up and down.

"Nothing," Kates said.

Rick's face fell. "Nothing?"

"Nothing *yet,*" Jillian said firmly. "We didn't go far."

"All right, everybody, back out," Ben said. "We're jammed up in here like sardines. Let's get some space and plan what we're going to do."

What they were going to do was simple. He had done some fast thinking while they were inside the tunnel. On the chance that they might have found the Stone City, he didn't intend to leave Jillian behind at the mercy of either Kates or Dutra. Where he went, she went. They couldn't carry the litters through there because of the twists and turns, but would have no trouble negotiating the corridor with backpacks in place. The loads were swiftly broken down and redistributed, almost weighing the men down. He hoped it wouldn't be a long trek through the tunnel.

He roped everyone together by the simple method of running the rope through a belt loop—a problem with Pepe and Eulogio, since they didn't have belt loops, but Jillian provided some safety pins and they improvised. Jillian insisted on carrying a small pack slung around her right shoulder, wanting to do what she could, and everyone carried a flashlight.

With the Glock firmly in his right fist and the shotgun within reach, Ben led them back into the tunnel. He had no idea what they would find. The tunnel might be a dead end, or it could be blocked by a landslide. Anything was possible.

Jillian transferred her flashlight to her left hand and surreptitiously slid her own pistol out of the pack on her shoulder. She had made certain it was close at hand.

Ben went first, followed by Jillian, with Pepe behind her. Pepe seemed very nervous about the proceedings, but she suspected it was the closeness of the tunnel that got to him. The more stolid Eulogio was merely interested, rather than fearful.

Sound echoed so severely, reverberating in their ears, that everyone quickly learned to whisper.

She estimated they had gone at least a quarter of a mile when the tunnel abruptly sloped upward, with wide, shallow steps that seemed to have been carved out of the stone. It wasn't a steep slope, but it took a toll on the men, since they were carrying so much extra weight.

The air became even cooler, and Jillian shivered. Ben's flashlight picked out nothing but more of the same. "How much farther can it go on?" she wondered aloud.

"The way it's twisting and turning, I'd imagine for quite a way. As long as we can feel that breeze, I'm not worried. There's fresh air coming in somewhere."

The endless darkness was unnerving. She wondered how spelunkers learned not only to tolerate the sensation of being buried in the bowels of the earth and to endure the oppressive darkness, but to actually enjoy it. This wasn't for her.

The tunnel evened out again, and Ben called a short break for them to catch their breath. After ten minutes he had them going again.

Jillian had noted the time when they entered the tunnel. She turned her wrist so the flashlight shone on the watch face. They had been walking for fifty-four minutes, minus the ten-minute break—say, forty-five minutes. If they had been setting a fast pace that would have translated to about three miles, but even at their slower rate she estimated they had gone two miles, at least. This was some tunnel. Someone had gone to a lot of trouble to cut it out of the heart of the mountain, though it was possible nature had begun the effort and man—or woman—had simply enlarged what was already there.

"Here we go again," Ben said, and they started climbing another series of wide, shallow steps. Each step was probably no more than an inch or so higher than the one before, but hundreds of them added up, both in height and in the effort it took to climb them.

Then suddenly they turned a curve and there was light ahead. Dim light, barely distinguishable, but there. As they neared, they could see that this opening was overgrown every bit as much as the other one had been, covered by thick lianas and bushes. This entrance was as wide as the tunnel itself, but there was still room for only one man when that one man was swinging a machete. Ben set his backpack down and began slashing with the lethal, razor-edged weapon, hacking their way out of the tunnel with brute force. The sunlight poured in, brighter and brighter.

Then they were outside again, pushing aside broad leaves that slapped at their faces, slicing away trailing vines. After the darkness of the tunnel they had to shade their eyes until their vision could adjust to the sunshine.

What they saw looked pretty much like what had been on the other end of the tunnel.

"Now what?" Rick asked in disgust. "Where do we go from here?"

Jillian was turning around and around. They seemed to be in a kind of bowl, with rock walls encircling them. Her trained eye picked out detail after detail, and a swelling sensation grew in her chest until she thought she would burst. She caught Ben's eye, and knew that he had seen the same things, but suddenly he was looking dead serious while she wanted to whoop and scream her delight.

"We don't go anywhere," she finally managed to say, her voice shaking with strain. "We're here. We've found the Stone City."

14

Rick looked around again. "This is *it?*" he demanded, obviously disappointed.

"Unless I miss my guess," she said. There was no guess to it; she knew what she was seeing. The stone walls surrounding them were honeycombed with chambers. The entrances had long ago been overtaken by the jungle, but she could still make out shapes and a certain regularity to the growth pattern of the vines.

"So where's this treasure you talked about?" he demanded.

She drew a deep breath. "If there *is* a treasure, it could be anywhere. We might not be the only ones to have found this."

Kates strode forward, scowling. "What do you mean, *if* there's a treasure? Why the hell do you think we came along? If you lied to us—"

Ben was suddenly at her side. "No one knows what's here," he said, his tone even but underlaid with a note of menace that halted Kates. "A lot can happen in four hundred years."

"What do we do now?" Rick asked.

"Make camp. That's the most important thing. This place isn't going anywhere, that's for sure."

Jillian was almost eaten alive with impatience to start

exploring, but she knew Ben was right. First they hacked out a huge clearing, putting her on tenterhooks that they might carelessly destroy some ancient artifact, but nothing went down under the flashing blades except bushes and vines and small trees. There were no extremely tall trees in the bowl, and she wondered why. There was plenty of sunlight, but the vegetation, though thick, didn't seem to grow to any great height. The reason behind this oddity, whatever it was, was part of the differences of the Anzar, and she could barely wait to begin discovering their secrets.

The tents were set up farther apart than they had been on the trail. She felt it too: a strange sense of security. They were safe here in this protected bowl. Ben, however, made certain her tent was placed right next to his.

She would not have expected any wind, enclosed as they were on all sides, but a light breeze seemed to swirl continually and the air was amazingly comfortable, almost cool. It would probably be distinctly chilly at night.

"Everyone watch where you step, please," she begged. "There could be bowls, pots, anything, just lying around." Any artifact would most likely be covered by hundreds of years of accumulated dirt, but she had seen them just lying on the ground, too.

There was still plenty of light left, and after the camp was set up, Ben slipped his arm around her waist. "Take a walk with me," he said, softly cajoling.

She gave him a suspicious glance. "Why?"

"We need to talk."

"About . . . ?" she prompted.

He sighed. "Damn if you're not the most untrusting woman I've ever met. Just come on, will you?"

"All right," she said grudgingly. "But don't get the idea I'm agreeing to anything else."

He sighed again. "When have you ever?"

Walking in the thick undergrowth wasn't easy; he carried the machete and carved out a path as they went. After a few minutes Jillian said, "Is there a point in this? Or did you just want some exercise?"

He looked back to make certain no one was behind them. They were well out of earshot, and anyone trying to slip through the brush would alert them. "It gets sticky from here on out," he said. "I've dropped a quiet word in the men's ears to watch out for Kates and Dutra. If anything starts happening, I want them to scatter, to get out any way they can. I figure we're still fairly safe, unless you do find some huge red gem of some sort, though gold is more likely and would get us killed just as fast."

"I know." She understood the ramifications of having actually found the Stone City, and despite what she had said earlier, she didn't think it had already been plundered. They were likely the only humans to have been inside this isolated bowl since the Anzar had died out.

"Playtime's over. Keep your pistol with you at all times."

"I will. I understand."

"If anything starts going down, don't wait to see how it turns out. Hightail it to the tunnel and get the hell out. Run as fast as you can and don't stop for anything. I'll catch up with you on the outside. Whatever you do, don't let yourself get trapped in here. This place makes me uneasy, with only one way out. I hope to hell I can find another exit."

"I don't think it's likely. That tunnel is what kept the Anzar so well hidden."

"And it didn't work, did it?" he demanded. "They died out anyway."

"I wonder what happened to them." She couldn't help it; her eyes began to glisten with tears. "It isn't just that this will vindicate Dad. A special tribe lived here, and one day they just disappeared. Finding out about them is . . . important."

"Probably disease, if they had any contact with Europeans." He wriggled his eyebrows, having been serious as long as he could. "Or maybe, if they really were all women, they died of boredom."

She glowered at him. "Sometimes I'd like to punch you in the nose."

"Any time you want to get physical with me, sweetheart,

just let me know. I'd be glad to wrestle with you any day."
He was grinning in that way that irritated her so much, as
cocky as it was possible for a man to get.

"Do you know what you are?" she demanded, narrowing
her eyes at him.

"No, what? A stud? The light of your life? The man of
your dreams?"

"A turd," she said distinctly, and stalked away from him,
leaving him bellowing with laughter.

Under her direction, the exploration of the Stone City
began the next day with slow caution. More underbrush had
to be cleared so they could find a way up to the almost
obscured chambers, and as they worked, small pieces of the
Anzar's daily lives began to turn up. Joaquim found a
section of chipped stone tile that, when more of it had been
carefully uncovered, seemed to be part of a fountain. Jillian
photographed it from every angle and made meticulous
notes.

Shards of pottery began to turn up, and those too were
photographed and cataloged. She had never been happier in
her life. They weren't making history; they were uncovering
it, learning about a hitherto unknown aspect of man's life on
earth. When she handled a broken piece of pottery that still
bore a glazed design, she was awestruck that someone
hundreds of years before had molded it, made it pretty so it
would decorate their lives, used it day after day. It was like
holding time in her hands, and it was oddly comforting.
Individuals died, but life continued.

Strangely enough, it was Dutra who, four days later,
found the first inclined pathway up to the chambers. He had
no interest in broken old pots, but after his confrontation
with Ben he had, without argument, used his brute strength
to clear out huge patches of underbrush. He poured his
aggression into physical exertion, taking out his hostility on
any branch or vine that got in his way.

The incline, after centuries of disuse, had begun to
crumble. It was covered with debris, but there was no
mistaking its use. They began immediately to clear it off,

though Jillian nagged them into a caution that slowed the work again. The incline led up to what seemed to be a wide avenue that circled the bowl, with chambers leading off of it. Since there were other chambers on higher levels, she guessed there were inclines connecting each level. The Stone City had been built in concentric layers, capable of housing thousands of people.

The avenue was as buried under debris as the incline had been and she suspected there were thousands of artifacts under there, but the main interest was in getting inside the chambers. The chambers were where the Anzar had lived, and they would hold the greatest riches. She knew that her idea of riches was different from that of the others, but the physical record of the Anzar was beyond price to her.

Animals had gotten into the chambers, of course. Birds had nested within, and various other creatures had used the shelters over the years. It would be wonderful if everything had been kept pristine, she thought, surveying the first chamber, but nature wasn't tidy.

That first chamber was small, no more than eight feet square, and though she carefully sifted through the debris she could find no hint of how the room might have been used, at least not on initial examination. There didn't seem to be any of the pottery that would have indicated cooking, or even a method of cooking. Nothing that looked like a brazier or fireplace, no soot or charcoal. All she found was a small snake that immediately slithered for cover when she disturbed its resting place with the stick she was using to probe the litter.

She refused to let herself be disappointed. There were hundreds of these small chambers; not all of them would be as empty. Finding nothing was as much a part of an archaeologist's job as finding something, though not nearly as emotionally satisfying or as exciting. She photographed the room and logged it into the journal.

Ben stuck his head in. "Don't poke around in these rooms by yourself," he said irritably.

"Why? Do you think there might be snakes?" she asked, opening her eyes wide.

"I damn well know there are snakes; you just haven't seen any yet."

She resumed raking the litter with her stick. "Of course I have. One little guy beat a retreat just before you came in."

Ben's jaw set, and for a minute temper glittered in his eyes. Then he relaxed and gave her a wry grin. "I keep forgetting you're an old hand at this. So you're not afraid of snakes?"

"No. I'm cautious, but not afraid."

"Snakes aren't the only danger you could find in a place like this."

"Agreed."

"You don't intend to pay the least bit of attention to me, do you?" he asked in exasperation. "You're going to continue just blithely walking into these rooms."

"It's my job."

"And my job is keeping you safe. From now on, if I'm not with you, one of the men will be."

"Fine with me," she said absently.

She really wasn't paying any attention to him, he thought. She was absorbed in poking around with that stick, squatting to examine some detail, her entire being focused on what she was doing. It was maddening, but he felt an odd softening as he watched her. That was just Jillian. She loved this stuff and tended to ignore everything else when she was involved. All he could do was watch out for her as best he could and remember that she was the most capable woman he'd ever met. She knew what she was doing, and she was solidly grounded in reality.

He couldn't help being dismayed that they had actually found this place. He would have liked it much better if she had been forced to admit that it didn't exist; that would have bitterly disappointed her, but all of them would have been much safer. As it was, he felt as if they were sitting on top of a volcano that could erupt at any minute. Everything seemed calm enough at the moment, but if that damn Empress was found, or any gold, the game would change. It never hurt to be ready for anything, so he had already made certain preparations and plans. If nothing happened, he would carry on as usual.

Since he wanted to keep an eye on Kates and Dutra, he assigned Jorge to stay with Jillian and help her, both for her safety and because her shoulder was still a little swollen. He didn't want her to use it any more than necessary.

Jillian was happy to have Jorge for company. He was pleasant, and a tireless worker. He wasn't enthusiastic about the broken pots and odd scraps that she found, but he was perfectly content to help her look for them.

Other chambers, happily, did contain more than the first one. She was extremely careful about noting the specifics of each find: the location, the description, the condition. She wouldn't be able to carry much, if anything, out of here, and she didn't want to destroy any evidence that would help in unraveling the puzzle of the Anzar and determining their level of advancement. The glazed and painted shards of pottery she had found so far indicated that they'd used a kiln, but she hadn't found any sign of one. It would take a long time to find and piece together the artifacts and evidence that would define the Anzar.

Kates became more impatient as each day passed without finding anything other than what he called "junk."

Jillian too was becoming, if not impatient, a bit disturbed at finding nothing *else.* Had the site been cleaned out long ago by scavengers? If so, they might never be able to learn much about the Anzar by what had been left.

She was carefully sifting through yet another pile of debris when she realized she had done something monumentally stupid. In the excitement of finding the tunnel, and what was surely the Stone City, she had forgotten about the instructions.

The instructions hadn't ended with the tunnel. There were other directions, which presumably would lead her straight to the Empress.

She halted her work and smiled at Jorge. "I think I'll stop for the day," she said. "My shoulder is bothering me and I'm tired."

"You should rest," he said with the shy concern he had often shown.

"I will," she said, and returned to the camp. Most of the men were already there, having grown bored with clearing an access route to those small chambers that seemed to be so much alike and produced nothing exciting. She was half a day behind them in going through the chambers, so it didn't matter. Ben was there, sitting cross-legged on the ground while he cleaned and oiled his weapons. Alerted to her presence by some sixth sense, he looked around at her. She smiled at him but didn't make any effort to converse, instead going to her tent.

Ben continued with his task, but his expression was thoughtful. During their weeks together he had formed the habit of watching Jillian, closely studying her in an effort to find some little chink in her armor of capability that would allow him to get to her. He had become an expert on picking up the slightest deviation in her behavior, and now all of his senses were alert. She was up to something, but what?

Jillian sat cross-legged in her tent, the coded instructions on the floor in front of her and the notebook open in her lap. Though she had memorized the instructions weeks ago, actually writing them down in English still helped to clarify her thoughts. Then she stared at what she had written for a long time. A sound just outside the tent alerted her and she swiftly tucked the sheet of paper under her sleep pad.

Ben opened the flap and crawled in, crowding her backward. "Come on in," she said sarcastically.

"Thanks." He winked at her. "I did. Okay, what's going on?"

He settled himself beside her, and she had the distinct impression that he wasn't going to budge until he had a satisfactory answer. That playful wink was merely camouflage for his iron determination.

She pulled out the sheet of notebook paper and gave it to him. "I remembered that there were more instructions, that they didn't end with finding the tunnel." She made certain her voice was so low that they couldn't be overheard from outside.

Ben read what she had written. "What are you going to do about this?"

"I don't know." She sighed, her indecision reflected in her eyes. "What I've found so far isn't exactly earthshaking, certainly not on the level with King Tut's tomb or the Ouosalla find. I've found proof that humans lived here, but nothing, absolutely *nothing*, to indicate that they were an unknown tribe. We have a miracle of a tunnel leading in here, but not much else. Oh, archaeologists will be interested, and eventually someone will fund a dig here, but I haven't found anything that's going to grab any headlines. I wanted something that would set archaeology on its ear, *force* them to give Dad the credit due him, and I haven't found anything that dramatic."

He lifted the paper. "Unless it's here."

"Yeah."

"And finding it could mean big trouble for us."

"Yeah," she repeated gloomily.

He cupped her chin and lifted it, a wry smile on his face as he looked at her for a moment. Then he leaned over and kissed her. "So I'll look for the jewel while you keep the bad guys diverted," he murmured. "If the Empress is there, I'll let you know and then we can decide what to do. No point in worrying yourself sick about the gem when it might not even exist."

"Oh, it exists."

"Then there's a good chance someone else carried it out of here centuries ago. People just don't leave huge gems lying around, even if there are superstitions attached. The Empress doesn't even have a good threatening curse to go with it."

"It could be a real curse for us, though."

"We'll make that decision later. Even if the thing isn't there, I might find something else you'll like. Who knows? Maybe these people hid all their interesting stuff away."

"They sure did, from what I can tell."

"Then we'll find out tomorrow."

She bit her lip as she stared at him. A month ago she wouldn't have trusted him with her lunch, much less something as important as this. Since then she had gotten into the habit of trusting him with her life. As her life was infinitely more important than the Empress, she didn't see any point in refusing to trust him to search for the gem.

"You'll be careful?" she whispered. "Make certain no one is following you?"

"I promise. And if I find anything, you'll be the first one to know."

Ben didn't do anything unusual the next morning. He went with the others up to the first tier of chambers and helped clear out several more, then left Jillian and Jorge poking around while they returned to the camp. Kates seldom let Jillian out of his sight these days, so he had remained above. Ben busied himself around the camp doing several small chores, then settled down in the shade as if ready for a nap. Dutra, after eating lunch, did go to sleep.

When the snores were issuing from Dutra's barrel chest with loud regularity, Ben got up, draped the shotgun across his shoulder as he always did, even though they hadn't found anything more dangerous than snakes in here, and ambled out of the camp. None of the others paid any particular attention to him. He had taken the precaution the night before of stashing his flashlight in a spot away from the camp, and he retrieved it, hoping he wouldn't need it.

They had begun their explorations, naturally enough, at the areas closest to the camp. Jillian's code placed the Empress in a special chamber directly across from the tunnel opening. When he studied the bowl, he saw that its far edge was slightly higher, giving him a visual reference once he was out of sight of the tunnel. The bowl was at least a mile wide and half again that in length; the floor was choked with trees and undergrowth. Those trees bothered him, for some reason. Why weren't they bigger? With so much sunlight flooding the bowl, there should have been some real giants in here. Though it rained every day, the heavy rains couldn't erode the soil as they did in the Amazon plain; the soil was retained in the bowl.

And just how did the water drain out? It had to, or the

floor of the bowl would be a lake, instead of the very rich soil beneath his boots. The richness of the soil made the size of the trees even more puzzling.

Unless the trees weren't very old.

He stopped in his tracks and stared at one lustrous hardwood, and a chill ran up his spine. Now, that was a spooky thought. Had the floor of the bowl been free of vegetation until the fairly recent past? Had the Anzar disappeared only a couple of decades, rather than centuries, ago?

Nah. Impossible. If they had been here that recently, there would have been a lot more evidence than what Jillian had been finding.

Unless they had moved out and taken most of their stuff with them.

He shook himself. He had to stop thinking like that. Just take care of the business at hand, which was finding the place indicated in Jillian's notes.

Crossing the floor of the bowl was hard work, for he didn't want to use the machete and leave a path even Kates could follow, but he figured it worked out about even, since slashing his way through would be hard work, too. He stopped occasionally to make certain he wasn't being followed and that used up time, too, but he made it to the other side of the bowl within an hour.

This close, he could see a cleft in the rock face, but getting up there would be a problem. There should be one of those inclines carved into the side of the cliff, if the pattern was carried out, so he began a systematic search for it. It had to be his lucky day, because he found it in only a few minutes.

He worked his way up it and at the top noticed something different: unlike the other inclines they had found, this was a double one; another incline rose from the opposite direction to meet this one in an inverted V at the first tier.

Directly ahead, according to Jillian's instructions, and built into the cleft, was the temple of the Anzar. He looked up, and another chill ran down his spine. Soaring high above his head were huge stone columns, carved out of the cliff itself. They were almost totally obscured by vines, but enough of the shape showed through for him to tell what they were.

He approached and began searching through the thick, living green veil for the entrance, thrusting a long stick into the vegetation. When the stick hit solid rock, he moved a foot to the side and thrust again. On the fourth try the stick poked into nothingness, and he knew he'd found what he was looking for.

He'd need the flashlight after all. He parted the vines with his hand and held them to the side, then switched on the light and played it over the enormous chamber revealed within. What he saw made him curse softly.

Statues. Oh, goddamn. Big statues, carved out of stone. The figures were larger than life-size, maybe seven feet tall before they were placed on the pedestals that supported them. Overall, they reached about ten feet.

The workmanship was superb, surpassing anything he had seen done by either the Incas or the Mayas, though the styles were similar. The features were less exaggerated, the proportions more normal. The chills were chasing up and down his spine big time now, and he became aware that he was holding his breath. He forced himself to exhale, but he couldn't shake off the almost overwhelming sense of awe and disbelief.

The statues were of warriors. Each was armed with a different weapon, some with spears, some with a bow and a quiver of arrows, some with clubs.

And they were all female.

15

He advanced even more cautiously than before, thrusting his way through the tangle of vines to stand in the cool darkness. He felt as if he were intruding, as if the blank eyes looking down on him knew he didn't belong. He was a man, alien to these halls. He'd never had this feeling before, even when on one memorable occasion he had followed a woman into the ladies' room.

Well, Jillian had her stupendous find. Even without the Empress, these statues would set the world on its ear, and not just archaeologists. Historians would be salivating to see these, to figure out just what their existence meant.

There were no booby traps, no crumbling floors. Solid rock lay beneath his feet. He simply walked down the middle of the immense hall carved out of stone, between the two rows of female warriors who stood eternal guard.

It was located in an alcove at the end. A sepulcher, also carved in stone. Covered with dust and cobwebs, as was everything in this silent hall. The likeness of a man was graven in bas-relief on the top. And above the sepulcher, in a niche by itself, was another guard. There, glowing even through the dust of unknown years, reflecting back the light of his flashlight in a red glitter that took his breath away, was the Empress.

It was huge, bigger than his fist, and roughly the shape of a human heart.

A fortune was staring him in the face. He knew something about diamonds, having lived in Brazil as long as he had, and this sure looked like one. He supposed there was a possibility it was a garnet, but he didn't think it was. There was too much fire, too much depth. It had been crudely cut, but even so, it was magnificent. Most colored diamonds were pale; the intensely colored ones were extremely rare, usually very small, and very expensive. He'd heard that red diamonds were the rarest diamond of all, and here he was staring at one that was not only a deep, rich red but had to be as big as the Cullinan, if not bigger. The gem was literally priceless.

But was it worth their lives? If Kates found out about this, there would be a killing. He'd either have to kill Kates and Dutra or risk not only his life and Jillian's but also the life of every man with them.

On the other hand, if he was the only one who knew about it . . .

He squeezed behind the sepulcher, shining the flashlight around to make certain the area was uninhabited. It wasn't. A snake was curled in a corner, sleeping off its last mouse meal. He prodded it with the stick and watched it slither quietly away. Then he reached up and carefully removed the Empress from its resting place.

It was surprisingly heavy; he guessed its weight at over a pound. He blew the dust off, then polished it on his pants, and the deep, rich red gleamed with a fire that enchanted him and drew him down into its spell. It was the most beautiful thing he'd ever seen, warm where most diamonds were icy.

Jillian didn't need the Empress to attract world attention; those statues out there would accomplish that. She wasn't doing it for the money anyway; if she had the Empress, and if they made it back to Manaus alive, she would just turn it over to the Brazilian government. But, God, what he could do with it! This thing meant more money than he could even imagine. He could buy his own boats and set up a charter service, maybe even venture into air charter. He'd gotten his pilot's license years ago, because many places in the Amazon were accessible only by air, and he'd seen the possibilities there. And he'd be able to provide Jillian with anything her little heart desired for the rest of her life. Not that she desired much. What did you buy a woman who was happiest digging around in dirt? More dirt?

His conscience didn't even whimper. He slipped the stone inside his shirt and carefully blew on the niche where it had rested, to redistribute the dust and cover the fact that something had been there until very recently. It wasn't as if he were looting a grave or destroying artifacts. If he had found the sucker while mining, no one would object to his profiting by it, and given the fact that their lives depended on how well he could keep it hidden—hell, that was no choice at all.

He looked carefully around. Any other kind of treasure could endanger them just as much as the Empress would. But he saw no gold, silver, or other gems. So far, so good. He would have felt better if he could have taken a closer look, but he didn't want to visibly disturb anything. Taking care of the last detail, he carefully obliterated his footprints behind the sepulcher.

He needed to get back. Jillian would be on edge, waiting for him. Not that she would let anyone else see her agitation, but she would sure let him know about it if she thought he had taken his own sweet time. He smiled, thinking of her excitement when he told her about the statues. Those green eyes would positively glow, and her face would get that absorbed, ecstatic look that both fascinated him and drove him crazy with desire, because he wanted to see that look on her face when he made love to her. He wanted her to want him with the same passion she showed for clearing her father's name and for finding broken pots and old bones.

The statues remained on guard as he walked between them, down the echoing hall toward the dim arch of light that marked the entrance.

On the way back, he reconsidered walking into the camp with the stone hidden under his shirt. The thing was too damn big. Instead he carefully wrapped it in his handkerchief and buried it in the same place where he'd earlier hidden the flashlight. He would retrieve it later, when he could better conceal it.

Jillian was sitting outside her tent when he returned. She lifted her head immediately, but she didn't say anything.

"Where the hell have you been?" Kates snapped. "It's your rule that no one leaves without telling anyone where they're going."

Ben ignored him and instead said to Jillian, "I found the temple."

She leaped to her feet, eyes blazing with excitement. "What's it like? Is it in good shape?"

"Sweetheart," he slowly replied, "it's something you have to see to believe."

Everyone was crowding around, and Kates grabbed him by the arm. "What did you find?"

"A temple," he repeated. "Statues. Shit like that."

Jillian's mouth formed the word. *Statues.*

Kates looked impatient. "Anything else?"

"A tomb, I guess. No treasures or anything like that, if that's what you're asking." The lie fell easily from Ben's lips.

He figured that the lack of treasure didn't matter to Jillian one whit, if the look on her face was anything to go by. Her expression was that of a kid at Christmas. He laughed suddenly and jerked her into his arms, swinging her around. "Want to see it?" he asked. "If we hurry, we can get there and back before dark."

No sooner were the words out of his mouth than she was struggling to be put down. "I need my camera," she babbled. "And my notebook. They're in my tent. Just let me get them and I'll be ready—"

"Okay, okay," he said soothingly. "Calm down. The temple isn't going anywhere. I keep telling you that, but you don't listen."

They all went, even Dutra, and this time they used the machetes to clear the way, making future trips easier.

"What kind of statues?" Rick asked. "Kinda small?"

Ben wondered what he was hoping for, a statuette like the Oscar, only made of gold? "No, they're pretty big. Carved from stone."

"Oh." Rick's disappointment was evident.

"I didn't snoop around much," Ben said. "There may be some smaller stuff in a side chamber, but I didn't see anything." God, he hoped there wasn't any smaller stuff. It was a risk he had to take, because keeping the temple from Jillian's knowledge wasn't something he was prepared to do.

When they were close enough to make out the columns, Jillian bit her lip to hold back a gasp. She was standing so close to him that Ben could feel her shaking. He put his arm around her waist and held her close to his side.

Vicente slashed his machete at the vines covering the entrance, and they fell to his feet in coils, like so many green snakes. The arch of light penetrated deeper into the hall. Ben turned on his flashlight and ushered Jillian inside. The others eagerly followed.

He let the light beam slowly play along the ten-foot figures. Jillian clutched his arm, her fingernails digging into the skin. She was utterly silent, her disbelieving gaze locked on the statues.

Both Pepe and Eulogio went stiff, their faces frozen as memories of ancient tales stirred, brought to life by the sight of these stone warriors.

For a long moment no one said anything, overawed by the immensity of the hall, the gravity of the silent stone guards. Even Rick, who revered nothing and whose interest in ancient cultures was nil, seemed to sense something—a solemnity, perhaps. There was no hint of danger; rather it was as if they had intruded on a sacred place, a place meant for peace.

Jorge walked over to the foot of one of the figures and stared up at it. Tentatively he reached out and fingered the stone. "Who are they?" he finally whispered, his voice full of wonder and curiosity. Even though he had whispered, the vast expanse of the hall caught the sound and amplified it, so the words were perfectly audible.

Jillian was still trembling and leaning against Ben's strength. "I think they really must be . . . the Amazons," she replied in the same wondering tone, as if this was more than she could take in. Ben knew just how she felt. He still hadn't completely recovered from his initial shock on seeing them.

Her mind was whirling, trying to cover all the angles, consider all the ramifications of what the existence of these statues meant. How had these women warriors come to be *here*, in the South American jungle? The Amazons were myth, nothing more. They were supposedly a tribe of warrior women who had once a year bred with a neighboring tribe of men in order to produce offspring, and who had fought for Troy in the Trojan War. No proof had ever been found that even hinted at their true existence, any more than proof of Atlantis had ever been found. Both were just myths.

And yet . . . here they were. In a place where there was no logical reason for their existence. How could the mythology of ancient Greece have somehow reached deep into these jungles, when there were entire tribes who had never seen a white person, or been exposed to any form of outside civilization until only a few years before? How *could* these statues be based on Greek mythology? Or was it just a similarity? Had tribes of warrior women once existed on both continents?

A tantalizing possibility was that somehow the Greek tales were based on the Anzar. Who knew how long the Anzar had existed? Perhaps, untold thousands of years before, some ancient wanderer had come across these female warriors and returned to his own land with the seeds of a myth.

"Oh, my God," she whispered.

"Yeah, I know. That's close to what I thought when I saw them," Ben said. "The sepulcher is at the far end." He used his flashlight to show the way, but the hall was too long for the light to penetrate to the tomb.

The party trooped down the huge stone hallway, dwarfed by the dimensions of the hall itself as well as the rows of silent guards. Any talking was still done in whispers, as if anything louder would disturb the sanctity of the place.

Then they reached the sepulcher, and the combined beams of their flashlights played over the tomb, over the bas-relief on the top. Jillian caught her breath at the male features etched in stone: strong, roughly handsome, calm and sure even in the long sleep of death. This was a man who would give his life without hesitation, without doubt, in defense of the woman he loved. This was a man for whom a woman would grieve a lifetime, around whom legends were woven. There was no hint of where the queen's tomb might be, but in the niche over the sepulcher was the place where she had left her heart, the heart of a warrior, to stand guard over her beloved through all eternity.

An empty, dusty niche.

Unable to help herself, trembling with relief, she turned her face into Ben's shoulder, and his arms came strongly around her. Thank God there was no Empress, she thought, no huge red diamond to endanger their lives with its worth. Kates wouldn't be interested in the statues, no matter how revolutionary they would be to the world of archaeology. They were of stone, without inherent value except as what they represented, and taken out of the context of the Anzar they were worthless. Each would weigh hundreds of pounds, probably half a ton or more, so they would be impossible to transport even if they did have a monetary value. Later on, once their existence was recorded and their context known, they would, like the Mona Lisa, be beyond price, but in this case value depended on the world knowing about them exactly as they were now, in their original setting.

Kates had shone his flashlight across the floor, looking at the footprints Ben had left earlier. He walked to the sepulcher and peered behind it.

"Watch out for snakes," Ben said casually.

Kates squeezed behind the tomb and shone the flashlight on the niche for closer observation. He ran his finger through the dust.

"Evidently there was a real Empress stone," Jillian said, finally finding enough strength in her legs to stand away from Ben. He seemed reluctant to release her, keeping his hand on the small of her back. "But there's no way of telling how long it has been gone or who took it. Since nothing else has been disturbed, it's likely the Anzar took it with them wherever they went."

"Well, if this goddamn tomb is so important, why didn't they take it with them, too?" Kates demanded. He was in a savage temper, and restraining it with difficulty.

Jillian eyed the sepulcher. It had to be eight feet long, or more. "There's no telling what it weighs, and it would be impossible to move it through the tunnel, anyway. From what I've seen, the Anzar didn't die out; it looks as if they left this place, carrying their personal goods and treasures with them. All that they left behind, other than a few pots, was this temple."

"What good is a stone tomb?" Kates yelled, his face twisting with rage at finding his dream of riches turn to nothing but dust. "And these goddamn stone statues?"

"You knew this trip was a gamble," Ben said coolly. "Nothing in the jungle is a sure thing."

Kates looked ready to explode, a muscle in his jaw trembling and his fists clenched. He was sick at the thought of the money he'd spent, the money he owed . . . the people he owed it to. His eyes fell on the tomb. "Maybe there's something inside," he said.

Jillian jerked visibly at the idea of disturbing the sepulcher. "Not likely," she forced herself to say. "They didn't leave anything of value that we've been able to find. No gold, no silver; nothing."

His tenuous control broke again. "Goddamm it, there has to be something!"

"Look around," she said sharply. "Do you see anything with even silver *plating?* There's nothing. If there was a treasure, *they took it with them.* It's gone. Maybe the Anzar were absorbed into the Incan culture; maybe that's what made the Inca culture so rich. Whatever happened, there's nothing here now."

He looked dazed, sick. "There has to be," he mumbled.

She waved her hand, indicating the surroundings. "Not that I can see."

Kates turned away and walked hurriedly toward the entrance, the beam of his flashlight bobbing. Dutra followed, but the rest of them remained in the temple, still awed by what they had found.

"Shouldn't you be taking some pictures?" Ben prompted, smiling at her.

Amazed that she could have forgotten, she began fumbling with her camera, but her hands were shaking so much she couldn't hold it steady. "I can't," she finally said raggedly, looking up at him. "I'm shaking too hard. Can you do it for me while I take notes?"

He took the camera from her, while she described how it worked. It was an "idiot" camera, with automatic everything, so simple to use anyone could operate it—assuming the idiot could hold it steady, which at the moment was beyond her. All Ben had to do was aim and press the button. The automatic flash and focus would take care of everything else.

He took several of the tomb, then walked from statue to statue while Jillian scribbled hasty notes by the light of a flashlight clumsily tucked under her arm. What amazed her even more, now that she noticed it, was that the statues all had subtly different features. That made her think these were statues of actual women, perhaps women who had in truth stood guard over the warrior's tomb. Their individuality made the statues all the more precious, unequaled anywhere else in the world.

"Happy?" Ben asked, looking down at her.

She turned a brilliant smile on him. "'Happy' isn't the word for it."

"I thought you'd like them."

"I never, never thought there'd be anything like this. These will be even more famous than the Elgin Marbles."

He gave her a quizzical look. "Some guy collected old marbles?"

She gave a low laugh. "Marble statues, not shooting marbles."

"Well, that makes more sense." He grinned, unabashed.

"Senhor! Senhor, look."

The urgent call came from Jorge, who had dug his fingers

into a crack in the stone and was tugging with all his strength. "Senhor, I think it's a door."

Jillian's heart leaped into her throat as they all went over to investigate Jorge's find. It did indeed look like the outline of a door, arched at the top. But tug as they might from any point, the stone door didn't budge.

"Try pushing on it," she suggested.

Ben placed both hands on the right edge and obeyed. Nothing happened. He moved to the left and pushed again. The stone slab creaked. He gave her an exasperated look and bent his strength to the door. Slowly the narrow slab creaked open, stone grinding against stone, and cool air rushed at them.

"It's another tunnel," Ben said, shining his flashlight into the darkness beyond. "So they did have more than one exit."

"Shall we follow it?" she asked.

"Not now; we don't have time. Let's finish taking the pictures so we can get back to camp before dark."

It was sunset when the group left the temple. Jillian was surprised that Rick had remained with them, but he had been amazingly interested. He fell into step beside her on the walk back.

"This is what Dad was trying to find when he was killed?" he asked after several minutes of silence.

"Yes. Proof of the Anzar."

"So he wasn't a crackpot?"

"No. His head may have been in the clouds, but his feet were definitely on the ground."

"What are you going to do?"

"Have these pictures printed up; notify the Brazilian government. This will clear Dad's name. Archaeologists will be swarming over this site soon, and it will all be because of Dad and his work."

He was quiet for a while longer. "Then I'm glad you found it, even if there isn't any treasure or anything."

"There is a treasure," she said gently. "It just isn't the type of treasure you expected."

"Yeah, I guess." Rick let himself drop back, evidently having said all he'd intended to say. Since she had risked her life to save his, his hostility toward her had disappeared, but he seemed ill at ease with her, as if they were two strangers forced to converse. She was glad that he no longer seemed to so bitterly resent her, even hate her, but she accepted that they would never be close. They were too different, without even the common memories of childhood to bind them together. Rick had been so wildly resentful when the professor married her mother that he had effectively sealed himself off from the family, with only minimal contact between himself and his new stepmother and, later, even less with Jillian. By the time she was old enough to really notice things, Rick had already moved out.

As soon as they reached the camp, Rick began telling Kates about the new tunnel they had found, but Kates didn't seem interested. He growled at Rick to shut up and took himself off to his tent. Rick shrugged and went over to the other men, who were settling down for a card game.

Jillian sat and wrote, totally absorbed in her thoughts as she explored various theories of the statues' existence. The ramifications were so enormous that she couldn't absorb them all. This opened up possibilities that seemed ludicrous, completely unreal. But the statues were very real; she had seen them, she had them on film. Perhaps, with careful exploration of the surrounding area, more information on the Anzar would come to light and their history would be known. She would have liked very much to know what happened to them. What had caused them to leave this place, and where had they gone? Had the tribe consisted only of women, or were the statues only of women because women had, for some reason, been dominant? If they had bred with a tribe of men, who were those men? Where had they lived? Were the men responsible for the disappearance of the Anzar? Had the two tribes simply merged, and if so, what had happened to them?

So many questions, and all of them fascinating.

It was later than usual when she retired to her tent, her mind still whirling. The men still sat outside, talking and laughing. She almost immediately began to doze, rather than lying awake for most of the night as she had thought she would. She couldn't remember ever having felt this happy before.

16

Ben slipped silently out of camp the next morning before dawn, while the others still slept. Unless he missed his guess, Kates wouldn't see any point in prolonging the stay here, since there obviously wasn't any treasure to be looted. It would be smart to retrieve the Empress while he had the chance.

In the camp Kates, who hadn't slept well all night, woke just in time to peer through his open tent flaps and see Ben disappear from view. He frowned; just what was that son of a bitch up to? He got his pistol and crawled out, then went over to Dutra's tent, taking care to make as little noise as possible. "Dutra!" he hissed.

The snoring from within missed a beat, then resumed. "Dutra!" Kates said again. "Wake up, damn it."

The snoring stopped, and Kates could hear the movement of Dutra's massive body as he sat up. "What?" came the sullen rumble.

"Lewis just sneaked out of camp. I'm going to follow him. If you hear any shots, you know what to do."

"Yes," Dutra said.

Kates didn't bother with any further explanation but went after Lewis, trying not to lose sight of the thin beam of light he could see, now that Lewis was away from the camp. He didn't trust Lewis out of his sight, and all night he had been thinking about the fact that Lewis had been in the temple alone before telling any of them about it. If the diamond had been there, would he have just *left* it there, or would he have taken it? Kates knew damn well what he would have done under the same circumstances, so why would Lewis have done anything differently? Lewis had never struck him as a man who played by the rules.

After Kates had left, Dutra crawled out of his own tent and stood silently with his pistol in his huge fist, his sharp incisors showing in a smile of cruel anticipation.

Rick, in the tent closest to Dutra, rolled over with a grunt, then settled into sleep again.

Pepe and Eulogio had both awoken at the first sound of Kates's urgent whispers. They lay very still in the darkness.

Jillian awoke suddenly, to an odd sensation of alarm. She listened, concentrating very hard. She couldn't hear anything close to her tent, but she could hear . . . something. Breathing. Had some predator negotiated one of the tunnels? Not likely, she thought. There was absolutely no light in the tunnels, and no animal would willingly go where it couldn't see. She reached for her flashlight, thinking of unzipping her tent flap a little and shining it on whatever was out there.

The others snored peacefully.

Ben went down on one knee and brushed the dirt away from the handkerchief-wrapped diamond, then carefully lifted it out of its hiding place. He removed the handkerchief and shook it out, so he wouldn't have so much grit inside his shirt, then rewrapped the diamond in the cloth.

"I thought you were up to something," Kates said viciously behind him.

"Shit," Ben muttered, even as he automatically threw himself to the ground, dropping the flashlight as he did so, but he sure as hell didn't drop the Empress. Kates fired at him, missing in the darkness.

* * *

At the camp, everyone came awake at the sound of the gunshot and began scrambling out of the tents. Pepe and Eulogio sliced open the rear of their tents and slithered out of view. Vicente was the first one out, and with a grin Dutra shot him in the head.

The sound of a shot rang out from the camp, echoing around the bowl. Ben's blood froze in his veins even as he drew his pistol. Jillian! He fired at Kates, but didn't take the time to aim. His shot went wide, though it served the purpose of making Kates hit the dirt. Ben scrambled up and started for the camp at a dead run, knowing that the poor light and heavy brush would give him cover. He'd take care of Kates later. Right now he had to get to Jillian.

Jillian was the second one out of the tents. Dutra pinned her with that animal grin but held his fire, thinking how much he would enjoy her in a few minutes. Jorge scrambled out and Dutra fired at him, but missed as Jorge dodged to the side. Behind him, Rick was already halfway out of his tent, his eyes wide with confusion. He saw Vicente, saw Dutra standing there with the pistol in his hand, saw Jillian, and yelled, "Jillian! *Run!*" even as Dutra swung on him. At such close range, Dutra couldn't miss. The first slug caught Rick in the middle of the chest and slammed him to the ground. He didn't even twitch at the second one. Jillian was frozen for one horrified second; then she dived into the foliage. She crawled, scrambling on her hands and knees, Ben's instructions ringing in her ears: Head for the tunnel. Don't let them get in ahead of you. Run like hell. *Ben!* she thought despairingly. Oh, God, Ben! She would do what he said and get out, but if he didn't follow shortly she would take her chances and return.

Shots were still ringing out. Then there was an eerie silence.

She reached the tunnel and flung herself into the darkness, running blindly and crashing into the wall before she remembered the flashlight in her hand. She didn't turn it on, for it would have targeted her if anyone was right behind her. Instead she placed one hand on the stone wall and used it for guidance, stumbling on the wide, shallow steps as if she truly were blind. She closed her eyes and found it was easier, as if the total darkness confused her brain when her eyes were open. She waited until her senses told her she had gone around a curve before she switched on the flashlight. The light seemed obscenely bright after the utter black, and at the same time very weak, a small effort against the overpowering night.

She ran, her heart thundering in her chest, her ears roaring, the blank rock walls rushing by, never changing. She felt as if she were caught in a maze without end.

Oh, God. Rick. *Ben.* The despair was almost paralyzing.

Ben bumped into Pepe and almost shot him before he recognized him in the deep grayness of dawn. "The senhora," he hissed, grabbing the little Indian by the shoulder. "What happened to her?"

"She ran," Pepe said politely. "Into the long black hole."

"Good man. I'm going after her. Take care of yourself, Pepe."

Pepe nodded. "We will wait, senhor. When the evil ones are gone, we will leave this place and return to Manaus. You must find the senhora."

"I will," Ben said grimly, and made for the tunnel. He knew Kates was still behind him, and Dutra was still in the camp, laughing as he fired at any imagined movement around him. Ben focused all of his attention on finding Jillian.

Jillian's lungs were burning like fire, and her chest felt as if it would explode when she finally plunged out of the tunnel. She fell against the huge boulder that kept the entrance hidden, gasping for breath. Birds, startled by her crashing exit, rose skyward calling their alarm.

It was dawn, the first dim gray seeping through the foliage. Higher up, it would be much brighter, but down on the forest floor it was perpetual twilight. She used the flashlight to find her way around the boulder and out into the open. She was breathing too hard to tell if anyone was following her, but she had to assume someone was. She had to find a hiding place, fast, because she was too breathless to continue. Disregarding the danger, she crawled into the thick foliage and went limp, exhausted by terror.

"Goddammit, what do you mean they got away?" Kates shrieked. "Lewis has the goddamn diamond! He could be anywhere in this damn place, but he's probably already on his way back to Manaus, laughing every step of the way!"

"I can catch him," Dutra said, his small head lowered like a bull about to charge. His mean eyes seemed to glow red.

"Yeah, sure," Kates sneered. "He's probably waiting right outside the far end of the tunnel, waiting for us to step out. He can pick us off without half trying. We're trapped in here, goddam— No, wait. Sherwood said there's another tunnel. They found it in the temple. We can get out."

"Yes," Dutra said, that strange smile showing his wolfish incisors again.

Kates gave the camp a disgusted look. "All you had to do was shoot them when they came out of their tents, but you fucked that up too. You only got two of them. Do you know how many we'll have to hunt down?"

Dutra shrugged, then lifted his pistol and calmly put a bullet in the middle of Kates's forehead. Kates collapsed, his feet twitching momentarily before stilling forever. "Bastard," Dutra said, and spat on Kates's body. "I will find Lewis faster without you."

Ignoring the three bodies as if they didn't exist, Dutra calmly began gathering supplies. He had let Lewis have his own way for weeks, but now his time of waiting was over. He would hunt the bastard down, kill him and take his rock, and then have fun with the woman before killing her, too. Kates had been a fool to think that he could ever rule Dutra, and Lewis would learn the same lesson. Lewis thought he was ignorant in the jungle, but he would find that this was not so. Dutra would track him down like an animal, and there would be no escape, for he knew where the bastard was going. All he had to do was get there first, and wait for him.

Ben plunged out of the tunnel, the handkerchief-wrapped diamond tucked safely inside his shirt and his pistol in his hand. That had been a nightmare trip he didn't want to repeat, accomplished in total darkness, for he had dropped the flashlight when Kates first jumped him. Sweat dripped from his forehead, and ran into his eyes. It had taken all his concentration to stay on his feet as he ran down those wide, shallow steps, and to keep from panicking at the sensation of being buried alive. Only the knowledge that Jillian had entered the tunnel kept him going.

The morning light that greeted him was like heaven; until he saw it, he'd had no idea how tight his nerves were stretched, and what a relief it would be to see daylight again. He edged around the boulder, out from under the thick latticework of limbs and vines, and the light became brighter, sunshine dappling the forest.

There was no sign of Jillian.

When they first reached the Stone City he had taken the precaution of slipping out during the night and hiding a pack of provisions at the outside entrance of the tunnel. Now he dragged his pack out of its hiding place, slipped the diamond into a pocket where it would be adequately protected, then swiftly lifted the burden to his back and buckled it in place. She couldn't be too far ahead, but if he didn't find her pretty soon, she would probably disappear into the jungle without a trace. His chest felt as if there were a tight band around it, continually pulling tighter. He had to find her.

Someone had come out of the tunnel. Jillian froze, not daring to lift her head for fear the movement would give her away. She lay with her cheek pressed to the ground, her eyes closed, her blood thundering loudly in her ears. She tried to hold her breath, to calm her pulse, so she could better track the person's movements by sound. Insects rustled in the moist humus beneath her ear, and her fingers dug into the dirt.

It might be Ben. The thought crept into her consciousness. The terror that he had been killed by that first shot had been so great, so paralyzing, that she had barely been able to think. But Ben was tough, and supremely capable; he knew that they would have to get through the tunnel ahead of Kates and Dutra. She had to take the chance of moving, just to see.

Cautiously, inch by inch, she lifted her head and moved a leaf out of the way. She still couldn't see anything. The sound began moving away from her.

Desperately she sat up and crawled halfway out of her hiding place. A set of broad shoulders burdened by a backpack was disappearing into the foliage, broad shoulders topped by a head with very dark, too-long hair curling over the shirt collar.

Relief shot through her, relief so sharp that it was almost as debilitating as the terror had been. She sank to the ground. "Ben!"

She couldn't put much force in her voice, but he heard her, or heard something, for he stopped and whirled, ducking into concealment. She grabbed her flashlight and struggled to her feet. "Ben!"

He stepped back into view and was beside her with three long strides, crushing her in his arms, his head bent down to hers with his cheek resting on top of her head. She clung to him, tears burning her eyes, the feel of his hard body safe and whole against hers so sublime that she never wanted to let him go. For an hour of hell in the dawn, she hadn't known if he lived or not, and the pain of it had been crushing. She had lost Rick; she didn't know what she would have done if anything had happened to Ben, too.

"Shhh," he whispered. "I've got you. Everything's going to be all right."

"Rick's dead," she said in a choked voice against his chest. "Dutra shot him. I saw it."

He stroked her hair. Personally he didn't feel that Sherwood was any great loss, but hell, he'd been Jillian's brother.

"I'm sorry." He began urging her forward. "Come on, sweetheart, we can't stay here. We have to move, and move fast."

She went, but her mind was beginning to work again. "Why can't we stay here and ambush them when they come out the tunnel?" As soon as she said it, she remembered the other tunnel. "No. We don't know which way they'll come out, do we?"

"I'd bet on the other tunnel, since we don't know where it exits the bowl. It would be safest. They'll have to work their way around, but they need to come back here so they can retrace the way we came. We need to take advantage of what time we have to put as much distance between us as we can."

"But what about Jorge and the others?"

"Pepe said they would hide, and wait until Dutra and Kates left. Then they'll make their way back to the river. They're experienced in the jungle, they'll be all right."

She fell silent then, saving her breath. Ben pushed her ahead of him at almost a run. Jillian shut her mind down and let her body take over. She didn't want to think, because if she did she would think about Rick and she couldn't afford the weakness of crying right now. There would be time for tears later on, when they were safe, when the cocoon of shock had worn off and could no longer keep the grief at bay. All she had to do right now was keep placing one foot in front of the other as fast as she could, without the usual caution of looking both overhead and underfoot before taking a step.

Finally Ben slowed her down with a hand on her arm, and moved in front of her now that the danger of a bullet coming at them from behind had passed. "We can take it easier now," he murmured, keeping his voice down even though he hadn't been able to detect any sign of pursuit. "Pace ourselves. We have a long way to go."

A very long way, she thought. Around a thousand miles, give or take a hundred or two. The thought of it was daunting; they had traveled that far to get there, but they would be returning under very different circumstances, without the support of a substantial party. Ben had somehow managed to get a backpack, but he couldn't possibly have enough supplies in there to last them all the way back. They would have to hunt for their food, and any gunshot could guide Kates and Dutra right to them. She had a heartening thought: Jorge and the others outnumbered Kates and Dutra; they might overpower them. She and Ben might not be pursued at all. But they wouldn't know, and couldn't afford to assume that they weren't.

She had gone to bed the night before thinking that she had never been happier. Now she was numb from shock. Her brother had been shot dead right in front of her, and she and Ben were running for their lives. The irony of it made her want to scream, but she didn't dare do that, either. She could do nothing but keep walking, for only by surviving could she hope to see Dutra brought to justice.

"We have to make it past the ledge today," Ben said.

She remembered the ledge, and her mind recoiled from it. "We can't cover that much distance! It's over a day's walk, remember? It was almost noon of the second day, after we got off the ledge, before we found the tunnel."

"We also set a very easy pace and took a lot of breaks because of your shoulder. It's about one day's normal walk, and we're going to do it faster than that. If they beat us there, we're caught. Once we're past the ledge, there's no bottleneck where they'll be able to find us."

"It took us several hours to walk the ledge," she pointed out. "We'll be on that thing in the dark!"

"I know," he said grimly.

Her protest hadn't been in argument, only to state the difficulty of the task he had set for them. Once it was said, she put it out of her mind and concentrated only on doing it. They had to get past the ledge, so they would. No matter what pace he set, she would keep up.

He paused briefly after about an hour and they each took a small drink of water. Neither of them had eaten, of course, but food could wait. Ben studied her face with sharp eyes; she was wan, but he could see the determination there. She would make it.

The morning had been one nightmare after another, and

the headlong dash through the jungle to the ledge was yet another. She marveled at how different the horrors could be and still be nightmares. Rick. The horrible fear for Ben. The tunnel, and the panic. And now this endurance race, when she was hungry and tired and dazed from everything that had happened. The textures and forms of the nightmares were very different, but they were all the stuff of bad dreams.

After a couple more hours they stopped for water again and ate some canned fruit. "We'll take the time to eat tomorrow," Ben promised.

"I know," she said, getting to her feet, ready to push on. "I'm okay."

His big hand touched her hair in a brief caress, and then they began walking again.

They kept walking through the daily rainstorm, though the wetness made them cold and miserable. They had a lot of time to make up, and even so, it was almost sunset when they reached the long ledge that had taken Martim's life and almost stolen Rick, too. She had saved her brother's life, only to lose him a week later. She tried not to think about it.

They paused for a moment, staring at it. "Remember," Ben said. "Stay close to the wall."

"We'll have to use the flashlight in a little while," she said. "Anyone coming up behind us will be able to see it."

"That's a chance we'll have to take. I came down that damn tunnel in the dark, but we can't walk this ledge like that." He had stashed a flashlight in the pack he'd hidden away, but he hadn't had the pack with him when he'd been barreling down the tunnel. All of the flashlights had heavy-duty batteries, but there was no telling how long they would last. They would use only one on the ledge holding the other as a reserve.

She walked. She had been walking since dawn, and it was sunset now. The darkness began to intensify, but she didn't let herself flag. She turned on the flashlight, hoping they had put enough turns between them and the beginning of the trail so that anyone following them wouldn't see the telltale beam.

Her legs were trembling with fatigue. The small can of

fruit hadn't been much fuel. "Do you have a candy bar?" she asked over her shoulder.

"No, but I have some cooked rice that I saved."

"Can you get to it?"

He did, and passed the pouch up to her. She plunged her hand into it, got a handful of rice, and squeezed it into a ball. She gave the pouch back to him. "Thanks." She began munching on the ball of cold rice. It wasn't very tasty, but it was food, and her body could use the carbs.

Behind her, Ben did the same thing. There wasn't much to be said for cold gooey rice, except that it stuck together really well, which made it easy to eat.

Her flashlight beam caught the gleam of yellow eyes and she froze, her scalp prickling.

"Easy," Ben murmured, drawing the pistol and clicking it off safety. "It's a coati. They're not particularly dangerous, but they do have nice long claws. Let's not crowd him."

She played the flashlight over the long-snouted animal with a banded tail like a raccoon's. "I thought they lived in trees."

"Usually. I don't know what this guy is doing by himself. C'mon, scat." He picked up a stone and threw it at the coati. It recoiled, but remained solidly in the middle of the ledge.

He threw another stone, striking it on the paw. "Scat!"

The coati remained, confused by the bright light shining in its eyes. Ben sighed and picked up a larger rock. "I don't want to have to hurt you, little guy, but you're moving one way or the other."

The third rock struck it on the haunch, and the coati made a high-pitched noise of pain and startlement. Swiftly it scrambled over the side of the ledge, out of sight. They heard the branches of a bush rustling, telling them that the cliff below wasn't completely vertical at this point.

Relieved, they hurried on. She wondered what they would do if they met a jaguar on the trail, or an ocelot. Who gave way then?

The ledge seemed unending. The day had been full of things she refused to think about, and here was another. She didn't let herself anticipate the end or try to guess how long they had been on it. All she had to do was keep walking, and when the time came, the ledge would end and the day would be over.

Ben's presence behind her was as solid as a brick wall. She kept walking. She knew they had spent hours on the ledge when they crossed it the first time, but they had also sat out a storm and been delayed by Martim's death and Rick's accident as well as by her own injury. Her shoulder barely gave a twinge now and then, having healed in the week that had passed. She was stronger, and they were moving faster. It wouldn't take much longer.

Her thoughts were so turned inward that she didn't even notice when the ledge ended and the jungle spread around them once more.

Ben halted her automatic strides, sliding his big hand under her hair and gently massaging the nape of her neck. "We did it," he said gently. "It's going to be okay. I'll find a place where we can sleep for the night."

17

How did you get the pack and all of these supplies?" Jillian asked in confusion, indicating the tent that Ben was swiftly and efficiently erecting.

"The tent and pack were Martim's," Ben said. "I sneaked most of this stuff out of camp not long after we got there. It seemed like a smart precaution to take, and damn if it wasn't. If nothing had happened, we wouldn't have needed it. I had it stashed in the rocks outside the tunnel entrance, because I knew if everything started popping, I sure as hell didn't want a pack slowing me down when I was coming through that tunnel."

The small tent seemed like heaven to her, a safe place where she could stretch out and relax for the first time that day. She had been dreading sleeping out in the open, and when she realized that Ben had managed to get one of the tents she had been almost giddy with relief.

"Are you hungry?" he asked. "I don't want to risk a fire, but there's stuff here that doesn't need cooking."

"No, I'm not hungry at all now." The rice ball, and anxiety, had taken care of her appetite. She had been thirsty, but the first thing they had done on stopping had been to drink water.

She held the flashlight for him while he finished setting up the tent. He had found a shallow overhang to provide a bit of shelter, and now he cut fronds and vines to drape over the tent, further camouflaging their position.

"After you," he said, indicating the tent, and gratefully she crawled in; he followed, and zipped the flap, closing out the jungle.

"Get settled, sweetheart. We can't afford to keep the flashlight on any longer than we have to."

Wearily she removed her boots and socks and stretched out on the thin foam pad, moving over to make as much room as possible for Ben. He shoved the pack into the far corner, placed the pistol close at hand, then removed his own boots and socks. He clicked the flashlight off, and darkness consumed them, darkness so complete it had a certain solidity to it. Ben lay down beside her, his big body hot and comforting.

Now that she had relaxed, all the things she had refused to let herself think about during the day came rushing over the barricades. Rick was dead.

"He told me to run," she murmured. "I wasn't blind to Rick's shortcomings; we were never close. Most of the time I think he actually hated me. But when he saw Dutra with the pistol and realized what was happening, his last words were for me to run."

"When you kept him from going off the ledge, it got his attention, made him think," Ben replied, his deep voice quiet. "He wasn't as much of a shit-ass after that."

"No," she said, remembering the short conversations they'd had. "He wasn't." After a minute of silence she said, "He stole one of my dolls once, when I was little. He destroyed it, hacked it to pieces. I was nosing around in his room one day and found it. I don't know why, but I never said anything."

"Were you scared of him?"

"No. He just seemed . . . not really part of the family. I was so close to Dad, and I know now that Rick wanted to be, but I was so like Dad in temperament and interests that poor Rick didn't have a chance. He got only the fringes of Dad's attention. No wonder he hated me."

"It wouldn't have made any difference if you'd never been born," Ben said. "People are what they are. He wouldn't have amounted to much under any circumstances."

"We'll never know now, will we?" she said sadly. After another short silence she spoke again. "Vicente is dead. He was the first one Dutra shot."

Ben swore, then sighed. Vicente had been a steady worker, a happy-go-lucky fellow always ready for a laugh. Even the strong warning Ben had given the men hadn't saved him.

Jillian began to tremble. Ben felt the slight movement and turned to her, taking her in his arms and holding her as she battled the shock of reaction. His vital animal heat was comforting, and she sought to get closer.

She felt him touch her hair, smooth it back from her face. Then his mouth covered hers, and she turned her face more fully toward him. She was quiescent, accepting both the kiss and the slow domination of it as his tongue penetrated her mouth. She began to breathe more deeply, a heavy languor stealing into her body. After all they had been through that day, she both wanted and needed him. A shock of recognition hit her: the sparring was at an end; it was time. He lifted his mouth and she sensed him leaning over her in the dark.

"I can't believe you've held me off this long," he said in a low, guttural voice. "Let me inside you, sweetheart. Now." There was no supplication in his tone, only primal male determination.

His hands were hard on her body as he removed her pants, unbuttoning, unzipping, sliding them down her hips and legs, and off over her feet. He swept her panties down in the same movement, leaving her naked from the waist down, trembling. She felt his movements as he stripped out of his own clothes, and shut her eyes as if the act would freeze time, give her an opportunity to think.

He was moving too fast, unwavering in his intent, and she couldn't muster any protest or denial, couldn't think why she would want to. Why slow him down? She had that feeling again, that sense of . . . waiting, as if the time had been long approaching and had now arrived. There was an inevitability to it. She loved him, and for a while that day she'd thought she had lost him to death. All of the squabbling competition seemed unimportant right now. He had called her his woman, and she lay there in the darkness feeling the final acceptance of it.

He opened her legs and moved between them, mounting her. Jillian clutched his steely biceps, her nails digging into the skin. She felt him brace himself over her on one arm, while he reached down with his other hand and guided his penis to her. The first heated touch made her flinch, and he murmured, "Easy, sweetheart."

She tried to relax, but somehow it didn't seem like an option she had. There was no time to prepare herself, no foreplay, only the basic act itself. He pushed into her with slow, inexorable force, squeezing his thick penis in to the hilt. She writhed beneath him, feeling unbearably stretched, on the verge of pain, her soft sheath quivering as she tried to accustom herself to his girth.

"Shhh," he soothed, and only then did she realize she was making small whimpering noises. He stripped her shirt off and let his weight down on her, the crisp curls on his broad, hard chest rasping against her tender breasts. She locked her arms around his shoulders, clinging desperately.

He withdrew a little and slowly squeezed forward again, testing her tightness, shuddering with the pleasure of it. He was so aroused that he felt almost ready to climax right then, a startling realization for a man who was accustomed to drawing the sex act out for at least an hour. His testicles were drawn tight against his body, signaling how close he was to orgasm. It was going too fast; he didn't want it to end so quickly. At last he had her naked, her arms around him holding as if she never meant to let go, her taut, firmly muscled body welcoming him, and he never wanted it to end.

But the Lorelei of irresistible pleasure beckoned, and his body, so long denied, refused to be denied a moment longer. He began thrusting heavily, groaning as he pounded into her, feeling her sheath grow moist and supple as she clung to him. She wound her strong slim legs around his waist and he lost it. His climax slammed into him like a freight train. He hammered into her with the violent rush of semen from his body, groaning deep in his chest.

It was over. In the silence afterward, Jillian lay still beneath him, feeling dazed and a little battered from the force of his passion. He had been overwhelming, so dominant in his need that her mind reeled from it. He lay heavily on her for a time, his chest heaving like bellows and sweat dripping down his side. When he had rested, he began slowly to thrust again.

She moaned, softly, and he kissed her, his tongue probing deep. "It's all right," he said in a soothing whisper. She was slick from his climax, accepting him easily, her hips rising in an involuntary little movement to meet each inward stroke. He could take his time now; he was still hard, and knew he would come at least once more, maybe twice, but not for a while. He could savor every inch of her, the smooth satin of her skin, the hot wet silk of her sheath.

He drew it out, with slow, steady thrusts. He felt the tension grow in her, felt the subtle vibration of arousal as her slender body tightened and lifted to him.

"Ben," she said, just his name, but laden with desire.

It was as perfect as he had known it would be, and yet it was more. Nothing could have prepared him for the intensity, the overwhelming need to brand her body with his, using the heat of ecstasy. No other woman had ever mattered as much, had ever fit him so tightly, been so wonderfully perfect. He'd never been this excited before, every inch of him alive, or so aware of every tiny sound and movement she made.

She began heaving under him, crying out in a soft, strained, mindless sound. He slid his hands beneath her to cup her buttocks and lift her up as he thrust more solidly into her. He felt the deep, delicate inner shivers around his penis as she convulsed in his arms.

He didn't stop.

The day had been an endless nightmare to Jillian. The night became endless too, but in a different way. He knew just how to wring another response from her, even when she thought it was impossible, when she wanted nothing so much as sleep. He whispered to her, lovemaking words, both sweet and raunchy. He lavished attention on her breasts, and between her thighs.

When they did finally sleep, he was still on top of her, still penetrating her. Several times during the night he grew hard within her and made love to her again. Or had he ever stopped? The darkness gave everything an aura of unreality, a drama conducted by feel alone.

She learned his body. She found that a firm touch on his nipples made him shiver with pleasure and that he loved having his back stroked. She cupped the soft, heavy weight of his testicles and he all but purred. He was a total sensualist, without a shy or modest gene in his body. And he learned her body, touching her in ways she had heard about but never before experienced, gentle as he led her into pleasure, then letting himself be as rough as he sensed she needed when her own desires rose beating in heavy rhythm.

The close, intimate darkness wrapped around them, allowing a lack of inhibition that would have embarrassed her had they been able to see. But the night was timeless, stretching on forever, their lovemaking guided solely by touch. He never left her alone for even one minute, holding her close, pushing away her sadness with the demands of his hard body. She felt infinitely secure and desired, cradled so close she could feel the strong pounding of his heart, the boundaries of the night set by his arms and steely thighs. His heavy weight pressed her down into the mat, and it was so wonderful she could have cried. Instead she forgot about the dawn.

She slept. They both did, finally. But she awoke and, without even opening her eyes, became aware of the light, very dim, creeping in through the thick canopy, edging past the layer of fronds he had used to camouflage the tent, seeping through the thin nylon to forever end this particular night. She lay very still, not wanting to face the day just yet. Ben lay sprawled on top of her, the weight of his torso eased a bit to the side so she could breathe, but he was still very heavy. His head was turned away from her, his chest moving in the slow, easy rhythm of sleep. Her thighs were open, his hips cradled between them. He had drawn one leg up, forcing her leg higher on his hip. He was soft now, but still nestled within her. The only time he had left her at all during the night, she thought, was to change position.

Monkeys chattered in the treetops. Ben woke; he didn't move, but she could tell because he swiftly grew erect within her, and a fine tension invaded his muscles.

Gently she stroked her hand up his back and curled her arm around his neck. Just as gently, he began thrusting. She kept her eyes closed, holding the dawn at bay for just a while longer.

Afterward he allowed only a few minutes of rest before saying, "We have to start moving. Kates probably stopped on the other side of the ledge last night, giving us a few hours, but we can't afford to waste time." He disengaged their bodies and sat up, running his hand through his hair. God, he'd have liked to stay here with her for a week or so, doing nothing but eating, sleeping, and making love.

Jillian opened her eyes and faced reality. Rick was dead, but she couldn't just stop. Life inexorably moved on, and she and Ben were still alive, and in danger. She would grieve for Rick, but only in a private place in her heart. So she pushed his memory into that private place and sat up, ready to go on.

Or maybe not so ready. She took immediate stock of the situation and said, "I need a bath."

He grinned as he lay back and began pulling on his underwear and pants. "I'd say we both do, but it'll have to wait."

"It can't wait very long," she muttered, wrinkling her nose in fastidious distaste as she too began dressing. "I'm sticking to myself. Why couldn't *you* have waited until we got back to Manaus where they have bathrooms and showers?"

He gave her a disbelieving look. "Are you kidding? I'd already waited so long I was having hallucinations. I'm allergic to abstinence; it causes all sorts of health problems." Then his expression turned serious and he cupped her chin, forcing her to look at him. "Are you okay? I forgot about your shoulder last night."

"My shoulder's fine." She moved it to show him, and added wryly, "I have a few aches and pains, but not in my shoulder."

His eyebrows slowly lifted. "Do tell. Anywhere that needs massaging?"

"No massaging until I have a bath."

Her voice was firm and he said, "Oh, hell." The appalled look he gave her said that he was taking her request for a bath much more seriously. "Okay, if we come to a stream that's safe, you can take a bath. A fast one. If not, we'll find a clear spot and stand in the rain. Will that do?"

She pulled on her boots. "Anything will be an improvement."

Breakfast was instant oatmeal and coffee, and five minutes after the meal began, Ben was packing up the tent and supplies and stowing them in his pack, taking care that the diamond was protected and that Jillian didn't so much as glimpse it.

God, he felt wonderful. Making love with her had been so much *more* than he had ever imagined. Powerful, intense . . . caring. His body was relaxed, marvelously sated and rejuvenated; he could take on the world and win. He felt violently possessive and protective, all at the same time. She was his now, and he'd never let her get away from him.

They didn't take the same path returning to the river as they had taken inland; on the trek inland they'd had to follow the directions and landmarks laid out in the map; not only would it have been dangerous to follow the same trail, but a more direct, and therefore faster, route was now possible. Ben figured they could cut their time by at least one full day, maybe more. They had to reach the boats before Kates could cut them off. He didn't have a minute's doubt that they were being pursued; Jillian had witnessed two murders, and Kates knew that he had the diamond. Yeah, they were being followed. The only question was how close behind them the hunters were.

He used the machete as little as possible, not wanting to

leave such clear sign. An Indian could easily have trailed them, but Kates and Dutra didn't have that degree of skill. Kates, in fact, had none. No point in helping them along by slashing at every bush that got in the way.

They splashed across several small streams, but they were too shallow and grassy for bathing. The daily thunderstorms blew up, but of all days for the storms to sweep by in the distance, that was the day it happened. Ben looked around once and saw that stubborn look on her face, the one that said she wasn't going to change her mind even if it wasn't his fault the storms had missed them.

"It'll be better if it's late afternoon before we bathe," he pointed out. "Neither of us has a change of clothes; that way we could wash these out and they would have time to dry before morning."

"You make it sound as if I've been nagging you every step of the way," she said.

"You have. Silently."

She gave him a long, level look. "When I decide to nag, you can bet I won't do it *silently.*"

He sighed. "No, I don't guess you will." Inwardly he felt cheerful at the prospect. With Jillian's rapier tongue, it was bound to be entertaining. What he didn't feel cheerful about, however, was the possibility of not being able to make love to her that night, and he had no doubt she would cross her arms and stubbornly refuse to let him touch her, if she didn't have her bath. Why did women have to be so damn fastidious? Cleanliness was great in its place, but they were in the middle of a jungle, for God's sake. A certain amount of grunginess couldn't be helped.

But Jillian wanted a bath.

To hell with leaving it to chance that they would come to a suitable stream. He began searching for one in earnest.

The one he finally found wasn't anything to brag about, certainly nothing to compare with the waterfall they had bathed under or the pools they had found at various times during the trip. But it was wet and safe, even if it was less than a foot deep and that only because it was filled with runoff from the storms that had passed to the northwest of them. He found a clear, rocky section, and they both stripped and stepped into the stream. Ben carefully placed the pistol where it wouldn't get wet but would be within reach.

One of the things he hadn't packed, not considering it essential, was soap. They had nothing but the clear, tepid water to bathe with, but it was enough. Jillian stretched out so she could let the water flow through her hair while she scrubbed her scalp with her fingertips, feeling her sweat-clumped hair unmat as she worked. Ben watched her with hunger in his eyes, for her naked body was fully exposed to him for the first time and his body plainly revealed his interest.

Under his amused gaze, she also washed out her underwear.

"Just what do you plan on wearing under your pants?" he drawled. "I didn't think to bring any extra pairs of panties."

"We won't be walking for much longer," she replied briskly. "I can manage to do without underwear for that length of time. Then tomorrow, when I get dressed, I'll have clean underwear to put on."

He was so relieved that she planned to undress that night, all he could do was grin at her. Of course, he'd have to find some way for them to clean up in the morning, or it would be the same routine all over again. It would be so easy if they had enough drinking water that they could afford to waste it, but he had only so many purification tablets and they had to preserve as much as possible.

"You're grinning like an idiot," she said as she stepped to the bank and leaned over to wring out her hair, then began wiping herself dry with her hands.

"Like a jackass eating saw briers," he admitted cheerfully.

"Well, the jackass part is right. I don't know what saw briers are."

"Neither do I. It was just something folks said back home." He smoothed his wet hair back and also waded out of the stream.

She watched as he dressed, and suddenly realized that he was enjoying every minute of this. He was an adventurer down to the soles of his boots—cynical, wily, and supremely capable. She was well aware how much more dangerous their situation would be right now if he hadn't taken the precaution of gathering some extra supplies and hiding the pack along the trail. Just the tent was a lifesaver in itself, protecting them from snakes, insects, and various other creatures while they slept. And the food he'd packed meant they didn't have to kill to eat, but could save his supply of bullets for protection. Come to think of it, he had been prepared for every danger they had faced, from the very beginning.

After dressing swiftly, they covered as much ground as they could for the remainder of that day. When they did make camp, however, he permitted a small fire and they ate a hot meal of canned fish and more rice. "Do you know what I'm craving?" she asked, sitting back with a sigh.

"Me."

"Good try, but wrong category."

"Not animal, then."

"Nope. Vegetable. Well, maybe with a little animal thrown in."

"Spaghetti and meatballs?" he guessed.

"You have the right idea. Pizza, loaded with ham and extra cheese."

He reached into the pack and tossed her a small can of fruit. "Have this instead."

"Thanks, I will. When we get back to Manaus . . . Well, I might not be able to find pizza in Manaus, but when I get back to the States, I'm going to order the biggest one I can find."

He didn't say anything, but suddenly his hard face took on a dangerous cast. He ate his own can of fruit without comment.

Jillian wondered what she had said to put him in such an obvious bad temper, but decided to leave well enough alone and not ask him about it. Instead she devoted herself to the fruit, savoring every bite.

Ben watched her with hooded eyes, his insides tightening a little bit more every time she licked the spoon with obvious enjoyment, with the unselfconscious, regal air of a cat. Damn her, how could she talk so casually about going back to the States? Not that he intended to let her go, but it was infuriating that she would even consider leaving. Had their lovemaking the night before been so commonplace to her that it meant nothing? He'd had plenty of commonplace sex, and he knew last night had been different. She should have realized it, too.

She stood up, yawning a little. One thing about hiking through the jungle all day: she didn't feel like staying up much past sunset. Of course, Ben had kept her up most of the night before, so that was a factor too. "I'm ready for bed. Are you going to stay up?"

His face was still grim as he stood and pulled her hard against him. Circumstances had forced them to stay on the move all day, and he had restrained himself from touching her, though the need had burned in his gut. Perhaps, because of that, she hadn't gotten the message that she was *his* now. The feel of her slim body in his arms brought an almost painful sense of relief, as if an aching emptiness that he hadn't even known existed had suddenly been filled. He bent his head down to hers and felt savagely triumphant when she went up on tiptoe to press herself against him, winding her arms around his neck, lifting her soft mouth to his. He could feel the excitement humming through her taut muscles.

"I don't guess you are," she murmured.

He'd lost track of what she had said. "Are what?"

"Going to stay up."

He managed a harsh bark of laughter. He took her hand and moved it down to his crotch, folding her fingers over his erection. "What do you think?"

Jillian sank against him, already weak with anticipation. She had craved his touch all day, but accepted that they had to keep moving. She trembled at the knowledge that she would soon be eagerly accepting his heavy thrusts. "Maybe I should clarify the question."

"I don't think it's needed." He kissed her again, hungrily. "We both know what we want."

HEART OF FIRE

She crawled into the tent while he doused the campfire, and was already half undressed by the time he entered. She left the flashlight burning while he stripped, delighting in the sight of his muscled body. He paused a moment to savor her nudity, too, then regretfully switched off the light and mounted her in the warm cocoon of darkness.

18

The days and nights fell into routine, though "routine" was a strange word to use to describe something that wasn't ordinary at all. They walked all day, usually even eating on the run. Ben seldom touched her during the day, keeping those touches he couldn't avoid to the briefest, most casual of contacts, but she understood. She felt the frustration too, the almost overwhelming compulsion not even to leave the tent in the mornings but to forget the urgency of their forced march in the fever of lovemaking. It was worse now than it had been before, as if reality were far more delicious than anticipation.

Sometimes she felt almost mindless from the pleasure of those long, dark hours. All of the brash, teasing comments Ben had irritated and taunted her with for weeks turned out to be true. His sexual stamina was unbelievable, while she doubted he knew the meaning of the word "inhibitions." He didn't have any. According to his mood, he would dominate her completely, holding her down, laughing softly at her struggles to reciprocate in their lovemaking, while he rode her with a strong, endless rhythm until she could no longer hold off her climax and was shuddering helplessly beneath him. At other times he was as playful as a cat. A big cat. A tiger, carefully restraining his strength. Then he would turn as lazy as a pasha, lying on his back and lifting her astride him, letting her enjoy him as she wished.

As a lover, he was irresistible. He had been truly aggravated and bewildered that she had held him off for so long, and now, looking back, she too was amazed. She could put it down only to not having known what she was missing. Every time she looked at him, tall and strong and confident, she felt such a surge of love and lust that she wanted to strip off her clothes and throw herself on the ground in front of him. Being Ben, of course, he would probably give a joyous whoop and leap on top of her. It was a tantalizing thought.

But they both severely restrained themselves, knowing that there would be time enough to indulge their senses once they reached safety. She was grimly determined to reach Manaus, for only then could she file murder charges against Dutra. She didn't know if they could implicate Kates in the murders, even though he had shot at Ben; she didn't even know if the Brazilian authorities would pay much attention to a charge made against an American by another American. But Dutra was a different case; the authorities had been trying to get him for a long time. It was possible that both Kates and Dutra had fled, but she intended to file charges anyway.

Often her throat would tighten when she thought of Rick. She would have liked to retrieve his body for burial, but as Ben had once pointed out, the jungle swiftly took care of that. There was also the possibility that Kates and Dutra would have moved the bodies, thrown them down a ravine somewhere, to destroy the evidence.

She tried to resign herself to the certainty that all she could do was report the murders.

She didn't let herself think about what she would do after that. She had found the Stone City, but failed to bring back proof of it. She had left all of her notes and the corroborating photographs behind; she didn't have so much as a pottery shard. She hadn't let herself dwell on it, because whining wouldn't have accomplished anything, but every day she'd had to deal with the hollowness of loss.

She couldn't think of any way to get back to the Stone City. Other archaeologists would not be any more interested in listening to her now than they had been earlier. She certainly didn't have the kind of money needed to mount an expedition; that was why she had been forced to go along with Rick and Kates in the first place. She thought about asking Ben if he could help her return, but discarded the idea. He wasn't a rich man; he was an adventurer, a river guide. He wouldn't have that kind of money, and even if he did, he wouldn't be interested in spending it for that, nor would she expect him to, just because they were sleeping together. Even if the government paid them a finder's fee, it probably wouldn't be enough to offset the cost of an expedition. No, she had failed, and she had to accept that.

And eventually she would have to get on a plane and go home. Perhaps Ben would be around to kiss her good-bye and give her a farewell swat on the bottom; perhaps not. To a man like Ben, who had so many women, what would one particular woman mean? She was here now, and his passion was white-hot, but things would be different when they got back to Manaus. She couldn't hold that against him; she had known the nature of the beast from the moment she first set eyes on him. In all fairness, how could she pout now, and demand that he change?

She would simply enjoy him while she could. A woman met a man like Ben only once in a lifetime . . . thank God. He could cause some serious disruptions in an otherwise orderly existence. Her own life wasn't what she could call ordinary, but since meeting Ben she had felt as if she were on top of a seething volcano. It was interesting and violently exciting, but how long could it last?

Back in the real world, she would have to decide what to do with her life. She knew now that she had no chance of advancement with the Frost Foundation, and in any case wasn't inclined to forgive the condescending way she had been treated. She didn't intend to give up archaeology; she loved it too much. Perhaps she could get a job with a university, though she wasn't taken with the idea of teaching. She would much rather be *doing*. But all of that was for the future; for now, there was only Ben and the jungle, and the danger behind them.

On the fifth day, a rumble of thunder made Ben stop and lift his head. "Sounds like it's going to go right over us. Let's find a clear spot and take a shower," he said. "We'll put up the tent and stow our clothes in it so they won't get wet."

She wrinkled her nose. "It wouldn't hurt them to get wet." She cringed every time she had to get dressed; their clothes were absolutely filthy. If she hadn't had the opportunity to wash out her underwear a few times, it would have been unbearable.

He gave her that lazy, flashing grin. "We should get to the boats tomorrow or early the next day. You'll be able to wash them then. Just think of lying naked on the deck while our clothes dry in the sun."

"Are you including your clothes in the category of what *I'll* be able to wash?" she asked, in the mildly curious manner of one who liked to be as specific as possible.

He gave her a hopeful glance, then sighed heavily. "I guess not."

They found one of those small, temporarily clear places where the solid canopy had been broken when one of the giant trees had toppled over, perhaps from its own weight. Fallen trees decomposed rapidly and new vegetation would grow to fill the gap, but while the clearing lasted, both sun and rain poured through with joyous intensity.

He set up the tent, then cleared out a section of the burgeoning undergrowth as the thunder steadily grew closer and the cool wind began whipping through the upper canopy. The denizens of that high world chattered and scampered for cover, to wait out the deluge.

They stripped and stowed their clothes inside the tent, then stepped into the small clear area just as the first huge raindrops began to fall. They stung Jillian's skin with surprising force, and she jumped at the discomfort. Then the storm broke, and the heavens opened, and a thick curtain of rain splashed down on them.

It was almost like being under the waterfall. She was pummeled by rain, her skin stinging. She tilted her head up and stood with tightly closed eyes, letting the rain sluice through her hair. Oh, how she would have loved to have a bar of soap right now! This was the most invigorating shower in the world, crisp and violent. Her nipples tightened under the chill lash.

A delicious sense of freedom grew, as did the same impression of overwhelming beauty that she'd had when she watched Ben bathe under the waterfall like some glorious, beautiful primitive man. Here she stood, naked, in the middle of the largest rain forest on earth, while the life-force of this huge jungle poured down on her from heaven. The wind whipped the trees overhead; lightning flashed and thunder boomed all around her, the sound echoing. It was dangerous to do what they were doing; all the other jungle creatures had taken shelter. But it was also exhilarating, and she wanted to shout with joy. She raised her arms high so the rain could more freely lash every inch of her body. She had the dizzy feeling that no other bath in her life, no matter how luxurious, could ever match the glory of this one.

Then, with a low growl that she heard even over the crash of the thunder, Ben was there. He wrapped his arms around her so tightly she could barely breathe, and he lifted her off her feet, his mouth grinding down on hers. Eyes closed, she grabbed at his shoulders, sinking her nails into his slick, cool skin. Heat quickly formed where their naked bodies touched.

Gripping her hips, he lifted her higher. Instinctively she locked her legs around his waist to steady herself. Fiercely he took one nipple into his mouth, his tongue darting out to circle it with heat before drawing it inside. Jillian gave a breathless cry, her blood already racing with excitement.

Then he slowly began to lower her onto his turgid shaft. It brushed against her soft flesh and she moaned, her eyes flying open. Her gaze locked with his. Rain poured down their faces, off their bodies. His black lashes were spiked with moisture, his pupils dilated, the blue of his irises as intense as the deep cobalt of the ocean.

"Look at us," he said hoarsely. "Watch it go in."

Quivering with almost painful desire, she did. The bulbous head bobbed with straining eagerness, dark red in color. The thick shaft was laced with raised, bluish veins. He lowered her a bit more, and the head pushed into her soft opening. It was a sensation she had felt often during these past days, but it was still jolting. His heat seared her. Inch by inch she sank downward, his shaft spearing upward into her, stretching her soft sheath to its limit. He felt huge inside her, nudging against the mouth of her womb. Watching his flesh disappear inside her, feeling it as it happened, catapulted her into climax. He held her while she convulsed, her hips rocking against him.

"Again," he whispered. "I want to feel it again."

He gripped her buttocks and began working her up and down, his powerful body braced to support them. The sensation was almost more than he could bear, and he ground his teeth, his head falling back. Each time her weight came downward, enveloping his straining flesh in heat and softness, his entire body shook with pleasure. The rain continued to pour.

Jillian clung to him. She started to groan as each thrust heightened the exquisite agony. "Please," she said, her voice barely audible above the downpour. "Please."

"Not yet, sweetheart," he panted. "Not yet. It's too good."

Her body felt incandescent, even with the cool rain washing over them. She fought him, trying to wrest control so she could grasp the culmination that hovered just out of reach, but she was helpless against the iron strength of that muscled body. He laughed, the sound one of fierce triumph rather than humor.

The sun broke through the clouds, streaming down into the clearing even though the rain still fell, bathing them in a glittering halo of light. It was like being caught inside a diamond. She kissed him wildly, grinding her entire body against him, refusing to accept defeat.

His fingers dug into the cleft of her bottom. He cursed thickly, feeling his climax rise inexorably. He moved her on him in several quick, hard thrusts and she cried out, going over the edge. Her trembling inner muscles grabbed sweetly at him and he threw back his head with a primal shout, shuddering, his seed spewing out of him.

His legs were shaking. It took all of his concentration to keep them from collapsing beneath him. Jillian was limp in his arms, her head lying against his shoulder, her legs still wrapped around his waist. The sunlight was dazzling, almost blinding. The rain stopped as the storm moved on; the only sound they could hear for a moment, suspended in time, was the steady drip, drip, drip of water from the leaves, all around them, like nature's applause.

After a minute she said drowsily, "We're steaming."

The entire forest was steaming, clouds of moisture rising toward the understory. Wisps drifted from their own overheated bodies. Still he held her, and she was content to stay there.

"I can't move," he finally muttered against her wet hair. "If I do, I'll fall."

She barely stifled a giggle.

"Think it's funny, do you?" He began lazily caressing her bottom.

"As long as I land on top."

"Mmmm." That deep purr was the only sound he made for a few minutes, other than that of his breathing as it slowly calmed. She thought she might go to sleep.

Then: "If I manage to stay on my feet, can you unlock your ankles?"

"Maybe."

"What are the odds?"

"Fifty-fifty."

"Meaning either you can or you can't."

"Right."

"If you can't, we'll probably have to go for another round."

And he probably could, too, but Jillian didn't think she was up to it. She couldn't remember ever having felt more replete in her life. All she wanted to do was curl up somewhere and take a long nap. Regretfully she unlocked her legs and let them slide down his hips, disengaging their bodies at the same time.

Carefully he set her on her feet, holding her until he was certain her legs would hold her. She swayed against him for a moment; then they walked the few feet to the tent, still holding each other. He didn't want to let her go even for a minute. He still felt slightly dazed in the aftermath of passion, a passion so intense he could barely believe what had just happened.

They dried off as much as possible by wiping their hands down their bodies. He held his handkerchief under a dripping bush until it was wet, and Jillian used that to clean herself. In the rapidly increasing heat, their skin was only slightly damp when they began dressing.

She was almost finished when Ben suddenly stiffened beside her. "Don't be scared," he said softly.

Her hands froze on the buttons of her shirt, and she lifted her head in alarm. Standing not ten feet away, barely visible in the concealing undergrowth, were several Indians, their faces inscrutable as they watched her and Ben. They were naked except for loincloths, and all were armed with bows and arrows. Their straight black hair had been hacked off in a brief bowl shape. They stood motionless, black eyes missing nothing.

"They're Yanomami," Ben said, still in that low voice.

"Are they hostile?"

"Depends on how much contact they've had with white people, and what kind of contact it's been. Normally they aren't actively hostile."

"What do we do?"

"We see what they want." He carefully kept his hand away from the pistol. This was a band of hunters; the six-foot arrows they carried were tipped with poison, probably cyanide, not a substance he cared to screw around with. He spoke with them in their language. The oldest of the Yanomami, a dignified man with graying hair, replied.

After a few moments of conversation she could see the Indians relax, the stern cast of their features easing into smiles. The gray-haired man said something as he slapped his hands together several times, and they all laughed.

Ben was chuckling too.

"What's funny?" she asked.

"Oh, nothing."

He couldn't have said anything that would have made her more suspicious, or more curious. "What? You'd better tell me."

"He just wondered why we were making slap-slap in the rain, instead of in our funny little moloca—that's 'house' to them, 'tent' to you."

Jillian could feel her face heat up as she realized there had been several very interested but puzzled witnesses to their lovemaking, but at the same time she had an almost overwhelming urge to laugh. "Slap-slap?" she asked faintly.

Ben's eyes were alive with merriment. "Yeah, you know." He lightly clapped his hands together, re-creating with devilish accuracy the sound of wet bodies moving together in hard rhythm. "Slap-slap."

Quickly she put her hands over her mouth, but the laughter gurgled out anyway. The Yanomami began laughing again, genially joining her mirth.

He looked smug. "I gather they were also impressed by both my . . . shall we say *presence,* and my technique."

"Shut up," she gasped, trying to gulp back the giggles. "Or I'll slap-slap your face-face."

His expression changed to one of pure ecstasy. "Oh, God," he said. "Would you?"

The band of Yanomami were pleased to offer their hospitality, and Ben decided it would be more dangerous to risk insulting them by refusing than it would be to go with them and risk Dutra and Kates reaching the boats before they did. The Indians escorted them to the moloca, the communal house where all the people in the band lived. It was a huge, round, thatched structure, undetectable from the air. The band was fairly small, Ben explained, only about fifty people, though the groups seldom numbered more than two hundred.

All of the villagers poured out to greet the two newcomers, the naked brown children shy and giggling, the women deftly separating Jillian from Ben, whom the men urged in a different direction.

"What do I do?" Jillian called, curious yet a little alarmed.

Ben looked over his shoulder and grinned at her. "Smile and look pretty,"

"Thanks so much," she muttered, then took his advice and smiled at the women. They varied in age from a toothless, wizened matriarch to lissome young girls with budding breasts. The women were bare-breasted; indeed, none of the villagers wore anything resembling a shirt. The men wore a sort of rolled breechcloth that tied in the back over their buttocks, while the women wore girdles, fashioned of many strings, that left their buttocks bare.

She didn't speak a word of their language but was relieved to find that a couple of them spoke a little Portuguese, so communication on a basic level was possible. Evidently they were in the midst of preparing the communal meal, and were happy simply to have her company while they worked. She was soon sitting on the ground with a baby in her arms and two toddlers crawling back and forth over her legs.

The men returned with Ben, all of them seeming in good humor. He winked at her but remained with the men while they ate. She continued to play with the baby while she ate the simple meal of fish, manioc, and fresh fruit. She knew about manioc. It was a tuber, an excellent source of carbohydrate and the staple of their diet. It was also an excellent source of cyanide, which they used to tip their weapons. Like the blowfish, one had to know how to prepare the manioc or eating it could be one's last experience. Since no one keeled over, she felt safe in assuming that it had been correctly prepared.

After the meal, Ben came over and squatted down beside her. "Hey, you look pretty natural doing that," he said, tickling the baby's foot.

She gave him her sweetest smile. "I'm so glad you think so, since I had to leave my birth control pills at the Stone City." She didn't bother telling him that she had been nearing the end of a cycle and thus the chance of conceiving was very small. She expected to start her menses any day, and only hoped they reached the boat before she did.

To her surprise, Ben only gave her a long, considering look rather than panicking as she had expected. "Would you mind having my kid?"

Her smile faded, and unknowingly changed to something much softer as she looked down at the squirming, cooing baby in her lap, then back up at him. "We'll talk about that if it happens," she finally said.

He gave a short nod, and changed the subject. "We're going to stay here tonight. I don't like losing the time, but they seem inclined to be friendly right now and I'd sure hate for that to change. We're safe enough while we're with them, anyway."

"But what if Kates and Dutra get to the boats ahead of us?"

"The headman said he and some of the men will take us to the river tomorrow. We're a little closer than I thought we were. They seem to think they can find where we left the boats; hell, they were probably watching when we came ashore. I told them what happened, and that we may be followed by men trying to kill us. Datta Dasa, the headman, said they would protect us until we leave. After that, we're on our own."

"Again," she said.

"Yeah. Staying here is a risk we have to take, though, so we might as well go with the flow. While we're here, we'll have a chance to clean up with the soap they make, and really wash our clothes."

"What are we going to wear while the clothes are drying?" she asked politely.

That wicked grin flashed. "Exactly what the Yanomami are wearing."

19

If he thought she would be discomfited, she showed him. Her profession had taught her to be at ease with other cultures, so she didn't protest. Instead she happily went with the women to their well-hidden forest pool where they swam daily, stripped off for the second time that day, and plunged into the water. They hadn't been in the pool for five minutes when a child ran up carrying a very recognizable bundle: Ben's clothes. Jillian was amused at how neatly he had outmaneuvered her, knowing that she wouldn't refuse to wash his clothes when he requested it in front of the entire village. These people would be shocked if she did so, for in their culture each sex, each person, had assigned duties and there was no argument about performing them. That was simply the way it was.

Before tackling the laundry, however, she indulged in personal use of the gelatinous soap the women provided, fresh smelling and pale green in color. It lathered without effort, and she scrubbed herself with it from head to toe. It felt wonderful to be really clean again.

She used the same soap on their clothes, and after they climbed out of the pool, a friendly young woman—whose name, Alcida, revealed contact with the outside world—gave her a kind of detangler and conditioner to work into her hair. The smell was sweet and delicate, like fresh flowers.

After she'd used it, the wooden comb the women produced almost glided through her hair.

She put on a string girdle, which left her entirely bare behind, as it consisted of a small band around her waist and a series of braided strings in front. With all of the other women wearing the same minimal covering, however, she didn't feel as naked and uncomfortable as she would have thought. Maybe she liked nudity more than she'd suspected before, but she thought it rather more likely that the faint glee she felt at being so attired—or unattired, depending on how one looked at it—was caused by the smug knowledge that she was going to cause Ben Lewis some uncomfortable moments. Served him right for the sneaky way he had forced her to wash his clothes for him.

The Yanomami men wouldn't pay any particular attention to her nudity, except perhaps to show an initial interest in the paleness of her skin, but Ben's reactions would be entirely different. Though he had been careful not to ogle any of the Yanomami women, not wanting to offend their newfound friends, *her* nakedness would be different.

Walking back to the moloca, she discovered that she rather liked the freedom of wearing just that string girdle. She felt the heat and humidity less with so much of her skin exposed to the air; she hadn't been aware of the barely stirring breezes until now, but she was exquisitely sensitive to their subtle brush against her skin. Her nipples rose in proud response.

That was the way she looked when Ben first saw her, when the genial group of women walked into the clearing surrounding the moloca. He felt as if an invisible fist had been driven hard into his gut, almost doubling him over. He was consumed by two equally fierce desires, the first to throw a blanket around her and conceal her from all these other male eyes, and the second to throw himself on her.

The second impulse was distinctly uncomfortable, for the snug loincloth he wore, rolled and tucked as it was, didn't allow much room for growth.

He couldn't stop looking at her. Her pale skin had a creamy golden hue, and she glowed like a cameo among the brown-skinned Indians. The smooth, strong muscles in her marvelously fit body moved like poetry. She was slim but not thin; her figure wasn't as sleek as those of models or starlets, whom Ben mentally categorized as "bony." Rather she was neat and taut, with enough flesh under her skin to give her the womanly softness that he adored. Her breasts, round and upright, delicious little nipples puckered—damn it, what had caused that?—made his mouth water. The sway of her bottom was powerfully enticing, and the female flare of her hips drew his gaze. He stared hard at the braided string flap in front, trying to see beneath, hungry for just a glimpse of that soft cleft.

He felt an irrational surge of anger at the naturalness of her manner. How could she be so unconcerned at being naked in front of so many men? Not once had she even glanced in his direction; he might as well not have been there for all the attention she paid him, and that made him angry too. He'd never been possessive of any other woman, so the force of his primitive reaction took him by surprise. She was his, exclusively his. No other man had the right to see her like this.

Finally she looked at him, and gave him a smile so angelic that he almost jumped out of his skin. The only time Jillian looked sweet was when she was being perverse, and a smile that glowing meant he was in serious trouble. With a flash of intuition, he knew it was the laundry that had done it. She had probably shredded his clothes or doused them with something that would make him itch. No, that would have been too easy, because he didn't much care if he wore clothes or not. This loincloth would do him just fine. No, she would come up with something more diabolical, something that would truly make him miserable—damn it, she had probably cut him off!

It wasn't fair. It just wasn't fair. He sat there silently fuming. Why had nature made women so damn irresistible to men, but neglected to build a reciprocal response in women? No matter what a guy did, no matter how small the transgression—bingo! women immediately brought out the big guns. Their noses would go up in the air, they would turn a delicate cold shoulder, and a man immediately got the message: no sex for you until you've properly groveled and apologized. Ben felt distinctly put upon, but panic was building in his chest. He thought about throwing himself at her feet and getting the groveling over with before night. Maybe she would relent.

Maybe pigs would fly, too. He wouldn't get away with it that easily. He mentally cursed himself for ever having had the bright idea of sending his clothes to her to be washed, in such a public manner that she couldn't, wouldn't, refuse, being too smart and too sensitive to the culture of their hosts. She would ignore him for at least one night, no matter how he groveled.

Datta elbowed him, and Ben turned to meet amused dark eyes. "Your woman is new?" Datta asked, indicating the uncomfortable bulge in Ben's loincloth, for of course he wouldn't have had such a violent reaction if he and Jillian had been together a long time.

Ben swallowed. "Yes, she is new."

"Perhaps she will walk with you."

I doubt it, Ben thought mournfully.

When he didn't move, Datta nudged him again. "Speak with her," he said. "How can she know, unless you tell her?"

Oh, she knew, the little witch, just as he knew his effort was doomed even as he obediently walked over to her. It didn't help that every woman there cast a discreet glance at his loincloth, then politely looked away.

Jillian looked up at him, still with that sweet expression on her face.

"Let's go for a walk," he suggested, hoping against hope.

She too let her eyes drift downward. If anything, she looked even sweeter. "We've been walking for five days," she murmured. "I'm glad of the chance to rest for a while, now that I have *our* laundry done." She nodded toward where their garments had been spread out to dry.

He felt like groaning aloud. "Don't hold that against me."

Her eyes were limpid green pools. "I don't plan to hold *anything* against you."

"I knew it," he said under his breath. "Damn it, Jillian, don't you think you're overreacting here? I know I was a little sneaky, the way I sent my clothes to you, but I couldn't wash them. The men here do *not* do laundry. It would have been a serious breach of conduct if I'd washed my own clothes."

"I know," she replied.

"You do?"

"Of course I do."

He drew a deep breath. "But you won't go walking with me?"

"No."

"Why not?"

She was still smiling, the sweetest smile on earth. "Because while *you* may be right, *I'm* the guardian of the gates to paradise."

He thrust an agitated hand through his hair. "You mean you'd do this to me even though I'm right?"

"Yes."

"For God's sake, *why?*" He thought he would explode with frustration.

"Because."

He thought about tossing her over his shoulder and carrying her off anyway; he'd have her wrapped around him and begging for it within five minutes. He was actually reaching out for her before he stopped himself. He could do it, but it would hurt her feelings. He had transgressed, not in what he had done but in how he had done it, and the score had to be evened up before she would feel comfortable with him again as an equal. This couple stuff sure could get complicated.

He made several abortive attempts to speak, all of which were cut short because he couldn't think of an argument that would make any difference to her. Finally he returned to sit by Datta, who seemed to find his frustration very funny.

"Your woman did not want to walk?" he asked gleefully.

"She said that she could not, so soon after the last time," Ben lied. No point in losing face.

"Ah." Datta nodded. "A man must take care not to hurt his woman."

From that, Ben understood that Datta thought he had been too rough with Jillian when they had made love in the jungle, therefore it served him right that she now refused to walk with him. He felt pretty glum about the entire situation.

Hammocks were slung for them in the moloca, where the entire village slept. Jillian gladly settled into hers, surprised at how tired she felt even though she'd spent half the day with the villagers rather than walking. The intense physical exertion was almost over; they would reach the river tomorrow. She thought of the long, monotonous days on the boat with a wistful longing she couldn't have imagined on the trip upriver. She would hang a hammock and spend the days gently swaying, more indolent than a slow-moving sloth. By the time they reached Manaus, she would be completely rested.

Ben swung into the hammock next to her. He had been moping around with such a hangdog expression that it was all she could do to keep from giggling. She had been thinking of putting something bitter in his food, knowing good manners and common sense would prevent him from spitting it out and insulting their hosts, but when he had approached earlier, he had so obviously expected her to withhold sex because of his maneuver with the laundry that the temptation to go along with it had been irresistible. It was the worst revenge he could think of, so of course he had jumped to the conclusion that it was the worst revenge *she* could think of. Actually, she hadn't thought of it at all, because she didn't believe in cutting off her nose to spite her face, but the amusement value of the situation more than made up for her sacrifice.

It was getting even funnier, because a mild, very familiar cramping had started a few hours ago. Sometime tomorrow, she was sure, Mother Nature would step in to further frustrate Ben.

"That guy you had sex with in a hammock," Ben muttered in the darkness, his tone low. "Do you still see him?"

She yawned, feeling content. "I've never had sex in a hammock."

There was a full ten seconds of silence; then his wrathful response seared her, although he kept his voice down. "What do you mean, you've never had sex in a hammock? You told me specifically that you had. We've discussed it at least twice. Are you saying you've been *lying* to me all along, just to make me jealous?"

"I never told you I'd had sex in a hammock."

"Yes, you did. On our first night aboard the boat."

"You asked if I'd ever 'done it' in a hammock. Since we had just settled down to go to sleep and you didn't specify what you meant by 'it,' I put my own interpretation on it and assumed you meant 'sleep.' Then you asked where I 'did it' in a hammock, and I said on my balcony. End of discussion."

"Damn it, you knew what I meant. You knew I wasn't interested in *naps*. And when we were at the waterfall, I asked if you'd been screwing on the balcony with some guy you barely knew, because you said—"

"I know what I said. I also know that it isn't my fault if you seldom think of anything except sex. That time I told you that I've never had sex on a balcony with a stranger, which is perfectly true, because I've never had sex on a balcony with anyone. Now will you hush and let me go to sleep?"

"No," he said. "I'm going to strangle you."

"Temper, temper," she chided, smiling in the darkness.

Ben wasn't smiling, he was positively fuming. She'd done it on purpose, tormented him all that time with nothing but lies, knowing that he was so jealous he could barely stand it. No doubt about it, men were at a severe disadvantage when it came to dealing with the so-called gentler sex. Women held all the aces. Of course, most women weren't as diabolical as Jillian Sherwood. She knew just which buttons to push with him.

He reached over and shook her hammock. "Okay, no slick answers this time, just the plain truth. Are you romantically, sexually, or otherwise involved with anyone back in the States?"

"The absolute, plain truth?" she asked.

"Yeah. The truth." He braced himself.

"It's been at least six months since I've even dated anyone."

"Good God, why?" He sounded shocked to the soles of his feet.

"Because I'd rather be alone than have to be polite when I'm really bored out of my skull. And I've never been much interested in sex."

"Bullshit." The word burst out of him. "You can't keep your hands off of me."

"It must be your elegant way of putting things," she said sarcastically. "Good night. I'm going to sleep."

He set his hammock to swaying gently, his good humor restored. She was obviously crazy about him.

They left the moloca the next morning, accompanied by Datta Dasa and four more tribesmen, and reached the river three hours later. The tribesmen led them unerringly to where they had left the boats. Ben wasn't very surprised to find that one of the boats was gone; he wouldn't have been surprised if both of them had been missing. The only thing that worried him was the possibility that somehow Kates and Dutra had gotten ahead of them and taken the boat to wait in ambush around some bend. It would make more sense to wait here at the boats; perhaps they were somewhere watching, but reluctant to do anything with the Yanomami there. If even one tribesman escaped an ambush, Kates and Dutra would be in trouble, for they couldn't hope to match the Indians in their jungle skills or knowledge.

The hidden rafts and cache of supplies hadn't been disturbed, though, so Ben felt better about their safety. If Kates had indeed taken the first boat, he would certainly have taken the supplies as well.

They loaded part of the supplies and one of the rafts. Kates and Dutra might get the rest of the supplies, but on the other hand Pepe and the other men might be the ones to use them. There was no way to tell. At last they said their good-byes, and Ben started the engine, slowly reversing the boat out of the cove and into the river channel. Jillian waved until the boat passed out of sight of the Yanomami.

Dutra pressed deep into the shelter of buttressed roots that rose several feet higher than his head, scarcely even daring to breathe for fear the Indians would hear him. If he hadn't lost his pistol, he thought viciously, things would have been different. But the pistol had disappeared when a mud slide caught him two days before, sweeping him into a ravine. As it was he had to cower in the bushes to keep those scrawny little bastards from knowing he was there. They were no match for him in strength, but those poison arrows gave them the advantage now that he was unarmed.

He had pushed himself to the limits, trying to get to the boats first, and he'd made it. But since he was unarmed, there was no point in waiting to ambush Lewis, and he had no way of getting another gun this far upriver. Instead he had taken the other boat and hidden it farther upstream, then waited for Lewis and the woman to show themselves. He had started to load some supplies, but realized in time that would be a dead giveaway, and would make Lewis even more wary.

Now all he had to do was follow them downriver, hanging back and waiting until he could find a weapon. Once they reached the more traveled waters, he would be able to jump some river trader and steal a gun. By then Lewis should be feeling nice and safe, and he wouldn't be paying attention. A couple of quick bullets, and the diamond would be his.

Dutra forced himself to wait an hour, giving the Yanomami plenty of time to leave the area and making certain he wouldn't accidentally come upon the other boat before he was ready. An hour's time would be easy to make up when he needed to.

Despite having lost the pistol, Dutra was satisfied with the way things were turning out. Since Kates had told him that Lewis had found the diamond, Dutra hadn't been able to think about anything else. If he had that diamond he would be able to wear fancy clothes and lots of gold jewelry, the way the people on television did. He would buy a big American car to drive around Manaus, and people would be afraid of him. He would never again have to hide upriver when the police were looking for him; he would simply pay a bribe, and they would leave him alone.

He dreamed about the diamond. He hadn't seen it, but he lovingly dwelt on the image in his mind. It would look like a piece of ice, shaped like those diamonds in a fancy lady's ring, only a lot bigger. It would blind him to look at it in the sun, it would glitter so. He had never wanted anything as much as he wanted the diamond. Lewis didn't deserve to have it. He would kill Lewis, and enjoy doing it.

The first thing Jillian did was sling a hammock in the shade of the flat roof and gratefully ease into it.

Ben looked around at her, feeling a sense of relief now that they were alone once more. He was glad they had met up with the Yanomami, but at the same time he felt as if his privacy had been invaded. He liked knowing that he and Jillian were alone.

"The captain expects more effort from his crew than that," he said.

"The crew will make an effort tomorrow," she said, closing her eyes.

"What's wrong with today? You had plenty of sleep last night."

"I'm always really tired and don't feel good on the first day of my period," she explained, keeping her eyes closed.

The silence was thick. Then Ben said, "I'm learning. You didn't actually say you were having your period. You simply made a statement that you get tired and don't feel good on the first day of your period. You're still punishing me, aren't you?"

"I'm having my period," she said flatly. "And I don't know any way I could have arranged that to coincide with your many transgressions."

Ben looked at her again, this time noting the circles under her eyes. She wasn't kidding. He felt a moment's dismay, then concern. "Do you have anything to take? What can I do to make you feel better?"

She did open her eyes then, and smiled at him. A real smile, not the angelic smile that made him shudder. "I'm okay. I don't feel sick, just tired. If you really need me, wake me up. And I promise I'll be better tomorrow."

He couldn't leave the wheel, not in this section of the river, or he would have taken her in his arms and cuddled her, held her while she slept. He always had this strange compulsion to baby her, and that was ridiculous, because she was one of the most capable, stalwart people he'd ever met, man or woman.

He said, "How long does this usually last?"

"What, my period, or your strange delusion that everything I do is planned specifically to keep you from making love as often as you seem to think you should? My period will last four or five days. I've seen no break in your delusion at all."

He grinned. Ah, he loved it when she talked sweet to him. "I don't know where you got the idea that having a period prevents making love."

"From the fact that I don't feel like it, don't want to, and won't let you."

"I guess that about covers the issue."

She chuckled at the rueful note in his voice and snuggled more comfortably into the depths of the hammock. "By the way, I hadn't thought of refusing to 'walk' with you until you made it so obvious it was what you expected. Thanks for the idea. I was just going to make your food taste bad."

He was very still for a moment. Then he began to laugh. "The next time, sweetheart, use your own judgment."

"I did," she said smugly, closing her eyes again. "I know how to recognize a superior idea when I hear it."

He was still chuckling. "Sleep tight, sweetheart."

"Thank you, I will."

Several minutes later he looked back again, and saw the evenness of breathing that signaled sleep, and he smiled. Even when she was being diabolical and cantankerous, he had more fun being with her than he'd ever had before in his life. He'd find some way to keep her in Manaus.

20

That night she slept in his arms. She had expected they would once again sleep in the hammocks, but he unrolled the sleeping pad and arranged the mosquito netting so it formed a small tent over it, remembering her dislike for sleeping totally unprotected from any stray insect. She lay with her head pillowed on his shoulder, and slept better than she had in days. The heat had become oppressive again once they left the mountains, but even though they would have been much cooler had they slept apart, neither of them suggested it or moved. She felt happier when she could touch him. Though she also loved to tease and irritate him, she was never more content than when he was holding her.

Their days together were numbered now, to about a week. She remembered that he had said the return to Manaus would take less time than the trip upriver, since they would be traveling with the current instead of against it. She wanted to seize every moment with him while she could. Things would change rapidly once they reached Manaus. She would do what she had to do, and then she would return to the States.

But for now she was in his arms.

Now that they were on the boat again, everything was so much easier that during the next few days she felt almost as if she were on vacation. The toilet facilities, which had seemed so make-do and inadequate before, now seemed positively luxurious. Cooking on the alcohol stove was a delight. Even the limited varieties of food were perfectly satisfying, since they could take their time eating each meal. They each had a change of clothes, having left one with the extra supplies as a precaution, and she had her personal items. Life was basic, but it was good.

They began passing tin and cardboard shacks, built on stilts on the river's edge, signs of encroaching "civilization." Right now there weren't many of the shacks, but the farther they went downriver the more there would be, lining the riverbank in increasing numbers. These were individual dwellings, but soon there would be the occasional settlement, groups of shacks huddled together and connected to the outside world only by the traders who plied the river.

Two children ran out of one isolated shack, waving wildly, perhaps thinking that Ben and Jillian were traders or perhaps just excited to see the boat. Jillian waved back at them. They didn't have much in their lives to get excited about.

"How often do you have guide jobs?" she asked idly, imagining a life spent permanently on the rivers and in the jungles.

"As often as I want. I usually like to take some free time between jobs, the length of the free time depending on the length of the job. If it's just a week with some tourists who want to experience the 'real' Amazon, a weekend off is enough. Most jobs last longer, though. The one before this one took a couple of months. I'd planned to take a full month off before signing up for another one."

"So why didn't you?"

"Curiosity. I knew Kates was up to no good, and I wanted to know exactly what he was after. And he paid good money up front."

She leaned against one of the roof poles, her expression pensive. "What happened that last morning in the Stone City? Why was Kates shooting at you? Was that what set Dutra off?"

"I guess." He felt uncomfortable. "They must have had it planned, that Kates's shot would be the signal to Dutra."

"But what happened to start it? We didn't find any treasure. There was no reason for it to happen."

He should have known that when she had time to think about it, her agile mind would start putting the pieces together and notice the gaps. "I woke up early and left the camp. Kates must have thought I was up to something, because he followed me. He took it pretty hard that the diamond was long gone, and that the temple wasn't full of gold."

"When I crawled out of the tent, Dutra didn't try to shoot me. He just looked at me and grinned."

"Probably saving you for last," Ben growled, rage building in him at the thought. "Literally."

"I wish I had thought to get my pistol instead of the flashlight. I can't believe I was so stupid."

"I'm just glad you didn't get into a shoot-out with him," he said, shuddering inwardly at the thought. "You did exactly what I had told you to do, and I'd have been pissed as hell if you hadn't."

"But Rick might still be alive if I had."

"And he might not. There's no way to second-guess what will happen when bullets start flying. You might have shot him yourself, by accident. Never play the 'if only' game; it's a stupid waste of time."

His rough logic made her smile, though a little sadly. Ben would never waste time with regrets; he would simply forge ahead, single-minded and ruthlessly determined. His playfulness and raunchy sense of humor sometimes masked that part of him, what she felt was the biggest part of him, but she never forgot it was there. People who underestimated him did so at their own risk; she had underestimated him at first, but had quickly realized her mistake and never let herself forget it. Ben was of that very different breed, the adventurer, the explorer. He made his own rules and was willing to enforce them. His edicts and warnings on the trail were so effective because no one was in any doubt that he would do exactly what he had said he would do.

How dull and bland life would be without him. Excitement crackled around him; he was lusty, dangerous, bigger than life. How could any other man ever measure up to him?

"I thought you were a drunken bum," she said, her eyes twinkling.

His eyebrows quirked. "I thought you were in desperate need of being laid."

"That would, of course, be your first concern."

"Yes, ma'am." He was drawling. "It was then and it is now."

"At least you're consistent."

"Persistent, too. Is today okay?"

As she had every day, she smiled and shook her head. "Tomorrow."

"If tomorrow is okay, why isn't today?"

"Because I said so."

"You've let this little taste of power go to your head."

She blew him a kiss, still smiling. His gut tightened and he began to get hard, but he found that he was smiling too. The shadows had lifted from her eyes and she looked happy. He wanted that expression to stay on her face; he wanted her to wake up smiling every morning, her eyes full of sleepy contentment as she turned toward him and put her hand on his chest.

The noon tropical sun was burning down on him, but suddenly it wasn't half as bright as the realization that slammed into him. His pupils dilated and the sunlight stabbed painfully at his eyes, almost blinding him. He gripped the wheel as if it were a lifeline, trying to regulate his breathing, trying to get the world to settle back on its normal axis.

He had been determined to keep Jillian in Manaus, to have a "relationship" with her, whatever the hell that meant. It was very simple and forthright for him: he wanted her around. He wanted to sleep with her every night. That logically meant living together. Though he'd never taken things that far before, he'd felt comfortable with the idea, even liked it. But in that overwhelming moment of realization everything had crystallized, and the blinders of habit were destroyed.

He wanted Jillian forever.

"Living together" suddenly seemed far too impermanent, too unreliable. He wanted the strength of legal bonds. His mind had never before even formed the word "marriage" in connection with a particular woman, but with Jillian it was the only tolerable situation. She was his, for a lifetime.

His hands shaking, he pulled back on the throttle and began idling toward shore.

She looked around in curiosity. "What are you doing?"

His entire big body was shaking visibly, and she was suddenly alarmed. She reached out to steady him, her arm sliding around his waist. "Ben? What is it? What's wrong?"

"Nothing's wrong," he said between gritted teeth. "I have to have you. Now."

This was different from the groaning, humorously inventive pleading with which he had entertained her over these past few days. There was no humor in his eyes; his expression was frighteningly intense. He was still shaking, the powerful muscles in his bare torso so tight she could see them rippling.

"Don't say no. Please. Not this time." He could barely talk. His entire body was consumed by overwhelming need.

She stood uncertainly for another few seconds, confused and a little alarmed. Then she knew what to do. She pressed a gentle kiss to his sweaty bare shoulder, then moved under the roof to prepare herself for him.

By the time the boat was secured, she was lying naked on the sleep pad, waiting for him. That curious blindness was still in his eyes when he came to her, shoving his pants down and sinking into her arms. He entered her immediately, pushing deep on the first thrust; she flinched from the pain, but held him even tighter, trying to ease his desperate urgency.

With penetration, the awful tension seemed to ease from his body, his muscles relaxing with great shudders as if this intimate contact with her relieved some unbearable inner pain.

Gently she stroked his shoulders and neck, sliding her fingers beneath his dark hair. After a moment he eased his weight up onto his elbows. His blue eyes were very dark. He brushed slow, warm, beguiling kisses across her mouth and throat, and then, with aching tenderness, he began to make love to her.

They lingered in the noonday heat, reveling in the exquisite intimacy. All of their previous heated lovemaking had only prepared them for this, for the slow ecstasy that caught them in its grip and wouldn't let go. Her senses were almost painfully heightened. Every brush against her skin made her moan with delight; he lazily licked her nipples and her wild, strained cry sent birds fluttering skyward in alarm. Time meant nothing. She wanted this moment never to end.

But it did. It had to; it was too intense to be sustained for long. Afterward he lay beside her, relaxed and drowsy, his hand rubbing absently on her stomach as if, she thought wryly, she were an alligator to be soothed into sleep.

She didn't want to talk, didn't want to ask why. She was afraid she would cry if she did. Emotion swelled in her chest until it was difficult to breathe. She loved him so much.

She thought perhaps they dozed, one of those periods of deep unconsciousness from which she awoke feeling as if no time had passed, though she knew it had. The sun had slipped from its zenith, the burning rays angling to reach beneath the roof. Ben stirred and stretched, then rolled to his knees and pulled up his pants.

She expected one of his provoking, smart-ass remarks, or at least a certain smugness, but his expression, though relaxed now, was still somber. He lifted her to her feet with that effortless strength of his and held her locked in his arms for a long minute, his cheek resting on top of her head. Then he kissed her, hard, and said, "Let's get you dressed before someone comes by."

"We haven't seen anyone since we passed that shack, and we haven't seen another boat all day."

Now that familiar grin showed itself again. "I thought you had a streak of exhibitionism in you, prancing around the way you did in front of the Yanomami."

She burst into laughter. "That was your idea."

"Yeah, but I thought you'd keep your undershirt on."

"It needed washing, too."

She dressed while they bantered back and forth, and then they decided they were hungry. She made a quick fish stew, simply stirring together the canned ingredients and bringing the mixture to a boil. Their appetites were easily satisfied these days, for they had become accustomed to a sparse, plain diet. Probably a full restaurant meal would have made them both sick. Their stomachs would have to be reaccustomed to civilization, too.

Ben started the engine and backed the boat away from the bank, then carefully turned it around and began idling out of the cove into the river channel. He saw another boat coming downriver and pushed the throttle out of gear so it could pass by ahead of them.

Jillian stared at the oncoming boat, shading her eyes with her hands. "That boat's built just like ours," she said. "It looks like our other boat." She narrowed her eyes and focused on the boat pilot, noting the massive shoulders and too-little head. "Dutra!" she gasped, in mingled horror and disbelief.

Ben shoved the throttle all the way forward and the boat surged in response, the motor roaring. At the same time Dutra must have realized whom he was overtaking, for he too pushed the throttle to full power.

"Get down," Ben said automatically. "And slide my pistol up here to me." Damn it, he was almost never without that pistol within reach whenever he was on the river, but this was one of those rare times. Violently he wished for a rifle.

Dutra fired, but he was too far away for accuracy and the bullet zinged overhead.

Jillian got Ben's pistol and crawled on her hands and knees, staying well below the sides of the boat, out of sight, until she could reach up and place it in his outstretched hand. "Get back. He'll shoot at me, since I'm the only one he can see."

"Then you get down too, idiot," she snapped, tugging at his pants.

The boats were surging toward each other at an angle, at

full power. Ben spun the wheel sharply to the right, hoping to save a few precious seconds, if only they didn't run aground on one of the numerous snags. The movement slung Jillian off balance, and she rolled into the boxes of supplies. Dutra fired again, and this time the bullet splintered the wood railing.

Ben lifted the pistol and fired, but Dutra dodged to the side. Ben shot once more, swiftly adjusting his aim. It would be pure luck if he hit anything, with both the target and his shooting platform bouncing across the water like broncos, but he could keep Dutra down.

Jillian struggled to her knees. Two bullets pierced the wooden side of the boat, and she hurled herself flat on the deck.

Ben returned fire, the shots cracking on the water. The stench of gunpowder drifted to her nostrils.

They swung into the river channel only twenty yards ahead of Dutra. Ben went down on one knee and turned to face the stern, which was open except for the toilet facility taking up roughly the same amount of space as a phone booth. Dutra was directly behind them, the other boat so close that it was inside their propeller wash, and gaining on them in the smoother water. Ben fired and hit the wheel, but Dutra had ducked again.

Ben looked forward just in time to swerve around a big log; Dutra, following in the propeller wash, had an easier time of it as the wash pushed the log away from him. He pulled even closer.

Ben swore violently. He couldn't steer the boat at top speed and at the same time trade gunfire with Dutra behind them. He had to get the son of a bitch before a lucky shot hit him in the middle of the back, and Jillian was left to face Dutra alone.

"Jillian, you'll have to steer the boat! Can you do it?"

She didn't hesitate, but crawled forward. "Be careful!" she yelled over the roar of the motor.

"You be careful! Stay down as much as possible, and to the side so you aren't in his direct sights."

She did as he said, crouching to the side with one hand on

the wheel, her head lifted just enough to peer over the bow. Ben swiftly crawled to the stern of the boat, staying behind the cover of the toilet housing.

A shot made him go flat on his belly, and he felt the boat shudder beneath him. He rose to his knees and fired three quick shots. Dutra screamed and fell to the side, but instinct told Ben it hadn't been a solid hit. He'd just grazed him. He waited, nerves stretching, and was ready a few seconds later when Dutra popped back up, his arm outstretched and steady, pistol muzzle flashing. Ben fired simultaneously. Dutra screamed again, holding his shoulder, and slumped to the side.

The boat shuddered wildly, and the motor's rhythm caught. The son of a bitch had been shooting at their motor instead of at them! The other boat kept coming, throttle locked forward, wheel secured so it didn't veer.

"Hold on!" Ben roared, lunging toward the bow. "He's going to ram us!"

Jillian cast a frantic look over her shoulder, feeling the wheel trying to tear out of her grip as the motor coughed and locked with metal grinding against metal. Desperately she pulled on the wheel with all her might, trying to turn out of Dutra's path. Sluggishly the boat swung to the side, without power, and almost immediately the other boat slammed into them. She was sent sprawling across the deck, her head crashing hard into the side. She saw Ben grab a roof pole at the last second, and that was all that saved him from going overboard.

She had turned the boat enough that it wasn't a head-on collision. The other boat plowed into them from the right rear, violently swinging them around. The stern of Dutra's craft swung forward, the motor still churning, still driving. Wood splintered; the bow of the other boat and the stern of their boat ground together, collapsing the structures, combining the two watercraft like two clumps of clay jammed together. The force shattered the wheel and throttle of the second boat, and the engine died.

The sudden silence was so complete, so nerve-racking, that it was only then she realized how loud the crash had been. Dazed, she tried to stand up, but everything was swimming around her and she sagged to her knees.

All of the supplies had been scattered over the deck. Ben had dropped the pistol on impact, but luckily it hadn't gone overboard. He snatched it up, whirling toward the stern of the boat, every muscle tense. "Are you okay?" he asked tersely.

"Yes," she said, though she wasn't sure. She would manage.

He struggled toward the rear of the boat, where the other boat had overridden their craft and smashed it to splinters. Black water was beginning to lap up over the deck toward the bow. Both boats were taking on water.

"Get the raft and inflate it," he called over his shoulder.

She fought off her dizziness and scrambled across the sloping deck toward the raft. The degree of list increased almost by the second, it seemed. They would have only a few minutes, at most, to get off the boat.

Water lapped over Ben's boots. He pushed a section of wrecked bow aside. Where was Dutra? If he had been in the bow, he should be dead, because that entire section was in splinters. He'd been tagged, twice. There was a piece of wood with blood on it.

But there was no Dutra, dead or alive. No sign of movement, no sound other than the creaking of wood as the boats rose and fell on the waves.

The impact could have thrown him overboard. If he had been unconscious, he was now dead. Could he have made it to shore, unnoticed, in that short length of time? Ben looked closely at the bank, searching for a fern frond waving with slightly more force than it should, signaling that something had brushed by it. But everything looked normal; the butterflies were flitting undisturbed.

He turned back to the wreckage, but the boats were so splintered, so ground together, that it would be impossible to search it in the few minutes they had left before the whole thing went under. He knew there was a possibility that Dutra was clinging to the wreckage on the other side, but he simply didn't have time to find out. They had to get the raft inflated, load supplies, and get off the boat.

The water was at mid-calf now. He sloshed through it up the steeply slanting deck to where Jillian had dragged the raft out onto the bow where she could have room to inflate it. There was a pressurized air tank attached to the side of the boat for just that purpose; she had unclamped the tank and dragged it forward, also, and attached the nozzle to the raft.

Ben helped her to brace the raft and she opened the valve. Air spewed into the raft with a violent hiss, swelling it to plump proportions in less than thirty seconds. It was big enough to hold six people, and it was all they could do to hold on to it. Quickly she shut off the valve and Ben closed the plug. Swiftly he looped the attached rope around the roof pole and shoved the raft overboard.

"Get in," he said, and Jillian scrambled over the rail and into the raft.

Ben gave her the pistol. "Keep a sharp eye," he said. "I couldn't find Dutra. He may have drowned, but we don't know for sure."

She nodded, holding the raft close to the boat with her left hand on the railing, while the pistol was in her right.

Ben grabbed his backpack and tossed it into the raft. He sure as hell wasn't going to leave the diamond behind, and they'd need the tent again. He handed the small outboard motor over the railing to her. It weighed a good fifty pounds, but she managed it even without letting go of the pistol. Damn, what a woman! He got the gas tanks, loaded them, then began grabbing boxes of supplies and tossing them over the railing, while Jillian set the motor into the brackets made to hold it.

The boat lurched, and tipped sharply upward. "That's enough," she said. "Come on."

"Oars," he said, and tossed them aboard.

She gave him a furious look. "The oars and the motor should have been first. Come on, *now.*"

Figuring he had better obey, he unlooped the rope from

the pole, then swung his legs over the rail and slipped into the raft.

Swiftly he moved to the stern and attached the gas tanks to the motor, squeezing the bulb to pump the gas. Over his shoulder he said, "Get a fresh clip from my pack. My gun's almost empty."

Jillian moved cautiously to the pack so she wouldn't rock the raft.

"In the front pocket, the one fastened with Velcro," he instructed. Praying, he pulled the cord and the motor coughed. He pulled again, three times in rapid succession, and the little motor fired, caught, then settled into rhythm.

Jillian found the fresh clips and took one out, but her searching fingers had felt something curious in the middle section.

Gurgling, the two smashed boats settled deeper into the water. Ben shoved them away, and used the tiller to guide the raft to a safe distance. As they pulled away, he sharply surveyed the wreckage, but there was still no sign of Dutra. He swung the craft in a complete circle around the boats, to no avail. Probably Dutra was on the bottom of the river, already being added to the food chain.

He settled next to the tiller, his thoughts already turning to the chore of getting them down this big river all the way to Manaus in a raft.

Jillian was searching through his backpack. He bit off a curse as, with a puzzled expression, she lifted out something wrapped in a handkerchief. The cloth fell away, and the sun was caught and splintered into a thousand bloodred rays.

She lifted dazed eyes to him. "It's the Empress," she blurted. "You found it."

21

"Why didn't you tell me?" she babbled. "It makes sense that you would hide it from everyone else, but why didn't you tell *me?*"

Swiftly he cut the power down to idle and locked the tiller in place. She was still sitting there, holding the diamond on her lap. Even as roughly shaped as it was, it was gorgeous. The size of it still stunned him, and evidently Jillian was just as stunned because all she could do was stare at it.

Moving quickly, he retrieved his pistol and the extra clip, shoving the weapon into his waistband and the clip in his pocket. Then he took the diamond from her unresisting hands and rewrapped it in the handkerchief before placing it once more in the backpack. Still without speaking, he carried the pack with him when he returned to the tiller and resumed his seat.

Jillian was no dummy. Far from it. She looked at the pack and at him, and her eyes narrowed. "What's going on?" she asked.

"You know what's going on. I found the diamond," he said flatly.

"Kates saw you with it that morning, didn't he? That's why he started shooting."

"Yes."

He increased the throttle and they picked up speed. The noise made conversation impossible. Jillian sat in the bow, the wind whipping her hair around, and silently watched the river for a while. Ben began to hope she was going to leave well enough alone, but then she stirred herself and moved to sit close enough so that he could hear her.

"I had to leave the film and all my notes behind," she said. "I have no proof of the Stone City or the Anzar. The diamond is a way of convincing people that the Anzar really existed. It'll get their attention, force them to listen to me. They'll send in another expedition, at least, and Dad will be vindicated. And maybe I'll be able to retrieve Rick's body."

"I'll take you back," he said impatiently. "You don't need the diamond to prove anything."

She just looked at him, those green eyes unwavering. "And I suppose you're going to finance the trip."

"Yes." He jerked his head toward the pack. "I'll have plenty of money from that thing."

"No, thanks," she said. "I won't use that kind of money."

Fury boiled in him. "What do you mean, 'that kind of money'? It isn't blood money. The diamond itself isn't proof of anything, except that Brazil has some damn big diamonds. I can use it to finance an expedition back to the Stone City and still make myself a big profit. You want to use it to convince a bunch of stuffed shirts to mount an expedition, and to benefit yourself at the same time by clearing your old man's name. I may be stupid, but I don't see a whole hell of a lot of difference there, except my idea is a lot smarter!"

"The diamond belongs to the Brazilian people," she said, "just as the pyramids belong to the Egyptians. Or do you think it was all right for grave robbers to loot the burial chambers in the pyramids? For history to be destroyed?"

"There's a slight difference here, sweetheart. The diamond is the least important part of the Stone City. The temple, those damn eerie statues, the city itself, even that damn bowl it's in—that's what's important, what people like you will be studying for the next hundred years. The diamond is meaningless."

"It's a priceless artifact."

"Artifact!" He gave her an incredulous look. "It's a shiny rock that people like to wear in jewelry. Put a garnet in the niche above the tomb and it would have the same meaning. What do you say that's what we do? Even a garnet the size of an ostrich egg wouldn't put a dent in what the diamond will sell for."

Her face was stony, unyielding. "Taking it is stealing."

"Ah, shit," he said in disgust. "Damn it, Jillian, do you think I went to all the trouble to get the damn thing just to turn it over to someone who didn't lift a finger to retrieve it? We risked our lives to find that place."

"You were paid to do exactly what you did," she pointed out. "And you couldn't have found it without me. In fact, I would have found it instead of you, if you hadn't talked me into playing decoy while you sneaked off."

"I didn't expect to find anything."

"Why not? Everything else was where I'd said it would be."

"I'm not handing over the diamond," he said coldly. "Give it up."

"Are you going to throw me overboard?" she demanded. "All I have to do is contact the authorities when we get to Manaus."

"How are you going to prove I have it?" His blue eyes were icy.

Jillian subsided in impotent rage. She knew exactly what would happen if she went to the authorities. They would check into it, and turn up the information that her father had been full of wild schemes, and that she was a chip off the old crackpot. They wouldn't take her seriously. They would assume she had made the story up in order to attract publicity for a wild-goose chase that would, like all of her father's adventures, turn up exactly nothing.

Ben was too smart to try to sell the diamond in Brazil. His contacts wouldn't be legal, but she would bet the Empress would surface in Antwerp. It would attract worldwide attention, but its origins would forever remain murky, adding to its mystery and value. And what if it ended up being cut, divided, and placed in settings to enhance someone's sense of importance? The thought of the Empress being cut was horrifying; it was the heart of a culture, and it should remain intact.

"Stop sulking," he advised. "I meant what I said. I'll take you back. What you wanted was proof of the Anzar and that's what you'll get."

She moved away and sat in the bow, watching the river. Again the distance between them prevented conversation, but now it irritated him. He wanted to shake her, force her to see his side of it. He was using common sense, but she was spouting idealistic bullshit. Damn it, why hadn't he been more careful? He hadn't expected her to start nosing around in the pack after she got out the extra clip.

He was savagely frustrated. If he asked her to marry him now, she would think he had asked just to keep her quiet about the diamond. The way things stood, he didn't have a snowball's chance in hell of convincing her that he really wanted to marry her. If this didn't just beat all; the first time in his life he had ever thought about getting married, and Jillian not only wouldn't believe him, she'd probably slap him if he even brought it up now.

What a son-of-a-bitching day. He'd been shot at, his boat had been sunk, he had realized he wanted to get married, and now Jillian was mad at him.

His patience was getting worn thin.

On top of all that, he couldn't shake the feeling that he should have made certain Dutra was dead. But he'd wanted to get Jillian away from there, and he supposed he would do the same thing if he had it to do over again. Protecting her came first.

There hadn't been any sign of Kates. Ben didn't figure there was much chance Kates was still alive. He'd made a big mistake in hiring Dutra, who would have turned on his own mother if there was money involved. Kates had needed Dutra, but Dutra hadn't needed Kates. It was that simple.

But even if Dutra hadn't been killed, he was wounded and had no way of coming after them, assuming he'd made it to the bank in his condition, and assuming his wounds didn't turn septic. Infection was almost a certainty here in the tropics, unless Dutra knew enough about the medicinal qualities of plants to doctor himself, which seemed unlikely. So why was he still worried?

Because it paid to worry about things like that.

Dutra clung to the wreckage, letting himself slip below the surface of the water when he heard the raft swing around. He was terrified, thinking of his blood leaking into the river and attracting predators, expecting at any moment to feel thousands of sharp teeth sinking into him. When the noise of the motorized raft faded away, he rose gasping to the surface, but the boats were sinking fast and he had to get away from them. He had no choice. He tore a strip off his shirt and bound it tightly over the wound in his right arm, then hurled himself into the water.

He could barely use his arm, but his brute strength got him to shore and he crawled, exhausted, onto dry land. He lay there using every curse he had ever heard on Ben Lewis. The fool, why had he stopped in the middle of the day, evidently for a long time? He had never done such a thing before, but this day he had. Probably he had been using the woman, the little slut. Why couldn't she have kept her legs together until night?

Because of that, Dutra hadn't been prepared. The attack hadn't gone the way he had planned. He had intended to slip up on them during the night, when they were asleep. How easy it would have been. Instead he was the one who had been surprised, and Lewis had nearly killed him.

But Dutra wasn't dead. And he had the advantage now, because they thought he was. He would still follow them. Even if they got back to Manaus before he caught up with them, the outcome would be the same.

When he had regained some of his strength, Dutra struggled to his feet and, after a moment's thought, turned upriver. He had passed a shack not so far back. There would be food, almost certainly a boat of some sort, and perhaps a weapon.

* * *

Ben would rather have spent the night at a settlement, but with the time they had lost he knew they wouldn't make it that day. He eased the raft out of the current and into a protected shoal. "Looks like we'll sleep one more night in the tent," he said.

These were the first words he had spoken since she moved up to the bow of the raft, for she had remained there for the rest of the day. She didn't reply now, but moved back so that the overhanging limbs wouldn't hit her when he nudged the raft against the bank.

He hid the raft as well as he could, for smugglers would consider two people, especially when one of them was a woman, a far easier and more desirable target than a party of twelve. They had to force their way inland, away from the thick undergrowth that lined the riverbank, to find a place where he could set up the little tent. Immediately Jillian unpacked a few supplies and began preparing a simple meal.

He finished with the tent and gave her a deeply exasperated look. He hunkered down beside her, determined to put an end to this silent treatment. "Look, you might as well stop pouting. You don't have to like it, but did you ever hear about cutting your losses? You aren't going to get the diamond, but you're still going to have everything else you wanted: proof of the Anzar and your father's name cleared."

"No, I won't," she said.

Initially he was so relieved that she had actually spoken to him that it took him a moment to think about what she'd said. "What do you mean by that?"

She shrugged. "I mean I refuse to have anything to do with an expedition financed by the sale of that diamond. I can't stop you from doing what you want, but I don't have to be involved. I'll get on a plane and out of your hair as soon as we get back to Manaus."

He'd had enough. His temper was ragged and he was holding on to it by only the thinnest thread. He gripped her arm, forcing her around to face him. "The hell you will," he said, a deliberate space between each word.

"Oh? How do you propose to stop me? Kidnapping?" Her voice was both angry and taunting.

"If I have to."

"I guess you would, at that." She jerked her arm away. "But you'd do better to take your own advice and cut your losses. So why don't you just forget about salving your conscience with another expedition, and save your energy, because there's no way you could force me to have anything to do with it."

"I'm not salving my conscience," he snapped. "I said I'd get that proof for you, and I'll do it, even if I have to drag you all the way back there."

"Oh, I suppose you're going to make me famous in spite of myself, and that's supposed to make it all better? Theft is theft. Nothing will change that."

"Just who in hell am I stealing from? The Brazilian people? Name one who would profit from the diamond being locked up in a museum, not even allowed to be seen because of security? Ninety percent of them wouldn't even hear about it, and wouldn't give a shit if they did. What if I had been mining and found the diamond? It's the same diamond, but would it be all right then for me to take it? Finders keepers, right?" He was yelling. He had never been more furious in his life.

"You would be stealing from history."

"Bullshit! You could put a goddamn piece of glass in its place, and the history of the Anzar would be exactly the same!"

"But it wasn't a piece of glass, it was the Empress. I was taught my entire life to respect the past, to treasure every little bit of history we can find because it's part of ourselves, who we are and how we got to where we are today. I've forced myself to stay awake more nights than you can imagine, with a gun in my hand, standing guard at a site to protect it from scavengers. Do you think I'm going to turn into one of those scavengers now?"

He wasn't getting anywhere. He felt as if he were battering his head against a brick wall. If God had ever made a more stubborn woman, he never wanted to meet her. This one was driving him crazy.

He gave up for the night. He'd said all he had to say. Let

her think about it, and eventually her common sense would take over. She wanted to vindicate her father, and he had offered her a way to do so. She would accept that something was better than nothing.

Complete silence reigned between them for the rest of the night. When they had finished eating and cleared things away, he indicated the tent with a brusque motion of his hand and she crawled into it without a word. It was difficult in such a small tent, but she managed not to touch him. Of all the things that had happened that day, that infuriated him most of all.

The next day began in the same fashion. It was as if she had wiped him from her thoughts, as if he no longer existed, or at least was no longer noticeable unless he spoke to her and gained her brief attention—*very* brief attention. It lasted only as long as it took her to reply, in as few words as possible. Her manner made it plain that she bothered to reply only because it was polite to do so.

He found himself holding the raft to a slower speed, to stretch out the time she was forced to spend with him. It would give her common sense more time to take over. He only hoped he could hold out that long, because he hadn't realized how hard it would be for him to restrain himself. Her deliberate aloofness outraged him. She was his; he would never let her go. He would do whatever was necessary to keep her with him, including the kidnapping she had so sarcastically suggested. If she thought he would stop short of that, then she didn't know her man at all.

That was the bottom line. She was his and he was hers. How dare she ignore that? How dare she deliberately try to destroy the bonds between them? He'd be damned if he'd let that happen.

There was still plenty of daylight left when they reached the first settlement. It was a ramshackle affair, though it had electricity, courtesy of a generator. Kids came running when he nosed the raft up against the dilapidated docks. There were about fifteen shacks and one larger building, big enough to qualify as a house, though it wasn't in much better shape than the shacks. There wasn't a glassed window in the settlement; all of the roofs, even that of the "big house," were thatched.

"Why are we stopping?" Jillian asked, for the first time breaking her rule about not speaking unless he spoke first.

"If they have a place for us to sleep, we'll be safer here. Too many smugglers in this part of the river for us to take any risks we don't have to." His own voice was curt. He was as angry at her as she was at him.

Some of the kids were chattering, some standing back a little shyly. The older inhabitants were also curious, but less friendly, watching from the doorways and open windows of their mean little dwellings. A tall, gaunt old woman came out of the big house and strode down to the docks. She was dressed in trousers and a sleeveless shirt that hung free of the waistband. A ragged straw hat protected her head from the heat, and a thin cigar resided in the corner of her mouth.

"Who are you?" she demanded in a gruff voice as deep as a man's.

"Ben Lewis. This is Jillian Sherwood. Our boat sank yesterday and we had to take the raft."

The old woman shrugged. "You were fortunate to have a boat *and* a raft. What do you want here?"

"A place to sleep, nothing else. This settlement is safer than the riverbank. We have our own food; we wouldn't be taking from you."

The old woman looked him over from head to toe. He was shirtless, because that was how he had been when the boat sank. Evidently his powerful torso found favor with her, for she smiled. It was disconcerting, like watching an act against nature. "I am Maria Sayad. This is my trading post. There is no extra room, but there are extra hammocks. You are welcome to sleep on my veranda."

"Thank you, Senhora Sayad."

Evidently she hadn't finished being gracious. "You will eat with me. No one has passed by this week, and I like to see different faces."

"Thank you, senhora," he said again.

The senhora kept what Jillian thought of as Latin hours; the evening meal didn't begin until nine or ten and lasted for a couple of hours even though there were only three simple courses. The big house had electricity, though the light bulbs were of such low wattage that oil lamps would have done as well. A big ceiling fan circled lazily overhead.

Jillian had difficulty staying awake. She made polite conversation and smothered her yawns, but as the clock edged toward midnight it became more difficult for her to follow the conversation. Ben seemed perfectly normal, talking with the senhora as easily as if he had known her for years. Jillian doubted that he often had trouble charming a woman.

All day Jillian had been sunk in thought. The hurt that Ben would so callously destroy her dreams like that, and expect her to go along with his plan, was so great that she'd had to force it to the back of her consciousness. If she had dwelt on it, it would have destroyed her. Instead, she forced herself to face reality. She had always known that this adventure could end only one way, with her return to the States. Whether they parted on good terms or bad terms wouldn't affect the outcome.

The only detail still undecided was what would happen to the Empress. Ben had his plans, but she didn't have to agree with them and she didn't have to stand by and let him go through with those plans. She had been racking her brain all day, trying to figure out how she could get the diamond, slip away from Ben, and return to Manaus with the Empress. No definite plan had presented itself. He kept the pack beside him and never left her alone with it. She would just have to stay alert and seize any opportunity that presented itself. She might fail, but not without trying.

It was after midnight when the senhora rose and bid them good night. Gratefully, Jillian went with Ben out to the open veranda, where two hammocks had been slung. She sank into one with a tired sigh, her eyes closing.

Ben arranged himself in the other, but he lay awake for a while, staring into the darkness. He wanted her. He knew better than even to suggest that they make love; there had been none of the teasing banter that he so enjoyed, no hint that she had relented so much as an inch. But even anger couldn't dull the ache, the need to hold her in his arms and know that she belonged to him.

He finally did sleep. A storm woke him a couple of hours later, thunder rumbling and lightning flashing in the depths of the clouds. The senhora had loaned him a shirt to wear, so the cool wind was comfortable to him. Jillian moved restlessly, hugging her arms in her sleep as she became chilled. Rain washed across the settlement in great silver sheets, illuminated by the frequent lightning.

Down at the river's edge a massive figure moved silently onto the docks. He had seen the raft and swiftly continued on down the river, slumping low in his stolen boat to make himself appear smaller. He had also stolen a broad-brimmed straw hat, and it had helped disguise him. No one had paid him any attention.

In the silent hours after midnight he had made his way back up to the settlement. The rain had started, further masking any noise he might have made. First he searched the raft, but there was nothing in it except a couple of boxes of supplies. He hadn't expected the diamond to be there, but he had searched anyway, not wanting to overlook anything. He would take the supplies with him; after tonight, Lewis wouldn't need them anymore.

Lewis and the woman would be up at the house. The machete in his hand glittered wetly as Dutra made his way through the rain, silently circling the house, looking for his targets.

22

Jillian shivered in the cool, damp air, and Ben swung out of the hammock. He began unbuttoning his shirt, intending to place it over her. Some faint noise, or maybe it was instinct, made him look up as the bull-like figure rushed out of the shadows of the veranda, eerily silent, machete raised high. Jillian was caught between him and Dutra. Ben screamed, a primal sound of fear and rage, and violently pulled her out of the hammock even as he threw himself back, scrabbling for the pistol.

He managed to grab it but he was off-balance; he fell sideways across his own hammock. Ignoring Jillian, Dutra leaped over the wildly swaying hammock and her sprawled body and grinned with evil delight as he slashed down at Ben. Ben rolled to the side and the blade ripped through the hammock, cutting it in half and dumping him to the floor. As he fell he used his legs in a whipping motion, catching Dutra at the knees and sending him reeling sideways, but not taking him down.

The fall jarred Ben's shoulder, making him drop the gun. He grabbed it up, knowing precious seconds had been lost. Dutra recovered and rushed again, blade raised high.

Ben got up on one knee. Jillian was struggling to her feet beside him. "Run!" he yelled as he pushed her. Then he didn't have any more time. Dutra swung the blade, and Ben launched himself, driving inside the shining arc, ramming his shoulder hard into the man's gut and simultaneously clamping his left hand around Dutra's blade hand, locking his arm so he couldn't swing the machete again. Dutra grunted explosively from the impact, but he had the strength of a bull. The smell of him was sharp and foul. Ben tried to bring the pistol around, but Dutra saw it and grabbed Ben's hand, holding it away.

They were locked together in mortal combat. The winner would be the one who could get his weapon free first.

Dutra was a seasoned alley fighter. He knew better than to roll backwards, throwing Lewis over his head, for unless he could manage to wrest the pistol from Lewis's grip at the same time, that maneuver would give the bastard the time and space to use it.

He slammed Ben into one of the wood posts that held up the thatched roof of the veranda. The sharp, unfinished edge of the post dug into Ben's back. Dutra's little bullethead slammed forward, trying to smash Ben in the face. Ben jerked his head back and braced himself against the post, using the leverage as he hooked his foot around Dutra's ankle and jerked. Dutra didn't release him, and they both rolled out into the rain.

Jillian had scrambled to her feet again. Seeing Dutra, hearing another man she loved shout "Run!" as he drew the danger to himself in order to protect *her,* had been so nightmarish that for a few seconds she stood frozen, her gaze locked on the two men rolling in the mud and slashing rain, illuminated only by the flashes of lightning. Thunder was rolling around them.

Behind her a light came on, spilling weakly across the veranda. The noise had disturbed the senhora.

The switch that turned on the light also released something in Jillian, as if the two were connected. Fury filled her that this should happen *again,* such an incandescent rage that she felt herself swelling with it, an incredible force demanding release. She wasn't aware of making a sound, but a low, inhuman howl vibrated in her throat. All she could see was Dutra, his ugly little head filling her vision, everything around him blacked out. Without thought, without effort, she was moving, plunging into the rain after them.

She leaped on Dutra's back, both hands clutching his wet, greasy hair and twisting savagely, hauling back with all her might. He howled with pain, his thick neck cording as he tried to resist the force jerking his head back.

She heard Ben yelling, breathless bursts of sound, but she couldn't tell what he was saying. She braced her feet against Dutra's back and lunged backwards, her fists still twisted in Dutra's hair. Great clumps tore loose from his scalp, and she tumbled to the mud, black strands hanging between her fingers.

Dutra was shrieking with pain, maddened with it. He was astride Ben, his heavy weight grinding him into the mud. On his back, unable to get any leverage, it was all Ben could do to hold his own against the enraged bull. He couldn't throw him off. Frenzied, Dutra began slamming Ben's gun hand against the ground, trying to dislodge the weapon. Desperately Ben hung on, all of his willpower focused on holding on to the pistol, because it was his only hope.

Jillian leaped to her feet. Behind her the senhora was shouting. The people in the shacks had awoken and were gathering around in the rain, silently watching.

Dutra was on his knees astride Ben, positioned too high for Ben to use his knee. Jillian's thought was very clear as she stepped forward with all the precision of a field goal kicker, her eyes focused on the target. She never paused, just moved in with her leg swinging at precisely the right point. Her boot crashed into Dutra's groin with all of her strength behind it, aided by the whipping motion of her leg.

Dutra screamed, the sound rising to an unholy shriek, his entire body arching back and to the side. Ben surged upward, bringing the pistol around. He shot once, the bullet hitting Dutra in the temple. The big man toppled to the ground.

Wearily Ben dragged himself free of Dutra's body and staggered to his feet. Jillian was standing a few feet away, rain dripping down her face, hair and clothes plastered to her. She hadn't taken her eyes off Dutra; her fists were clenched, her chest heaving, as if she waited for him to move again.

"Jillian?" He approached her cautiously. "He's dead."

She didn't reply. He remembered the low, chilling sound she had been making when she leaped onto Dutra's back like a small Fury, like an animal's snarl. Very gently he touched her arm, bringing her out of it. "He's dead, sweetheart. I shot him."

She hesitated, then gave a small jerky nod.

"You saved my life," he continued in a low, calm voice. "What did you hit him with? It sure got his attention."

She didn't speak for a moment, and then she turned to him, her eyes glassy. She met Ben's gaze and said, "I smashed his balls," in the polite little voice of someone in shock.

Ben controlled his automatic flinch. "Come on, sweetheart, let's get out of the rain." He slipped his arm around her waist.

She slid right out of his grasp, sitting down in the mud and leaving him holding air. He started to lift her in his arms, but something in her expression stopped him. He knew what she was feeling, having been through it himself. She had been in a killing rage; she had to get herself back. She wanted nothing more than to be left alone right now.

The senhora shouted at him from the veranda. She was wearing a long white nightgown and held a machete in her right hand.

He looked at Jillian. She was just sitting there, shoulders slumped and head bowed, rain pouring down on her. She was already soaked to the skin, so she wasn't going to get any wetter. Reluctantly he left her and walked to the senhora.

"Do you have some explanation for this?" she growled in her deep, harsh voice. "Who is that man?"

"I'll tell you everything," he said. "Would you make a pot of coffee, please? Or tea. Jillian will need something."

She drew herself up, glaring at him as if he had suggested

her hospitality might be lacking. "Of course. I'll bring towels out." She turned her glare on Dutra's body. "That will have to be disposed of." Practically everyone from the settlement was out in the rainy night now, standing grouped around, staring at the body. She shouted at them, "Take him to the shed," and several men stepped forward to take hold of the thick arms and legs, and they dragged Dutra off to be stored in the shed until morning.

The senhora went back inside, and Ben returned to Jillian, crouching by her side. "Come on, sweetheart. The senhora is bringing towels. We'll get dried off and drink some coffee. How does that sound?"

Her gaze lifted to his. "Mundane," she said.

He managed a tight smile. "It is. That's what you do after a crisis. The mundane things help put everything back in focus."

"All right." She sighed and climbed to her feet, moving slowly and with great care, as if her muscles weren't working all that well. He put his arm around her waist again as they walked to the veranda. The rain was ending, the storm moving on, and he looked up to see stars through a break in the clouds.

The senhora came out with a couple of towels. Jillian took one and wiped her face, then began rubbing her dripping hair. They had no dry clothes to change into, so that was about all she could do to repair herself.

But the senhora was regarding them, her lips grimly pursed. "Perhaps I can find clothes for you," she said. "My husband was a big man like you, senhor, God rot his nasty soul. And I have a skirt and blouse for you, poor little chicken."

Jillian felt like a poor little chicken. She was wet and muddy and exhausted. The senhora brought out the clothes, and Jillian went with Ben to the other side of the house where they changed clothes on the veranda in relative privacy. The senhora's skirt was too long and too big, hanging to the middle of her calves, but the old woman had provided a gay sash and Jillian wrapped it around her waist like a belt, tying it in a snug knot. She had discarded her muddy boots but had no other shoes to put on. Ben was also barefoot.

Here too the senhora came to their aid, producing two pairs of old leather sandals. The smaller pair was still too big for Jillian, but she could manage to keep them on her feet.

Then they sat at the table and drank hot, sweet coffee, the caffeine moderating the effects of crashing adrenaline levels. Jillian sat in silence, her face pale, as Ben related to the senhora the bare bones of the situation. He left out most of it, certainly not mentioning the Empress, explaining only that Dutra had killed Jillian's brother on the expedition and had been trying to kill them, too, as they were witnesses. It wasn't much of an explanation, but the senhora didn't press any further.

Instead she said with a rather shocking casualness, "My people will carry the body inland in the morning. It wouldn't do to bury him too close to the house. The smell, you know."

Ben wasn't sure Dutra could smell any worse dead than he had alive, but kept that comment to himself. Neither of them mentioned notifying the authorities. The people in these isolated settlements tended to handle details like this themselves.

"Senhora," Jillian said, "please, may I use your facilities?" It was the first time she had spoken since thanking the senhora for the coffee.

The old woman nodded graciously, and directed Jillian to the rear of the house. Jillian left the table. Ben watched her go, noting the bowed head.

"She will be all right," the senhora said. "She is strong; she attacked without hesitation and did not waste her time with silly squeals or wringing of the hands."

"I know," Ben said, and smiled. "She has more guts than any ten normal people combined."

Ten seconds later it hit him, and he shot to his feet. "Goddammit!" He ran out onto the veranda where they had been sleeping. His pack was gone.

"What is it?" the senhora asked, rushing out after him.

He sprinted for the dock, cursing with every step. He

could see Jillian already stepping into the raft, silhouetted against the glassy river by the starlight. He yelled as she began jerking the cord to start the motor. The reliable little motor coughed into life on the second pull, and the raft began moving away from the dock. By the time his feet thudded on the planks, she was fifty feet away and increasing the distance with every second. Ben stood there, helpless, and watched her disappear in the night.

His fists were clenched, and he was repeating every curse he knew when the senhora reached his side. "Why did she run?" she demanded baldly.

"We had an argument," Ben said. He thrust his hand through his damp hair. God, he couldn't believe he'd been so stupid. He had just gotten the words out of his mouth about Jillian being so gutsy; he should have realized she wouldn't accept defeat so easily, and expected something like this.

"It must have been a serious disagreement, instead of just an argument."

"It's pretty serious, all right," he muttered.

"What would you do if you could catch her?" the senhora asked suspiciously.

Ben thought of several violent things, but then discarded them. "Kiss her," he finally said. "And make love to her." His knees wobbled, and he sat down hard. "I'm in love with her," he said blankly, staring at the black river.

"Ah!" The senhora laughed. "Perhaps you aren't as foolish as I thought. It will be dawn soon, no more than an hour. You may go after her then."

"I don't have a boat, senhora."

"Why waste your time with a boat?" she boomed. "It would be much faster to use my aircraft! I will fly you myself."

Ben looked up, hope flaring in him with white-hot intensity. "I have a pilot's license, senhora."

"Then you may fly yourself, but if you don't return my craft, I will find you and deliver a fitting punishment. Hah! You must ready yourself. How much petrol does she have?"

"Enough to get her to the next settlement, but she'll have to refuel then."

"Then that is where you will wait for her."

Jillian kept to the middle of the river, following the wide, gleaming ribbon. She had done it, but she didn't feel any wild triumph or exhilaration. She felt tired, more so than ever before. The events of the night had been draining. She knew how dangerous it was for a woman alone to brave the river in a raft, but she hadn't been able to think of an alternative. Once they reached Manaus, she would have had no opportunity to get the Empress away from Ben. This had probably been her only chance, so she had taken it.

She might not ever see him again. In fact, she expected to do so only if he somehow caught her, and she didn't think that would be possible. She had seen the watercraft there at the settlement; there had been a few old motorized boats, but nothing capable of catching the agile raft. Her last mental image would be of him standing on the rickety dock, cussing a blue streak.

She didn't know how many more days it would take to reach Manaus. Food was no problem; they had left their supplies in the raft. Fuel would be her only concern, because she had no money. She would have to barter her food for fuel. Ah, well, going hungry wouldn't hurt her. And if she wasn't able to get fuel, she would use the oars. That would definitely give Ben a chance of catching her, but that was a bridge she would cross if she came to it.

The gray pearl of dawn began to lighten the sky, and then in a matter of minutes the darkness had been dispelled. The jungle filled with color, deep, vibrant colors, more intense than in the northern climes, chasing away the monochromes of night. Perhaps, in a few weeks, she would be returning to the interior, this time on an expedition sponsored by the government. They could carry a global positioning device and, once in the bowl, get their exact coordinates from the orbiting satellite. Thereafter they could reach the bowl by air, perhaps clearing out a helicopter pad or constructing a short runway; the bowl was easily long enough to accommodate a runway. The Stone City would never be the same again, but the people exploring it would be properly reverential of the secrets held there.

Her chest was throbbing with pain, but she knew she had done the right thing.

A small airplane droned overhead, startling her. She had just been thinking of helicopters and airplanes, but only in the abstract. It had been so many weeks since she had seen such a sign of civilization that the sound was jarring.

She stopped to check the fuel; only a few inches left in one tank. If she didn't make it to the next settlement, she would try to barter with the inhabitants of the river shacks. One way or another, she would get to Manaus. She simply refused to give up.

She had no watch, no way of telling time, but she had become adept at gauging the sun and it was a little after midmorning when another settlement came into view, ramshackle huts perched on their stilts, lining the bank. There was less than an inch of fuel left, so she had no choice about stopping.

The scene was much the same as the day before, the children running to the dock, their parents hanging back. But this time it was a man who came to greet her, a portly gentleman dressed in tropical shorts, sandals, and a wide straw hat. His bare chest hosted a veritable forest of curly gray hair.

Predictably, his first words were "Senhorinha, you are alone?" His bushy gray brows snapped down in disapproval.

"By accident, yes," she said. "I must reach Manaus."

"But this is not good. It is very dangerous. And you need a hat."

"I need petrol—"

"Yes, yes, of course," he said. "But you must come in the house. My wife will give you a hat and something cold to drink."

She hesitated only a moment. "Thank you, that would be lovely. But I have no money, senhor . . ."

"Moraes," he replied. "Bolivar Moraes. My wife is

Angelina, and she is truly an angel, as you will see. Do not worry about money, senhorinha. You are alone; you need help. We will manage. Now come, come."

He told one of the children to secure the raft, and extended a courtly hand to help Jillian onto the dock. She picked up the backpack and accepted his aid.

A very attractive woman, at least twenty years younger than Senhor Moraes, came out onto the veranda. "Bolivar?" she called.

"We have a guest, my angel," he bellowed in reply. "A lovely young woman in need of our help."

Senhor Moraes must need glasses, Jillian thought, amused in spite of herself. Lovely? She had to be haggard with strain and fatigue, and her hair hadn't been combed in two days.

Angelina Moraes came forward and deftly rescued Jillian from her exuberant husband. "My dear, do come in where it is cooler. We have ice; would you like something to drink?"

The thought of an iced drink made her almost dizzy with anticipation. "If it wouldn't be too much trouble," she managed to say.

Senhora Moraes led her into the deliciously cool interior of the house; ceiling fans swirled in every room, and there were screens and shutters on the windows. "What is your name, dear?" Angelina asked as she poured a pale green liquid into a glass and added several ice cubes.

"Jillian Sherwood." She sipped the cool drink; it had a tart lime taste to it, both sweet and sharp, and utterly delicious.

"You must have a hat," Angelina said, echoing her husband. "Would you like to freshen up while I find one for you? We have ridiculously modern plumbing; Bolivar insisted on having it done when we married. I am from the city, and he did not want me to feel deprived."

Modern plumbing? Jillian numbly followed her hostess, who directed her to a small bedroom with windows shuttered against the heat. "For guests," Angelina explained. "With its own private bath. I will leave you alone while I search for a hat, yes? Please make yourself comfortable."

Jillian found herself left alone in a room that seemed

sharply alien. It had been weeks since she'd seen a bed. She had experienced culture shock before and knew that it would soon fade as she adjusted to once-familiar things, but for now she was almost wary. She put the pack down and moved gingerly into the bathroom. There was a flush toilet, a basin, an actual bathtub. It wasn't luxurious, but it was functional.

It was remarkable how silly she felt.

But the running water was nice. She washed her face and hands, and borrowed the comb left on the side of the basin to bring order to her tangled hair. She forced herself not to linger, for fear she would be tempted to make use of the bathtub. When she left the bathroom, she found herself facing the bed again.

She gave a faint smile. Would she have to gradually accustom herself to a bed, or would it feel like heaven?

Hoping Senhora Moraes wouldn't mind, she sat down on the edge of the bed. With that action, fatigue almost overwhelmed her. Just for a moment, she promised herself, and leaned back against the headboard, swinging her legs up onto the bed. The mattress was a little too soft and a tad lumpy, but she closed her eyes in delight. It did indeed feel like heaven. Despite herself, she felt her body begin to relax. . . .

Suddenly she sensed that she wasn't alone. Her skin prickled with alarm, and her eyes flew open, her reactions still in time with the jungle even though her common sense said that Angelina must have come to see how her guest was doing. But it wasn't Angelina. Ben stood in the doorway, his shoulder propped against the frame, his eyes brooding and dangerous as he stared silently at her.

Her heart gave a massive thump and her mouth went dry. She couldn't say anything, couldn't move. All she could do was lie against the headboard, caught in the curious paralysis of fear, her gaze locked with his. She had never thought she would be afraid of Ben Lewis, but she was. Her thoughts scattered like fireworks, sparks shooting in all directions.

His face was hard, his jaw set. She was acutely aware of

the pack lying on the floor. All he had to do was pick it up and walk out, and there was nothing she could do to stop him. But he didn't even glance at the pack; he never looked away from her. She had never seen that expression in his eyes before, so savagely intent that she shivered in primal alarm.

"B-Ben?" she managed to gasp.

He straightened away from the doorframe and stepped inside the room, soundlessly closing the door behind him. With two paces he was at the side of the bed. His big, muscular frame seemed to blot out the rest of the room. Her breath came in quick, shallow pants as she raised her hands to protect herself, knowing the gesture was useless.

He bent down, ignoring her action, and slid his big hands under her skirt. His hard fingers hooked in the waistband of her panties and peeled them down her legs. The coolness of air on her bare flesh made her acutely aware of her nakedness, her vulnerability. Shock reverberated through her with the realization of what he was going to do. He pushed her legs apart, opening her to him, and stared down for a moment at her exposed female flesh. Then his gaze lifted, to lock with hers once more and remain there. He moved between her spread thighs, placing one knee on the bed while his other foot remained firmly on the floor. Silently he unbuttoned his pants and opened them, freeing his erection. With one hand braced on the mattress beside her, he shifted deeper into the notch of her legs and positioned himself.

She couldn't stop herself from tensing in anticipation. His entry was rough and inexorable, jolting her, and all of her inner muscles tightened in reaction to that deep intrusion. The heat of his body wrapped around her, drawing her own heat to the surface. He held himself in her to the hilt until he had overcome that inner resistance, until it had softened to a clinging caress all along his shaft that she knew he wouldn't mistake.

"Put your arms around me," he rasped, and mindlessly she did.

As her arms slid around his broad shoulders she felt him

shudder, perhaps with relief. He leaned over her and she pressed her face to his chest, catching her breath at the slow, deep power of his thrusts.

She was stunned, disoriented. She felt the overwhelming possessiveness of his lovemaking and was keenly aware of the claim he was staking. He was refusing to let her go.

He tilted her face up with his free hand, cupping it, holding her gaze with his as he thrust into her with increasing power and speed. The headboard thudded against the wall. She clutched his rib cage as he drove her higher and higher toward climax, the glorious, maddening tension coiling in her muscles. She could feel him getting even harder inside her, and she heard her own small cries as she lifted her hips to better receive him. He never let her look away, and when she climaxed, when he pounded into her with his own release, it was with those fierce blue eyes holding hers, forcing her to accept that she was his.

Afterward he gently bullied her into the bathtub and turned on the shower, getting into the tub with her. "But what about Angelina?" she mumbled, leaning against him. Her legs would barely hold her, they were trembling so much.

"They won't bother us." Hungrily he kissed her. He couldn't bring himself to stop touching her. "I've been waiting for you. They understand. They think it's very romantic."

"You've been *waiting* for me?" she asked numbly. "But how—"

"Airplane," he said succinctly. "Senhora Sayad has one. Haven't I ever told you that I have a pilot's license?"

"No." She couldn't respond to the gentle teasing in his tone. She stood under the tepid spray, her arms hanging at her sides. The water was wonderful; she felt so weak and limp that she thought she might swirl down the drain, too. She swallowed. "Why didn't you just take the pack and leave? You know I couldn't have stopped you. You didn't have to do . . . this." She was very much afraid that he had made love to her merely to soothe his ego, wounded when she escaped with the Empress.

"You don't seem to get the picture. It was *you* I came after." He rubbed the soap into a rich lather and began sliding his hands over her body. "You won't get away from me again."

"But why aren't you angry?" she asked helplessly, struggling to understand.

"I am. I'm so damn angry I just might fuck you again."

She sputtered with laughter; then the shock and the strain caught up with her and she began to cry. Ben held her close, rocking her in his arms as they stood under the spray. He murmured soothingly, his head bent down to hers. At last it seemed the only thing he could do to comfort her was to make love to her again, so he did, lifting her up and sliding into her. Her sobs caught on a gasp; then a moment later she made a deeper sound of pleasure.

The raw sexuality of their joining soothed him, too. For a few hours he had been terrifyingly aware that he might have lost her forever—until she accepted him into her body with that stunned acquiescence, until her arms closed around him, he had been the most frightened man on earth. He didn't intend to let her out of his sight for the next year, at least. It would take that long for him to recover from the panic.

23

Manaus was overwhelming. There were too many people, too much noise. Using Senhora Sayad's small airplane, he had flown them into Manaus, an abrupt transition that had taken too little time. Instead of days, the trip had been accomplished in a few hours.

He arranged for the senhora's plane to be returned to her; then they took a taxi straight from the airport to the hotel where she had stayed before. At least they were fairly presentable, she thought wryly; thanks to Senhora Sayad and the Moraeses, both they and their clothes were clean. Angelina Moraes, practically beaming that she and her husband had helped bring two lovers together again, had even insisted that Jillian use her makeup.

Ben held her at his side as he checked them into a suite at the hotel. "A suite?" she murmured. "I don't have that kind of money."

"I do. Don't worry about it."

They retrieved the belongings she and Rick had left behind, and the relieved manager also returned the letters she had written, beaming at her as he congratulated her on having returned safely. He asked about the two gentlemen, and behind Jillian, Ben gave a warning shake of his head. Understanding, the manager quickly made another comment and didn't give Jillian time to reply. Then he personally escorted them to their suite.

Ben put Rick's belongings aside, and while Jillian was unpacking her clothes in the bedroom he called down to the manager and quietly explained the situation to him. He told him to do whatever he wanted with Kates's belongings. Then he arranged to have some of his own clothes collected and brought to the hotel.

Jillian could hear him on the phone, but didn't go to the door to hear what he was saying. They hadn't discussed the Empress at all. She was tired, tired to the bone. Ben had changed the rules of the game, and she didn't know what to do anymore. All she wanted to do was sleep for a very long time, and maybe when she woke up she would feel like beginning the battle all over again.

Ben walked into the bedroom. "We'll have room service tonight. Stay in and rest."

"What do you usually do on your first night back?" she asked idly.

"Buy a bottle of whiskey and get laid."

"You're deviating from tradition?"

"You're exhausted. I can wait," he said.

She nearly fainted at hearing those words come from Ben Lewis's mouth. He scowled at her exaggerated double take and swooped her up in his arms, then placed her on the bed. "Let this stuff wait until later," he said, slipping her shoes off and just as easily sliding her out of the rest of her clothes, then deftly tucking her between the covers. "Take a nap, and that's an order."

"Alone?" she asked in astonishment.

He looked sheepish. "If you want to sleep, it'll have to be alone," he admitted, pulling the curtains shut and setting the thermostat lower. "I'll be in the other room."

Jillian settled herself in the large bed. She practically sank into the pillows. Her last drowsy thought was that she bet Ben could be marvelously inventive in a bed like this. Perhaps she'd find out. . . .

Ben peeked in half an hour later to make certain she was

asleep. Her breathing was deep and regular. He quietly closed the door, then sat down and began making phone calls.

They had just finished their room-service breakfast the next morning when another knock sounded on the door. Ben answered it and took delivery of one large box and a suitcase.

"What's that?" Jillian asked, following him into the bedroom where he placed both box and suitcase on the bed. A bed that had yet to be properly used, she thought. He had held her in his arms last night, but insisted that she sleep.

"The suitcase is mine," he said. "I arranged for some of my own clothes to be delivered. The box is yours."

She looked at it. "That isn't my box," she said positively.

"Yes, it is."

"I've never seen that box before in my life."

"Would you open the damn box!" he said in exasperation.

Satisfied by the response she had provoked, she lifted the lid off the box and took the contents out. It was a suit, the type of suit that very rich women wore to society luncheons, with a slim, slightly-above-the-knee skirt and a long, gracefully cut jacket. The skirt was pale pink, the simple blouse was white, and the jacket had vertical, narrow pink and white stripes. No clunky business suit, this. Everything was silk. She estimated the cost at well over five hundred dollars. Silk hosiery and matching shoes were included.

She stared blankly at it. "What is it for?"

He had placed his own suit on the bed and was taking off his clothes. "It's for wearing," he said. "Get dressed. Sorry about the stockings, but that isn't the kind of suit you wear bare-legged."

"But what's it *for?*" she demanded.

"For me." He looked at the clock. "You have twenty minutes."

"To do what?"

"To get dressed."

"What happens if I don't?"

"For God's sake, just do it!" he yelled. He was getting more nervous by the minute.

He bullied her every inch of the way, out of her clothes and into the new ones. He insisted that she do a full makeup job, and stood in the bathroom with her while she did it.

"You're making me nervous," she complained.

"*I'm* making *you* nervous?" he muttered.

"What are you up to, Ben Lewis? I know you. You're sneaky and underhanded."

"Agreed. No, I don't like that lipstick. I like red. Use the red."

She gave him an impatient look in the mirror. "Not with a pink suit."

"Oh. Okay. How do women know about stuff like that?"

"Simple. You put on red lipstick with a pink blouse one day and see that it looks wrong. You put on a lighter lipstick, and it looks all right. What did you think, that the ability to coordinate colors is a side effect of ovulation?"

He wisely didn't answer that question.

She barely had the lipstick on before he had her by the hand, dragging her out the door.

In the elevator she pinned him with a glare. "What's going on? I don't like not knowing what to expect. I don't deal well with surprises. I usually don't like them. It's safer just to tell me what you've planned."

"Jesus," he muttered.

The elevator doors opened and the hotel manager rushed toward them. "Is everything satisfactory, Senhor Lewis?"

"Perfect, Senhor Jobim. Everything is arranged?"

"Yes, senhor. Everyone is waiting."

"Who is 'everyone'?" Jillian growled.

"You'll see." His hand firmly gripped her waist, propelling her forward. In the interest of dignity, she went.

Senhor Jobim, the manager, led them to a large meeting room and opened the door. As Ben ushered her inside, a group of about thirty people, mostly men, rushed toward them. Ben deftly stepped in front of her, holding them back as he continued to steer her toward a dais set up at one end of the room.

The bright lights clicked on, bathing them in heat and brilliance.

Questions were being shouted at her in a mixture of English and Portuguese. She heard the words "Anzar" and "Amazons" and gave Ben a murderous look. He was going to make her look like a fool. He might have gotten these people here, but without proof, she would be a laughingstock.

There was a cluster of microphones on the dais, as well as a table and two chairs. Ben seated her in one of them, then took the other.

"Be seated," he said into the microphones, his deep voice booming around the room. "The sooner you all settle down, the sooner your questions will be answered."

In a relatively short time, the room was fairly quiet.

"Some of you are representatives of the Brazilian Department of Antiquities," he said. "Some of you are press. Miss Sherwood will make a brief statement about her discovery, then she will take questions first from the government representatives. I'm sure you ladies and gentlemen of the press realize that this will give you more to report, as the Antiquities people know the right questions to ask, so we'd appreciate your indulgence on this."

He turned and nodded to Jillian, and under the table, his big warm hand covered hers and gave it a comforting squeeze.

She wasn't uncomfortable speaking before a group, having done it before, but she had to fight down a queasy sensation. Very plainly, she outlined how she had found her father's notes about the lost city and the lost tribe of the Anzar, and she related the myth. She explained how she and her brother, and another associate, had put together an expedition to follow the coded instructions in her father's notes. Both her brother and their associate had lost their lives in the expedition to the interior.

Videotape cameras were whirring quietly.

"We found it. We found the Stone City of the Anzar. It is literally carved from stone and would have housed thousands. There are not many everyday artifacts to be found, suggesting to me that the Anzar abandoned the city and carried their possessions with them. But they left behind a most amazing temple. There is a single tomb inside it, a tomb with a man carved on top in bas-relief. And the temple is lined with statues of female warriors—"

She got no further, for the room erupted into a buzz like a swarm of angry bees. As she had expected, the press didn't respect Ben's request to let the people from Antiquities ask the first questions.

"Are you saying you found the Amazons, Miss Sherwood?" a wire-service reporter asked.

"That's for historians to say. The Stone City will take a lot of study. All I'm saying is that we found statues of female warriors."

"Just how big are these statues?"

"Including the pedestals, about ten feet tall."

"This code your father used," another reporter shouted. "Was he connected with military intelligence?"

"No. He was a professor of archaeology."

"Cyrus Sherwood?"

"Yes," she said, and braced herself.

"Wasn't he known as Crackpot Sherwood?"

"Yes, he was. But this proves that he wasn't a crackpot at all. He was right."

"What kind of code was it?"

"A code he devised when I was a child. It's based on the Lord's Prayer." Beside her, she sensed Ben giving her an incredulous look.

"Senhorinha Sherwood," said a bearded gentleman in a double-breasted suit; she immediately assumed he was a member of the Department of Antiquities. "What proof did you bring back of this fabulous find?"

Silence fell over the room. "Photographs, perhaps?" the gentleman persisted. "Examples?" When she didn't answer, he sighed. "Senhorinha, I very much suspect that this is exactly the type of . . . of joke your father was famous for perpetrating."

"Perhaps," Ben interrupted gently, "you owe both Miss Sherwood and her father an apology. We have proof."

Jillian went white. In that instant, she knew. She turned stunned eyes on him as he leaned down and pulled a bundle from beneath the dais.

She turned her head away from the microphones. "Ben," she said weakly.

He winked at her, his eyes bright and mischievous as he set the bundle on the table and gently began unwrapping it.

The cloth fell away and the red stone glowed with incredible warmth under the blinding lights. "The Empress," Ben said. "A red diamond, one of the rarest gems in the world." Cameras were clicking madly, and reporters were shouting. The gentleman from Antiquities was staring at it with mouth agape. "Though for my money," Ben continued, "I think it should be renamed the Jillian Stone."

"I can't believe you did that," she said numbly. They were back in their suite. He had finally extricated her from the madhouse downstairs. The Empress was now in the loving and fanatical custody of the Department of Antiquities, frantic efforts were already being made to put together another expedition, and phone lines were humming as archaeologists everywhere tried to be included. The Empress would be featured on news programs around the world that afternoon.

"A bit dramatic," he agreed. "But good showmanship. It got their attention more than if the rock had already been sitting there when they went in."

"Not that," she said. Her eyes were huge, and she looked as if she might cry. He didn't want that to happen. Quickly he grabbed her and threw her across the bed, following her down and pinning her there with his big body.

"It wasn't that hard a decision," he confessed. "When you cut out on me like that, I knew I had to make a choice between you and that damn rock. I'd rather have you, period."

"But the money—"

"Yeah, the stone would have brought in a lot of money, but I'm not broke. Far from it. I guess I have a quarter of a million or so in the bank."

She stared at him. "Dollars?" she asked faintly.

"Well, of course. I had some big plans for the Empress, but instead I'll keep guiding. I'd have gotten damn bored, anyway."

She looped her arms around his neck. That misty look was gone from her eyes, and he relaxed. Well, sort of.

"And I won't be able to take a month or so off between trips this time, either," he said. "How long do you reckon it'll take those folks to get their ducks in a row?"

"A week, maybe less," she said.

"You feel like another trip?"

"I can make it."

"But this time we'll have a double tent."

"Sounds good to me."

He glanced at the clock. "We have another appointment. Damn, I didn't mean to get you wrinkled."

"What now?" she wailed. "Ben, I can't take another surprise."

"We're getting married," he said, getting to his feet and hauling her up. "Well, maybe not today. I've never done it before, so I don't know how long it takes. But we'll get the ball rolling, at least."

She froze. "Married?"

He gently engulfed her in his arms. "Yeah, married. I'm as shocked as you are. I'd been planning to ask you, but then you found that damn diamond. I knew you wouldn't say yes with that rock standing between us, so I got rid of it." Then, slowly, an anxious expression crept over his face. "You will marry me, won't you? I know I'm not the best husband material in the world—hell, probably not even on this floor of the hotel—but I'm a lot of fun."

"Lots," she agreed weakly. She thought her knees would give out, and her head fell forward to rest against his chest.

"So what's the answer?"

"Yes."

She felt his chest expand beneath her head as he took a deep breath of relief, and she said, "I love you, you know."

"Yeah, I know." He rubbed her back and kissed the top of her head. "I love you too. I have to love you a hell of a lot, to give up a diamond like that for you. Remember that the next time you're giving me hell."

The telephone rang. Jillian was sitting cross-legged on the bed, a pile of newspapers on her lap. Ben was stretched out beside her, absorbed in a soccer game on television. The Brazilian announcer was shouting with excitement. She leaned over to lift the receiver.

"Jillian Sherwood . . . Lewis," she added as an after-thought. She still wasn't used to her new name, having been married only one day. She had thought about not taking Ben's surname; then she'd considered hyphenating it. Ben frankly didn't care. He had what he wanted; she could call herself anything she liked. She thought Jillian Sherwood Lewis had a nice ring to it.

She listened to the caller for a moment, then said, "I tried to interest the foundation in the expedition, but was laughed at."

She listened for a while longer. "But I'm not here as a representative of the Frost Foundation. I had to take a leave of absence and make this trip on my own."

She listened some more. Brazil had just scored, and the fans were screaming in jubilation. She said, "Just a moment. Let me speak with my husband."

Mischief sparkled in her eyes as she held the phone a little away from her mouth and said, "Ben, this is the director of the Frost Archaeological Foundation. Since I'm technically still an employee of theirs, they want me to state that the expedition was done under their aegis. In exchange, of course, I would get a wonderful promotion. What do you think?"

Knowing exactly what his response would be, she thrust the receiver out toward him. He didn't see it; his eyes never left the television screen. "Tell them to fuck off," he said.

She managed to stifle her laughter as she put the phone back to her ear. "My husband doesn't think it's a good idea," she said gravely. "Good-bye, Mr. Etchson. I'll mail you a formal letter of resignation. . . . Yes, I do think it's necessary. Good-bye." She hung up, glowing with satisfaction, and went back to her reading.

When they settled down to sleep later on, Ben said, "Do you regret resigning?"

"Not in the least. I love archaeology, and I won't be leaving it behind. The Brazilian Department of Antiquities has offered me a position and I'm going to take it. Think you might be interested in going on another dig?"

"Why not?" he asked lazily. "My first one was a real piss-ripper."

"And we'll go on guide trips, too."

"Yeah," he muttered. "To wind down." He yawned, and thought of something that had intrigued him. "So your dad's code was based on the Lord's Prayer, huh?"

"I'll show you how it works," she said, turning her face into his shoulder. His warm male scent made her want to burrow closer, so she did and was instantly rewarded by the possessive tightening of his grip. "In the morning. It's a little hard to memorize."

"The Lord's Prayer? I've known it since I was a little kid."

"Well, this version is a little different."

"How different?"

"It's in Old Scots."

"Old Scots?" he repeated faintly.

"It goes like this." Lying in his arms in the dark hotel room, she began to recite: "*'Uor fader quhilk beest i Hevin, Hallowit weird thyne nam. Cum thyn kinrik. Be dune thyne wull as is i Hevin, sva po yerd. Uor dailie breid gif us thilk day. And forleit us uor skaiths, as we forleit themquha skaith us. And leed us na untill temptatioun. Butan fre us fra evil. Amen.'*"

"Good Lord," he muttered.

She smiled in the darkness. "Exactly."

Epilogue

"Senhor Lewis!"

Ben turned, searching the crowded docks for whoever had called his name. Jillian was on the boat they were in the process of loading for a return trip to the Stone City, seeing to the storing of her own supplies. She looked up and gave a sudden shriek, then bounded off the boat and raced past Ben, her arms outstretched. A black scowl knit his brows as she grabbed a man and hugged him enthusiastically. Then he recognized not only the man Jillian was hugging but the one behind him, too, and the scowl changed to a grin.

Jillian released Jorge and threw her arms around Pepe, who looked alarmed. By then Ben had reached them, and he shook hands with both of them. "When did you get back?"

"Last night," Jorge said, still blushing at Jillian's greeting. "All the talk on the docks was about you and the senhora. We learned that this is your boat, so we knew we would find you here today."

"Let's find a quiet place where we can talk and have a beer," Ben said, and by mutual consent nothing more was said about their adventures until they were all sitting in a dim bar.

"Did all of you make it back?" Jillian asked.

Jorge nodded. "Except for Vicente. We buried him and

your brother, senhora, before we left. The other one, Kates, we did not worry about."

"What happened to Kates?" Ben asked.

"Dutra killed him, there at the camp."

"I wondered. Since Dutra was alone when he caught up with us, I figured Kates was either dead or had been injured and Dutra had left him. Either way, I wasn't worried about him anymore."

Jorge's dark eyes were serious. "What about Dutra, senhor?"

Ben shrugged, his blue eyes clear and cold. "I'm not worried about him, either."

From that, Jorge correctly guessed that Dutra would never be seen again, a prospect that he seemed to find most pleasing.

"We're resupplying to go back," Jillian said softly. "I had thought I'd try to bring Rick's body out, but now I think I'll let him stay where he is." It was there, in the Stone City, that her brother had finally reached out to her, there that he had made the one caring gesture of his life. The professor hadn't made it to the Stone City, but his children had; it was fitting, in a way, that a Sherwood should be buried there, becoming part of the legend that had lured them all.

Ben's arm was draped across the back of her chair, and now she felt him rubbing her shoulder blade in silent comfort, a light, automatic touch that didn't need words. Their days had passed in frenzied activity as they organized the expedition, which seemed much more complicated now that the government was involved, but whenever she got frustrated or tired, or when the inevitable moments of sadness would creep up on her, he instinctively knew, and his touch would tell her that she wasn't alone.

"I'm going to be expanding my operations," Ben said. "I'll have steady work for you on my crews if you're interested." He grinned. "Most trips *aren't* like this last one."

"Thank you, senhor," Jorge said. He looked delighted by the offer. "I will tell the others."

Pepe had said very little, and now he murmured something to Ben in his own language before sliding silently out of his chair and leaving the bar.

"What did Pepe say?" Jillian asked.

Ben leaned back in his chair. "Well, Pepe has worked for me a few times before. The gist of it was that he prefers to stick to the rivers, thank you very much. If I want to help you find empty dead places, he will happily stay behind."

They all laughed, and the conversation drifted into the reminiscing common after a shared adventure. Then Jorge had to take his leave, and Ben and Jillian had to get back to the boat.

"I have a surprise for you," Ben said as he and Jillian walked back to the docks.

That alone made her suspicious. "You know I don't like surprises."

"Have I disappointed you yet? Just trust me."

She hooted with laughter, which earned her a hard, quick kiss. Ben kept his arm around her as they continued. "Have you ever done it in a hammock?" he asked slyly.

She wasn't about to be caught in her own trap. "Define 'it,'" she said warily.

He did, graphically.

"You know the answer to that."

He had a very satisfied expression. "You will tonight."

"Oh, yeah?" Since they had just that afternoon loaded hammocks onto the boat, she stopped dead and crossed her arms. "I'm not sleeping on that boat tonight."

"Of course not. It's at home."

Home was now Ben's place; she had decided the hotel was too expensive, and he had decided that there were too many interruptions there. His place would never grace any magazine covers, but it had all that they needed: a kitchen, a bed, and functional plumbing.

"Let me be very clear on this," she said. "Exactly what is at home?"

"The hammock. I had one delivered today."

"I see." She did, and her imagination was already getting her excited. One look at Ben told her that he was feeling the same way. "But why bother with a hammock when we have a nice big bed?"

He grabbed her and kissed her again, and this time there was nothing quick about it. "We'll start out in the hammock," he said. "Who knows where we'll end up?"

She laughed, throwing her head back with sheer delight. With Ben, everything was an adventure.

"AN EXTRAORDINARY TALENT."
—*Romantic Times*

LINDA HOWARD

"Linda Howard writes such beautiful love
stories. Her characters are always so
compelling....She never disappoints."
—Julie Garwood

☐ A LADY OF THE WEST .... 66080-2/$5.50

☐ ANGEL CREEK ....66081-0/$4.99

☐ THE TOUCH OF FIRE ....72858-X/$5.50

☐ HEART OF FIRE ....72859-8/$5.50

Pocket Books
Proudly Announces

DREAM MAN

Linda Howard

Coming from Pocket Books
Spring 1994

The following is a preview of
DREAM MAN . . .

Marlie jerked the door open on his fifth knock. She stood squarely in the doorway, her posture plainly denying him admittance. "It's ten thiry, Detective," she said coldly. "Unless you have a search warrant, get off of my porch."

"Sure," Dane replied easily, and stepped forward. She wasn't prepared for the maneuver, automatically moving back to give him room before she caught herself. She tried to recover but it was too late; he was already over the threshold.

He didn't take his eyes off her as he shut the door behind him. She was wearing a pair of cutoffs and a flimsy old T-shirt that draped over her braless breasts as faithfully as her own skin. Very pretty breasts, he noticed, making no effort to hide the direction of his gaze. High and pointed, with small, dark nipples peaking the fabric. His loins tightened, the same reaction he had every time he was in her company. The casualness of her clothing jolted him, making him suddenly aware of the prim facade she normally projected. The more he knew about her, the more intriguing she became. She had more layers than an onion, but she was determined to keep them hidden beneath that prickly shield she had developed. Instinctively he knew that was part of the reason she was so hostile right now; she was naturally angry at his suspicions and less-than-gentle questioning, but part of her dismay was caused by the fact that he was seeing her like this, without the armor of her bland disguise.

Marlie flushed angrily as he continued to stare at her breasts. She crossed her arms in a half-belligerent, half-defensive gesture. "If you don't have a good reason for this, I'm going to file a complaint about you," she warned.

"I've been to Denver," he said abruptly. "I just got back an hour or so ago." He paused, watching for any flicker of expression. She didn't give much away, but he was learning to read her eyes. She hadn't quite learned how to shield her eyes. "I talked with Dr. Ewell."

Her pupils flared wildly, and there was no disguising the dismay in her expression. She stood stiffly, glaring at him. "So?"

He moved closer to her, so close that he knew she could feel his heat, close enough to intimidate her with his size. It was a deliberate tactic, one he had used before in interrogation, but he was acutely aware of a difference this time in his own attitude. Questioning her was still important, but underlying it was a powerful sexual need to make her aware of him as a man. The closeness of his body shocked her; he saw her waver, saw the sudden color in her cheeks, saw the alarmed flicker of her eyes. She didn't allow herself to retreat, but she went very still, her nostrils flaring delicately as the heat of his skin reached her.

Her own feminine scent wrapped subtly about him, drawing him even closer. It was a clean, soapy odor that told him she wasn't long from her bath, mingled with the warm sweetness of woman. He wanted to lean down and nuzzle her neck, to follow that faint scent to its source, investigate all the intriguing places where it might linger.

Later.

"So, the good doctor had a lot interesting things to say," he murmured. He began to slowly circle her, letting his body brush hers, the light touches tingling through his nerves like electricity. "It seems you're some kind of miracle of ESP. If you believe in that kind of stuff."

Her lips tightened. She had herself under control again, not even glancing at him as he continued to circle her, ignoring the fleeting contact of his arm, or his chest, or his thigh. "You don't, of course."

"Nope. Unless you can prove it to me. Why don't you give it a try? Come on, Marlie, read my mind or something." Slowly, slowly, around and around.

"There has to be something *in* your mind."

"Nice shot, but it doesn't prove anything." He kept his voice low. "Make me believe it."

"I don't do parlor tricks," she snapped, goaded.

"Not even to prove yourself innocent of murder? This isn't a party, babe, in case you haven't noticed."

Her head whipped around and she gave him the full force of her glare, blue eyes narrowing. "I *could* change you into a toad," she said speculatively, then shrugged. "But someone has already beaten me to it."

He gave a bark of laughter, startling her. "You've seen too many old 'Bewitched' shows; that's witchcraft, not ESP."

The slow circling finally got to her. Abruptly she bolted, toward the kitchen; he let her go, following closely behind her. "Coffee," he said blandly. "Good idea."

She hadn't planned on making coffee, but seized gratefully on something to do, as he had known she would. She was rattled, and fighting it every inch of the way. He was beginning to realize how important control was to her.

She halted with the coffee in her hands, her back to him. "I don't read minds," she blurted. "I'm not telepathic."

"Aren't you?" That wasn't what Dr. Ewell had said, exactly. He felt a tinge of triumph. Finally, she was starting to talk to him, rather than resisting him. He wanted to put his arms around her and hold her close, shelter her from the trauma of her own memories, but it was too soon. She was physically aware of him now, but she was still frightened, still hostile.

"Not—not a classic telepath." She looked down at the coffee. He could see her hands shaking.

"So what are you?"

Look for DREAM MAN
Coming from Pocket Books
Spring 1994